Lc
re:
Lib
wi!

PL

Hannie Bennet's Winter Marriage

Kerry Hardie was born in 1951, grew up in Bangor, Northern Ireland and read English literature at York University. On returning to Ireland she worked for the BBC in Belfast and for the Arts Council. She has published two books of poetry with the Gallery Press and is the winner of the Friends Provident National Poetry Prize [Ireland]. She now lives in Co Kilkenny with her husband, the writer Sean Hardie. This is her first novel.

ALSO BY KERRY HARDIE

POETRY

A Furious Place (Gallery Press)
Cry for the Hot Belly (Gallery Press)

Hannie Bennet's Winter Marriage

KERRY HARDIE

HarperCollins*Publishers*

This novel is entirely a work of fiction.
The names, characters and incidents portrayed in it are
the work of the author's imagination. Any resemblance to
actual persons, living or dead, events or localities is
entirely coincidental.

HarperCollins*Publishers*
77–85 Fulham Palace Road,
Hammersmith, London W6 8JB

www.**fire**and**water**.com

Published by HarperCollins*Publishers* 2000

1 3 5 7 9 8 6 4 2

Copyright © Kerry Hardie 2000

The Author asserts the moral right to
be identified as the author of this work

A catalogue record for this book
is available from the British Library

ISBN 0 00 225920 6

Set in Stempel Garamond by
Rowland Phototypesetting Ltd,
Bury St Edmunds, Suffolk

Printed and bound in Great Britain by
Clays Ltd, St Ives plc

For Sean
Without whom there'd be no book

~ *Acknowledgements* ~

My grateful thanks to all the following, who helped or read or advised:

Carmel Cummins, Olivia Goodwillie, Paddy and Dorothy Jolley, Barbara and Irene Kelly, Kieran Lineen, Val and Marian Lonergan, Pat Murphy, Helen Parry-Jones, Helen O'Brien, Paddy and Fintan Ryan, and all those at the Butler House.

The author also wishes to thank the Tyrone Guthrie Centre at Annaghmakerrig.

∾ *Chapter 1* ∾

She met him at a wedding she had gone to only because she needed a husband and a wedding wasn't a bad place to begin looking.

She didn't try to hide much from him, which was sound judgement because he didn't know much about women and he couldn't have talked to a woman who wasn't straight with him. But more than judgement, Hannie had luck. She met Ned when he was looking anyway, so most of the work was done for her. And he took to her, he liked her crooked straightness from the start.

She came from nowhere, had no family, no country and no background. None of that would have mattered only she had no money either so she needed somewhere to live, something to live on. She was fifty-two, she made no secret of it, nor of the fact that her need for a husband was overwhelmingly financial.

That didn't put Ned off. Nor did the fourteen-year-old son she'd left in Africa while she came prospecting for their futures.

Ned didn't know what he wanted when he met her, he'd only just admitted to himself that he wanted anything at all, so her directness eased things for him. He didn't know it, but he couldn't have coped with a woman of delicacy who left him to do the running, and he couldn't have coped with a woman who wasn't an outsider.

So the way of it was she decided Ned might do and she got round Tom and Beth so they helped her, and Ned went along with it not because he was trapped by her as his friends thought, but because she was what he wanted all along.

Social situations were what she needed, and introductions to the right sort of men: men who didn't know her history or reputation, who might be charmed and cajoled into taking her on. By luck a widow this time not a divorcée, she still had a few respectable connections to exploit, so when she decided on taking this trip to England she phoned the Grenvilles from Kenya and asked Beth for a bed.

'For the wedding,' she said. 'Maybe a day or two after, I'm not sure of my movements. So much to be taken care of – Andrew's English estate – London – Andrew's solicitors ...' She left it vague.

Strictly speaking, she hadn't asked, she'd just said her piece and then waited, knowing that Beth wouldn't be able to let the silence run on. Beth was soft, everyone knew that, most of all Hannie, who was anything but soft. There were other people she could have asked, but she didn't. If you were going to use someone, best choose someone trustworthy who assumed that you were the same until they were reminded that you weren't. It wasn't long before Beth was reminded, but by then it was too late.

The wedding invitation was more luck. The bride had been Andrew's god-daughter, the embossed invitation had come in the post a bare six weeks before he died. Andrew had answered at once: congratulations to his little Sophie (not so little any more, it seemed); he and Hannie would most certainly be there to see her married. Between this acceptance and his death a few weeks later he had issued his ultimatum and Hannie had left.

But Sophie didn't know this and neither did Sophie's parents, who wrote their commiserations when the death-notice appeared in the London *Times*. The letter was addressed to Andrew's widow, Hannie Bennet.

Hannie wrote back that she would be in England on

business matters and she very much looked forward to this meeting with Andrew's old friends and his god-daughter at her wedding. Andrew had spoken of them so often, she felt it only right to be there as his representative.

She sealed the letter, trusting they wouldn't yet have heard the gossip. Even if they had, they'd hardly write and tell her so. Or make a scene when she turned up at the church.

She was still an attractive woman, Beth thought, watching Hannie sitting at a table on the lawn. There was the usual wedding marquee but the day was fine and dry, the tables had all been moved outside.

Very attractive, whatever Tom might say. Tom liked more grooming: nice hair, a little make-up, something finished in the look. Yet he woke up when Hannie was around, he pretended he didn't, but he did.

Any fool could see she was trouble, Tom used to say; there were always nods and murmurs of agreement from his listeners. Beth thought men saw the trouble and they liked it, even Tom. They liked the aloofness, the lack of involvement, the way she walked by herself.

Hannie had kicked off her shoes under the table, her hair was sun-bleached and she wore a not-new dress in faded grey. Beth pulled the floral frock she'd thought she liked so much down over her stomach. She wished she'd tried for elegance not prettiness. She wished she didn't care that her waist had broadened and her stomach bulged. She wished that, like Hannie, she didn't try to hide it.

Funny how it looked all right if you didn't care. Except it probably wouldn't on her. She resolved to eat less, walk more. She knew she wouldn't. She resolved to stop worrying so much about what she looked like, to 'accept' herself (that curious language that her children spoke). Hannie had just done that thing she did when she stopped being interested by whoever it was she had been being interested by. Switched off the light and gone out. Beth had almost forgotten that trick, the way she could not-be-there, like an abandoned puppet, a rag-doll left out in the rain. Men always fell for it, they suddenly got frantic that she wasn't listening any more, wasn't interested when she had been, so intensely. Funny how easy it was for some people.

It didn't feel easy to Hannie. It was all smooth and smart and understated, all grooming and opinions. She had to wrench herself up to the mark, make herself perform, not give up and go under. She felt blunt and shabby and old. And tired, really tired.

She met Ned through a young woman called Jessica who'd sought her out and introduced herself.

'My mother knew your husband. She said you might be here. I'm to offer you her sympathies.'

Hannie hovered for a moment on the edge of paranoia. She dismissed it. This Jessica would neither know nor care about the marital gossip of another generation on another continent.

'She knew the family. Years ago in Oxfordshire. She had a thing about the oldest brother.'

'Edward,' Hannie said.

'Edward,' Jessica agreed. 'You must tell me how he is. She'll want to know in detail –'

'He's dead. Died before I ever met him.'

'Really?' Jessica sounded quite interested. 'My father will be relieved. Edward was her untravelled road. She does rather tend to let herself regret him out loud when she's cross.'

Jessica was tall and slender with grey eyes and perfect skin and perfect self-possession. A woman, not a girl, nearer thirty-five than twenty, her voice was clear and well-bred and she wore a loose green linen dress which showed off her wavy, fair hair. She was like daylight, Hannie thought, not liking her.

She had a man with her, following a few paces after like a dragged anchor, so that he didn't seem to be with her though he was. He caught up with her and stood almost beside her and she introduced him. Ned Renvyle.

Hannie shook hands. He was very tall and bony, with a full head of fine grey hair. The hair was much younger than the face, which was tanned and folded into long broken creases like the wandering courses of wadis in the dry season. The eyes were withdrawn and almost invisible between deep lines and puckers.

Jessica had finished with Hannie, she had enquired about her mother's old flame and was ready to move on, but a sudden eddy of people pressed into them and the space for retreat closed. Resignedly the two women began again. Ned Renvyle stood and listened.

Jessica worked in broadcasting, a producer not a secretary, Hannie's assumptions smoothly corrected. She spoke briefly of a series she was executive-producing, throwing in a couple of observations that were meaningless to Hannie but made Ned Renvyle nod appreciatively. It was all gracefully done: self-aware, modest, informative. Hannie glanced at the hands. Jessica wore no rings.

'What do *you* do?' she asked Hannie. Her tone was pleasant, conversational. Your turn, it said, I've done my bit.

What you don't do, Hannie thought. Live off men. When I get the chance.

'Marry,' she said starkly.

Jessica looked startled. Hannie was startled herself, she probably hadn't intended to say it aloud, she wasn't entirely sure. The bony old man twitched slightly, the wine jumped in his glass. He had been watching Hannie closely while seeming not to.

Jessica laughed. She lifted her glass as though to drink to Hannie but it was empty. Ned Renvyle automatically held out his hand for it. 'Perrier water,' Jessica said. He held out his hand for Hannie's glass. 'Red,' she said. He turned and bored his way through the crowd.

'So you're currently out of a job?' Jessica asked lightly.

5

Hannie nodded. 'I am looking for a new position.'

'Oh?' Jessica said. 'That must be tedious. Wouldn't you rather a break?'

'Economic necessity,' Hannie said.

Jessica looked at her curiously. It seemed to occur to her that Hannie was serious. Her interest was almost caught – it was the tastelessness of Hannie's remarks. She seemed about to speak but a tall, impeccably dressed man with a thatch of straight brown hair was shoving his way furiously through the crowd.

'That was Ned Renvyle,' he accused as soon as he reached her. 'I saw you talking to him, couldn't get near you ... Honestly Jessica, why didn't you hold on to him? You knew perfectly well I wanted to meet him.'

This was not a boyfriend, Hannie realised, nor a lover awaiting divorce. This was a consort or a partner or whatever these things were called now; a husband she hadn't yet bothered to marry. Jessica introduced Hannie, but the man hardly glanced at her.

'He didn't want to meet anyone,' Jessica continued calmly. 'He wanted to hang on to someone so he didn't have to. I can't think what he's doing here. He's terribly shy –'

'Shy? You're talking about a man who marches up to head-hunters and invites himself round for a year or two. He's not shy, Jessica, explorers aren't shy, for a halfway intelligent woman you do talk a load of crap.'

'Shy in this sort of company. Stop making such a fuss and go and find him yourself. He's gone to get us drinks, but he's probably forgotten by now. Mine's Perrier water, Hannie's is red wine.' She spoke like a mother ignoring a child's petulance.

He glared at her and headed off after Renvyle. Then he stopped, turned on his heel and came back. He addressed Hannie.

'Sorry,' he said. 'Very rude of me. Bit of an obsession.'

He wheeled and stomped off again, ignoring Jessica.

'It's true,' Jessica said. 'The obsession bit. He read the books when he was a boy and just completely fell for them.'

'What sort of books?'

'Travel. The Gentleman Adventurer. More Thesiger than Fleming, but slightly later and not so well connected. Quite obviously incredibly brave, only never ever written like that. Touching, really.' She paused, her eyes on a woman who seemed anxious to shepherd them towards the lunch tables.

'Of course, they're hopelessly out-of-fashion and out-of-print and cluttering-up-the-second-hand-bookshelves. I shouldn't think Ned Renvyle's royalty cheques are exactly keeping the mice from his door.'

'Where is his door?'

'Oh, Ireland somewhere.' Jessica spoke in a neutral voice. 'Old family. You know the sort of thing. Nettles and decay.'

Hannie didn't, and it didn't sound very promising. Still, she wasn't exactly being bombarded with opportunities; she might follow it up for want of anything better.

She scanned the tables, found her name on a bit of card and picked up the one from the place-setting next to it. Three tables up, she found Ned Renvyle's name-card. People were beginning to take their seats but she ignored them, leaned over and changed his card for the one in her hand. She went back to her table, sat down, and put Ned's card on the setting beside her.

Jessica was right, Ned Renvyle lived in Ireland. Hannie had listened for an estate but heard only a house, a farm.

A family farm?

No, not a family farm but the next best thing. A farm near the places and people he'd known in his childhood. He'd bought it when he left off roaming around the place and came home.

Home? He was an Irishman?

His family had lived there for generations, he said, not answering her question.

But he wasn't a farmer?

He was now. Before that, he told her, he'd mostly travelled, written the odd book, given lectures, that sort of thing. There'd been some rooms in London where he'd lived when he wasn't away. Now he farmed a few acres. Nothing much, but it kept him occupied. He lived alone. Been married once, his wife had died. He was over for this wedding. And to see his publisher, visit friends.

They were snarled in a long line of traffic with no visible reason for the hold-up. Hannie sat in the back of the car, staring absently out of the window while Tom and Beth bickered about Beth's choice of route.

Ireland. She hadn't thought of Ireland, had never been there. It might be the answer. He was on the look-out, she knew that, just from the things he'd said this afternoon. And he'd taken to her, she knew that too.

She'd have to find things out, she decided: how much land, if there was money to go with it, if there were any commitments.

You couldn't rely on family any more, Andrew had said. Or schools. A chap could sound right and have nothing. These days, there was more likely to be money if he sounded wrong.

Ned Renvyle would definitely have sounded right in Andrew's book. Hannie didn't care what a chap sounded like as long as he wasn't flat broke.

She could probably hook him if she played him right, she thought, and he might be the start she needed. She could always leave him if she couldn't stand him, but he must be pushing seventy, he couldn't live for ever, she might just stick it out till he died. With a bit of luck he'd leave her somewhere to live or enough to live on. With a lot of luck he'd leave her both.

If he turned out to have anything at all.

But she'd have to let him do the next bit. She wondered how fast he would move if he made up his mind to it. She wondered how fast she could move in her turn. If he did as he'd told her he planned to do and went up to London, she'd have to follow him, invite herself on someone. She couldn't afford a hotel, couldn't put all her eggs in one basket at this stage when nothing might come of it.

But he might not go to London, he might stay on. And if he did, she'd stay on too. She'd tell Beth the truth, or a version of it, ask for her help. Beth would understand. Not like that blonde bitch at the wedding with her career and her salary and her future.

She would explain about the separation which she hadn't so far mentioned. She would tell Beth there'd be no money coming, even after the will was settled, Andrew's children would inherit; she was broke and needed to marry again.

They'd hear it all anyway, and there was no predicting when. Africa gossip, it might take a while, but it would permeate through in the end. Tell Beth, but ask her not to pass it on to Tom. She would of course. So if they heard before she was ready, she'd be covered.

But she wouldn't tell her about Joss or the reasons for the separation.

The traffic began to move. Tom stopped telling Beth she'd chosen the wrong route and started complaining about the cold supper she was planning. All that fidgety food they pushed at you at weddings. You needed a decent dinner to settle you down, he said. He was quite drunk.

For once Beth stood her ground and stuck to her cold meats and salad. She was tired, they'd eaten a massive lunch, and the help had the evening off. It wasn't like Africa, she said over her shoulder at Hannie. Africa, where everyone had servants. There was nostalgia in her voice.

Hannie said nothing . Where everyone like *you* had servants, she thought, remembering days when she hadn't had enough to feed herself and Joss, much less a servant.

Ned Renvyle. Only if she was desperate. Maybe not even then. The next move was his, anyway.

'Oh, the Woodburns,' Beth said. 'Minster Lovell, beautiful house, Jacobean, been in the family for generations. Jessica's the youngest. Nice, isn't she?'

Hannie said nothing.

'And terribly successful.'

More silence from Hannie. Beth began to waver.

'It must be wonderful,' she said, 'to be like her.'

Hannie looked at her.

'Oh, you know . . .' Beth flapped her hand around vaguely. 'Not having to wait for the right moment. A job. Confidence. Beautiful clothes . . .'

'Career.' Hannie corrected her.

'Career?'

'She has a *career*, not a job. She told me so.'

The two women sat outside in the sunshine, helping the help. And Hannie was working on Beth, she was re-establishing herself and gathering information.

'I never liked stringing beans,' Beth said. 'I always slice my fingers as well as the beans. Shelling peas is different, I like shelling peas. The little bump-bump-bump noise in the bowl. Mummy made us volunteer but we never minded.' She picked up the next runner bean from the pile on the table and looked at it balefully. 'I bet Jessica Woodburn *never* strings beans.'

'Are there many like her?' Hannie asked. Her voice was neutral.

Beth sighed and leaned back in her deckchair. 'It's the way things are now,' she said carefully. 'Women like us . . .'

Hannie waited.

'Anyway, I like my life,' Beth continued, 'I don't really want to be like that. Except sometimes. Sometimes it's hard – feeling you haven't done anything. You have to *do* something, you know. Not just marry and have children and run a house. Sara says I'm a bad role-model. That means an example for her to base herself on. She says it won't be her fault if she turns out just like me.'

Hannie laughed. Then she remembered herself. 'What does Tom say?' she asked tactfully.

Beth cheered up. She sat forward, waving a runner bean around as she talked. 'Tom? He just wants things to go on as they've always done. His home the way he likes it, food the way he likes it, me here to look after him. To "service him", as Sara says. Even the boys talk like that since they went to Cambridge. And they're right, of course they're right, and I wish I was different, I'd so like them to be proud of me, especially Sara.'

'These Jessica Woodburns,' Hannie said, 'do they have children?'

'Oh, yes. One or two. Late. It's all wonderful. Then they get a nanny and go back to work. Just like our mothers, my dear, only they went back to their social lives. Which is what work is to them anyway, as far as I can see. Still, it gives the lie to the men laying down the law about the sacrifice they make for us, slaving away in the office all their lives. These women simply can't wait to get back there.'

Beth stopped suddenly. Hannie was looking across the lawn, that still, empty expression on her face. Beth heard herself and blushed to her hairline. So stupid, she'd forgotten for a moment about Hannie. She was always so poised, her English almost flawless, she had been so very much at home in Andrew's world where they had met her.

And it might not have been true, it could have been just spiteful gossip. She tried desperately to think of something to say but nothing came.

Hannie rescued her. 'What do the men think?' she asked lightly.

'I don't know. They don't seem to have much choice. They're not really allowed to say anything, whatever they may think. Which is about time, really,' she finished, brightening. 'But *we're* not allowed to say anything either. Not even discuss. We've wasted our lives and we're jealous. But I'm not jealous, really I'm not, and I don't mind if that's what they want to do, I just don't want to have to start doing it myself . . .'

Sara appeared in the doorway behind them.

'There was a man on the phone for Hannie. I said I'd get her but he got in a panic, said he'd ring back in an hour.'

Beth swivelled round in the deckchair. She addressed her daughter. 'What was his name, darling?'

'I don't know, Ren-something,' the fifteen-year-old replied. 'First he wanted her and then he didn't. Couldn't make up his mind.'

Hannie couldn't, either.

❦ *Chapter 2* ❦

Ned Renvyle sat on a bench by the river in the late afternoon sunshine. He hadn't gone to London as he'd first planned. Instead he'd left his friends the Langtons and their hospitality for a timbered pub one village away from Hannie. He knew Jean and Alasdair Langton were perfectly aware of what he was about, knew this attempt at concealment was both foolish and futile, but he felt, at least, less overlooked.

Courting was never a dignified business. Women might thrive on it, but it made men look like fools. A bit late to start worrying about that now, he decided. The river was narrow with dirty, thick-looking water and mown banks, the grass worn thin by picnickers and courting couples. There were litter bins and benches and lifebelts on stands. Fishermen stood in line all day and threw back what they'd caught when they'd caught it. Hard to see what they got out of it. A travesty of a river. He should be grateful for the benches, he supposed; saved his piles.

He shut his eyes and a warm orange glow of sunny darkness closed over him. He dozed or dreamed, saw the small rushy meadows of home, the ragwort and the dampness, the cattle wandering about in them. He heard their quiet trampling and chomping and the harsh cry of a heron in the reedbeds.

He felt miserable, weary and old. He wanted her all right, but almost as badly he just wanted to get finished up here and go home. Suddenly he hardly cared about the outcome. With or without her, he'd go back to the farm and the fields and the river.

Yet at the same time he had wanted her badly enough to

have sat it through this far, he had to remind himself of this in his dejection. Why he wanted her, he hardly knew. It wasn't for anything he could put into words and say aloud to someone else.

He had a picture that was really more of a vision at the edges of his mind. Sometimes he called it up deliberately, but more often it came when he wasn't thinking and floated in front of his eyes. He saw a hallway with dark wood, sunshafts, dust-motes. And flowers leaning out of shadow into light.

With the picture came a jumble of sense-impressions: morning and a garden, dew and dewy grass in the early sun, the swish of skirts. Then a china jug pulled from a wooden press and water gushing in till it ran over.

The sense-impressions settled and stilled. The scent of flowers, the quiet drop of petals on old furniture.

Then a feeling of simplicity. Of his life inhabiting his body. Of his body sitting simply wherever he was when the picture came. Of this being enough.

He knew that this yearning vision of flowers was a yearning for home. Not the house he had now, but the home he had left fifty years ago to sit on the bare ground beneath unknown stars with strangers, with unfamiliar tongues and smells and sounds about him, and a peace in his blood more intense than fire or wine.

And nothing would do him then but to have those stars, that peace, and no price to be paid was too high. And nothing would persuade him that his life lived in Ireland wouldn't be narrow and diminished beyond endurance.

There'd been flowers too, in his wilderness places: carpets after rain, a white bloom clenched in a rock.

Only now he wanted what he'd left behind him all those years ago. Or the ghost of it. He was neither so old nor such a fool as to imagine that anything could be again as it once was.

He'd spent too many years in search of himself, confronting

himself, till it was like living in a high altitude where the visibility is always intense and clear. Now, an old man, he found that he could not altogether bear this. Nor the losses time brought: that intense sweet peace only a memory now.

The truth was he was lonely, as simple as that, he told himself. Finally, after almost a lifetime away, he'd decided to come home. He had bought a house in the place he'd known in his childhood and now, five years later, he was still waiting for it to turn into his home.

Somehow he'd got it into his head that a woman might make the difference, and he couldn't get it out of his head, though he knew that acquiring one would solve nothing, the yearning would simply transfer itself to something else, he'd be led by the nose to follow another dream. That had been the way of it all his life. In the meantime he wanted a wife, so there was nothing to be done but to go and find one. But Hannie? The woman was a nomad, not a homemaker. Had he taken leave of his senses altogether?

The sun had left the bench where he sat and the coolness of the evening was upon him. It wouldn't be much longer now, he thought. He'd ask her. She might have him or she might refuse him. Either way, at sixty-nine, he'd look a bloody fool.

And he'd look a worse fool, bringing her back with him, than leaving her here and no one any the wiser. Fortunately his few close friends were scattered. If she said yes he would write to them, tell them his news by letter. Then they could let off steam, calm down, write him a civil note. No need to tell anyone at home, might as well just turn up with her. They'd know soon enough, probably before he knew himself.

Well, if he'd minded men's opinions he'd have lived a different life. Let them think him a fool, he supposed that he could bear it one more time.

And when he was with her, he didn't care. She had that effect on him. Caution left him. It was her attitude. *Why not?* she said, as others might say, *Why?*

She had a lopsided walk. He liked that, he didn't know why. He'd asked her about it and she'd laughed. No, no injury, she'd said. Just the way she was. Didn't seem offended.

He liked her, that was all he could say. Liked her untidy hair and the way she took her shoes off under the table and went fishing around for them when it was time to go. Liked the hearty way she ate and the way that she laughed with her head back and her mouth open. She got under his guard.

Oh, he knew she was untrustworthy, unsound, knew she was running, though he didn't know from what. If pushed he'd have said she was a selfish woman of loose morals and bad habits. But also courageous, strong-minded, energetic. She didn't try to cover or apologise. He recognised her as he would have recognised a man.

And he might have befriended such a man, but he'd never have let him come too close.

Then why was he letting *her*? Holding the door open, inviting her in?

He thought about this one for a long time and the answer he came up with confused him with its simplicity. He felt warmer in her company.

He'd cut his London plans. No point. He had no desire to sit in his club and talk to the other old fogeys. The London part of his trip had only ever been an excuse to go looking for a woman. The whole thing was, if he was honest. But he'd taken her up for the day when he went to see his publishers.

Publishers. Hadn't published anything for years and then there was a letter out of the blue.

Backlists. Something might be done about backlists. Perhaps lunch? Next time he was in London?

As though he was in and out of London every second week. As though he lived that sort of life.

She'd worn her good dress, the same one she wore for the wedding. He'd liked that, that she'd thought enough of a day out with him to wear it. Not that he liked dressed-up women, he didn't. But he liked her in that dress, and he was flattered.

She impressed the publisher fellow, that was clear enough, though he'd been a bit put out when Ned first introduced her, had muttered something about business, and not knowing they'd have company ... Ned had ignored him, he'd reached the age when he didn't hear if he didn't want to.

Anyway, the petulance didn't last long. When the publisher fellow was doing his stuff she sat quietly and listened in and when he'd finished she joined easily in the small-talk. He asked her about Africa and she told him. When he started asking her what she read, she said she read nothing, she used to read, but she hadn't for years. He started dropping names then – people he knew, people they published. She should read this, read that. He wrote the names down for her and she laughed and folded them into her handbag. She said she probably wouldn't read them, but she might. If she did she would write and let him know what she thought.

Ned liked it that she was honest, that she didn't need to seem to be what she wasn't. He hadn't any time for people who said with pride that they never read, but she didn't say it with pride, she just said that she had once, but she didn't now. She didn't explain why.

Ned smiled to himself. Publisher fellow wanting her to himself, trying to work out what it was about her, was she with him, what was going on? Chap half his age, too. Hannie with a good few years on him and not pretending that she hadn't.

He didn't think anything would come of this backlist business. Still, it was a decent place, she'd enjoyed it, and he'd enjoyed having somewhere to take her.

Afterwards he couldn't keep it to himself. He fancied you, he'd said and, I know, she'd said, and laughed as though it was a good joke and made him buy her an ice-cream to eat in the sun outside the National Gallery though she'd just eaten two puddings off the trolley.

She'd never been to the National before, knew nothing about pictures and never had. He said he'd write her a list to go in her handbag and she smiled. He had planned to take her to the English section, to the Turners and the portraits, show her the things he liked, but he couldn't remember the way and he couldn't get her to walk past anything that caught her eye. She spotted the Monet water lilies through the arch from the room before and once she was there he didn't want to move her away. She didn't say anything, just stood looking. He told himself he could see how she'd have looked when she was a girl, and it wasn't so different. He wondered why she'd never seen pictures when it was plain that she liked them.

She didn't bother to look at anything that didn't attract her right away. There was a Holbein she went for, a woman full-length in a black dress on a dark-green ground, a fine painting.

Christina of Denmark, he told her. Painted for Henry the Eighth to see if he liked the look of her. Lucky for her, he didn't.

But Hannie didn't know about Henry the Eighth and his six wives. He was taken aback. You didn't learn British history in Dutch schools, she said, especially when the schools were in obscure Dutch colonies.

She might not know much about history or pictures, but she didn't miss much.

When he asked her why she liked the picture she said because the woman owned herself. And then she said wasn't it funny she should go on owning herself even hundreds of years later when she was long dead. He knew what she meant if he didn't think about it.

When they came out and they hadn't looked at what he had wanted to show her, she said she was sorry but she'd been excited and had forgotten.

He didn't mind. He had enjoyed watching her excitement. She had taken his arm walking down the street. He was pleased. The expedition was a success.

He smiled to himself now, remembering. The picture of

Hannie in London faded. He saw again the river bank in the evening light. People strolling, a loiter of dogs and children. A little cloud of midges danced by his left ear. He scratched, reached down for his hat, got up and set off up the path to the village pub where he was staying.

'Been enjoying the sunshine?' The landlord was cheerful in his polished bar parlour. Ned thought of Keoghs, its wooden shelves and stacks of untipped Carrol's cigarettes and dusty bottles of Guinness. Mrs Keogh coming through from the back, drying her hands on a dirty cloth. Serving him in silence, leaving when it was done.

He thought of the wide Blackwater, its wooded banks and hidden farms and windy skies.

He'd ask her, get it over with. Then he could go home.

✎ *Chapter 3* ✎

*H*annie had made her move as soon as it looked as though Ned Renvyle might come through. She'd told Beth she wanted to take her into her confidence, put all her cards on the table. Then she'd told her about the separation and the will.

She might get something in the end, she said, but then again, she might not. That was all in the future anyway. For now she was broke and she needed to remarry. She asked Beth for help.

Beth couldn't let a kitten drown, much less a scrawny old cat like Hannie, and anyway she knew the facts of life for women of their generation. Or rather she knew that she didn't. She had always lived in comfort, was terrified as to her future should Tom ever decide to abandon her, she had an acute imaginative sympathy for Hannie's dreadful position.

Tom didn't, but Tom let it run on because that was what Beth wanted and anyway he didn't mind having Hannie around for a bit, she livened things up, added spice to the daily fare, though that wasn't what he told his wife.

Tom was a dull man; he'd been dull in Kenya, and he was duller here. If she hadn't been at such a low ebb, Hannie thought, she couldn't have stood it for two hours, much less two weeks.

'Invite them,' Andrew had said to Hannie years ago in Kenya. 'He's a bore but he might be useful.' Andrew had had an eye for useful men.

So she had. A little racing and a lot of booze – Tom and Beth, letting their hair come unpinned for a year or two, far from the Home Counties. Well, now they could pay for their fun.

'He's too old,' Beth said. 'They'll say you're marrying him for his money.'

'Who'll say? I don't know anyone any more. Besides, he hasn't got any money, or none that you'd notice. If he had, I wouldn't be dithering around like this, would I?'

'Oh, Hannie,' Beth wailed, 'I wish you wouldn't do that! You know how slow I am. I always think you're serious.'

'I am. Totally.' She got up, took out her cigarettes, remembered and put them back. She walked round the room to calm herself. Ned had been to the house for a drink. Now Beth was having second thoughts.

'He might die,' Hannie said. 'He's pushing seventy. At least then I'd have a house.'

Beth shot her a swift look. She stabbed at the needlepoint she was working. 'I do hate this cat,' she said passionately. 'All these marmalades and browns. I have such a lovely one waiting for when I've finished this.' She gazed at Hannie, her eyes wistful and large.

'Roses and honeysuckle on a green ground,' she went on. 'Beautiful colours, all shading into each other. Andrew died, Hannie. It won't necessarily help –'

'True,' Hannie said, ignoring the tapestry. 'Andrew died. And no house. Not so slow, my dear Beth.'

Beth flushed with pleasure.

'And it's not true that you don't know anyone, Hannie,' she said, taking courage. 'It's never true. One always knows someone, no matter where one goes. It's one of those laws.'

Hannie said nothing. Beth retreated.

'Well, at least you wouldn't have to cope with sex.' She had the air of one trying to look on the bright side.

Hannie stared. Then she roared: 'Oh Beth, you great booby, how can you be such an innocent?'

It was Beth's turn to stare. 'At his age?' she said weakly. 'Oh no, Hannie, surely not?'

'At his age, either he can't or he'll rut like a baboon. At least till the novelty wears off. He won't be any good, though –' she stopped abruptly. She'd gone too far, had offended Beth's sensibilities.

But it seemed not. 'Won't you mind?' Beth asked, concern in her voice.

'Why should I? That's not what I want him for.'

'I don't mean that. I mean if he wants to do it all the time.'

'I know that's what you mean. It won't make any difference either way. It's not what I want him for. Sex isn't the problem.'

Her voice was indifferent. She glanced at Beth. Now she *had* gone too far. Too bad. She'd asked Beth for help, not counselling.

But Beth hadn't finished. 'I couldn't bear it.' She shuddered. 'Someone one didn't know. At our age . . .'

Hannie looked at her. 'How married you are, my dear Beth,' she said lightly. 'Only to have sex with someone one's known for twenty years . . .'

Beth blushed. She picked up her needlepoint. Hannie could be quite cruel.

'If you hate that cat so much, why are you sitting there martyring yourself over it? Why don't you just dump it, start a new one?'

'Sara,' Beth said hopelessly. 'Sara gave it to me for my birthday. Tom helped her choose. He said he thought I'd *like* cats with pansies in the border.'

'Let me see.'

Beth handed her the frame. Hannie carried it over to the window and studied it briefly. 'Horrible,' she said. 'Why don't you have an accident?'

'Oh, Hannie, I couldn't.'

'Why ever not? Spill something. So disappointing. But Sara would forgive you. You could console yourself with the other one. Would you like me to do it for you?'

'Oh no, Hannie, no. Please give it back. I don't mind it, really I don't.'

Hannie shrugged. She handed it over.

Beth bundled the wools up together and pushed the whole lot out of sight.

In case I make a grab for them, Hannie thought.

Beth gathered herself. 'Where is this house, anyway?' she asked, determinedly.

'Somewhere on a river called the Blackwater,' Hannie said. 'Near a town pronounced *Yawl* and spelt Y–o–u–g–h–a–l. It's where Sir Walter Raleigh planted his American potatoes. He seems to think that's important. But it's a farm, not a house. A farmhouse.'

When Tom came in from the office looking for attention and a drink he found the two women on their hands and knees on the floor, pouring over an atlas. Beth scrambled to her feet, talking about the time and how she hadn't noticed. Hannie stayed where she was, elbows on the rug, bottom sticking out, chin cupped in her hands, staring down at the opened book. When she'd finished staring she shifted her gaze up to Tom and regarded him balefully.

'We were just looking for somewhere,' Beth was explaining vaguely. 'The children had the atlas out – some argument they were trying to settle.'

'We're trying to find where Ned Renvyle lives,' Hannie said. She straightened up and sat back on her heels. 'With a view to deciding whether or not I should marry him.'

'Has he asked you?'

Hannie grinned. 'Not yet,' she said. 'But he will, and I want to be ready with my answer. We're just adding up the pros and cons, working out his assets. If he's got any, that is. Or at least enough to make it worth my while. You couldn't help, could you, Tom? All your contacts? The Langtons? Somebody must know?'

'No, I couldn't,' Tom said. 'And I'd stay well clear of the Langtons. They're fond of Renvyle by all accounts, won't want to see him taken advantage of. Any more than I do,' he added pompously. 'It's not decent, what you're doing, Hannie, you should lay off him. I've a good mind to ring him up and tell.'

'But you won't,' Hannie said, getting to her feet and giving Tom an affectionate pat on the arm on her way to the drinks tray. 'You're much too English to go interfering. Besides, if you do that you'll never get rid of me.' She handed him a drink. She poured herself a refill and fished out the glass that Beth had quietly pushed behind a vase out of Tom's sight. She poured a large gin into that, too, and held it out to Beth. Beth flushed and took it, not looking at Tom.

'I could throw you out.'

Hannie shook her head. 'You'd upset Beth. The house would be unsettled for at least a week. You'd hate that. Better marry me off to Ned.'

Beth gaped at her when she said such things, but Hannie knew it earned her keep with Tom.

'Anyway,' she went on, 'I can't see what you're taking such a high moral tone about. Ascertaining assets is all I'm doing. Perfectly sensible and respectable and it's always gone on. I bet Beth's father wanted to know exactly what *you* proposed to keep her on. And if he didn't it was only because *her* mother had it all off your mother long before you even knew you liked her.' Hannie sat herself down on a leather pouf. She looked intently up at Tom.

'Well, I haven't got a mother and I'm not thinking of marrying Ned for reasons of altruism. He'd understand. He'd probably show me his bank statements if I asked him. And he's quite mediaeval enough to believe in dowries and exchange of lands.'

'Neither of which you happen to have.'

'True, but if I had I wouldn't be thinking of marrying him at all, would I?' she said shrugging. 'He's no catch, Tom. He's nearly twenty years older than I am and he wants a wife. He can't have it all ways, he'll have to deal.'

'My God, Hannie, I'm glad I'm safely married to Beth. Is this what you did to poor old Andrew?'

'I didn't have to with Poor Old Andrew,' she said. 'Poor Old Andrew liked my terms. I married him in the nick of time to stop that Clayton woman he was screwing from leaving her husband and landing in on him. Remember her? Janine Clayton? Looked like Zelda Fitzgerald with a temperament to match? Poor Old Andrew was just begging to be saved from Janine. Anyway, it was a straight deal. A wife in his house and a mother for his children. Someone to tidy away his women. I needed a home for Joss.'

'Andrew and Janine Clayton?' Tom was caught irresistibly. 'But didn't she kill herself around . . . ?'

'Around that time? Two weeks after Andrew and I were married. Booze and pills. Got out of that one by the skin of his teeth, didn't he? And it nearly came out. Husband hysterical, wanting to tell the world, show Andrew up for what he was. Poor bastard loved her, you see. Under a lot of financial pressure, though. Got leaned on by the Powers-That-Be. Tell, and we won't lift a finger keeping off the vultures –'

'And did they?' Tom was unwilling to let the story go.

'Indeed they did. Helped him sell up, ship himself home.' Hannie shrugged her shoulders, took a mouthful of gin. 'Didn't you know all this? It wasn't so long after you left –'

'Who killed herself?' Sara stood in the doorway, her face young, blank, deceptively innocent. A strand of dark hair lay over her shoulder. She picked it up and chewed at it absently, her eyes intent.

Hannie swivelled lazily round on her stool. 'A woman we knew once,' she said.

'Because of your husband?'

'Partly. Partly because she was a mess.' She swivelled lazily back, catching Beth's tightened mouth in the turn of her eye. The little bitch didn't like her. The little bitch was the apple of her mother's eye. Beth was shooing her out now, a good sheepdog, careful of its charge, firing darts of reproach at Hannie as she went.

Sod, Hannie thought. Now Beth would go all prim and

proper on her again, remember she'd said she'd help Hannie find a husband but only if Tom didn't know. But she had to feed Tom the odd titbit, keep him diverted, stop herself from dying of boredom. This way he'd forget to grouse at her living in his house and drinking his gin and leading his wife astray.

❧ *Chapter 4* ❧

Ned took her for dinner that night, to a place someone had recommended. It offended him – the thick carpets, the starched damask, the fancy words in the menu. And he didn't like the prices.

She watched him, his crotchety reaction. She saw his age, the setness of his ways and opinions. She refrained from soothing him or playing up to him. No sense in bringing him to the point, if she wasn't going to be able to live with him.

He studied the menu while the waiter hovered. He looked up, caught her eye, flushed.

'We could go somewhere else,' she said neutrally.

'And have you think me a cheapskate?' He made an effort, smiled self-consciously.

She raised an eyebrow, not returning the smile.

'What do you want, Hannie?' Ned asked her. The waiter was approaching.

She picked up the menu. 'Whatever's most expensive.'

'Is it a test?'

She nodded, not looking up. The waiter was standing there, silently waiting. She ordered the lobster. Ned did the same. The waiter wrote it down.

'Did I flinch?' Ned asked when he'd gone.

'Hardly at all,' she said. 'Call him back and we'll change it.'

'No we won't.'

'Yes we will. Try and hide your relief, Ned. The waiter will despise you.'

'Do you?'

'Hardly at all. And I don't like lobster.'

The food was better than the surroundings. Afterwards, they sat on over the coffee. Ned had offered her information over the past days, not an account exactly, but a beginning: his family's ascendancy origin in Ireland, his childhood in his grandmother's house following his soldier-father's early death, the world war he had gone to fight in. Then his marriage, his travels, his books. An outline had begun to emerge.

Hannie had told him almost nothing and he hadn't asked. He had waited. Now she sat, folded arms resting on the table, telling him her story or the bones of it.

She had told it many times and many ways and it surprised her a little, how she was telling Ned now. She told him less than the whole but far more than she'd meant to, and she told it nearer the truth.

Perhaps it was her age, she thought. At fifty-two she had little appetite left for pretence, could not be bothered any more with best behaviour. Perhaps it was her desperation or the way he took it. He sat there quietly, looking at her as she talked, accepting what she told him without comment or apparent judgement. It eased her and it loosened her tongue. It made her think there might be more between them than she'd expected, that this plan of hers might be marginally less deranged than it seemed.

She didn't hide her origins, her past marriages or her need now for a new one. She didn't hide her financial situation. She spoke briefly of Joss, her son, whom she had left in Africa. She made it clear that she wanted him near to her when she settled, that she didn't care for smartness or reputation, just that the school was steady.

She had thought of looking for a job, she said, but she had no experience, references or qualifications.

'Do you have friends?' he asked, leaning back in his chair, his legs stretched out and his feet crossed under the table.

'Influential friends? No. I have acquaintances. A few people I can fall back on in a crisis. I had a friend once but she's dead.' She didn't explain further. He nodded gravely. They both knew the sort of job she could get at her age and in these times.

'You'd better think about marrying me,' he told her. 'No great shakes. I'm sixty-nine. No money to speak of. Farm takes every penny and all my time. Quiet sort of a life, not much in the way of excitement, not very social.' He paused. His eye swept the crowded restaurant, the muddle of smells and voices, the busy faces.

'But at least you can breathe there,' he added passionately, 'at least it's a life. Not like *this*.'

Here Hannie held up her hand as though to stop him.

'We've had a week together, Ned, a pleasant week. It doesn't have to go any further, you don't have to solve my life for me. You could just get on your boat now and go back to Ireland. We could put all this down to experience, leave it at that.'

He regarded her gravely. 'Are you trying to save me the pain of rejection, Hannie?'

'I'm trying to make you think before you speak.' She lit a cigarette, leaned back, inhaled. 'I'm not in this for my ego, Ned, I'm not collecting skulls. If you ask me, I'll probably say yes.'

'I'm asking you, Hannie.'

'I'm not much of a catch,' she said quietly, looking straight at him.

He liked that, that she wasn't doing the coy wistful thing and looking at the table as another woman might.

'You wouldn't be sitting here if you were.'

He smiled suddenly, his face twisting. 'Your loss, my luck,' he added. 'Whatever it was that you lost.'

It wasn't a question. He knew there was something and he wasn't going to ask. Hannie sighed deeply. She rested her head heavily on her hand, the heel of her palm pushing up her cheekbone, and stared at him with a weary intentness.

'Can I have till tomorrow, Ned? I want to go through it one more time. I want to be sure.'

He nodded. Her words didn't leave much room for illusion. He didn't quite know how it had come to this but still he didn't want to draw back.

'Just the same,' Tom was saying, 'there must have been something. Hannie ran a tight ship and if that was the deal she had with Andrew, there must have been something big to break it.'

'Someone else?' Beth's voice came softly. Hannie stood breath-still in the hallway.

Tom snorted. 'It was an arrangement, you heard her. And Andrew liked things that way. Divorce too expensive, too disruptive, liked his women as mistresses and no fancy ideas about becoming wives.'

Beth's voice, softly again. Hannie couldn't catch the words.

'Wrong tree there, old girl. He'd have turned a blind eye, part of the deal. He'd only have asked for a bit of discretion.'

Beth, anxious now: 'Tom, I'm sure I heard a car, I'm sure she's back. It's making me nervous, talking like this.'

'Nonsense, we'd have heard her coming in. Anyway, she's living off us, isn't she – using us – what're you worrying about? Have you written to Kenya lately? Might be an idea. See what happened to make Andrew dump her. Drop Martia a line, or Dora Seaton. Don't say she's staying, just that we saw her at the wedding.'

'Tom, I couldn't, I really couldn't . . .'

'I don't see why not. I don't see why you always have to be so wet about things. She'd do it in your place without so much as stopping to catch her breath.'

'Oh Tom, she wouldn't.'

'She damn well would. And if you think otherwise you're a bigger fool than I took you for. Write tomorrow. Don't push for an answer but make it clear you'd like one.'

'I can't, you shouldn't ask, it's not right, Tom, Hannie's my friend.' Beth's mutiny ended on a low wail.

Very softly, very quietly, Hannie stepped back through the panelled hallway, back through the door through which she had come. Then she stood in the darkness, waiting. Noisily she re-made her entrance.

Hannie poured another gin and set herself to go through it all again. How easy he'd been to bring to the point, she thought. A word or two here, a sentence left hanging. Ned Renvyle had rushed into the breach.

Not so easy to work the same process on herself. Especially in the long insomniac nights when she paced about her room. Already she'd been over and over it, arguing it backwards and forwards, all the time knowing it was so much wasted effort because the truth was you couldn't ever know. Life with another human being – marriage, call it what you would – was always more than the sum of its parts, and it was always the small unknown, unnoticed things that made it unbearable or redeemed it. Beth, worrying about sex, had seized on the least of her problems. She didn't marry for sex, though fortunately most men did.

But she didn't think it was sex that had brought Ned Renvyle to the point. Clearly he could do without it, or he'd have lived a different life. And he wasn't queer, she was sure of that. So if it wasn't sex, what was it, and why her?

Companionship most likely. And to complete his picture of himself, his life. Return to his roots, a home, a wife in it. Romantic. That was his pattern.

He'd never lived with a woman, not really, but he thought he had. That brief marriage, all those years ago. Isobel, a distant cousin, become an army nurse for the war that had over-run the world. He'd met her again in India afterwards, and they'd come back on the same troop-ship in 1947, happy to be thrown together, a childhood friendship renewed. They'd been married not long afterwards in London. Six months later she was dead. It seemed she'd gone home for a visit, this Isobel, and fallen off a horse. A hunting accident. A grim look on Ned's face as he'd said it.

Idly she worked out how old he'd been, wondered what he'd been like then. Tongue-tied, she guessed, all suppressed feeling. Twenty-four, a melodramatic age. Astonished deep down inside himself that he'd survived at all.

Funny the way he talked about Ireland as home when he'd hardly ever lived there. She never spoke of Java as home, nor Africa either, she never spoke of anywhere. She would lay money he always had that look when he spoke of Isobel. Years of habit. A candle always burning before the shrine.

He had a portrait, he'd said; she could see it in her mind's eye. Some girl with dark cloudy hair, a pale, arrogant face. His class, one of his own.

He'd been lucky. What price his precious expeditions if she'd stayed on her horse?

And he'd never remarried. Had it all gone into his journeys? Perhaps. Perhaps he had a low sex-drive, perhaps he'd just done without . . .

But he liked women, you could tell that, for all his asceticism, he liked women. Well, nothing unusual in that. Men who loved hardship often loved softness between. They just liked it earned.

Prostitutes? Possibly. It went with his class. Maybe he'd bought sex the way he'd hired porters to carry his gear? Or maybe it was married white women, the wives of the men he stayed with in out-of-the-way places.

No. She shook her head to herself, the gesture underlining the mental negative. Not other men's wives, that wouldn't be done in Ned's book, not unless they threw themselves at him. No, not then either. He'd be pompous about that, would think them predatory, be ashamed for their husbands, for himself . . .

Hannie stopped herself, this wasn't the point, she was getting side-tracked into stupid speculation. Sex wasn't difficult.

He might have odd ideas, plenty of men did, but all she had to do was find them out and pander to them. And they'd have separate bedrooms. That, too, went with his class. For pleasure there were always other men.

She brought herself back to the problem. Marriage to Ned. Or not. She walked herself round the room as the thoughts walked round in her head. She stopped, lit another cigarette, poured more gin. The house was quiet beneath her.

She could marry again in Kenya, but she'd have to take a step down, perhaps quite a big step down. She moved in a small tight caste and her history was becoming too well known. Correction: Joss's history was becoming too well known.

And it wasn't only Joss and his reputation that worried her. It was Africa, the demise of the glory days of white colonial Africa. Which she'd lived on like a tick on a sheep's back, sucking the rich blood.

Well that was all changing now, even South Africa no longer a sure bastion of privilege and ease. Mandela was free, apartheid was crumbling, once the factions left off quarrelling and pushed together they'd be hard to stop. Time to pack your bags Hannie, time to move on. Survivors couldn't afford to hang around to see how things panned out.

Hence this trip. Getting started was the hard bit. She could marry Ned and as Ned's wife she'd be in. After that she could take her time, look around, see what else was on offer . . .

She walked across to the mirror and stood squarely in front of it, meeting her own eyes. Who was she kidding? She was no Jessica, tending an immaculate C.V. She grinned at herself, a painful, self-conscious grin. She was getting older, less employable, already there were too many job changes. And there was Joss.

Reality. She might as well start getting used to it because this was the way it was going to be from hereon in.

And if no alternative offered itself, if she had to stay with Ned?

A farm again. Well, she wouldn't starve, it would be a home

for Joss. And she was older now she might settle. Who knows what you can settle to if there isn't a choice? Certainly she, Hannie, did not.

And he might not be too bad. Beth said she didn't know anything about him, but Africa was full of men like Ned Renvyle, men who found the world noisy, suburban and over-crowded, with the wrong people running things. Romantics who couldn't accept the world as it was now.

But he was decent and straight and he wouldn't be cruel. And he had a hundred and thirty acres, some of it 'marginal', whatever that meant. It didn't sound much, not when you were used to Africa, but there must be enough to live on or he wouldn't be asking her. She had made herself quite clear about Joss from the start and he'd accepted it: a reasonable, fee-paying boarding school until he was eighteen.

She couldn't leave Joss where he was much longer. The school was only letting him stay on over the summer because she had written and begged them, using Andrew as her excuse, his recent death, his empty place on the board of governors, promising that she was making other arrangements.

Other arrangements. She said the words aloud, her voice full of mockery and self-disparagement. Ned was her other arrangement, the best she could do for the moment, perhaps the best she could do at all. She went for the bottle, slopped more liquid into the glass. It was nearly four in the morning, the sky had lightened, sunrise was not far off. She no longer had any assets, only a liability, it all came down to that one thing. Joss, her fear for Joss, her need to build a life that would protect him.

And how would Ned react if Joss did something again? *When* Joss did something again.

He would stand by her. That's how he was, how Andrew wasn't, despite the schools, the lineage, the family history. Ned would stand by her because that was what he'd expect of himself. That was why she had come this far with Ned. None of the other reasons mattered a damn.

34

She crossed to the opened window and stood with the cool air of dawn flowing round her.

Or maybe she'd let him go, take a chance on another one . . .

With the years closing in, the mirror giving her relentlessly back to herself?

Who was she kidding, she asked herself again. He was the best she could get, so she'd take him. Against the time when she would take what she could get.

She leaned her elbows on the sill and stared out at the thinning darkness. The security lights still burned, the swimming pool glowed blue by the shrubbery, pale rectangles of light lay over the shaved grass. And beyond the lawns and walls the orange glow of habitation and the low roar of traffic that had not ceased all night.

She felt her hopelessness, the fight gone out of her. In her mind the soft thick darkness of another continent, the great, soft stars that bloomed through the turning night. Who knows, she thought bitterly, she might have more in common with Ned Renvyle than she thought. She longed for Africa, its endlessness and space.

'So Beth thinks I'm too old for you,' he said. 'What does Tom think?'

'He thinks I'm taking advantage of you. He thinks you'll rue the day you met me. Or something like that.' She spoke carelessly, her eyes on the rows of lichened graves lining the path they walked.

Ned turned to her. She wore a dark blue blouse and a sand-coloured skirt and her feet were tanned in her leather sandals. She looked well, strolling about in the dappled churchyard, he was proud of her.

'Do you?' he asked seriously.

'I wouldn't be surprised.' She grinned up at him. 'Would you?'

'No,' he said thoughtfully, not grinning back. 'I think I

wouldn't be at all surprised. We may both rue the day. Do you want to back off?'

They'd stopped in their walk to stand by a sloping gravestone. She laid her hand on its mossy back. She looked at him, her dark eyes gone distant and unreadable.

'No. Do you?'

He didn't speak for a minute.

'Oddly enough,' he said, 'I don't.'

He smiled then. He meant it. He thought, for all their mutual warnings, that it was straightforward. He didn't realise he would come to love her.

~ *Chapter 5* ~

'*T*he Mona Vullagh Mountains,' Ned said. He waved his hand at a long blue line of hills to the right. 'And those are the Comeraghs beyond.'

Hannie looked. She thought she was seeing foothills. She sat waiting for the mountains to appear.

'Irish mountains are small,' Ned said. 'Small and blue, small and brown. You'll get used to them, once your eye adjusts they'll seem quite high.'

Ned was smiling all the time now as he drove. Hannie watched these mountains that weren't mountains and said nothing. They crested a rise and below was a bay with a town built round a harbour.

'Dungarvan,' Ned said, as though they'd reached somewhere significant. They drove into the town and he parked on the quay under a battered notice offering boats for hire.

'Dungarvan's our nearest town,' he said. 'We'll get out, take a look around, you can see where it is you'll be living.'

Hannie got out. The air was sharp with the stench of fish and seaweed. She stood looking down into the harbour.

'Tidal,' Ned said. She nodded.

The harbour was deep and wide and empty of water. There were beached half-deckers under the wall and four small sailing craft lying about on the muddy sands. It was quiet, all but deserted. The tide must have turned, she could hear the trickle of the water running back into the harbour, seeping in around the beached boats. Wading birds dug in the silt, a few gulls rose and fell on the moist air, a single grey heron stood watch by a lone puddle.

Smallness, quietness, soft grey light. Whatever she had expected, it hadn't been this.

'King John's castle,' Ned was saying, waving his hand to the right where abandoned warehouses and high walls of dark stone crumbled against the greying sky. 'Important town in the fourteenth century.'

The weather was breaking up, the day going cold. He walked her through side-streets, past rain-stained, stone-built houses, often dilapidated or deserted, the slates off, the gutters full of weeds, saplings sprouting from the chimneys. Away from the harbour the town revived. The main square looked almost prosperous, the tall, elegant old houses painted up in pastel shades, the clear colours lending them a raffish, down-at-heel gaiety as they leaned in together, disdaining the street life below.

Hannie stood on the pavement surveying the shops and businesses. A bank or two, a heating supplier, a gents' shoe shop, a building society. The rest was pubs, take-aways, small plain grocers with not much in them.

Nowhere you'd want to linger, nothing you'd want to buy.

It had started well, she reminded herself. Setting off last night there'd been the expectation, the excitement and flurry of departure, standing in the darkness by the packed car she had felt her spirits soar.

It was movement, the release in movement, the scrunch of feet on the night gravel, the map and sandwiches and torch lying ready on her seat.

'Oh Hannie,' Beth had wailed, 'I feel as though you're going away for good, as though I'll never ever see you again.'

And Hannie had laughed, free at last of this house, this friendship, free of herself as she had had to be here.

It continued well. She liked the night drive, the three a.m. boat, the snatched sleep on the cramped seats of the crowded lounge, the dawn light seeping in from the sea through the uncurtained windows. They had stood together on the deck as the land drew close; Ned, eager, showing her Ireland, pointing out the Wexford landmarks.

The ship had moved slowly in, long unbroken ripples fanning out across the sheened water with its passing. Hannie had stared at a herring gull perched on the railing, its unblinking yellow eye, the red stain marking its long hooked beak. It slid off as the ferry pulled in, dropped to the water, swept high again to join with a clamouring cloud. It was a perfect morning, the air vivid with salt, the empty harbour pearly and pale in the shining stillness.

They'd stopped when they got to Waterford. They bought breakfast, then walked along the quays inspecting the trawlers and tugs and the big cattle boats with their foreign names and foreign flags loading up with hay. She'd seen worse, she thought confidently. She liked the busy port, the wide river, the tugs and buoys and pilot boats. There was a world beyond this place.

A buoyant mood. Standing here in Dungarvan, it was hard to remember the feeling. She had fallen into the old trap, she told herself, the trap of thinking that once she got through the thing in front of her then all the rest would somehow be all right.

And she had got through. She had found Ned, she had married him, she'd embarked on another life in another world.

But had she thought enough about that world?

Ned touched her arm. She woke from her reverie and followed him back to the car.

A few minutes out of Dungarvan and the town, such as it was, might never have been. They headed north away from the coast, each time leaving the road they were on for one that was narrower, more winding and more pot-holed. The hedges closed in. They were high and dense and thickened with full-grown trees. Where the hedges broke there were old walls, long crumbling stretches breached like broken teeth in a rotting mouth, great ivy-burdened trees pressing up against them from behind.

Sometimes there were neither walls nor hedges, but little low-lying fields and boggy stretches of rock and rushes. Sometimes there were farms, the houses hidden, the outbuildings blank against the roadsides. Once or twice a bit of a field held a gaggle of unfinished bungalows. Then hedges and trees again for miles, their high wild branches cutting off the sky. Hannie sat very quietly in her seat, looking, saying nothing. She felt as if she were burrowing down, away from life as she knew it, back into some overgrown and forgotten past. Ned, sitting so close beside her, noticed nothing but his own emotions at returning.

'They'll want to know your maiden name and who your mother was,' he said suddenly. 'It's so that they can work out who you are.'

She looked at him, but didn't speak.

'It isn't personal,' he said, 'don't take offence. They'll just want to find the connection.'

'What connection?'

'That their mother's second cousin had a house off your great-aunt's brother-in-law in Kildare in 1926. Or better still, a horse.' Ned laughed, pleased with himself, her bewilderment. 'Ignore it, they'll lose interest once they find you're not from here at all.'

Hannie watched his profile as he drove. She didn't know what he was talking about and she didn't care, but she noticed his anxiety and his excitement. At first she thought they were for her, were about arriving here and having her see the life he wanted her to share. Then she saw that it was something altogether simpler. He was nearly home, in the place he liked best, where he liked himself best.

She saw that she was the one being shown the bride.

A figure walking the road ahead called a sheep dog in to heel. Ned slowed and raised his hand in salute. The man saluted back.

'Best not mention the previous marriages,' Ned said to her suddenly. 'Catholic country, and all that.' She looked at him sharply but he was edging the car round a deep bend and over a little bridge.

'This is it,' he said, 'this is home.'

The house was built of rough stone, rendered with plaster, and sat in a muddle of yards and sheds. It was long and narrow, with a newer wing built on at right angles, mature trees around it and a short shrubby drive to the road. The whole impression was not so much shabby as workman-like and a bit down-at-heel. Probably mid-nineteenth century, Ned said, though he wasn't sure, he wasn't much interested in houses except for the big Georgian piles of his class and childhood. It was her domain, he said, she could explore it thoroughly herself and do what she liked within reason.

As soon as he'd done with the house Ned had taken her down to the river. It was tidal here, he explained. At low tide the pull of the sea all but emptied the river. A thick silt of pale mud called a slob lay wherever the water had been.

Step on to this slob, he said, and you went to your knees before you stopped sinking. Bring the boat in on an ebbed tide and you waded through mud like the Somme.

He had pointed to the middle of the water where it was flat and almost still, the current there curiously stationary. That was sea-water pushing back up the river, meeting the river's flow, he said, the one briefly cancelling out the other. Then the stronger sea-flow won and by high tide you'd think the river ran backwards. There was six or eight feet of a drop between tides, and except at the lowest point of the ebb the water was brackish with salt.

It seemed he couldn't get enough of showing and explaining. There was his boat, called a 'punt', on a very long mooring because of the tidal drop. Here was the 'cut' where it lay, a little man-made creek sliced at right-angles into the bank.

You had to know what you were doing at every moment on this river, he said. The ebb tide was worse than the flood, the rip of the current made fierce by the pull of the sea.

The near bank where they stood was rough grassland falling off into rushes, grazed by ambling sheep. At the river's edge a few saplings clung, ash and alder and willow, their roots knotting themselves frantically into the eroding soil. A path wandered between meadow and water.

She stood with her arms folded and her feet in the boggy ground. A light chill wind tugged at her skirt and hurried the sky. The weak sun shone in a vague glory, luminous behind the moving cloud. A squall of rain blew over, pocking the water, and was gone. The river went smooth and pewter-coloured and white gulls dropped out of the sky and dipped to kiss other white gulls waiting under the water. Rings of black light spread out where they touched.

She looked across the sweep of the water. The far bank was bosomy with great, still trees, their deep green just bronzed with late summer. Downriver these trees thickened into dense woodland. Upriver the trees thinned and the river bank lost itself in stretches of tall flagged reeds that moved with the wind.

You could see the house from where they stood. Its raggedy outline of roofs and buildings peered over the hummocky meadow like an old woman too anxious to see to be altogether discreet about not being seen.

The river flooded easily, Ned said. Heavy rain, big tides, the waters ran fast and furious over the banks and into the woods and the meadows. That's why the house was built up and back like that. He was proud of this strong dangerous river and its complexities, she heard it in his voice and in his words.

Hannie looked and listened but said little. She was tired now from the night journey and the stress of expectation. It was all smaller but oddly wilder than she had expected. She hadn't grasped what he'd been saying about seas and tides. How could she, what had such things to do with this place? It seemed so lost and inland – how could so short a journey bring her so far away from anywhere?

❧ *Chapter 6* ❧

Niamh moved down the washing line, feeling the clothes as she passed, lifting a shirt here, the leg of a pair of jeans there, pressing the fabric to her cheek to test the stage of drying. She liked to iron straight from the line, liked the burning off of the last damp, the slight glaze, the smell of the fresh, folded clothes that she carried to the hot-press. As a student she hadn't ironed, it was hardly done to be creaseless in Fine Art, but left to herself she liked ironing and she liked shaking out pressed trousers in the morning and pushing her long arms into smoothed and folded T-shirts.

Nothing dry enough yet. The afternoon was damp and still, it smelled of grass and leaves and growing things. She ran her hands down her sides, down the narrowing-in of her waist, till they rested firm on her hips.

She stood so, liking the feel of her hips under her hands, absently inspecting the swelling apples on the mossed tree behind the line. Further back, on the straggle of lawn that was more like a field, Ned had planted six young apple trees, old-fashioned varieties local to the area, the strains carefully mixed for pollination.

'Worth the trouble,' he'd said to her. 'All this homogenis-ation.' He'd shaken his head in disapproval of the easy-grow, heavy-cropping varieties the garden centres sold.

It was like Ned to select carefully, to plant carefully leaving the right distance between each tree, to stake and to label. He was thorough in everything to do with the farm, never just settling for what was to hand. He'd get an idea, read up on it, ring someone who knew, then he'd write off and order exactly what it was that he'd decided on.

Often as not her father was the someone-who-knew whom Ned consulted. Her father liked Ned, he was considered capable of learning and forgiven his inexperience.

Her father would most likely have heard by now about this marriage, Niamh thought. Ned's latest acquisition, and one he certainly hadn't been consulted on. She'd maybe not phone home for a bit or she'd get the benefit of his opinion.

Niamh bent to pick fallen pegs out of the springy grass. A widow with a teenage son who'd been living in Kenya, Mrs Coady had said. Not African but Dutch.

Afrikaans?

No, not Afrikaans and not Dutch from Holland, either. Some island that used to be Dutch but wasn't any more. Part of Indonesia. God knows what she was, a mix-up like that. Never been to Ireland in her life before.

They'd said Hawaii in the post office. Niamh had been in buying stamps and they were all talking about it, the old people tut-tutting and the young ones enjoying it: Ned Renvyle had a woman half his age and he hadn't married her either.

A young lad with a lick of black hair falling over his eyes and a pale, clever face said he'd seen her. He was down by Haydn's cross, he said, bringing in an old cow, and she'd come round a bend in the road with nothing on her but a grass skirt and a big long loop of flowers around her neck.

Ned Renvyle had her from a newspaper ad, he said. And there were more where she came from.

The whole post office was sniggering but the postmistress had spotted Niamh out of the corner of her eye. She threw out a hard warning look, someone had jabbed the black-haired lad with an elbow and they'd all gone silent. Later when Niamh was coming out of Foley's with the paper she'd seen the same boy and he'd started rolling his hips as if he'd a hula hoop on them. Niamh had grinned and he'd grinned back and then she'd remembered herself and looked away.

An old love, Niamh guessed. He'd probably known her for years, loved her for years, the husband's death Ned's opportunity. In her mind Niamh saw a letter in a wooden drawer in a woman's desk, a foreign stamp on the envelope and petals pressed into its fading pages.

Funny the way these clichéd images came up strong like that every time, she thought. Funny the way they kept their potency despite the tired and corny symbols. If you painted them you'd be laughed out, and yet they had something – a fragrance – all those women hoping and dreaming down all those years.

Maybe if you made it like a tiny installation you would get away with it. Drawers from an old desk, letters falling out of them, flowers and sealing wax and broad-nibbed handwriting. Everything real and old, the colours enhanced, a bit over the top.

But not by itself, by itself you'd never throw off the cliché.

A whole show of clichés, that's what you'd need, she thought. Women's dreams of love set in the narrow context of the lives they'd lived.

She could see the roof of the house and a slice of the gable-end wall from where she stood now, a column of smoke from each of the chimneys rising straight up into the still air.

The new wife, lighting fires to air the place. Mrs Coady would be offended, she'd lit them all the day before, and anyway the place wasn't damp.

She was offended herself, she decided. This little romance-fantasy she'd been dreaming up was only a way of pretending to herself that she wasn't.

If only he hadn't gone and done this.

And if he had to do it, if only he'd married someone his own age. She made herself stop. She supposed you could be as lonely at seventy as at any other age.

It was no good, she was too angry. He was old, he had had his life, why did he have to be grabbing for more?

Niamh tucked back a loop of the dark straight hair that was working loose from the knot at the back of her head. Should she go over now, she wondered, or should she leave them alone a bit longer? The uncertainty was making her anxious, destroying her pleasure in the washing line and the tree. She didn't want anything to change now, just as she'd settled in, just as she'd fallen in love with her little house and its raggedy garden, just as she was doing what she wanted to do. These last weeks had been as close to perfection as she could have imagined.

She would go over this evening, she decided. She would take the fresh loaf but not the wild flowers, the bunch she'd picked before breakfast, now drooping in a jam jar on the table.

To hell with it, she'd go now and get it over with. She straightened up out of her indecision, lifted her arms and stretched, her back arched, her round breasts in the blue T-shirt pushing forward like the figurehead of a ship.

'She's only just got here,' Ned was protesting into the phone. 'No, I'm not hiding her, of course I'll bring her over, but not yet.' He was looking at Hannie. Hannie was shaking her head.

'No, she's not sick and she hasn't got three legs.' He was laughing into the phone. 'Perhaps in a day or two.' He looked at Hannie again but he was still getting a negative. 'When she's got used to the place, found her feet a little . . . No, you don't need to ring again, I'll ring back as soon as she's ready.' He put the receiver down.

'It hasn't stopped since we got home,' he told Niamh. 'It's like Christmas, everyone ringing up, asking us over.'

He sounded embarrassed and pleased at the same time. Niamh glanced at Hannie. She was smoking and drinking tea, a full ashtray on the table beside her.

'They want to get a look at the new wife,' she said, addressing Niamh for the first time. Her voice was light, her eyes mocking.

'It's only natural,' Ned said, a little defensively.

'Of course, it is,' she agreed. 'But it's for their benefit, not mine. They can wait till I'm ready.'

'I doubt they'll do that,' Ned said. 'If we don't go there, they'll come over here, you'll see. Might as well do as they want, go and drink their whiskey, it's the same difference.'

Niamh's loaf lay on the table beside Hannie's elbow. Its greaseproof wrapper was unopened. She wished she'd left it sitting on her own table, the flowers drooping beside it.

'It's a lovely house, isn't it?' She heard herself and cringed. It was a plain spare house with an ugly roof and not much grace to it. She sounded stupid and over-eager to please.

Hannie reached across for the teapot. 'It needs re-painting.'

Ned looked surprised. 'Does it? I put a new roof on last year. Everything stripped right down, new beams, cement tiles, it's completely sound. Plaster's a bit stained, I suppose, but it'll do a few years yet.'

'Inside,' Hannie said.

'People go on about slate, can't understand why. Cement's tougher and cheaper.'

Niamh opened her mouth to protest and closed it again. Ned was a funny mixture. In ways he was almost cool, and then he'd come out with stuff that would have shamed even her father.

'This kitchen's dark,' Hannie said deliberately. 'Another window would make a difference, don't you think? In the end wall, perhaps?' She was looking at Niamh, challenging her to agree. Niamh couldn't believe she was being hooked in so fast.

'It will all seem dark,' she said stupidly. Now they both looked at her. 'Ireland, I mean. After Africa. Mrs Coady said you came from Africa.'

'I was born in Java,' Hannie said. 'But it's many years since I lived there.'

Niamh stared. She couldn't think what this woman was doing in Ned's kitchen, nor could she think of anything else to say to her. A few minutes more and she'd go. Leave them to argue about the house or his friends or whatever else they were into.

She'd draw those flowers, she thought. Try and get that half-alive, half-dead look wildflowers had when you picked them and put them in water. The I-can't-thrive-look. And maybe she'd look up Java in the old school atlas that she'd brought from home.

'You didn't mention a cottage with a tenant.'

'It was empty.' Ned was surprised to feel that he was justifying himself. 'It needed a tenant. Fires lit, windows opened, that sort of thing. No damp course, you see.' He put down the paper and smiled patiently at Hannie. 'Ireland's not like Africa.'

'Niamh,' Hannie said as though trying the word on her tongue. 'Eve with an N. Who is she – this almost-Eve, and what's she doing here?'

'N-I-A-M-H.' Ned spelled it out. 'It's an Irish name, nothing to do with Eve, or not that I know of. Her father farms near here, he's by way of being a friend. And he's been a great help to me, so when he asked if I knew of anywhere to let ...'

'You thought of the cottage and it suited everyone?'

'Exactly. Three birds with the one stone, so to speak. A favour for John, a tenant for me and a place for the girl till she finds her feet.'

'It's a strange place for a good-looking girl to come to find her feet,' Hannie said. Her voice was neutral. 'Or is Ireland unlike Africa in that way, too?'

Ned smiled. 'No, not in that way, but she wants to be an artist and she needs a quiet place to live and paint. John's against it, but he doesn't want to play the heavy-handed father. He thinks if she has a go she'll find for herself that it's no way to live.'

'Enough rope to hang herself,' Hannie said. 'And you don't agree with him?'

'No, I suppose I don't. It's outside their ken, painting, she's stepping out of their world and he's afraid for her. He says she's an odd sort of girl, too soft for the farm, the sort who'll be on at you and on at you to save a calf then when it can't be saved she'll give you no peace till it's killed. Can't bear the waiting in watching it die. Well, the girl's by way of being John's calf, the youngest, the gentlest. They wanted a steady sort of life for her but when she wanted to go to the art school in Dublin they didn't stand against her. They thought she could train and then teach in a country school near home till she married . . .' Ned trailed off, shrugging his shoulders.

'And she has other plans?'

'Exactly. John says he'll pay for a year while she has a go. When the year's up she can do teacher training. He says she's a good girl at heart and too responsible to be idling. All she needs is a little time and she'll see things his way.'

'And you want to help her to be a painter?'

Ned nodded. 'I'm looking out for commissions for her. People's houses, children, that sort of idea. Things that will help her to pay her way while she learns her trade. I want her at least to have the chance to try. She's a good tenant,' he finished defensively. 'She's turned that cottage inside out, everything's been stripped and aired and washed to an inch of its life. She's a worker all right.'

'That is not quite the same as a painter.'

'Perhaps not. Time will tell.' Suddenly he didn't want to discuss it any more. He picked up the paper. He liked Niamh, was charmed by her lovely, old-fashioned face and her quiet, serious ways. But more than that, he liked young people who dreamed of making their own lives in their own fashion. Suddenly he felt a little foolish and he wasn't quite sure why. He tried not to mind but his pleasure in Niamh's presence was diminished.

❧ *Chapter 7* ❧

*T*he incoming tide was almost full, the river ran wide and dark, its surface swollen with little eddies and currents that creased and dimpled the water. The great trees on the far bank leaned forward and dipped their green boughs in the river. They made with the living waters a closed circle of surrender and completeness. At night there were no lights here, no sounds but the river's flow, the night birds, the scufflings and death cries of small animals. The valley had an atmosphere that was dense and secret, knowing nothing but itself.

Human absence. But an absence altogether unlike that of Africa where men and beasts moved light as thought across the land. This absence was more like presence, it conspired with the centuries of human occupation, denying their passing. Everyone who had ever lived in this valley was still here, still moved in its light, still lived in its emanations of water and land. Standing here was like stepping back to meet them, Hannie thought, stepping back into a past that was also present and future. The place was thronged and dense with lives lived.

A little evening wind had got up. The river shone and shifted, flakes of white light seemed to float on the moving water. Standing beside it, Hannie remembered another place and another river, a greener, sunnier river where it merged into the sea.

It was the place, she decided, the lostness of it. The sense that fatally she must be taken in or rejected and no compromise offered, that the life here would close over her or push her out.

The fifth time a bride, she remembered the first time. Suddenly, and with no warning, in a country more remote from that Indonesian trading station than even the flatlands of Holland, she was beset by her memories.

Piet Boonjes stood before her. Piet Boonjes, solid, Dutch, an island trader; the age those years ago that she was now. Piet, his small blue eyes, his fatty freckled shoulders, his sagging dugs and sagging belly and legs gone skinny, handing her money to add to the store of cash she'd been skimming from his takings for the past two years.

His money, her cut. But mostly she hadn't bothered to justify it like that. She'd just stolen what she could, taking care it was never so much that he'd notice.

But he'd noticed every penny and when the time came for her to leave he'd known how much she had and given her more.

'Tell me where you want to go, Hannie.' He'd held out a bundle of dirty notes. 'I will speak to the captain and arrange your passage. Put this money with the rest, you'll have enough now for a decent start.'

She had taken the money without looking up. She couldn't, it was too far beyond her comprehension. His acceptance of her, his acceptance of life. She couldn't believe he'd just open his hands and let go of her, letting his money go with her.

He'd laughed at her, but not unkindly. 'I thought a year at most but you've stayed two, Hannie. A girl like you, less than half my age. Take it, it's not a gift, it's yours, I owe it to you. On this deal I can truly say I haven't lost.'

She'd looked up then, meeting his eyes in his round clown's face with its comic-sombre air of burden and sadness. The tufts of grey hair stuck out all around like a small boy just climbed from his bed.

'Go, since you must, but write to me from time to time. I will miss you, but only a little. I will have compensations . . .'

He had always had compensations, though she hadn't at first noticed or understood this. Half-caste children ran round the tea gardens. Benign watchers followed her course, knowing she could not last. Everyone knew, even him. Only herself thinking it some secret she hatched and tended alone.

Piet was Indonesian-born Dutch, a hard, shrewd trader, with kindness only for women and natives and small children, shunning the fellow Europeans he despised. He had taught her books and storekeeping, who to cheat and who not to cheat, how to deal. Her mother had brokered the marriage and he had acceded to it; she saw now that she had merely played her cast-part. Piet had married her without expectation, she saw that too. As he might have taken a bale of cloth against his judgement. Wanting it, knowing it would not sell.

Her passage was arranged and did not cost her. She hadn't written, though he'd sent money to a poste restante in Jo'burg those first years. She'd thought of him, but mostly only when she refused a man. In the end the letter she'd sent had asked for a divorce.

The letter back didn't come from Piet. She could marry whom she liked, it seemed, for Piet was dead.

She was astonished then; somehow it hadn't occurred to her that Piet could die. He'd been in a Japanese camp in the war and she knew he would not easily let life go.

'There's a time when it's nothing to die,' he had said. 'You're so weak and the door stands open and all around they're walking through that door. But if you come back to life after that, it's a different story. My God, you hold life so tight in your hand, you'll never loosen your grip.'

His clenched fist had beaten softly on the flesh of his thigh as he spoke and his narrowed eyes had stared furiously ahead of him at nothing. Hannie recognised what she was seeing. Her mother had been in a Japanese camp for women. Her mother, too, had survived.

She was sorry then, for herself as much as for him. She had lost the last anchor mooring her to her first life. She had lived these months without it, never even knowing it had gone.

Sometimes in the early evenings, Piet had gone with her to the river to bathe. He would stand waist-deep in the sunny green waters, watching the shadows of fishes move over the sand. The fish floated above, bright and translucent, attached as by wavering threads to these more-real, darker, deeper selves. She would stand beside him, watching the shapes on the sunlit, sandy bottom. He would point and chuckle, he never tired of it. It was his indulgence, his gentlest time.

Would it come to that for her too? Could she ever be so satisfied?

She'd been nineteen then, her whole life ahead of her. Those shut-away years with Piet had been painful with impatience, but not with fear. Now here she was with Ned in just such a closed and forgotten place. Ageing, with no money with which to escape, no place to escape to. And no hope for the future to make it easier to bear.

But also with Joss. They were seeing the school next week, she wanted that done before he arrived from Africa. Get him in on Ned's clout before they smelled a rat and asked for an interview.

Briefly she acknowledged to herself the mistake she had made in coming here. Then she set the knowledge aside. She turned from the river and walked back up to the house.

❦ *Chapter 8* ❦

Mrs Coady threw the sheet out from herself like a sail thrown to the wind. Hannie caught it with practiced ease. They settled it on to the bed, smoothing out the starched whiteness. The slanting sun laid a window of soft light across it. The window repeated itself on the blanket they threw over it, and on to the next and the next.

The same sun pulled rich gleams out of the polished furniture. The two women bent and stretched, lifted and spread, the house quiet and empty around them.

She knows what she's doing, Mrs Coady thought, it's a pleasure to work with her. They'd been at it all day now and there was the rhythm of harmony between them.

Her son was expected, they were changing things round, preparing a room for him. They seemed to have done nothing but change things round since she arrived.

Move this, Mrs Coady, move that. If she needs a dressing table, she must have one. Whatever she wants, Mrs Coady, whatever it is that women need.

She'd shifted things here and shifted things there, his mother's dressing table from the house in Fermoy, the picture from the study that she'd taken a fancy to, the curtains with the knots of faded flowers folded away in the attic, now unfolded, washed, pressed, hung.

Mrs Coady knew the signs. She'd see her walking around the house looking, and then she'd be walking around with him, pointing here and pointing there, planning. There was to be a new bay in the drawing room and a glass-covered porch by the back door and the kitchen was to be opened out to take in the two little end rooms with a window looking on to the garden. The new garden that Joe Casey's digger was manoeuvring into being. And last week an automatic washing machine had arrived from Waterford.

Ambrose Power, builder and odd-job man, said as how he might as well move in. 'Fair play to the women,' he added hastily. 'I never saw a bachelor change a house though he lived in it sixty year. If it wasn't for the women I'd hang up me hat and stay home.'

There'd been no money before. Only for roofs. Always had a thing about good snug roofs, had Ned Renvyle. Anything else you could whistle for.

'Can't have what you can't pay for, Mrs Coady,' he'd say. Which was news to her. And there was no shifting him till this one turned up and persuaded the money out of him.

'It's not that he's mean, exactly, Mrs Coady,' she'd said, swishing the dregs of her coffee around in the mug and knocking it back.

'It's just he's got out of the habit of spending. It may even be it's a habit he never picked up in the first place.' She stopped, looked thoughtful, and then spoke again in that voice that was not foreign like the Dutch and the Germans, but not English either and certainly not Irish. You wouldn't know, listening to her, where it was she came from at all.

'Still, it's never too late to teach an old dog new tricks, now is it?' she was saying. 'And I wouldn't say he'd had much of an example, living around here?'

'No example at all,' Mrs Coady agreed. 'Unless it's a horse they'd be wanting.'

'They' meant his class, the Anglo-Irish, who lived in the great mouldering houses scattered about the valley. This one never pretended to be one of them, she never pretended to be anything. No airs and graces to her, but a distance like a wall when she'd a mind to it. She'd sit you down and she'd be talking or you'd be talking and the next thing she was somewhere else altogether and you'd be left hanging there, the ladder pulled away, the sick feel of empty space under you. You never knew where you were with her.

Any more than his friends did when they came calling in their wellington boots and their padded jackets and their old cars held together with bits of twine. It just depended how the mood took her. He didn't say anything. He was keeping his head down, ignoring the talk, pretending it wasn't happening.

But he was disappointed when she wasn't how he wanted her, you could see that. Well, he might as well get used to the feeling. She was like a wrong horse. One minute all pretty ways and gentle as you please and the next away off with herself and no holding her.

She was no one's, all right.

He looked a fool, standing there beside her, and he'd look a bigger fool before he was through with her. It was hard to watch – a decent straight sort of man as he was. He was proud of himself and proud of her still, for all she wouldn't behave for him.

They were finishing up the room now, she looking around, checking that everything was just so. It looked well. She'd had the broken sash on the window fixed and the chimney swept and she'd painted the walls and the ceiling herself. She'd sanded and re-stained the floor and waxed the boards till they shone. She wasn't afraid of dirtying her hands when she'd a mind to, you could say that for her, if you said nothing else.

It was funny she'd chosen this room though, away down the end of the corridor and looking out over the back field. And funny she wanted a school up there in the North, and no bringing him home at weekends and half-terms till he got a bit used to the way of things here. The empty room at the front of the house got the sun in the morning and longer into the day. There was to be a fire lit in here, for the boy was coming from Kenya and would have to adjust to the climate. Fine, settled weather they were having, and she always on about damp and cold. What would she say when winter came, what would she make of February?

Mrs Coady had asked for a photo but she'd said she had none. No photo, no stories, and no great rush bringing the lad home from Africa, either.

She was sorry she'd asked, she wouldn't do it again, she'd only opened her mouth out of kindness, pitying Hannie's strangeness in a strange place. Whoever heard of a woman with no picture of her own son?

✑ *Chapter 9* ✑

*H*annie watched the new life shaping up around her. She smoked more, said little. At least now she could smoke where she liked, when she liked. Sometimes it seemed the only compensation.

Ned also watched. He'd been pleased by her interest in the house till he realised she was serious in her talk of alterations. New windows here, walls knocked down there, floors torn up and replaced. Now. Not some time in the future when it suited. His pleasure quickly turned to apprehension.

At first he'd tried to warn her. It wasn't easy getting building done in Ireland, he said. Especially not fidgety bits of alterations, when the builder couldn't see what was wrong with the way it was to begin with. He'd start all right, but when a job came up on the farm he'd tack a bit of polythene over the hole in your wall and go off and attend to it. Priorities were priorities. When a better job came up he'd be gone for a month, calling now and again to say he'd be with you the next day for sure.

'I've dealt with natives all my life,' she said.

His heart sank at the statement. He wondered how many fences he would have to mend, how many hard-won understandings he would have to re-negotiate. He didn't look forward to the process. As he had learned not to look forward to introducing her to his friends and neighbours. Not that it always went wrong. Sometimes, for no reason he could see, she would decide she liked someone, or that they were worth an effort. And she'd leave them dazzled and amazed as she had him. But he never knew what to expect.

Ambrose Power seemed to like her. Joe Casey traded cigarettes with her and told her things that made her laugh. When they didn't come she didn't seem surprised. Watching her, it began to dawn on him that she didn't need to learn the ways of the country. She wasn't particularly sympathetic or patient. It was more that she was like that herself.

For Hannie the activity of the building work was enough. It kept her occupied, kept her from brooding too much on the place and on what she had done to her life and to Joss's. She refused to think about Ned, though she knew that she wasn't as he wanted her to be, she knew he was disappointed. Tough. He'd just have to get used to her the way she was. She had put so much effort into reassuring him, into appearing light-hearted when she didn't feel it. At least now they were married she could stop all that. Besides, she was doing up his house for him, he had nothing to complain about.

Joss looked taller, older; it was a shock. Somehow in her mind she must have lopped off a few inches, dropped a year or two. Babied him.

So he'd seem easier to manage, more amenable to her needs and wishes?

He hadn't seen her, or maybe he had and she just couldn't see him seeing her for the Ray-Ban wraparound look. He was wheeling his luggage trolley slowly out through Arrivals. Fair hair, grey cotton sweater, off-white trousers, and those black mirror-sunglasses, very appropriate for Cork airport. He looked cold and tense and tired underneath the tan.

Which meant he'd be angry and aggressive with her. She felt herself flooded with tenderness and dread in equal parts. Thank God she'd persuaded Ned to stay at home.

'Of course I'll drive you, you don't know the way.'

'I'll find the way, Ned, it'll be good for me to begin to get to know my way around.'

'You might break down. The Volkswagen's not reliable any more, it needs handling.'

'I'll learn that, too.'

Ned had walked across the kitchen, stared out of the window, then walked back and stood over her.

'I ought to be there with you when he arrives, Hannie,' he said. 'Make sure he knows he's welcome.'

'He hasn't seen me for two months and he's been travelling all night and half yesterday. You can make him welcome when he gets here.' She had spoken carefully and reasonably, as though addressing an over-persistent child. Finally he had accepted her refusal.

And all the way here there'd been the tenderness and the dread that Joss inspired in her these days. An aching tenderness, a compound of cherishing and love and pity. The dread was simpler.

She had tried to think clearly while she still had the chance. What was she going to tell him if he pressed her? A firm line? That this was it, the future, whether he liked it or not, and he'd better start getting used to it?

But if he was vulnerable and frightened, if he pleaded with her, saying it was his life too? If he wanted her to reassure him, to promise not to make them stay here if he hated it? What would she say then?

Would she crack and comfort him and say it was the best that she could manage? That it was only to be going on with, that it might not be for ever?

She'd anticipated it backwards and forwards, taut as a bow-string with the strain.

'Hallo, Mother.' He took his glasses off, pecked her on the cheek, looked at her out of his light-blue eyes, put them on again. 'What have you done with the geriatric?'

The fine weather persisted – days of hazy gold sunlight and warm sweet air. The river moved against the great still trees and the fields swam in the dreamy light. To the north the blue mounds of the Comeraghs lay drowsy and heaped.

Everyone smiled like idiots and sighed and said over and

over how lovely it was. Hannie thought they'd taken leave of their senses. Joss shivered in his cotton clothes, refusing the woollens that she'd bought for him. He walked the farm and the river banks without comment and spent long hours in his room. The mirror-sunglasses he never left off.

Joss hardly spoke in Ned's company. He was well-mannered and replied readily enough when directly questioned, but somehow the end of his answer was also the end of the conversation.

Ned let him be and did not press him. If Joss wanted to take his time and get to know him slowly, that was understandable. He approved of old-fashioned manners; he was almost relieved the boy wasn't a chatterer. He supposed Joss and his mother talked when they were alone together, and in time they would learn to accept him, too. Meanwhile the boy was only settling in and everything was strange to him. Ned set himself to patience.

He did very well, or he thought he did, interfering only when it came to the wearing of sunglasses at the table. He requested discreetly through Hannie that meals be eaten without them. She looked at him steadily, saying nothing. He felt her will against him. The next day Joss sat down to lunch, removed the glasses and laid them on the table to his right. Hannie looked at her plate. When the meal was over and the chairs pushed back, Joss picked up the dark glasses wordlessly and replaced them on the bridge of his nose.

After that Joss always removed them for meals with a careful ostentation. Ned stubbornly refused to think his request unreasonable, but he found himself disconcerted by the expressionlessness of his stepson's revealed blue eyes. He began to wish the glasses back in place.

∽ *Chapter 10* ∽

'*T*hey're protected,' Naimh said, looking up from her stance on her hunkers at Joss. 'You can't just kill it and get it stuffed, it's illegal.'

'So?' Joss sneered out the word.

Niamh flushed. If you said illegal someone always let on you were chicken. And if you said cruel, they let on you were soft.

Bad move either way with a weirdo like Joss: words like that only encouraged him.

The small owl in Joss's tight hands roused itself suddenly and struggled frantically in his grasp. It lunged at him with its beak but he held on, his knuckles showing white through his tanned skin, the blood springing up where the beak had struck home. It subsided. Joss didn't loosen his hold for a moment. Despite herself Niamh was impressed.

'We'll have less of that,' Joss said to the owl, his voice low and reassuring. 'We don't want to be damaging ourselves, do we? Nor spoiling our pretty feathers?'

He stroked at it awkwardly with his forefinger, still keeping the vice-tight grip.

'There's a whole long future ahead to be thinking of. Posterity, presentation. All that shite. Think of a nice glass case on the wall in Joss's bedroom, eh? It's not going to look very good now, is it, owl? All this flaffing about, breaking things.'

'Danno won't touch it if you kill it,' Niamh said flatly. 'He won't stuff an owl that hasn't died naturally.'

'But maybe it *will* die naturally, Niamh,' Joss replied. 'Maybe it'll starve to death on account of its poor broken wing.' He laughed softly, still stroking the bird with his finger, then looked up into Niamh's tight face.

'Of course it won't starve to death, stupid. What would be the point of that? A mangy poxy little owl that looks like it just flew out of Belsen? Squinting at you out of its glass case? Towit, towoo, a merry owl. I-am-the-ghost-of-a-Joss-starved-owl.'

Joss made his eyebrows go round and raised and his small mouth pouted forward with his owl-sounds. He looked so funny, Niamh laughed.

'Towoo, towoo, towoo, Niamh! What a merry way to scare yourself shitless in the small hours, eh . . . ?' Joss laughed, Niamh couldn't stop, their young fresh voices blithe and easy in the sunshine.

Hannie, flattened against the byre wall, ears stretched for every nuance of the conversation, sighed with relief and let her head fall back to rest on the warm stone. He wanted to talk to Niamh, that was it. That was what all the circling and inspecting had been about, the signs that she knew of old, the small details of obsession that she had to be constantly on the watch for. He had wanted to attract Niamh's attention.

And now it was done, and they were there together, Joss sitting on an old plank set across two drums, the bird in his hands, his back against the byre wall, Niamh squatting on her hunkers beside him.

Ned was wrong in supposing that Joss talked much to Hannie. Joss talked to no one, had talked to no one for years as far as his mother could see. But this not-talking didn't mean detachment or indifference. For stretches – sometimes long stretches – Joss was with her, as silent and close as her own shadow. Then suddenly he'd be off, his needs driving him, his attention totally elsewhere. The process was invisible, psychic not physical, but of an intensity that made her feel almost deranged. What she did know – instinctively, unmistakably – was the precise moment of his psychic arrival somewhere else.

Not half an hour earlier she had known it. She had stood in the yard in the empty sunshine and as surely as she knew the colour of his hair she had known that it had happened, that Joss had stopped circling and had settled.

She didn't know where, she never knew where. He might have fallen down a well, he might have drowned himself in the river, he might have killed someone. She had stood there, quite motionless, a flat empty feeling of despair settling back inside her, a rat settling into its familiar nest. Then her ear had caught voices and she'd followed those voices around the side of the byre.

'Take it to Danno,' Niamh was saying now. 'He'll put a splint on its wing, he knows about owls, he'll save it if he can.'

And then he'll release it back into the wild, she thought, keeping the thought to herself. Joss was weird all right, he might have other plans, but then again he might not. He knew about birds, you could tell that from the way he held the owl, the way he was liking looking at it, the same as she was. This talk of his might all be an act.

'Who is this Danno that Niamh speaks of?' asked Hannie.

'Danno? Taxidermist. Poacher. Lives in a sort of shed by the river. Does a bit of this and a bit of that. Odd fish, Danno. Why?'

'Joss found an owl with a broken wing. Niamh says he must take it to Danno, that Danno will fix it.'

'I expect he will. And if he doesn't fix it he can always stuff it. Badly. Danno stuffs everything badly, but he doesn't seem to notice. No more do his clients, they keep taking him things, James Beresford's pleased as punch with a pike Danno did for him, doesn't seem to notice how grotesque it looks.'

'Pike are supposed to look grotesque, are they not?'

'Frightening-grotesque, not lumpy-grotesque. How do you know about pike, Hannie? Don't have them in Kenya, do they?'

64

'Andrew had one on the wall. A family heirloom from some Scottish river.'

They were sitting outside on a bench by the wall, drinking coffee in the hazy Sunday morning sunlight. It was quiet and still, a day off from Ambrose Power and his sledges and drills. Joe Casey's digger had finished its work and beyond the little garden where they sat the new lawn lay raked and waiting to be sown. Joss was off visiting Niamh, or she hoped that was where he was.

'Didn't know Joss was interested in birds,' Ned said. It was half a question. Hannie stretched up her hand to pull at a late rose on the wall.

'He is. Birds, and also insects.' She turned the rose this way and that, inspecting the shaggy pink flower, the round black indentations on its smooth green leaves. 'This rose needs spraying.'

'It does, they all do, I just haven't got round to it. So you know about roses. Andrew had those too?'

'The English must have their roses, even in Africa. I looked after Andrew's roses, or rather the gardener did, and I instructed him. Would you like me to look after your roses, Ned?'

'Yes, please,' said Ned. 'The spray's in the shed, and I'm sorry there isn't a gardener to be instructed.' He paused a moment. 'I believe I am a little jealous of Andrew, Hannie,' he said, surprising himself with the remark.

She smiled vaguely, letting go of the rose. It swung, a diminishing pendulum, on the still air.

After that Joss was around Niamh like a shadow.

Or a cat, Mrs Coady thought, as she watched him prowl and stalk and sidle close. Very like a cat. So sleek and still. Not a hair out of place. The small mouth, the neat small tongue to lick cream.

A thief too, she wouldn't mind betting. Not the son you would think she would breed. But you never knew what would come out, you couldn't choose, and you always loved the bad ones best, for they'd no one else.

Niamh didn't seem to mind him. But Niamh liked cats. At least till they brought something in half alive and half dead and sat themselves down to torment it.

She slung the mat she was carrying over the line and beat at it with the back of the broom. Satisfying clouds of dust flew out of it. She wondered about the father.

~ *Chapter 11* ~

*H*annie took Joss to Cork to buy clothes and kit for school. Not all of it, but the bulk of it. There were specifics she'd have to get in the school shop when they took him North.

She'd asked Ned for money and he'd taken out his cheque-book and written a cheque out to cash. She could change it in Cork, he said, he didn't keep cash in the house.

She knew that already. And that he had no time for credit cards and didn't like banks, though he paid all his bills by cheque.

She could buy what she liked when she liked, he had told her. If she wanted anything she had only to ask and anyway all the local shops kept books under the counter, he would settle her bills when they were presented. There was to be no joint account.

She went first to the bank in Cork to cash the cheque and then to the school outfitters that Ned said everyone used. Methodically, she worked her way down through the list that the school had sent.

It seemed an enormous amount to amass, everything dark and heavy and thick. Joss was docile, almost co-operative, only occasionally attempting sabotage and never refusing out-right. She was so surprised and relieved that she told him to choose something for himself when they'd finished. He gave her a long look and said there was nothing in the shop he'd wear unless he had to.

When she came to pay she found that Ned's cashed cheque wasn't enough to cover their purchases. She had no other money, no credit cards or chequebook to fall back on. The last of her own money had gone on Joss's fare from Kenya.

She picked up the list and began to edit. Joss drifted off to another part of the shop, leaving her to sort out the situation. She knew from the turn of his head that he was despising Ned for under-providing and despising her for landing them both with him.

Abruptly she stopped trying to work out what to keep and what to put back and instead she wrote out Ned's name and address and asked that their purchases and the bill be sent on. The assistant who was serving her disappeared to consult with a senior. Out of the corner of her eye she watched the two heads scanning the paper, the older one nodding assent. Ned's name was good for something, after all. When the young man came back she asked him to recommend a good restaurant.

They ate lunch off a starched white cloth with a good bottle from the list and waiters in attendance. Joss helped himself to the wine and she said nothing. He watched as she paid the large bill with cash from Ned's cheque. She felt defiant, placing the notes on the salver, she wanted to spend Ned's careful money wastefully, to dissipate it in ways he would certainly not approve. And she cared nothing for such surroundings, was indifferent to the manicured food, the snobbish, over-priced wine list. Joss liked it, but she wasn't doing it for Joss.

Why *was* she doing it? she asked herself. Why did she suddenly mind Ned's minding his wallet? He hadn't minded it when it mattered. When it came to paying the school fees, he hadn't hesitated. Why had her gratitude so quickly turned to vindictiveness?

Because now it was all settled.

Ned had arranged things and gone with her to the school and made it all possible. The school had taken Joss because of Ned: Ned's name and Ned's presence, they'd hardly bothered with her at all. She had sat in her good suit drinking tea and keeping her thoughts to herself while the headmaster and the housemaster and the matron all ignored her and basked instead in Ned and in Ned's modest, admirable reputation.

They hadn't even queried the choice of a school so far from where they resided. Ned had served the Empire, it was natural that he should want his wife's son educated in its territory. Besides, he was a Protestant. There were Protestant schools in the South of course. Some would consider them dubious.

She had been so anxious on the drive up, so grateful for his willingness to help her and for his unspoken decision to accept what she asked for and leave her motives unquestioned. It was all she had thought of. She felt that if Joss was settled she might even be grateful to Ned, for ever. Or grateful enough to get by on for at least a bit longer.

Well, that had been then, she thought sourly. It seemed that her gratitude had worn thin before Joss was even despatched.

Ned tried not to blame Hannie for her loyalty to Joss and he tried not to imagine pacts between them. He tried not to notice that the boy's politeness was often a form of rudeness and he told himself it was perfectly natural that Joss should resent a new authority, at least initially. He had known Joss would be a problem.

Nevertheless, he was disappointed. Gradually he became aware of the cause of his disappointment. Joss did not inspire affection, nor did he seem to wish to have affection extended to him.

Ned found himself blushing at this realisation. What had he wanted? A son to love and be loved by? He got up and went out to the near meadow. The old mare he occasionally hacked around on came to the gate whinnying softly and blew into his hand. He liked the comfort of her. He grew calmer and tried to think more clearly. He didn't like this alliance of mother and son and he didn't like being shut out by them. And he didn't like this blank-faced boy in the mirror glasses, yet he wanted to like him and be liked by him. Most of all, he realised, he didn't like what he was learning about himself.

He knuckled the mare's bony face and she rubbed for more. Hannie had married him for a home for the boy, he knew that, she'd as good as said it, and he had accepted it. But already it seemed he'd begun to forget it.

Things were bound to be difficult at the beginning, he told himself; her loyalty was divided, that was where her coldness came from. The boy would be gone in a few days, he and Hannie would get used to each other, the school would settle Joss down.

It was a good school, straightforward and disciplined, with a sound reputation. He was relieved she hadn't wanted Joss nearer and home every other weekend, the way it seemed to be done now. He'd been surprised at the time but she seemed sure of what she was doing, and maybe it didn't seem far to her, being used to Africa. Then again maybe she was thinking of him and of their marriage, breaking him in gently, aware that Joss was difficult. Ned was pleased at this thought. He rubbed Connie's face again, dismissed her with a final pat. Yes, Joss would settle at school, make friends, get used to the climate. He'd be easier when he came home for the Christmas holidays.

Hannie, too, would be easier. He must be patient, he must give her time.

Hannie was aware that Joss was making things more difficult for her with Ned. With the boy standing watching and challenging, it was hard not to question her judgement in making this arrangement for their lives. She knew that this line of thought wasn't useful to her and she didn't want to be wasting her time in futile rebellion and resentment. She wanted to accept Ned as he was and thus be free of him: the chameleon's trick that had served her well in the past.

But when she was with Joss it was as though his wraparound glasses were clamped to her own nose. She criticised Ned with her actions and with her eyes. She allied herself with Joss against him.

It was partly because the stakes were so high for Joss. A new life, a new school, different influences. This was a chance for him and there might not ever again be such another. Her instinct told her to stay close to the boy, to support him sympathetically and emotionally and not let him be isolated through any intimacy of hers with Ned.

But it was also an emotional reaction against Ned and against the place she now found herself in. She hadn't anticipated so closed a life, nor that Ned's expectations would weigh so heavily upon her. At night she dreamed of blocked holes and locked rooms, of sealed and shuttered windows. She escaped from dream into consciousness and lay awake in her trap. She felt this life bearing down on her like a pillow pressed over her face and her panic and suffocation unbalanced her. Joss also unbalanced her. Try as she might she could not get through his refusal of her. She could not read him or reach him and his anger and avoidance of her enraged her and worried her sick by turns.

He escaped her to Niamh who accepted him without comment, like a cat that had wandered in and might perch on her sill or wind itself round her feet for a day or a week before disappearing.

He was there now. Hannie rose from her work of sorting and labelling and packing and crossed to the window. For a long time she stood scanning the deserted yard and the empty sheds as though they held some clue to Joss's heart that she might read if she looked hard enough.

Then she returned to the piled underwear, the marker pen and the labels. She was glad Joss was going in the morning, though she dreaded the pain and apprehension she knew she'd feel on his behalf once he'd left and her anger had subsided. Nonetheless she might be less emotionally swamped. She knew she would have to create some sort of a working relationship with Ned soon or the life here would rapidly become unbearable to them both. With Joss gone she might regain sufficient equilibrium to try.

Or to decide not to.

She knew Joss wouldn't write her letters or phone her. For a moment she wished she'd chosen a school that was nearer, that she could visit and be visited from. She refused the thought. The further away the school, the easier the damage-limitation. That was the hard-learned fruit of experience. She mustn't start now on fantasies that Joss was other than he was.

At least he'd had Niamh to hang round while he was here, Hannie thought. At the same time she hated Niamh for the intimacy that Joss had bestowed on her. An unsought intimacy, probably also unwanted, she acknowledged bitterly to herself.

Niamh had a passion for moths and butterflies. Joss, too, liked insects, though ants and beetles were more in his line. It was a bond between them, this shared interest that wouldn't be most people's taste. Niamh had books that Joss consulted, they discussed species together, she could tell him what was rare, what common as mud.

But Niamh's interest was essentially more aesthetic than lepidopterous and she especially liked moths and butterflies in death. It was the way death inhabited them that fascinated her, the way it lived in them, invisible but for its stillness, yet intensely respectful of its own power. The small corpses she collected seemed to her to collude with some aspect of death's sense of itself: a sense altogether different from that which she'd seen displayed in its grosser occupation of human beings and farm animals. There was a propriety in its dealings with these insects. It was as though they'd been given notice and had served as their own undertakers. They had laid themselves out, wings spread, feet neatly crossed, bodies sleek in their furred coats now doubling up as shrouds. Then, having prepared themselves, the master had been invited in.

Niamh collected up their spent bodies wherever she found them. She perched them on windowsills and shelves as she passed, she laid them carefully on the flat surfaces of stones. Sometimes she retraced her steps, gathering in her harvest. Sometimes she just left them where they lay. Ned had noticed her preoccupation and begun to collect for her. A dusty saucer, full of his gleanings, sat on a scullery shelf.

Joss also joined in the game but instead of adding to Niamh's stores he raided them, creating tiny dramas that were parodies of the living forms. Meticulously Niamh's corpses were re-distributed and resurrected. Furred brown moths clung by their stiff dead legs on to climbing roses, butterflies crawled the bright faces of late marigolds, small silvery moths hooked the porch geraniums. Niamh liked this, the way it made you look afresh at both corpse and flower, the way Joss sometimes changed things into art. But she wasn't so sure about all his insect activities. And she didn't share his fascination with fungi at all.

There were growths everywhere: it was the warm early September weather, the light night rains and heavy morning dews. He asked her endless questions but she didn't know the answers. She knew only the big horse mushrooms dotted about the fields. She liked picking these, easing them carefully out of the ground, breaking them open to check them for grubs. Not so Joss. These edible growths were too plain and serviceable for him, he only kicked and hacked at them, scattering soft shards of flesh across the bright grass. It was the stranger growths that he liked: their rich discolouredness, their spongy fluted branches, whiter than death.

Best of all he liked the big dense fungal clumps that grew in the rough grass on the edge of the pot-holed drive. These were not single forms but multiple manifestations, accretions of chestnut-coloured platelets, layer on spiralling layer.

'Like cities,' Niamh said, kneeling in the damp grass, peering into brown streets and alleyways. 'Or those old walled towns in Italian paintings. You know the ones. Improbable. Like snail-shells. The houses all glued to those lumps of rock sticking out of the planes.'

Joss didn't know, but he liked these impermanent cities. He lay on his belly for hours inserting ants and grasshoppers into their maze of alleys, prodding them into activity with long blades of meadow grass.

Niamh observed with a detached interest. She was getting

73

used to Joss, making assumptions about him. His weirdness might just be loneliness, she decided. He might be an artist looking for a form.

Hannie also observed, but she did not disturb Niamh's assumptions. Niamh was a grown human being, old enough to be making mistakes and learning from them. Old enough to be acting her age.

Hannie slipped her hand into the last name-tagged sock, grasped its fellow and pulled the first one over it to make a pair. She tossed the bunched socks into the open suitcase. Then she rose and went downstairs, trailing her hand down the polished banister, feeling the lonely emptiness of the late-afternoon house. She wanted to go and fetch Joss out of Niamh's, to harry him over this packing, to force him into sharing these last hours with her, but she made herself hold back.

What was the point? There'd be no confidences, nothing he'd say to her now in intimacy, but wouldn't say tomorrow with Ned there. He was punishing her, she was fairly sure of that, but whether for Ned or for school or both she didn't know. And he seemed all right about tomorrow's journey. He'd be into crossing the border, he'd said, and seeing this famous North with its bombs and guns.

'Less boring than here, Mother. At least there'll be something going on.'

But he didn't know how far it was, he didn't know how he'd feel when he saw them turn the car and drive away.

Neither did she, she told herself. He might like it. On past form it wasn't beginnings that were the problem, it was what happened after he'd begun.

She crossed the hall and on an impulse went into the drawing room and looked out over the front. They were there, both of them, standing on the edge of the drive, Joss doing something, Niamh watching. Hannie moved closer to the window, careful not to be seen.

It was a ceremony. Joss had gathered together a pile of large

74

round stones and was meticulously bombing his cities, his face impassive as the brown walls fell.

Hannie stood a few moments longer. Then she turned and went to the kitchen to prepare the evening meal. Fried chicken, his favourite dish. He'd be angry with her for doing it, angry if she didn't.

'Condemned man eats hearty last meal, eh, Mother?'

That's what he'd say when he'd finished.

❧ *Chapter 12* ❧

On the day following Joss's departure the weather broke and it rained for three days. Hannie watched the water running down the clouded windows and gathering in puddles on the leaky sills. Draughts blew through the ill-fitting frames, bad-tempered winds plucked at the guttering, the tall Scots pines at the back of the house moaned and complained. Rain swept the valley in wavering curtains and the river lost itself in a hissing blur of grey.

Hannie walked from room to room, smoking too much and hating this dank sodden world she had come to. The kitchen was full of dust from the walls that Ambrose Power and his mate Liam were knocking down, the floor was mud from the wet that their boots had tramped in. For once she was narky and short with them.

The Change, their looks said, women are divils at the Change. They were disappointed in her, that was clear. Where had she gone and who was this harridan left behind in her place?

It was ever so, she thought. Women raged and men mis-understood. Then they felt injured and hard-done-by. She put on wellingtons and a waterproof and went outside to tramp about in the drizzling rain.

She walked up the drive, away from the house, and came on the rain-blackened ruins of Joss's bombed cities. They were crushed and pulped now and smelled of excrement and decay. She stood over them, thinking of Joss in the rain in that grey Northern town on the wide grey lake. Despair settled upon her, the rain ran down her face and dripped off her hands.

76

Despair changed to rage and she kicked at the cities, scattering the ruins till all that was left was a blackened pulp in the long wet grass. She felt no satisfaction. The ugly feeling that had driven her was still in her. It was no use, nothing was any use, she could not protect him, nor keep him safe from himself. Strange growths came up out of the dark earth, they blossomed and decayed and you could not change that, no matter how you kicked and raged and trampled.

Finally the rain stopped. It was a different landscape: colourless, sodden, beaten down. Overnight a whole world had vanished. Hannie stood by the paddock fence and stared at the mud and the dying vegetation. Nothing was as it had been. The tall ghost-stands of willow herb were battered and flattened now, the fluffy seedheads that last week shone in the light like silk threads were all matted and draggled and done. The rain had stopped, but the sun had not returned. It was cold, the day was dark.

Hannie stood on, staring blankly at the rain's aftermath. She was awaiting a huge sun, floating up over the rim of the land, throbbing the life back into this cold spent world.

It would not come, she realised. That sun lived in Africa, there was no such sun here, nor ever would be.

A grey Cortina drove up, battered and muddy. Hannie watched as a woman got out, opened the boot, and stood looking down into it with an air of quiet satisfaction.

Alison Beresford. A small grey woman in her late fifties, deep-bosomed and slender, wearing trousers and clean wellingtons and a plain, light-green headscarf. Hannie recognised her at once. One of Ned's oldest friends, she lived with a husband called Vere in a crumbling grey house just a few miles away. Hannie watched her now as she straightened up and scanned the house front with quiet, determined eyes.

The boot of the Cortina bulged with muddy polythene bags that had leaves and bits of cut stem sticking out of them. Alison was rummaging about in there, opening bags and closing them, obedient to some order of things hidden in her mind. Hannie stood silently beside her.

'Oh yes,' Alison was saying as she found the bag she was looking for and heaved it out of the boot, 'since we were children. Or rather, since I was a child – he must have been in his teens. They'd just come to live with Mrs Valender at Oldcourt. His grandmother,' she added, with the air of one making clear things clearer.

'Of course he seemed terribly grown up and glamorous. And tragic. His father had just died, you see, Oldcourt was his mother's home. About fifteen, I suppose he must have been. And I must have been about five.' She hauled at another bag.

'Geraniums, cobalt blue. Masses of foliage, very fast spreaders. So useful in the right place, but you do have to be careful. Bullies, really, they'll take over the bed if you let them. Heavenly blue flowers, but only for about two weeks in June. Some people hate them, say they're not worth their keep.'

On some of the bags Alison had scrawled clues as to content with a black felt-tip pen. She would look at the words, then open the bag anyway, and stare hard at the tangles of root and mud and leaf.

'He went to the war of course, but afterwards, after Isobel died, we thought he might come home ... But he didn't. He began on his journeys instead. This one's a little white saxifrage, so dainty, good on a wall or under a tree.' She handed Hannie a bag and waited for her to open it and look inside.

'There's a small pink geranium in there with it. Quite dull, but makes neat little clumps and flowers for ages and ages.' She dived back into the boot.

'He always came backwards and forwards, all through the years. Then when Mrs Valender died, Oldcourt was sold and his mother moved into Delaney's – which was only a step away, so it made no difference really, we saw as much of him as ever. Then she died too, but he still came when he could. He would go to West Cork for his cousins, but he'd always come here for a few days at the end and he always stayed with us.'

Alison dumped the last of the bags with their fellows by the Cortina's back wheel. She straightened up, tightening the scarf under her chin in a gesture at once absent and automatic.

'There,' she said with quiet satisfaction, 'that should keep you busy. And don't be disappointed if the bearded irises don't flower straight away. They will when they get round to it – they simply hate being moved.'

'Alison came,' Hannie said, setting the casserole down on the table. 'She wants us to go there on Friday. "Family-supper-in-the-kitchen", whatever that means. I said we were busy.'

Ned frowned. He stabbed a potato, then reached for the butter. 'Remind me,' he said, not looking up. 'I've forgotten.'

Hannie said nothing. He looked at her.

'We're not busy,' she said, 'I just said we were. She wants me to help with church cleaning and flowers.'

Ned lifted the lid off the casserole. 'And will you?' he said neutrally, spooning lamb and mushrooms on to her plate.

'No,' Hannie said, moving the lid out of the way, still not looking at him. 'She'd been doing her border, splitting up her perennials. She brought us a bootful of off-cuts for our new beds. A bit of everything – even things she doesn't much like, or thinks probably won't grow in our soil. She says it's so much nicer, having plants from someone else's garden. You think of where they came from and they give you extra pleasure.'

'You don't like her,' Ned said.

Hannie looked at him, a long straight look. She picked up her knife and fork and began to eat.

'She's a nice woman.' Ned said, 'It was kind of her to bring us plants, and she's absolutely right about associations.' Hannie kept eating. 'Besides, it would have cost a fortune, buying perennials from a garden centre.'

Ned reached for the salt in the silence. 'You have to give

people a chance, Hannie,' he said reasonably. 'You'll never make friends if you won't try.'

'Why would I want to make friends?' she asked. 'I have Joss, I have you, I am busy all day, why would I want friends?'

Ned sighed. 'It will be easier if you make friends,' he said carefully. 'Easier to settle.'

She put down her knife and fork and rose from the table. She picked up the phone.

'What're you doing?'

She didn't answer him. 'Alison?' she said into the phone. 'Alison, this is Hannie Renvyle. Change of plan. We can come on Friday after all . . . About eight? That will be fine. Yes. I, too, am delighted.'

She sat down and resumed eating.

'I asked her if she'd help with the church flowers,' Alison said.

'And would she?' Vere was sitting at the long table, riffling through the new edition of the *Farmer's Journal*.

'She said she didn't qualify. She said she was an animist.'

'A what?'

'An animist. She comes from Java. She said in Java animists are the norm.'

He looked up, almost interested despite the fresh attractions in the journal.

'A Protestant animist or a Catholic animist?' He smiled, pleased with his little joke.

'A Lutheran animist.' Alison put the boiled kettle and two mugs on the table and sat down.

'She won't get out of it that easily. Tell her Lutheran equals Protestant and as such she's expected to do her bit.' He had lost interest, had already returned to the journal.

'She said her father was a Lutheran. The animism was on her mother's side.' Alison was pouring hot water on to the instant coffee in each of their mugs. 'What do you suppose she meant by that?'

80

Vere sat up, looking startled. 'Was she serious?'

'Totally.'

'I wouldn't know,' Vere said slowly, reaching for his coffee and abandoning the journal altogether. 'But if I was guessing, old girl, I'd say she meant a touch of the tar brush.' He looked at his wife speculatively. 'I wouldn't put it past old Ned, either. Would you?'

That night Ned came to her room. Afterwards, instead of going back to his own as was his habit, he stayed and slept beside her. Hannie dreamed, this time not of locked rooms and blocked corridors, but of Piet.

She woke in the darkness, Piet there in front of her eyes, Ned snoring gently beside her. The dream was a strong thick taste in her mouth. She lay finding her way back out of it, not wanting to return there when she slept again.

The dream was short. She was standing beside the river here, very early in the morning. It was like grey glass, and a mist crept up from the water in little trails and puffs. In the intense quiet a bird rose, its wings beating the still surface, breaking the smooth grey glass. She saw Piet standing, his feet astride, his hands clasped loosely together behind his back, his belly sagging. He lifted his head and glanced sideways at her. She wanted to ask what he was doing here, so far from home, but she couldn't speak. She saw that he was laughing at her. He rocked his weight from foot to foot, his belly jiggled. He would not tell her why he laughed, she had to guess. She could not. She looked down at her hands. They were greenish-grey and covered in small shiny scales like the skin of a fish. Then she knew she was waiting for something but she didn't know what. She knew that Piet knew, and she looked up from her hands to ask him, but he'd gone.

❦ *Chapter 13* ❦

*A*utumn was fully upon them. The river shone, a moving sheet of light. More and more she abandoned the house, Ambrose and the alterations. She would be outside and halfway down the avenue almost before she knew she'd gone. Above her the poplars, golden-green and thinning, streamed in the high blueness. A pheasant walked over the green meadow. The burnished oak trees stood against the thin, intense sky.

She learned to walk everywhere with her head tipped far back for the sky that was up there like grace, shining with light and swept empty and clean by the wind. She thought she could stand anything as long as there was this grace, this light. Only the wet grey days were too hard.

There were layers to the wind. Low down it was still and breathing, but throw your head back and you saw another world. Winds romped the sky, possessing the tall poplar trees, riding them, throwing them about like ships thrown about on the sea.

She would come home buoyant. She had been to the harbour: she might not yet sail on the ships, but she knew where those ships lay. It was like seeing the seagulls on the river. It promised that there was somewhere else.

Some days. On other days this illusion of escape eluded her. All illusions eluded her. What was the use of somewhere else if you were never in it? She would flee from the house and the yard and the half-planted garden and walk about for hours. Then she would trudge back across the fields, feeling the thinning grass, the dying light, the dense suck of the trampled mud where the cattle had clustered.

Every day the year's change came faster. The air thinned and the trees thinned and the colours sobered. The skies closed down. She felt bereft, shut in. She ranged further, pushed beyond the meadows and into the stands of ancient woodland that clung, here and there, to the river. She liked these at first: their secretness and their neglect. But each day the light died a little sooner and somehow she began to fear them. The snapping of twigs, the frantic dusk alarms of the roosting birds, the patter of leaf-fall, the wet black smell of decay. They seemed full of small shiverings and dyings.

Thirty calves bawled and cried in the sheds by the house, refusing the meal that was brought to them. Ned spent hours in there, calming and coaxing, trying to wheedle them into feeding. It was no good, they wanted none of him: they were desperate for milk and their mothers.

'Try the treacly stuff, they love that ... in the yellow bags ... You know the one, the stuff that's got loads of molasses in it.' Niamh hung around, throwing out vague suggestions, getting on his nerves.

Ned didn't know, but everyone else did, so every time he drove out through the gates he came back with a different sack that someone or other had recommended.

'Leave them alone,' Hannie said. 'They'll stop bawling when they're tired enough. They'll eat when they're hungry enough. Just let them be.'

Ned said he knew that, but they'd lose condition fast when they were upset like this and anyway they were his calves and he didn't want them to suffer. Hannie heard the annoyance in his voice, so she folded her arms and shut her mouth and went back inside, banging the kitchen door to behind her.

Ambrose was sitting at the table with Liam, having their morning tea-break.

'They do be missing their mothers,' he said into his mug.

'Missing their food, more like. Bloody calves, bloody fuss, shouting their bloody heads off. Empty bellies is what's wrong with them, they'll forget their mothers the minute their bellies are full again.'

'Ah no,' Ambrose said gently, 'it wouldn't be just milk, it's their mothers, too. 'Tis hard for them all, and some show it more than others.' He was still staring into his mug, avoiding looking at Hannie.

'Sure I mind a calf the brother had,' Liam said. 'Weaned and grown and away from the cow for a year or more. And then didn't he put him into the same field as the mother and wasn't he trying to suck her right away? A big, lump of a bullock, as if he was only a calf again.'

'Exactly,' Hannie said furiously. 'Bothering her long after he's grown up and well able to fend for himself.'

Ambrose kicked Liam under the table, finished up his tea and rose to return to the job. Liam, looking surprised, did the same.

'Twould be noisy inside as well as out today, Ambrose told her. All the old stuck-down lino was to be chipped away, then the floor levelled up and the new skim of concrete poured.

'No point in laying new tiles on a bockety floor,' he said. 'We'll be all day getting that old stuff up. Sure we might as well get all the noise done with in the one go.'

Hannie put on her boots and abandoned ship. The yard was loud with the bawling of calves as she walked away. The house reverberated with hammers hitting on chisels.

On the edge of the woods she chose a path that was new to her. It ran through stands of old hardwoods, dense with tangled undergrowth and unthinned saplings, opening here and there on to patches of neglected planting. She followed this path till it petered out. Off to the left behind a tangle of laurel and rhododendron, she found another one. It was narrower and windier than the first, more an animal track than a path, but she followed it stubbornly, ducking under branches, crashing through brambles, skidding on timber hidden in falls of moss and leaf. The path ended abruptly in a thin screen of leaves. She burst through and stumbled into a once-cleared clearing, cluttered now with mossy piles of abandoned logs.

Near the centre of this clearing rose a big old spruce, dead but still erect, the upper part of its trunk snapped abruptly off at twice her height. She walked around it, expecting the dark marks of a lightning-strike but finding none. Instead she saw fungal growths like red-brown misshapen kidneys, near to the ground but climbing the trunk in tiers.

There was something shocking about them, indecent, she felt she should turn her eyes away. Like coming on a bad car accident unawares, she thought. People with bits of themselves on the outside instead of the inside, their private internal organs casually on display.

Growths everywhere. Perhaps it was the damp? She reached out her hand and made herself touch the flesh.

She had expected softness, a slimy dissolving, but the fungus was dry with the hollow hardness of old wood. She pressed harder into it with her fingers, but still it did not indent. Something at once frightened and violent rose up in her and she had to damage it, to break it or mark it, it didn't matter which. She tried to snap off a piece but it was like twisting thick old leather. She wrenched, but nothing happened and the violent feeling grew more frantic with each failed attempt. She wrenched again. It gave abruptly and she staggered back, a piece of the leathery growth clutched in her hand.

She regained her balance without at once realising that she still held it. When she did she started, then hurled her malignant trophy furiously away. It arced from her and smashed into the thinning brambles.

There was a short burst of silence, then a sudden wild crashing. A black dog rushed from somewhere behind her and threw himself at the undergrowth in pursuit. Two more Labradors appeared and danced and circled around her and the empty place was suddenly filled with noise. A man stepped from between the trees, calling the dogs. The first dog emerged from underneath the brambles, the half moon clutched in his mouth, his tail thrashing in triumphant pride. He circled the man again and again, neck arched like a horse's to show off his trophy. He was fully grown, she saw, but still very giddy and young.

The man bent to the dog and removed the fungus. He turned it over and back, inspecting it, his face without expression. Hannie knew at once that he'd been watching her. Watching from a place of concealment and not intending to be revealed. It was like Africa, this place, eyes hidden everywhere. Only the missile and the young dog's exuberance had flushed him out.

'Root fomes,' he said quietly, weighing the thing in his hand. 'Always a killer. You think it's only external, but it rots right through to the heart.' He shifted his eyes along the broken trunk, noting the other growths.

'That's why the tree died, d'you see? You didn't break it off, you couldn't have. The tree's so deeply rotted the wood crumbled when you pulled.' He reached down and rubbed at the tree where the wound from the ripped-away fungus showed. The wood powdered off under his touch.

Surreptitiously, Hannie watched him. He was tallish and lean and not ill-made, but curiously without presence. His features were regular, his hair dark and just touched with grey, his eyes grey and veiled behind heavy glasses. He wore wellingtons and an old, torn waxproof and trousers made out of some brown stuff, long discoloured and stained. He was camouflaged, she realised. Everything about him was somehow damped-down, concealed, restrained. Only his thick dark eyebrows were energetic, even when he was saying nothing.

'The owl died,' he said. 'I thought she'd make it but she didn't. Boy settling all right, is he?'

For a moment Hannie thought she had misheard him, then light dawned. This was Danno, the man who stuffed birds.

'I haven't heard,' she said bluntly, surprising herself with the flash of bitterness in her own voice.

He heard it too, she could feel his recoil. He didn't like emotion or contact with people, she realised. She could feel

86

him wanting to get away but by effort of will making himself stay. He was like one of those large shy brown deer she sometimes glimpsed here at dusk: blundering and ungainly when startled, their first instinct always flight.

That he knew who she was did not surprise her. At first she had thought herself invisible here for no one stared or even seemed to register her presence, but she had soon learned the reality. Everyone knew her, it was as though her photo had been pasted up in the post office and passed through the houses and farms.

'The owl was doing well, or well enough, tell him. Something happened, I don't know what. She lost heart and I couldn't turn her round.'

'Like the tree.'

He looked puzzled.

'Heart rot,' she said, gesturing towards the growth he still held in his hand. 'You said it rotted right through to the heart.' She stopped. She had a sudden strange impression that they were talking about Joss. She shook her head to dispel the illusion.

'Heterobasidion annosum,' he agreed. 'There's a fair bit of it in these woods. They're old and neglected, they need thinning and replanting, but no one gives a damn –' He broke off and involved himself with rounding up the dogs. His eyes, she noticed, had not once rested on her directly.

Ready to make his escape now, she thought. The instinct for flight again. Like a lizard. A flick, and it was gone into its crack. No, not like a lizard, there was something overtly sexual about a lizard, there was a curious, damaged sexuality about this man.

She would hang on to him, she decided, make him show her the way back. She felt easy with him suddenly and faintly contemptuous but also hostile.

❧ *Chapter 14* ❧

'*Who will lend a dipper of water to save a fish in a carriage rut*? He quoted that to me. Then he paid my passage and let me go. He was a strange man, I didn't understand him, I still don't. He said he had dropped me into the rut, so it was only right he should lift me out.'

Niamh was warming the teapot and gazing at Hannie with her big, shiny dark eyes as she sent the water swishing around in its base.

'Black tea or jasmine?'

'Black.'

She was very self-possessed, Hannie thought, with her neat clean kitchen and her laid table and her choice of teas. Hannie took out her cigarettes and began to smoke.

'I dreamed my hands were covered in scales like a fish,' Hannie said. 'The dream wouldn't leave me alone, it kept coming back to me. I thought and thought but still I didn't connect it with that saying. Then I came walking here through the mud and the ruts and Piet's little fish dropped into my mind. He liked Confucian philosophers – their little stories and homilies. He often quoted them, he didn't mind their neatness or their smugness. He liked that, he said, it helped ward off life's pain.'

She was here for tea at the girl's repeated invitation. Young woman, she should say – that was how the girl referred to herself. Hannie ignored the proffered chair and mooched around the kitchen, talking and looking at things. Briefly, she wondered at this insistence on being a woman. Her own generation called themselves girls relentlessly till they died.

Niamh filled the teapot and settled the cosy down over it. She somehow couldn't quite grasp that this woman was Joss's mother, but she liked having her here, liked the funny jumps and disconnections in the way she talked. She felt a bit awkward with her but not shy in the way that she did with Joss or Ned, she was too interested. She didn't ask questions or interrupt in case Hannie noticed she was talking about her life and stopped. Niamh wanted to hear all about Piet and their marriage. She wanted to hear all of Hannie's crowded, exotic past.

'I hated these Confucians and their homilies. He used to say them to me all the time because he knew how much I hated them. I knew by looking at him when another one was coming. His mouth would go pouted and shiny as though he was sucking a boiled sweet. Then he'd laugh at me because I looked so sour. *Better a boiled sweet than a lemon*, he'd say . . .

'There was one I liked, though. I haven't thought of it for years. About a man on a white horse in a whirl of red dust. A young man, handsome and distinguished, and all the people coming out to watch. Lord Tung – that was his name – Lord Tung. He rode about the place looking for adventures and fine women. Piet knew he only had me till Lord Tung came riding by. I think perhaps he said it so often because he wanted me to know that he knew. And I never realised. I was too stupid and too young . . .' Hannie's voice trailed off into silence.

Niamh waited, hoping for more, but nothing came. She called Hannie to the tea table. She talked as she poured tea, buttered bread and sliced the apple tart. She spoke of her pleasure in the cottage, and her appreciation. She spoke of her work, the back room she was sorting out, the paintings she would make from the drawings done in the fine weather. The rain ran down the window panes, the fire danced. It was like a painting on a plate, Hannie thought. So smooth and shiny and clean. She ate nothing. She smoked and drank tea.

Niamh was very attractive, Hannie decided. She had fine eyes, a wide mouth and smooth dark hair pulled into a knot at the nape of her neck. She was tall, her figure was slender but full, and she had slim, strong wrists and large graceful hands. There was something of the Madonna about her, an effect curiously accentuated by the jeans and sweaters she wore. Did she know this, Hannie wondered, did she deliberately cultivate the Madonna effect?

Probably not, she decided. Mostly because it wouldn't occur to her that she needed to. Niamh expected the kindness and indulgence with which she was treated, it had clearly never crossed her mind that the world might have been a harder place had she been plain and spotted, or buck-toothed with a cast in her eye. She was artless because she could afford to be.

Niamh's assumption that she was loved for herself alone offended Hannie, who had grown up without any currency other than that provided for her by her youth and her looks. She knew, very exactly, the value of this currency.

Niamh used this currency, but she used it unconsciously and her behaviour produced in Hannie the same reaction that people who have had to scrape for every penny feel when they watch the next generation using unearned money thoughtlessly. To spend such currency idly was bad enough, but it was careless to the point of criminality to use it without ever being aware of what it was: a finite quality that won affection and privilege but would, with time, expire.

Watching Niamh now, Hannie came closer to understanding precisely how much indulgence she had been granted on that score in the past herself. It was a painful realisation, for with it came the knowledge that the currency in which she had traded was all but spent.

So perhaps it was simply envy she was feeling? Well, so be it, she didn't care. She was happy to dislike Niamh, she enjoyed her own ill-will.

'Do you like jasmine tea?' Niamh was asking. She picked

up the box on the table. 'I don't much myself, but this is the real thing. One of my sisters went to Hong Kong and brought it home for me – thought you'd like this, Niamh, she said, it's a bit peculiar. That's my family. If it's peculiar, give it to Niamh. I like what it says on the box, though – there, look, on the side –' She pointed at the words and read them out. 'Aromatic infusion. Homely refresher. Ideal gift.' She laughed, her voice blithe.

His blouse was the pale yellow of gosling down;
his face and figure were fine as a painting.
Always he rode a snow-footed horse,
whirling whirling up the red dust . . .

Tramping back through the rain, Hannie recalled a snatch of Piet's verse. Remembering it, she fell upon another painful little revelation. She was still waiting for Lord Tung.

'Because they are wasteful and stupid,' Piet would say of his fellow Europeans if you asked him why he shunned them. 'Because their greed is endless and they do not have the sense to be content with a full rice bowl.'

Well, it seemed that neither did she.

She had a full rice bowl now, why else had she married Ned? Yet she wasn't content, she never had been. It was always the same. At first the marriage – the full rice bowl – was a big deal, but before very long the same deal looked smaller and when it did she found herself a lover.

You're a fool, Hannie, she told herself now. You can't just go on doing the same things over and over all your life. The same things now, when you're fifty, as when you were twenty, or thirty, or forty. Look around you, where is this lover, this dashing Lord Tung of yours?

I'll tell you where.

At home by the fire, smoking his pipe and scratching his belly and counting his snot-nosed grandchildren.

She pushed open the back door, kicked off her wellingtons and flung them at a corner. But she could not kick off her thoughts so easily, no matter how she tried. They itched at her like flea bites.

She'd begun on the house because it was what he wanted, however he might resent the expense and complain of inconvenience. He'd said as much. He wanted a garden, flowers on the table, the place made into a home. A living life in the house that existed whether he entered it or not.

For her it was part of the deal, her way of earning the shelter provided. It meant she was not compromised.

But she saw now that deep in herself there was another reason. She was doing the house for the man who would come here and see her work and know this was what she could do. She was advertising, displaying her wares. So that the future might be different.

But no one was going to come, she saw that too. Her life here was a closed loop and would not change: Ned's friends, their modest, badly cooked dinners, their modest, penny-pinching lives. The same people, the same conversations: farm subsidies, the price of feed, what breed for the perfect cross, what had happened to what once-great house, the way things were now, the better way they'd once been.

And there was to be no salvation from outside, no wild card dealt into her hand, no young Lord Tung to take her up on to his horse and whirl her off. Lord Tung was grown elderly and married. She'd have to find her own alternative to Ned. Or walk away from him on her own two feet.

She stopped doing the house. She sent Ambrose off and told Ned she'd changed her mind about the shower and the new bay in the dining room. It was enough to be going on with, she said, she might think again in the spring. She wasn't short-changing him. She would still cook for him and clean and help him on the farm when needed. She'd run his house and go to bed with him and entertain his friends. But the things that were still unfinished, she left unfinished.

Ned made no comment. He couldn't help but see how she'd

improved the place, and he liked to open the door and see that a woman lived there. But winter was coming on, he was glad to have the house private again, Ambrose gone, and no more expectation that he find the money to pay for what she wanted. He accepted that he should provide, but it was money he was convinced he did not have. Except for the farm.

❧ *Chapter 15* ❧

You could get to Danno's by one of two ways. There was
a path through the woods that followed the line of the river,
or an old, narrow road, its thinly tarred surface broken by
roots and rain and years. Hannie came by the path on her
first visit.

Danno's house was built on a narrow strip of ground that
dropped very steeply down to the edge of the river. It was
small and old and single-storeyed, white-washed a long time
ago and roofed in slate. The site was dank and awkward and
everywhere there were steps and little runs and platforms,
inexplicable except to the initiated. Cages and wire enclosures,
some empty and some holding injured raptors, clung like mol-
luscs to its walls. It was dark and damp, with a cluster of
lean-to sheds huddling off to the left and the woods pressing
in close, shutting out the light. Beyond it the river flowed,
high and fast with the autumn rains, sinuous and muscled like
a salmon.

Hannie banged on the door and then waited with her back
to it. She had no explanation for her visit, had brought no
excuse in the form of an injured bird or the ubiquitous pot
of jam. She'd been walking over this way and thought she
might call. Just curiosity. She thought she might take a look
and then never come back again.

Nothing. She knocked again. A voice called something from
inside but no one came. She knocked a third time. The door
opened abruptly and Danno appeared, a scalpel in his right
hand. He took in her presence without once looking at her
directly.

94

'There's a knob on the door and it turns. Have you no hands?'

After that first visit Hannie came often. She would open the door and let herself in and sit in his dusty, chaotic room that smelled of outdoors and feathers, smoking and talking as he worked.

He never once called her Mrs Renvyle, it was Hannie right from the start. He never asked her questions or offered her anything to eat or drink, he never welcomed her, nor invited her back, but she came anyway, relieved of some burden by his privacy and his indifference.

Autumn and winter were his busiest times, he told her, the times for indoor projects and making the money to last him through the year. People brought him game birds to be stuffed, sometimes a frozen wild bird or the corpse of a pet, sometimes a big boastful fish from the river. He tied flies to sell to the fishermen, he carved the tops of the ash plants he'd cut and dried in the summer, he soaked the bundled sallies from last autumn and wove them into baskets.

He was busy. She could sit if she liked but he probably wouldn't talk to her and she wasn't to look at the hawk directly. If she wanted tea she could make it herself.

She sat. The room was untidy and plain and roughly finished. The walls had been painted a dark-cream colour a long time ago but were discoloured now and marked with big shambling patches of damp and dirt. Leather leashes and nameless tools hung from nails on the walls, photos of owls and hawks were pinned roughly about the place, there were grubby reference books on a long high shelf and assorted piles of things lay in heaps on the floor and the seats. A door gave off each end of the room and a single window, much larger and more recent than anything else in the house, ran most of the length of the back wall. This window was full of the river, of its moving mass of water. The river dominated the room and was its meaning.

At the left hand end of the room there was a sink with a kettle and a wooden draining board. On the dirty tiled floor three dogs sprawled. At the right hand end was his long wooden work table and an old blue office chair, battered and torn but still revolving. Beside it, between desk and window, was an open-fronted box about two and a half feet high with a length of old blanket pinned across the window behind it. In the box an injured female sparrow hawk was recovering. Leather jesses loosely bound her feet but she could move around within the box and fly up on top of it to perch if she'd a mind to it. The blanket, Danno said, was to stop her flying straight at the window and knocking herself cold.

Hannie never saw beyond this room and the small one to the left of it. She presumed the one to the right was where he slept, but the door was always shut and she never saw him come out of it or go in. He might have slept in a cupboard for all she knew – on a bit of old mattress or a nest of rags, it would have been like him. There was a lavatory built on at the back, but no sign of a bathroom.

The small room at the left hand end of the house was a sort of store where he kept unworked ash plants and big bundles of sallies and any sort of work-in-progress. On long shelves running all around the room, were the birds and animals that were being stuffed, some all but finished, some with splints on legs and necks, some with clips and bits of wires sticking out of them. On the very highest shelves were the finished items awaiting collection. Also the ones that had never been collected. He told her this lightly, with a flick of his head at a pair of chub that swam in a painted box. She couldn't tell if he was angry at this omission. He was always secret and impenetrable. Like the river, its wide opaque surface, its unknown depths.

She didn't care, she didn't need to like him or know who he was; she sat talking about her life before she came here, aware that he couldn't see the pictures constantly forming and dissolving before her inner eye, but relieved nonetheless to be describing them. He worked silently on a bird or an ash plant as she talked, and when she got up to leave he barely nodded. She didn't know if he had listened but it didn't matter, his silence was not unaccepting. It helped her to emerge from the sense of non-existence she so often had here, and it meant she could begin on the process of joining things up.

∾ *Chapter 16* ∾

Mrs Coady was washing the new tiled floor in the kitchen. It looked well now, she thought, a big long room with the light coming in from both sides and the new window facing south for the afternoons. The curtains were new and the walls were a warm egg-yolk yellow. 'Like the sun, Mrs Coady,' she'd said. She'd made the curtains and painted the room herself.

That was before. She'd no interest in the house any more, she'd no interest in anything much any more, she just walked around the place and wrote letters to the boy and sometimes she visited Danno or Niamh.

It was hard for her, he was a fine man but he wouldn't be everyone's cup of tea, and her so much younger. She never said anything or complained but sometimes she spoke of the light going and the shortness of the day. 'I just can't get used to it,' she said, 'it feels like death.'

She was always cold, she wore anything that came to hand, often his clothes, she didn't have enough warm ones of her own. Mrs Beresford had hinted a bit but he didn't catch on, in the end she just said out straight it was time his wife had some new clothes. He'd looked surprised, and then the next thing they'd gone off to Cork and she'd come home with sweaters and a pair of trousers in a heavy cord. She should have had winter underwear, nothing like an extra layer to keep out this damp cold, but there was no sign of any around, no vests or leggings on the line. She wouldn't complain, and sometimes he didn't see the nose on his own face.

*   *   *

A letter came, a queen's head on the stamp and a Northern postmark. Ned handed it to her, he watched her careful blank face and saw how her fingers trembled as she took out the single sheet and read.

'All well?'

'So it would seem.' She lifted her coffee cup and drank. 'But he needs more sports kit, he's sent a list, he's on a team.'

'Which team?'

'He doesn't say, just that he needs it by next week.' She put down her cup and began buttering a piece of toast. 'If I send him the money he'll buy what he needs himself from the school stockists in the town.'

Ned understood. She wanted a cheque. He went and got his chequebook and wrote one for the sum required. That was all she really wanted from him, he thought, not knowing why he minded so much; it had, after all, been the deal.

When he left the house she got out the writing pad. She wrote urgently, though there was no urgency, she knew that Joss would already have opened a charge account at the school suppliers, would already have acquired whatever he wanted and sold on what she'd bought only weeks before. When she had finished she sealed the envelope and addressed and stamped it. She had to stop herself going straight out to the post. It was pointless: the only post of the day left at four.

That evening she told Ned she thought she might try her hand at poultry. Ducks for the table and a few hens for eggs. He approved, it was traditional for the farm wife to rear poultry, it fell into his scheme of things.

'And we can give away what we don't eat.'

Hannie nodded. She didn't intend that so much as an egg be given away or eaten without first being paid for, but she didn't say so.

When she thought of what she might earn she was discouraged. It seemed so little she was nearly ready to give up before she started but she had no choice. She needed no ready money so he gave her none. Even if this poultry scheme earned her nothing, at least it would give her access to Ned's chequebook and bank account as a matter of right. And she saw the time ahead when she might need money badly. Money she didn't have to explain or account for.

❧ *Chapter 17* ❧

'*A* poofter? Danno Tuomey? Not bloody likely. More like old Brandy, I'd say: N.B.I. Not Bloody Interested. Happens sometimes – not a lot, but more than you might think.' James Bering stood in the crush of people by the parade ring at Clonmel races and bellowed his opinions down at Hannie. She gazed up at him, her gloved hand sharing his race card, her shoulder pressed comfortably against his chest.

It was as Ned had said; they all knew Danno, the taxider-mist-fella-who-stuffed-things. They went to him with dead animals for their walls and mantelpieces. Sometimes they wanted to know what he thought of a dog.

Not a bad-looking woman, James was thinking. Tanned still, but been living out there for years, could take time to wear off. Or Vere's tar brush theory might be true . . . Could do with a visit to the hairdressers, something decent to wear . . .

James's brother Vere stood on the other side of him, not speaking, absorbed in the horses as they appeared. Ned was across the ring with the rest of their party.

James had been explaining the going to her, translating the marks he had made on his race card about the runners and their past form. He had been enjoying himself – in full flight and oblivious of the carrying power of his voice in the quiet, soft-spoken crowd.

No one looked at him directly and you would not have known that the neutral faces around him listened at all. But from time to time a pencil hovered and a card or a folded newspaper was marked. Racing crowds were the same anywhere, Hannie thought. Suckers for a tip. Scouring the place for Someone-in-the-Know. Ready to ditch their most cherished fancies and bet all on a thrown word.

Hannie knew about racing – every colonial society had a racecourse so she knew how to look at a horse in the parade ring and how to read form. She let James know she knew – at least enough to whet his interest in explaining the local situation to her. She was flirting with him in a low-key, idle sort of way. She knew he did not like her. For the moment it amused her mildly to wheedle her way round his dislike. And it pleased her to annoy his wife Marjorie, who didn't much care for him but knew her rights.

'Don't know why it happens,' James was banging on from above her, still on the subject of Danno's lack of sexual orientation. 'There'll be theories, of course. Traumas and rot like that. All nonsense. Had Brandy since day one and never a flicker out of him. No mystery to it – born that way.' Brandy was an ancient liver-and-white spaniel who dozed all day by the range in Marjorie's kitchen, living proof of Danno's situation.

She nodded now and laughed because she wanted to, which was an unfamiliar way of feeling these days. She saw Ned's eyes on her from across the ring. He was watching the circling runners with Alison, just as she was doing with James. Hannie grinned at Ned and waved. She watched his beaky contained face break open with sudden pleasure. She was surprised – embarrassed almost. She turned her eyes back to James.

James's gaze was on the ring and the led horses swinging their way moodily round the rails. 'Danno Tuomey, a poofter...' he was saying, shaking his head and chuckling softly. 'That's a good one.'

A big bay was led in, the number 12 emblazoned in red on his grey stable blanket.

'I like him,' Hannie said, referring to Danno, aware that James didn't. He looked at her with sudden strong approval.

'Good woman, yourself,' he said warmly. 'Red Kestrel. O'Shaughnessy trained. All heart. Fast, but carries a lot of weight.' He lowered his voice. 'Only his third time out. Another Arkle in the making, so I've heard. Keep it quiet. I'm off to see what the bookies are saying . . .'

James pushed his hat firmly down on his head and plunged off through the crowd. Vere, who had been standing quietly on the other side of James, expanded slightly to fill up his space. Despite being twins, the two men were not physically much alike. Mentally they were even further apart, though this was not so immediately obvious, as Vere's voice was seldom heard above the noise James made wherever he went. Now Vere smiled vaguely at Hannie and returned his gaze to number 12, who was making a mutinous progress around the ring.

'All heart and no discipline,' he said, quietly. 'That's why they brought him out late. And hates this sort of going. So you like Danno Tuomey, do you? And why is that?'

Hannie shrugged. 'He's easy to talk to. I tell him about my life in Kenya and he doesn't change the subject. Then I remember I existed before I came here.' She smiled up at him, the slight foreignness in her voice and diction accented. 'That can be a pleasant reminder.'

Vere smiled back. Peculiar woman, he thought, where on earth had old Ned found her?

'Are we really so parochial?' he asked.

'On the journey here,' she said, 'Ned told me you would all ask my maiden name. Then when you didn't know it you would ask me my mother's maiden name. When you found you didn't know that either, you wouldn't ask me any more questions at all.'

'What else did he say?' asked Vere, suddenly interested.

Hannie looked at him, unsmiling. Then, with a slight wilful toss of her head, spoke with deliberate indiscretion.

'He said, "Best not to tell them about the marriages. Catholic country, and all that."'

Vere roared with laughter. From across the ring, his sister-in-law glared at him ferociously but he didn't notice.

* * *

The last race was over, the crowd was dispersing, the darkness coming up out of the ground like smoke. A traveller woman thrust oranges at Alison. Giving them away, she said, dragging her emptying black pram across the rutted ground. Alison shook her head but James bought a Mars Bar apiece off her, though no one much wanted them. Red Kestrel had fallen at the last fence, but had got close enough for James to feel he'd had a race. He was resigned but not discouraged.

They tramped across the muddy parking field, looking for where they'd left the cars. Ned handed round a hip flask. Hannie had lost her high spirits, they'd slunk off like the daylight. Her wet feet burned with cold and her hands were numb through her leather gloves. This was not racing, this rite held in mud and bounded by darkness. She tramped along, her head bowed and her shoulders hunched against the cold.

Glancing across, Ned noticed her with sudden clarity, as he might have noticed a stranger. He saw that she was utterly discouraged and slowed his pace. Then he remembered her flirting with James and with Vere, ignoring him, ignoring their wives. She hadn't wanted him when she was full of herself, he decided, so why should he help her now? A stubborn self-righteousness possessed him. He stuck his chin out and pushed on over the freezing mud.

They thawed out in Marjorie's kitchen with a couple of bottles of red wine, a reheated casserole and some dubiously labelled whiskey. Hannie got as drunk as she could manage. Now, she sat huddled in the corner of the car, not moving or speaking, just glad to be through with it all and going home.

Home? Was that what it was? Not home as others would mean it, but something all the same. A refuge. She closed her eyes and rested her head against the frozen window of the elderly Volkswagen. Her car. Or at least the car she drove unless Ned wanted it. Ned used the Land-Rover, but only for short distances. It drank petrol.

Ned was looking straight ahead, his eyes intent on the unravelling ribbon of twisting road which ran beside a once-great estate. The headlights discovered it out of the darkness: the bare, over-arching trees, the crumbling demesne wall, the clusters of houses where pockets of land had been sold off. Beech and ash and lime. Old trees, sufficient and unstriving in the deepening night. Over and over the lights gathered them and let them go.

Hannie sank further into her own dazed state. The heater blasted out hot thick air, its warmth poured over her. Her kicked-off shoes, stiff and dry now from Marjorie's Aga, lay in the caked mud on the floor and her thawed-out feet throbbed and itched with vicious persistence. She'd have worn wellingtons if she had known. She wasn't asleep, but somehow she was separated from herself, time and place dissolved into this unending tunnel of lit darkness. It was a sort of reverie of aloneness: a curious, stale aloneness, informed by night, discomfort, and hot, beating air.

She came to herself with a jerk. The car had stopped and Ned was getting out to open their gates, his movements careful so as not to awaken her. She went on pretending to sleep. He drove the car through, then got out quietly again to close the gates. She sat up. He appeared beside her, smiled at her, touched her hand.

Driving home through the night Ned had glanced across at her huddled form and thought her asleep. He had turned his gaze back to the unwinding road but with that small shift of attention something had changed in him. This was not just some fellow traveller behaving unreasonably, he realised, not some tracker or bearer deliberately making things difficult. This was Hannie, and she was his wife.

He had felt her there then vividly, the unlikeliness of it: her life curled up in the corner, her slack limbs, her body softened by sleep and age. If only they could pull together they could make some sort of a life for her and she could be happy or at least content. He had been flooded with a heightened, almost impersonal tenderness. His self-righteousness had dropped away.

He stood on the step now, fiddling the key in the door. The lock was stiff or the key needed filing down, it was always awkward. He was thinking he must see to it and at the same time he was trying in his mind to find some way of telling her his thoughts from the car. It had all seemed so obvious and simple when he was driving, but now he didn't know how to begin to speak.

He got the door open, groped for the light switch and felt her pushing past him. He called her name softly but she was already on the stairs and she didn't answer. He mustn't put it off and just let things drift, he decided. He'd get the whiskey and some glasses and take them to her room and they would talk.

But Hannie didn't go to her own room; she went to Joss's room and she locked the door. She pulled off her clothes, drew back the covers and got straight into bed. The sheets were icy and damp. There was a soft knock and she heard Ned's voice calling her name, but she didn't answer. She switched off the light. A few minutes later she heard his footsteps withdraw. She gathered the bedclothes tight round her neck and made herself small in the cave in the freezing bed.

It was no good, she would never sleep, it was too cold, she was too over-wrought. She switched on the light again, got out of bed and pulled on her discarded jumper. Then she rooted in Joss's drawers for clothes and socks, glimpsing herself in the speckled mirror of the dressing table as she searched. She stopped rooting and stared at her dim reflection. She pulled her hair back from her face and held it like that with both her hands. Even in the poor light she could not avoid the truth of herself. Hair greying and losing its curl, throat sagging, skin gone spongy and white. Nothing bankable there any more, nothing that might help her. She pulled on a pair of Joss's tracksuit bottoms, got back into bed and lay there with her eyes tight shut, too low for sleep.

There was an incident from the afternoon that she could not get out of her mind. A thickening, tallish man of about her own age had bumped against her in the crowded bar, jolting her arm and causing her whiskey to slop itself down his shirt. He had apologised promptly then disappeared, re-appearing a few minutes later to put a double into her hand.

That done, he had stood back and stared at her. An open, arrogant gaze, a blatant assessment he did not bother to hide.

'Richard Thornton,' he said, introducing himself. 'You must be the new wife.' He nodded his head towards the back of Ned's. 'Welcome to sunny Ireland.'

He was dressed in a thick sweater, worn jeans, leather boots and a torn, fringed suede coat. He had grey curling hair and a confident self-satisfaction. She knew at once she was being patronised and insulted. She knew he had come back with the drink to size up her sexual potential, knew that already she had been dismissed as too ramshackle, too close to his own age, too old.

'Glad to see old Ned's got himself shacked up at last. Do him the world of good, a woman about the place. Hope you won't die of boredom, though. Not everyone's cup of tea.' He grinned a big easy grin and jerked his head to where James and Alison stood with Ned. They looked glum and diminished in the warmth and life of the crowded bar-tent. They looked in-bred and shabby and austere. None of the energy of power remained, only the habit. They looked what they were – the end of their line.

Hannie heard the note of easy contempt in Thornton's voice. They were old buffers. So was she, for the company she kept. Hannie hated him – his curls, his self-satisfaction, his fringed coat. She would rather have Ned, she thought furiously. At least he was honest and not cruel. She turned her back on Richard Thornton and walked away.

Now, in the cold bed, it was not so easy.

The music business, Vere had said. He had made a pile, could live where he liked, do what he liked. He had the old

Cantelon house but he wasn't here much. America. A womaniser. Young women, half his age, one after the other. Seemed to have no trouble getting hold of them. He'd had a lot of work done on the house – everything as new. God knows what it had cost. The last word, or so they said. Locals very impressed.

Vere, clearly, was not. But he was wistful about the young women; the wistfulness of a life not fully lived. Then he had shrugged his thin shoulders slightly, letting it fall away. She saw that he settled for less without much struggle. Most likely had always done so. She felt his defeat.

Now, in the freezing night bedroom, she felt her own. She had met Lord Tung – not nodding by the fireside as she had fancied, but abroad still and roving. And he had seen her from up there on his fine white horse and had coldly passed her by.

Dust and ashes were in her mouth and she could not spit them out. In the arrogant eyes of Richard Thornton she had grasped what her life ahead must be. The future – whatever future she might have – lay where it had always lain, in marriage. But not, as she had imagined, in some marriage as yet unmade. It lay in the marriage she had now, with Ned.

Change of plan, she thought, grinning bitterly into the darkness.

She must knuckle down. She must stay married to him until he died and left her what he had. Then things would be different. She would be able to live for the rest of her life without being married to anyone at all.

❦ *Chapter 18* ❦

*T*here was another letter from Joss. Hannie read it, Ned watched. She finished the letter, replaced it in the envelope and held it in her hand as she talked.

'He wants to stay with a friend for half-term.'

'He must be settling in then, making friends.'

'Yes. A place called Omagh. He says it's not far from the school.'

'About fifty miles.' Ned pushed back his chair, aware that he wasn't being shown the letter. 'It's a bit soon, don't you think? And we don't know this boy.'

'Girl,' Hannie said flatly.

Ned looked startled. He still hadn't really grasped the facts of co-ed boarding. There was a short, tight silence. 'He can come home now and go to Omagh in the summer,' he said finally. 'He can't just go traipsing off to strangers –'

'Why not? They've invited him.'

'It's too soon.'

'So you just said.' Hannie'd got to her feet and started vigorously clearing the table.

'He lives here now, Hannie. He can't just go gadding about the place, he has to come home.'

'Why?' she challenged. 'There's nothing for him to do here, no one his own age to talk to, why must he come? Because you say so?'

'Because *you* want to see him,' Ned said quietly.

There was another silence. When Hannie spoke again she didn't look at him. A knife danced on a plate as she lifted it on to the tray.

'Yes, but I also want him to be happy. He'd only be here and he'd have to go again. There are several of them going to Omagh. If it makes him happy to be with other young people then I want that for him too.'

'It will do him good to be here, Hannie,' Ned said reasonably. 'He's not a child now, he can't just do what he wants, he'll have to learn –'

'He *will* learn. Life will teach him, it always does. And he's tired of travelling, tired of traipsing around.'

'He'd have to travel to get to Omagh, too.' Ned's voice was suddenly sharp with irritation. 'He's only been in Ireland a couple of months, Hannie, it will disorientate him going to Omagh at this stage. He should come home, get to know the place, settle in.'

'Listen to Ned Renvyle the famous explorer. I must settle, Joss must settle – all you ever think about is settling! Why must we settle? Because it suits you? Because you want it that way?' She banged a cup furiously down on the table. 'He can go to Omagh for two days, then come here for the rest of the time. And don't worry, you won't have to pay for extra petrol, he can get a bus direct from Omagh.'

'There may not be one.'

'There *will* be one.'

'– cutter ants,' Joss was saying. 'Big dark ants with jaws like scissors. They eat vegetation. You'll see a line of them trailing through the grass and you just think ants. Then a minute later you look again ... There's a line all right, but not an ant in sight, they've mown that grass right down to the roots, cleared a highway. Amazing!'

'Like locusts?' Niamh asked vaguely, not moving her eyes off the large dead moth that lay on its back on the windowsill.

'No, stupid, like veggie ants. What do you call this moth?'

'I don't know, I never saw one before.' She pored over the moth. 'It's huge, isn't it? And look at its horn-things.'

'Huge?' Joss sounded derisive.

'Huge for here,' Niamh said.

'Nothing here's huge. Everything's small and brown. Insects, birds, flowers. Small and brown . . .'

The smooth black eyes that stretched round Joss's face pointed in her direction. He's like a moth himself in those glasses, Niamh thought. The blank, expressionless eyes.

'The flowers aren't brown.'

'Might as well be,' Joss said. 'You should go to Africa, see some real insects. Everything's bigger, stronger, more interesting.'

'I like it here,' Niamh said steadily.

'Lucky you,' Joss sneered.

Hannie's hand moved of its own volition to wave, but she realised in time and lowered it. Joss didn't like waves, kisses, fuss, didn't even like her standing waiting for the bus to leave. She turned to go.

To hell with him, she thought suddenly, she needed it even if he didn't. She turned back and stood at a decent distance, stubbornly watching the back of his poised blond head behind the glass. Joss looked round once, saw her and turned resolutely away. He was wearing his dark glasses so she couldn't see what his face said. He didn't look round when the bus moved off.

It hadn't been an easy visit, she thought wryly. It had started badly, and then got worse. She hadn't been very clever about it either. She'd dug a big hole over the Omagh trip, and then jumped into it in plain view of Ned. She had wanted to believe Joss, that was the problem, wanted the picture he offered her, everything healthy and normal, everyone young and blithe. At the same time she'd known perfectly well it was just a ploy. Joss wouldn't go to a happy teenage house-party in some country town called Omagh. He'd go to a city, find himself company, stay away till things fell to bits. Then he'd come home.

And it wouldn't be the first time, either.

But Ned shouldn't have interfered, it was his instant assumption of authority that had angered her so. Joss was hers, for good or ill, the only thing she had that was wholly hers. No one was going to order him around but her.

So despite her defiant words she'd written at once to Joss saying he had to come home and he mustn't accept any invitations. Then she'd phoned the school and said she'd pick up the boy herself at the start of the half-term break.

So he wasn't to be sent to Belfast after all, they asked innocently?

No, he wasn't to be sent to Belfast. She'd collect him and bring him home. And she'd phone again if there was any change of plan.

She told Ned the Omagh girl's mother had rung and cancelled. She'd broken her arm, she said, and just wasn't up to all those kids. Ned made no comment. Joss was getting bolder, Hannie thought. She'd have to watch or he'd outwit her.

She had collected him herself from the school but he wouldn't speak to her at all on the journey. At home he'd produced only monosyllables and he'd spent all his time with Niamh. She'd been beside herself. When he was at Niamh's she'd ached to have him with her, but when he was with her and all she got were blank yeses and nos she fumed with helpless rage. Ned had said nothing. It was just as well, there was nothing he could have said that wouldn't have made it all worse.

She'd planned to drive Joss back, but the clutch had gone on the Volkswagen and Ned said he needed the Land-Rover, he hadn't said why.

She wished they could have driven. On the long monotonous journey he might have tired of his silence and opened his heart.

Pigs might fly. Suddenly, all her anger evaporated and she saw him in her mind, not difficult and devious as she'd been thinking him, but a vulnerable, awkward boy, sitting alone in a crowded bus, a tinny trickle of music spilling from his headphones, the empty miles opening out before him. She would drive him the next time, no matter what, she told herself. And she'd fetch him as well.

A child ran across the empty tarmac. By the bus shelter his mother waited, her hand outstretched. The child took the hand and together they moved away. An old man in a shabby dark suit and a cloth cap also moved away.

The bus had gone, the other witnesses to its going had gone, there was nothing left for her to do but leave as well. Instead she crossed the street and pushed open a door and went into a bar. It was dark and quiet with only a couple of men on stools at the counter and another reading the paper at a table by the fire. They glanced up discreetly, looked away again. She crossed to the counter and stood waiting for the barman to appear. She looked around her. From the mirror behind the bar stared a white-faced woman with untidy hair. She stared back, not realising at first that she was looking at herself. Then the barman came out of a door at the end, polishing a glass as he walked towards her. Suddenly she remembered she'd given all her cash to Joss.

Even a month ago, finding herself in a bar without cash wouldn't have bothered her. She'd have ordered a drink, waited to have it set up, opened her bag – no purse. What a surprise.

And some man would have offered to pay.

Not now. Suddenly she didn't blame Lord Tung or Richard Thornton, or whatever it was he called himself. She wouldn't have bothered with herself either.

❦ *Chapter 19* ❧

She was losing her looks, Mrs Coady thought, but she didn't seem to care. The warm-brown colour had faded from her skin, it was going yellowy-looking and stained, and you'd notice the grey coming through in her hair where before it was bleached by the sun.

'The sky's fallen down, Mrs Coady,' she'd say, standing at the back door, staring out at the low damp day and the cling of moist air in the yard. Then you'd see her around the house, her hand moving to switch on lights she'd already switched on, wanting more brightness, unable to thrive in this squinting daylight.

'I miss the colours, Mrs Coady,' she'd say, her face all strained and pinched up with the cold. She was sorry for her then; there were many that found the short days hard, and them not used to the warm sun and the bright air the way she was.

Tom was on at her to pack in the job and stay home. They didn't need the money, he said, and he was tired of her coming in so dispirited and out of sorts. She was tired of it herself, and she wasn't working for the money, though she let on that she was, that she liked having money that was hers alone to spend or waste as she wanted.

She didn't tell him the truth, that she still couldn't face the house every day because it reminded and reminded of Joanna.

She'd get over it, the same as she'd got over the sleeplessness, but she had to take her time, to find her own way out of the dark maze. It was two years before she'd slept the night through after Joanna died, but she'd got there in the end.

Tom thought she didn't talk about Joanna because she was protecting him; that she didn't want to be reminding him on account of him thinking the accident mightn't have happened if he'd thought ahead.

But it wasn't that, she wasn't protecting him, an accident was an accident, a mistake, no one's fault or intention, that was what the word meant. It was just that she needed to be private, even from him – especially from him – she needed to manage it in her own way. And you had to go on living.

People had said she was wonderful, she was so brave, but she knew that behind her back they had said she was hard and it wasn't natural and they'd have liked her better if she'd taken on like Tom. Well, the world hadn't stopped, though for a while there she'd thought it had, and it wasn't as if Joanna was their only child.

Still, she was the youngest, the afterthought, there'd been a special sweetness. It was five years now, the world had all but forgotten Joanna, but she hadn't, there wasn't a day when she didn't see Joanna in her mind and think of her.

Hannie'd cut back her hours, there wasn't enough work for the two of them. Which was true enough, there wouldn't have been any need for help at all if she'd spent less time traipsing about the place and rolled up her sleeves. And she was able for it, she had proved that from the start, she was a worker all right when she'd a mind to it.

Hannie hadn't told Ned about the hours, Mrs Coady was certain of it, she'd seen him leave out the money for wages on the table, the old amount, and Hannie had said nothing. Then, when he'd gone out, hadn't she subtracted the extra and taken it and hidden it away in a drawer?

She was saving it for Joss most likely, for the times when she would need it and she didn't want him knowing about it.

Hannie was withdrawn and morose. It didn't worry Ned overly, he thought it was worry over Joss or the pain of adjustment and the season pressing in on her, the sombreness of it.

Sometimes he hatched schemes and plans but he never really tried to realise them because he didn't know what she wanted or how to change things, and in the end it was easier to stay quiet and watch and wait and endure. He endured as he would have endured the hardships on one of his journeys: stubbornly and without surprise or complaint. Knowing that either it would pass, or it would not.

It should have been easier, once she'd realised her fate, Hannie thought, but it wasn't. Decisions were one thing, living with them was another.

The problem was that of a life which has been lived in action and movement and then finds itself abruptly arrested. Hannie felt like a victim of shipwreck or marooning. She had survived, but the price was this existence with Ned in a hidden valley from which there seemed no escape. Profoundly she didn't want this break in her life, this empty space that was like a mirror showing her back to herself. She was not reflective or used to reflection. She had no wish to confront herself or to understand herself or her life as far as she'd lived it.

More particularly she didn't want to be understood by Ned. She didn't even want to be seen. And she felt him constantly watching her and waiting, drawing conclusions, trying to fit those conclusions together. She felt her privacy violated by this meticulous, attentive observation.

Farm life threw you together, she knew that from her short-lived farm-marriage with Stan. But Stan had only wanted her sexually; apart from his frequent welcomed invasions of her body, Stan had been totally taken up with himself. Ned was different and that difference was more than a different land-scape and different time of life. Ned not only wanted to under-stand her, he wanted intimacy and he wanted to incorporate her into his life. She hadn't expected this, and she hadn't expected to feel so pressurised and observed.

When she couldn't stand it or herself any longer she went

to Danno's and talked about Piet or Africa. Danno didn't take any notice of her. He just got on with carving the knob of an ash plant into a fox's head or putting the rand on a log basket or whatever it was that he happened to be doing when she landed in.

Besides he was growing used to her, her fiery energy which burst out in anger and complaint and then suddenly left her and leaked away into nothing. He didn't try to reassure her or placate her. He didn't know what it was she was trying to figure out or think through and he didn't care. He just let her come in and walk around his room, talking and talking until it was enough for the time being and she could leave him and return to her life.

She talked about Piet a lot but she never once spoke of Ned. 'My first husband,' she called Piet, making it clear she'd had several. He liked to hear her talk of him, his trading station, his time in the Japanese camp, his little homilies and sayings. Sometimes he'd wondered that Piet should be so vividly there in the front of her mind after all these years, but he didn't ask.

'A fish in a carriage rut.' That was what she said she felt like. It was an apt enough image, he thought, but he doubted Ned Renvyle would ever do as her Piet had done. He'd think she'd get used to the carriage rut, would grow to like it, wouldn't even realise she needed water not air. But she'd only herself to blame for it. She'd jumped into this rut of her own accord and she didn't seem to be about to find a way of jumping out of it.

❧ *Chapter 20* ❧

Cold winds blew from the North and winter came early. The river was burnished where the sun reached – a dull, matt gleaming, like hoarded silver paper smoothed with a child's wet finger. The trees were emptying. Ned loved the ash best – its slender nakedness. A stripe of soft light followed each limb, each twig, where the weak sun shone. Here and there, in the copses of cherry, tattered red leaves hung on. There was a poignancy about them, a defeated courage – the pennants of lost armies trailing home, the winter pressing. The oaks under the lea of the hill still clutched their old brown leaves. The rest were swept bare, the leaves gone.

Colour leached from sky, woods, fields. Only the ivy kept its strong dark green, it glittered in the pale light, burdening up the hearts of the trees in great hanging masses that swung in the cold winds like gallows fruit. The ash were mauve-grey on the hill, the spindles had lost their leaves, their last berries stood in pinpoints of cerise against the grey. By the river the tall buff skeletons of charlocke and thistle rattled in the bleak wind. On the paths, black sludges of fallen leaves.

Even the sounds thinned and grew monotonous: the hungry bleating of sheep, the wing-whir of pheasants in the mornings, the dry rattle of magpies all through the short, dark days.

Late one afternoon, the light dying, Ned decided to talk to Danno about shooting the vermin on his land. He had done it himself at the start, had liked walking the land with a gun in the early morning, but the farm took more of his time now and Danno wasn't above poaching across his bounds. Might as well legitimise the situation, make an arrangement, Ned thought. Danno could go on shooting the odd bird in return for a haul of dead crows and the occasional fox.

Danno was agreeable, the business was done and he should have gone but he hung on, trying the sentences this way and that in his head and liking none of them. Danno sat at his work table fiddling with a half-stuffed pheasant and saying nothing. No matter what way Ned tried he couldn't slide over the fact that he wanted to ask his wife's friend what could be done to make her happier.

'You could get her a dog,' Danno said, when he'd got the gist of what Ned was saying. He heard himself, and a twisty little smile worked his mouth. 'Not a house dog or a pup,' he went on. 'A grown trained dog she has to work and exercise. One she can be proud of.' He looped a fine wire under the wing-feathers and chose his words with care. 'She shoots, she can handle a gun, can't she? I've heard her speak of game-shooting in Africa? Well, she can go along with you when you shoot. As a gun or as a picker-up, it doesn't matter. So long as she's there in her own right, not just stuck in a corner with the wives.' Danno paused; he was glad Hannie couldn't hear him.

'She might not take to it,' Ned said, his hands deep in his pockets. The pause in the room lengthened. 'There's no telling with her,' he added, staring intently out of the window at the deepening gloom beyond.

'She rides, you know. Sits a horse as well as any woman. Marjorie Beresford offered her the use of those two mares of hers any time she wanted, said she could use a bit of help exercising them since her back went. As good as begged her.' Ned waited, but Danno did not comment.

'No interest,' he went on. 'I told her if she doesn't want to go to Marjorie's there's always old Connie. I might as well be suggesting she go to mass. How do I know it would be different with a dog?'

'You don't,' Danno said. He didn't say anything else but kept his eyes and his hands on the pheasant he was wiring.

He was angry and embarrassed at this conversation. Ned should have known better than to ask him – did know better – but chose to ignore what he knew. Ned should have kept it to himself that his relations with his wife were not all they should be.

He knew, of course, and Ned knew that he knew. But Ned shouldn't have brought it out and set it there in the middle of the room for them both to look at, it was a gross intrusion. It hadn't been Danno's idea that Hannie come calling on him.

'It's a shot in the dark, but it might be worth a try,' Ned said. He had cheered up, his voice had regained its confidence. It was the opposite for Danno. His hands shook as he worked and he knew he'd have to re-wire the legs when Ned had gone. Who did these people think they were, he thought furiously? Those days were long over and done.

And if Ned believed a dog would solve Hannie's problems he must be either desperate or stupid.

Ned turned it over in his mind as he drove back home. Odd fish, Danno, difficult childhood, there were stories. Mrs Coady said he was an outside child. Some said he was a spoiled priest as well.

Somehow he gave the impression that he didn't much like Hannie. That she'd taken to visiting, though he didn't want to be visited.

It was typical of her, Ned thought. She wouldn't like the people who wanted to be her friends and she took up with someone who didn't. Maybe he shouldn't have gone there, shouldn't have asked. Danno certainly hadn't made it any easier.

✎ *Chapter 21* ✎

'Wonderful woman, Alison. Been the making of old Vere, don't know how he would have managed without her. How any of us would have managed, come to that.' James stood at the fire, one arm resting on the high mantelshelf. He stared moodily into his half-drunk whiskey, swirled it around in the glass. Then he sighed, tipped back his head and threw in the remains. 'I'll have a word,' he said, as though that sorted the problem. 'Get Alison on board . . . Give Hannie someone to talk to . . . Shouldn't be running around with oddballs like Tuomey and girls half her age . . .'

Ned said nothing. He avoided looking at James. He knew the avoidance was cowardly, but there was nothing he could say, certainly not that Hannie didn't seem to like Alison. He wished sincerely that he'd talked to Hannie himself when he'd meant to, and left his worries unshared. James was about as sensitive as a concrete bollard, but even James would have kept his mouth shut and his thoughts to himself if Ned hadn't started in on it. Wives were wives, in James's book, and you pretended it was all roses and sunshine even when you could feel the flood water lapping around your ankles. Unless the husband raised the thing, and declared the subject open.

James was pleased with his solution. He sincerely admired his sister-in-law and was confident of her tact and abilities, which had been exercised on her husband's family over the years and as the need arose. She was neither bossy nor managing and could be relied upon to gently insinuate herself into your affections and equally gently to nudge you in the right direction when you needed it. She was intelligent and self-deprecating and still reasonably presentable in late middle age. As a young woman she had been a beauty. She was, in James's view, the perfect wife.

The only thing that was quite beyond his understanding was why she had saddled herself with Vere and, in time, with his extended family. She must have 'fallen for him' he would say to himself, or Marjorie, when he had cause, once more, to examine the puzzle. 'Falling for people' was something women did. Marjorie said nothing. She was grateful for Alison's influence on James and her as yet undefeated ability to call him back from the bottle. She did not much care for Alison and she thought her dull company, but she knew a good thing when it came and sat down under her nose.

James strolled over to the drinks tray and helped himself to another whiskey. You could wait all night before old Ned would think to offer you one. Fellow was a natural ascetic. Tents and camp beds and deserts and all that. Made an ass of himself over this Hannie woman. A baggage, if ever there was one. A strap, as the country people would say. Must have got carried away with himself. Plenty of time to regret it now.

Ned watched James quietly and followed all his assumptions. He was neither surprised nor offended by them, but Hannie certainly would be. He was aware that talking to James – even to the limited extent that he had – had been both unwise and disloyal. But it was done now and couldn't be undone. He just hoped that Hannie wouldn't appear before he got rid of James.

They had been at the mart together, had run into Niamh's father, and somehow the result had been this misplaced confidence. With James at his elbow, Ned had steered his way out of the building and down through the pens for a last look at the calves he'd just let go. The cattle were anxious and unsettled and a steady reek of shit and fear was acrid in his nostrils. The mart was busy and he could hear the echoey boom of the auctioneer's voice on the Tannoy. The wintry sun had all but gone; its last rays lifted the wet concrete yard and the metal rails of the pens to a cold glory, and aureoled men and beasts with radiant light.

The air smelled frosty and keen above the cattle-reek. Ribbons of peat smoke from the chimneys of all the little houses round the mart ran straight up into its clear stillness. The sky to the west was lemon, the night was ready to fall. Something in Ned quickened. He felt the timelessness of this life, the ancient repetition of ceremony and act and season. He had spent so many years searching for myth in other lands and among other peoples, yet it was here all the time and could be lived from the inside.

John Comerford was standing over by the mart wall watching him with the quiet steady gaze of a man who has been doing it for some time and knows that his attention will be rewarded. When Ned saw him he nodded quietly and smiled. Ned made his way over to him.

'That's a fair price you're after getting,' Comerford said.

'I've done worse,' Ned said, his spirits rising at this approval.

The mart was always an ordeal for Ned. He knew that his inexperience showed, that he didn't yet know the nuances of pricing, of when to sell and when to hold back from selling, and he was afraid that he was mocked behind his back. He told himself that he didn't care what these farmers thought of him, but he was lying, he cared a great deal, and all his prickly pride was invested in the regard of one or two men.

'You were selling yourself?' he asked, though he'd seen Comerford's calves under the hammer just after his own. Asking was courtesy, it was part of the ritual dance of the conversation.

'I was,' John Comerford said. 'And I'm not sorry either.' He looked up and then down at his feet. 'There's a change or two in your life, or so I'm hearing?'

Ned agreed that there was. 'Will you thank Mrs Comerford for the jug? Hannie was very pleased with it, she said she'd be writing.' He must remember to tell her to do so.

James appeared. He nodded at Comerford but he didn't join in. It was clear he was ready to leave and was waiting to extract Ned. James was a dogged companion, if you were with him you were with him, there was no getting rid of him.

'Kathleen would have me ask if Niamh is being a trouble to you?' John Comerford asked. 'She was home there last week and she talked a lot about Mrs Renvyle. Kathleen says you're to tell her straight if she's under your feet.'

Ned assured him that Niamh was not being a trouble. On the contrary, he said, she was company for Hannie, who was lonely in this new country with her son away at school. It was good for her to have a young face around her, good for them all.

Comerford nodded and seemed satisfied. They shook hands and he thanked Ned again for his care of Niamh, and Ned said again that it was a pleasure and a small return.

James's old green station wagon was parked off a side-street, the passenger door secured with a knotted length of rope. Ned had to get in on James's side and shift himself across under the steering wheel. The awkward movement caught at his hip and a sharp stab jarred through his body, making him suck in his breath with the pain. James heard the sound. He passed over the hip flask he'd been nursing in his gloved hands.

'Arthritis,' he said cheerfully. 'Goes with the climate – happens to us all. They'll saw you up when it gets bad enough – doctors all butchers at heart, no interest in a pill if there's a chance they can get to cut holes in you, fire out the bones, stuff you with plastic instead. Seems to work, though. Have to live with it till then, that's the problem. There's a healer fella over at Coolnabawn you could try. Lays you out on a table and pulls you about. Some Johnny out of nowhere, married the mistress after old Henry Nairn passed on. Englishman, or so he says. Definitely not an officer. Funny ideas about food. Not half bad with animals, though – Marjorie uses him on her ponies, believe that's how he wormed his way into the grieving widow's graces. Or there's a Seventh

Son of a Seventh Son over Clonmel way. Bit too close to voodoo for my taste, but the country people swear by him. Peasants. Rag trees and water out of a holy well and a bit of clay from a saint's grave under your pillow when you sleep. Superstition.'

James rattled on in a steady flow as he twiddled the choke and crashed the gears and negotiated his way awkwardly on to the road. Ned sat back and listened and nodded. It would probably have been all the same to James if he hadn't, but he was fond of James, despite Hannie's contempt for his company. Hannie couldn't seem to grow fond of those she disliked or was disappointed in. She couldn't put away her expectations and let them grow on her like that old coat of his she took down off the peg and wore about the farm.

'What was all that about Comerford's daughter?' James asked suddenly, changing tack. 'Heard you'd let her a cottage. Marjorie said she painted houses. What's the sense of that, I said – a slip of a girl setting herself up to paint houses? – she'd never be able for it. Marjorie said I'd got the wrong end of the stick, as usual. Said the girl paints pictures, not rooms. Pictures of houses. I said well she'd better not go painting Ned's house till Hannie stops messing it around, better find her something else to paint. Houses the only thing she can do? What about animals? I've a dog she could turn her hand to, that black setter I have off O'Reilly. Wouldn't object to her having a go at Jacko if she'd a mind to it. Strange-looking creature. A Gordon setter, O'Reilly called him, but I'd say there's retriever in there and more besides. Looks like the wrath of God and hunts like an angel. Never had a dog like him, the softest mouth I ever saw. He'll lift a hen pheasant out of the nest and bring her home and lay her in my hand. "Dead, Jacko," I say, and he unhinges his jaws a fraction and out rolls the bird. Dead, my arse. Not a mark on her. Gets up and flies away once she's over the shock.'

Ned had listened more than once to the wonders of Jacko. He allowed himself to distract James.

'She may do animals, I don't know, you could ask her. She'll say no if she doesn't want to – not shy about that sort of thing. It might depend on how much you were thinking of paying her.'

James looked shocked. Ned could see that payment had never crossed his mind. James had volunteered Jacko as a favour, he was trying to be helpful.

Ned pressed on. 'It's by way of an experiment, all this. She wants to see if she can earn a living at it.'

James gathered himself. 'And what's she living off in the mean time?' he asked. 'What's she living off while she's experimenting? Comerford, I dare say. And Comerford's fobbed her off on you till she comes to her senses. Daughters! Worse than sons. Come on at you all eyes and tears. Yes Daddy and no Daddy and butter wouldn't melt in my mouth, Daddy. Before you know it you have them so spoiled they think it's your duty to keep them for life.'

James spoke with feeling. He had two daughters of his own and their maintenance in the style which both they and their mother considered appropriate had long been a sore point. Handing them over to husbands had temporarily eased the situation, but hadn't solved it.

'So if she wants to keep on at this painting game,' Ned was saying, 'she has to start making it pay. I'll mention Jacko to her if you like, sound her out?'

But James was not to be pinned down so easily.

'Bloody stupid name,' he said grumpily. 'Don't know what's come over people. Bloody stupid fashion for Impossible Bloody Irish Names. Surprised at the man. Nothing Irish about Comerford. Good Norman name, papist or no. Next thing you know she'll be changing her surname, putting the whole damn lot into some sort of unpronounceable caterwaul, won't even know who she is, who her people are. Hannie like her, does she?'

It was Ned's turn to be discomfited.

'Not much,' he admitted.

'Humph,' James responded. 'Thought Comerford said the girl couldn't stop talking about her?'

'Hannie's at a bit of a loose end, just now,' Ned said quietly. 'Niamh made friends with her boy when he was here. Hannie's taken to calling in with her from time to time. Bored, I'd say. And I'd rather she was there than spending her time with Danno Tuomey. At least the girl's educated, comes from a decent family.'

'Heard about Danno,' James said, for once not taking his eyes off the road as he talked. 'Wondered how much there was in it?'

And that was how Ned had got himself into this mess, with James tramping round the study, helping himself to whiskey, immune to all attempts to get rid of him, and Hannie due to walk in at any moment.

Life was simpler before, Ned thought. He thought it without regret or recrimination. It was simply a statement of fact.

❧ *Chapter 22* ❧

*A*lison had been got 'on board' and was quietly doing her best. 'Hovering around like a bad smell,' as Hannie, exasperated, had put it. 'Persecuting me with invitations.'

Hannie had said no to beagling in Tipperary, to an afternoon's pruning course in Kilkenny, to the selling of Armistice-day poppies to people-who-might-be-thought-to-be-sympathetic. She had refused invitations to inspect graveyards and once-great houses and poke around in ruined gardens. But she had agreed to a tree walk and to shopping in Cork. Of the two she had marginally preferred the tree walk.

'You can always tell ash,' Alison said. 'Those lovely smooth limbs, beige-grey, and the arms spread and just raised in that gesture like wonder. Ash is the masculine tree and hazel the feminine since ancient times. You'll see them together at holy wells, the ash and the hazel, the masculine and the feminine. Odd really, ash is so graceful. Perhaps it's because hurleys are made from its wood . . .'

Hannie was leaning against a crumbling wall, smoking a cigarette and staring at the blowing sky behind the empty branches of the small grey tree. From time to time Alison would pass her a twig or a bit of bark and she would glance at it absently, then drop it into the mud and resume her staring. She didn't know what hurleys were, or holy wells, and she didn't care. She was used to the foliage and blossom of Africa, its spontaneous extravagance, she couldn't see what Alison saw, what stirred in her voice and lit her face.

'Beech,' Alison said, moving on. 'Isn't it lovely? So graceful and wide and all those lacy twigs like fine hair standing out from a head. We don't have so many here, but they're very common in England. They blow down in the gales. Big wide shallow roots, the winds rock the trees and they just keel over.'

Alison was absorbed in her subject. She would reach up to catch hold of a branch, pulling it down to show twig structure and shape and buds already forming for the spring. She would rub the moss off bark to show its pattern, and suggest ways of remembering names by associations which mostly depended on an intimate knowledge of nineteenth-century English literature and meant nothing to Hannie. Hannie mooched along behind her kicking at sludges of dead leaves, hearing Ned's voice in her mind.

She's a nice woman, she means well, couldn't you just go for a walk with her?

Well she had, and this was the result. She was disappointed in Ned over Alison. She had thought him more honourable, had thought that at least he wouldn't have discussed her, would have left her to work out her own fate. She cursed herself now for letting him persuade her into this.

Alison stood at the sink, scrubbing and disinfecting flower pots to put away for the spring. They needed doing and she always cleaned something when she was worried or upset, it meant you could think things over without getting too overwhelmed by them and even if your conclusions were completely depressing at least you'd done something useful while you were reaching them.

Vere appeared in the doorway in his stockinged feet, rubbing his hands and blowing on them to get some warmth into them. He took off his damp coat and arranged it on the rail in front of the Aga.

'Good walk?' he asked. 'Interested in trees, was she?'

'Not much,' Alison admitted without looking round. 'But it got her out of the house.'

'Hmph. Wasting your time, old girl. Ned married her. Let him look after her.'

Alison scrubbed hard. 'The Jeyes fluid's finished. I must put it on the list.'

'Getting on, are they? No, well I expect he's regretting it now.'

'I don't think so. She's an unusual woman. And think how Ned's spent his life. He's always been fascinated by nomads.'

'Nomads? You're an incurable romantic, Ali. The woman's not a nomad, she's a tramp.'

Hannie woke the next day and stood back from herself. Something had nudged at her introversion and suddenly she was critical of the habit of drift she'd slipped into. She felt she'd done nothing for weeks but exist in a torpor of walking and staring. She must act, she decided, if only to defend herself from Ned and Alison. Joss was blessedly quiet but the silence couldn't last for ever, already it felt ominous. She'd have to get started on something sooner or later, be it hens or theft or prostitution. She went to the library in Dungarvan for a book.

She asked at the desk and the librarian waved her to a shelf marked DIY. Obediently she went through its contents. There were books on geese and on bees, there was nothing on hens. She went through the shelf again then crossed to the desk, annoyed, for she'd set her mind to action.

'It is odd, is it not, this omission?' she asked, her voice at its most foreign. 'And in a country library?'

'Dungarvan isn't country,' the librarian said haughtily. She stood looking at Hannie, daring her to contradict. Hannie glared back. There was a moment's impasse, then the librarian relented.

'Sure, why would we keep books on hens?' she asked. 'Doesn't everyone know how to rear them?'

Hannie picked up the book on bees and opened it. 'I don't,'

she said, looking at a diagram of a beehive and not at the librarian. 'That's why I wanted a book.'

In the end she got out the volumes on bees and geese on Ned's ticket, reasoning that their presence in the library must mean a wider ignorance than there was over hens, and a wider ignorance might signify a hungrier market. And she took out a book on herbs as well; it was sitting on the counter looking at her, Ned wanted to diversify, he'd been talking about lavender and scented herbs, she might as well show willing.

Ned came home with a pup, a little Springer bitch straight out of the litter. He put it into Hannie's arms and said it was hers. Hannie looked at it and smelled Alison. She put the pup down on the floor and it peed with fright. She prodded the pup with her foot. The little creature caught hold of her shoe and chewed at the leather. She lifted her foot and the pup fell over on to its back.

A baby will settle her. That's what was always said of a new wife. This would be Alison's version: a pup for a woman past child-bearing. She picked up the empty washing basket, put on her boots, and went out in the dusk to the line. She hauled at the wet clothes that had hung all day in the damp air. Well, Ned had bought it, he could look after it, she would not.

Later she watched as the pup played into his hands and would not eat.

'What shall I do?' he asked her, trying to involve her.

'Whatever you like,' she said sourly. But she went to the fridge and took out an egg and some milk and broke bread into the beaten-up mixture. She gave it to him.

Ned came back into the kitchen, holding out the empty bowl. The pup had eaten it all. He was pleased and relieved. Already he cared for the puppy. She was pleased, too, despite herself. For a short moment they were both pleased at once and they smiled at the little warm creature, puffed up with milk and bread, and forgot themselves.

Hannie bent down and put out her hand. The puppy came

to her and placed her neck on Hannie's wrist and her head on her opened palm. She gazed up at her out of round black eyes with only a sliver of white at their lower rim. Hannie allowed this, knowing that in letting the pup love her she would be letting herself love in return. She let herself. She was holding out against so much in this new life, for once she did not resist the softening.

A knock came to the door. Niamh came shyly in to look at the pup and dropped to her knees. 'Oh, the darling,' she crooned. 'Oh, the doaty little puppy.' She was on the floor, the puppy squirming and wriggling in her arms, biting at her fingers and her nose and the loose strands of her hair. Ned stood, smiling and watching. Hannie watched too. For a moment the kitchen was full of firelight and warmth and young things.

'What are you going to call her?' Niamh asked. She sat back on her heels with the puppy in her arms, looking at Ned. Ned looked at Hannie.

Hannie turned away, the softness going from her face which grew calm and neutral and watchful again. 'Alison,' she said decisively.

Danno smiled a small bitter smile to himself when he heard. A trained dog, he had said, not a pup. He didn't himself care for the innumerable small shoots that were littered around the country, but Ned liked his day out with a gun.

Perhaps Ned didn't want to bring his wife along just yet, Danno thought. It was a risk all right. She might or might not behave herself.

But the pup couldn't even begin to be trained for another few months, it would be a year at least before she was ready enough to be useful.

A year's grace to break Hannie in.

Danno shrugged his thin shoulders and went out to feed his Labradors. Hannie would just have to stay in her rut and learn how to like muddy water, he thought. It was her own fault. The people of Abel should not walk with the people of Cain.

Ned called the puppy Pippa. She was around the house in the day, chewing things and piddling and making sorties into the yard, but it was Ned who fed her and dosed her and played with her, she was his, now. He had tried to back off, to be cold and restrained, but when he saw how studied was Hannie's indifference to her, he gave it up and was unashamed in his affection. Someone had to love the little dog and teach her. If Hannie would not, then he must.

Besides, he liked having Pippa around, he looked forward to coming in to her when darkness had closed down the day. He would stand in the doorway between the scullery and the kitchen drying his hands on a raggedy towel, watching her thumping her tail and wriggling in anticipation. He liked washing his hands and drying them, taking his boots off, placing them together in their place beneath the hooks where his coat hung. He liked all these slow, thorough actions, the glow of the lighted kitchen in front of him, the smell of mud and bran and old flower pots in the scullery behind.

He would feed her, then he would play with her. He had given Pippa an old glove and nightly she fought battles with it.

'Look, Hannie, the glove's pretending to be dead, it's set an ambush, it's going to trap her!' The glove would be lying silently on the floor with Pippa crouched in front of it ready to pounce.

'The glove's going for her, look, the glove's attacking...' With a sudden wild leap Pip would be on the glove and thrashing it furiously backwards and forwards as though it was indeed alive and attacking.

'It's winning, the terrible glove's winning! No, it isn't, Pip's fighting back! She's got it by the throat, she's trouncing it – Little David's beating up Goliath...'

Nightly Hannie was irritated by this joint performance and

resented her role as audience. He looked so satisfied, so happy in his home and in his homelife. She felt outside of it all. She felt like a chattel.

'He might as well have bought a dog instead of a wife in the first place, Mrs Coady,' she said not long after Pippa's arrival.

Mrs Coady had raised her eyebrows at the word *bought*. She wondered if Hannie had said it to Ned. More than likely. For a survivor, she lacked sense.

Hannie hadn't, but what she didn't say spoke almost as loudly as what she did. Sometimes Ned was as exasperated with Hannie as she was with Alison. Why had she married him if she was going to refuse to participate in his life, he thought bitterly? She had misled him in their brief courtship. She'd been so different then, easy and open, an unconventional and independent companion. He hadn't misled her, hadn't pretended beforehand that he would be other than he was. Why was she always so difficult? He would go over it in his mind, rehearsing his arguments, nursing his anger.

His exasperation was exacerbated by guilt over Alison. He liked Alison and he respected her and he felt that he had trespassed on her, not least because he couldn't bring himself to tell Hannie that the pup hadn't been her suggestion but Danno's.

Sometimes though, his feelings swung the other way and he would be contrite. He should be supporting her, he told himself, not trying to convert her into something appropriate. If he had wanted appropriateness he would have chosen differently. He must help her to get used to things, explain his life and what he wanted from her. Tentatively, he tried to speak of his disappointment over her attitude to his friends.

'They're your friends, Ned, not mine, and I don't have to like them because you do. I'm not saying I won't see them. I'll invite them when you want them, cook for them, talk to them, entertain them. I'll even go to their houses with you and eat their badly cooked food and listen over and over to hilarious stories about people I've never met and never want to.' She looked at him out of those deep brown eyes that went so strangely with her light hair. '*Make an effort* you said, so I'm making an effort, but I still don't like them. Why would I? They've been looking through the same window at the same few fields for hundreds and hundreds of years, they've forgotten long ago there might be other windows, other views and other ways of being. And they don't like me either, we have nothing in common, they know what they like, and it isn't me.'

'They do like you, Hannie, Alison –'

'Alison is doing all this for you, not me. Alison is, as you said, a very nice woman, but one whom I don't happen to be interested by, Ned, and I don't want to go riding with her or walking or shopping or looking at gardens or other people's houses. Nor do I want to have tête-à-têtes with her about trees.'

'Then what will you do, Hannie?' he asked.

'Don't worry about me, I'll find something to do.'

But that wasn't enough for him. He should leave her alone, he knew he should leave her alone, but he couldn't. He wanted to talk to her, to show her what he loved and what he thought. All his life he had held back from intimacy, now he wanted to speak and have her understand what he said. And he was convinced still that she could, despite the signs, despite his friends' unspoken compassion. It was for this, he realised, that he'd married her and not someone else.

And Hannie felt smothered by him and by what he required of her. She felt burdened down by his constant efforts to close the distance.

❧ *Chapter 23* ❧

*H*annie got out of bed as soon as she woke and pulled on a sweater. It was freezing cold in the room and her breath came in visible clouds. Like smoking, she thought, shaking a cigarette out of the packet and reaching for the lighter. She padded about in the heavy socks that she wore now in bed every night for her chilblains. The window was opaque, the glass patterned with flowers of grey ice. She reached out her finger to touch and the glass seemed to jump out and burn her. Ice on the inside as well as the outside. She dragged the rickety sash as wide as it would go, then knelt on the floor and stuck her head and shoulders out into the morning.

The sky was a length of stretched silk. Lemon silk, translucent and shot through with pink. The grass was grey-white with frost and the trees were furred on every branch and twig with a coating of tiny frost-hairs. A white mist lay over the river.

Hannie threw her half-smoked cigarette out of the window and breathed in the clear empty coldness. She liked the promise in the air and the brief extravagance of colour in the sky. As she watched the sun broke through and the avenue poplars shone like white flames where the light caught their frosted branches. A momentary glory. Almost before her eyes the ice thawed and the white splendour dulled. Still, she felt better, defeat leached from her.

'Geese,' Ned said over breakfast.

Hannie looked at him. She'd forgotten all about the library books. As far as she knew they still lay unopened on the window-shelf beside the sink.

'You could start in the spring,' he went on. 'Less complicated than bees and at least there's a sure market for Christmas.

'I looked at the books,' he explained. 'My cousins keep geese, know all about them, we'll go and see them. Good time of year for it, just before slaughter, they'll tell you all you need to know.'

It seemed he had cousins who kept geese over Kenmare way. Their mother was his mother's youngest sister, he said, and he owed them a visit.

'The old girl's eighty-six, she can't live for ever. You'll like Ellen, she does all the hands-on work, Lettie runs the show.' He poured himself another cup of coffee from the cafetière Hannie had bought in Cork on her shopping trip with Alison. 'We could go for the day,' he went on, 'I'll find the time, you might as well learn all you can before you start.'

Hannie agreed. She had no desire to inspect hordes of geese or to question wellingtoned female cousins on fattening, but at least it was an outing. Ned seemed pleased. To her surprise, he got up at once to ring his cousins. She remembered it was Sunday. Cheap rate on Sunday, she toyed with the idea of phoning Joss, but resisted the temptation. Joss hated being phoned for a chat, he'd just stand there saying nothing till she got the message and fell into silence.

'The old girl's got pleurisy,' Ned said, coming back, 'she's been in hospital.' He sat down shaking his head. 'Extraordinary thing, Ellen was on the point of phoning, she had the number in her hand when I rang her.'

Aunt Cecily had been sick enough, Ned said, Ellen had held off phoning till the news was good because she hadn't wanted Ned to feel he had to visit. She was doing well now, Ellen said, she'd been wanting her own bed, but the doctor had ordered a week in a nursing home where she'd be warm and quiet and properly looked after.

She'd had a fit. Properly looked after? Of course she'd be properly looked after, she'd told the doctor, what else did he think she had two daughters for?

Poor Ellen. She was the youngest and most bullied of Ned's cousins and he was very fond of her.

Anyway, the old girl had caved in in the end, must have been weaker than she thought, and they'd found a place in Kenmare that would take her.

'House and geese no longer on the agenda, I'm afraid, Hannie,' Ned said. 'I'll go anyway of course, see Aunt Cecily, meet up with the girls in Kenmare for some lunch – but there's no need for you to flog all that way,' he continued. 'No one will be offended.'

But Hannie said she would come, geese or no geese. Ned seemed pleased. If he felt any apprehension he concealed it.

'You look very nice, very smart, Hannie, but we're not lunching at the Court, we're only meeting there, we'll find somewhere in the town that's less expensive.' Ned looked at his watch. 'You've got time to change.'

Hannie said she would come as she was. She was sick of sweaters and trousers.

'It's a four-hour drive,' he told her, 'you'll be cold on the journey.'

'I'll bring a coat.'

The roads were frosty but dry and they made good time, arriving early. Hannie was pleased, she wanted to sit in the hotel with a drink, looking and being looked at. She smoothed the fine dark skirt of the expensive Italian wool suit she had bought four years ago for a winter business trip to Germany with Andrew. She had worn it on their first visit to Joss's school but after that it had sat in the wardrobe and would have gone on sitting there for ever if Ned had had his way. She didn't care if he thought it unsuitable, it was the best thing she owned and she wanted to look quite unlike a woman who might be considering keeping geese.

The hotel building was grey and stately and there were other cars scattered about the dark-green grounds and parked under the ancient yew trees. They got out, Ned locked the car and they walked slowly across the drive to the stone steps. Hannie glanced down at her feet, liking them in their beautiful suede shoes on the dark sweep of the drive. She straightened, the sway crept back into her walk. Looking at them gave her confidence and helped her remember who she'd been before.

The wooden outer doors of the building lay open and there were soft daytime lights glowing behind the glass inner doors. The glass was old and fine and when you moved your head it had ripples in it like running water. Ned reached forward and turned the handle. He pushed but the door wouldn't give. He pushed again.

'There's a notice,' Hannie said, pointing to the paper taped to the glass.

'Closed until April,' she read, and looked around, dismayed. Ned was still fumbling in his pockets for his glasses. 'But it can't be closed,' she said, unable to accept it. 'The lights are on, there are other cars . . .'

'I expect people like to meet here,' Ned said. 'Meet here, walk round the grounds . . .'

'Why?'

'Why not?'

She felt like a child whose treat has been taken away. She stiffened herself. She would not be disappointed, she would not. And over so small a thing.

'Peculiar country,' she said calmly. 'People want to meet in December at a hotel that's closed?' She shrugged and sat down in her beautiful suit on the damp stone steps. She reached in her bag for a packet of cigarettes, took one out and lit it slowly, ignoring Ned's look. Ladies don't smoke in public outside good hotels, even closed ones, the look said. Too bad. She wasn't a lady.

'People here are content with nothing,' she said lightly.

A rackety station wagon burst through the open gates and charged to a halt. Moth-eaten dogs and women in tweeds and cardigans erupted out if it. Ned looked relieved. He hugged his cousins, rumpled the dogs, patted the car and called it by name.

'Glad to see Rosemary's still on the road.'

Hannie was introduced. The dogs were called back, introduced, shut into the car. They would walk to the nursing home, Lettie said. A dreadful place, frilly and pink, but it wasn't far. Then they would find some lunch.

They set off in a little straggle, Ned in front, talking to Lettie and Hannie with Ellen bringing up the rear. Hannie didn't bother to talk. Ellen looked as if she would have liked to have done the same, but her training wouldn't allow it.

'Ned said you want to know about geese?' she opened shyly.

It was very cold already, and would freeze again as night fell. Lights were coming on in the scattered dwellings; here and there yellow rectangles pushed forward through the gloom. Ned opened the window an inch, smelling the fields and the frosty air, watching the folded land fade into the four o'clock dusk. From time to time there were hamlets strung like beads down the side of the road, but mostly it was just fields and farms and boreens running off into twilight. Sometimes a creamery. Sometimes small towns, empty and quiet, the wide streets crossed with coloured lights that swung in the windy dusk. Once they waited while two old men and a girl-child drove a few cows home for milking. Once they stopped for travellers' horses: big dark shaggy shapes grazing loose by the road in the dying light.

Ned felt his love for this shrouded country, these small lost roads, this people he had known from childhood. Nothing in his life had moved him like this, not even the deserts, and he wondered that he'd journeyed so far to see what had always been here. He resolved not to leave again, he was home at last and he wanted nothing else.

He glanced across at Hannie. She sat slumped into herself, staring out of the window, seeing fields and mud and beasts and hedges pass before her eyes. For a moment he saw it as she saw it and for the first time he didn't blame her or condemn her because she couldn't be satisfied as he was. He would think of some way to make her happy, he decided. He felt very tender towards her, very patient and protective.

Then he stopped thinking and abandoned himself to this joy that was filling him. He could see the twin lights of a car away down the road in the valley. He could see darkness thicken and hold the land.

❧ *Chapter 24* ❧

'*M*aster them?' Danno said. 'Put that out of your head, there's no mastering them.' As he talked he was slitting open the blackbird Tommy Moran had found dead on the road and brought to him the night before. The sparrow hawk in the open-fronted box watched him sideways out of her yellow eye.

'Some men try it,' he went on. 'Whole books have been written about one man's struggle with one raptor. They're always the same. Man tries to master hawk. Fails. Tries again. Fails again. Gives up. Masters himself and leaves the hawk be.'

The sparrow hawk moved suddenly, sidling rapidly along her perch in the direction of the blackbird. There was a clicking noise from her claws and a dry scrabbling sound as she shook out her feathers.

'It's a fine line. To work a raptor you have to get its respect but you mustn't break it or even come close to breaking it or you'll drive it mad. They can't bend, you see, can't learn to come to hand like a dog and live submitted. But you have to drive it hard just the same, and no mercy, mercy is weakness, and weakness will always be taken advantage of, that's its nature. And you must get it at the right age and in the right physical and psychological state and not damaged by hunger. Then maybe you have some chance.'

'So why do you do it?'

'I don't. I patch them and feed them up a bit and cage them while they're healing. Then I let them go. To live or to die. Which is all they understand anyway.'

He stopped talking and concentrated on working the black-bird's carcass free from its feathered skin. Hannie was quiet today, he thought. Mostly she paced about, smoking and talk-ing, disturbing the hawk. He would tell her to sit still, or if she had to move around not to wave her hands or look at the bird, but she took no notice. She did what she wanted to do, charged noisily around till she tired of it, then sat herself down, deflating like a balloon that is losing its air.

Danno snipped a last tendon and pulled out the carcass. He placed it in front of the hawk, making little noises of encouragement and endearment. The sparrow hawk stared at it coldly and didn't move. Then with incredible swiftness she shot out her foot, pinned the skinned blackbird, and began systematically pulling off the flesh in long bloody strips with her beak.

Danno lifted the bundle of blackbird feathers and skin lying on the table, opened it out and sprinkled its fleshy side with plaster of Paris. He blew off the excess carefully. He looked up at Hannie, a swift sudden look, one eye opened and one closed, one eyebrow raised in a vivid inverted 'V', the other flattened over the closed eye. He looked down again.

'Hannie,' he said, 'why did you marry Piet?'

Hannie stared.

'You were young. You must have been beautiful. Why did you marry him? Were you in love with him?'

Hannie started to laugh. She'd told Vere she liked talking to Danno because he didn't change the subject when she talked about the past and it was true, but that wasn't to say that he listened to what she said. Danno didn't listen, or if he did he never responded or commented or asked a question, there was never anything to indicate that he'd heard. Until now. She stopped laughing.

'Because my mother told me to,' she said quietly. Danno had the blackbird skin spread out, feather-side down, and he was working one of its wings on to the inside. At the same time he was scraping at fragments of left-behind flesh and feeding them straight to the hawk. He nodded without looking up.

'She thought it would give me a future,' Hannie continued, 'and that I wouldn't have one otherwise. She said there weren't so many people who'd marry me and Piet wanted me, he didn't care what people thought.' She paused. 'For me, Piet was a stepping stone,' she said, shrugging her shoulders as though she were getting rid of something. 'I had to get away from her and I didn't much mind how.'

'Why weren't there many people who'd marry you?'

'Because of her. We weren't respectable.' Hannie reached for her cigarette packet. She extracted one and lit it carefully, leaning into the flame and inhaling deeply. 'And because of me, I was making it worse. I didn't care what I did, you see, she was afraid of how I'd end up.'

'What had she done that made you not respectable?'

'Sailed too close to the wind. In Java, in the war,' she added, as though that explained everything. Danno glanced up.

'The Japanese came,' she said. 'All the men who were Dutch were taken away to a camp. Then it was the women's turn and my mother also was put in a camp, but one for women and children only. She wanted to live, she was very determined, and it wasn't respectable to be so determined, to fight so hard to survive. It was a colony, you see, everyone must pull together, live together, starve together, die together. She didn't want to die. She was beautiful and the guards were men. When the war ended people told stories and the stories followed her around.'

Hannie's accent had thickened. Danno wondered if it was involuntary, if she heard the change herself. 'Were you in the camp too, Hannie?'

'No,' she said, 'or I wouldn't be here now, I was only a baby, I was with the Amah for those years. *When the Japanese came*, people say, as though everyone just woke up one day and it had happened, but it wasn't like that. First there were rumours and panics and people tried to get away. My parents tried. They got a passage on a cargo ship, crammed in with thousands of others, but I was too little to survive such a journey so they gave me to the Amah till the war had ended. Then the ship was turned back so they went to the camps anyway and my father died there. Afterwards, my mother came and got me from the Amah. I was lucky, the camps were very hard, I wouldn't have survived them. Or I'd have been like that hawk you said couldn't be worked. Damaged by hunger. And fear. As she was . . .'

'Why didn't she go somewhere else afterwards?'

'Where could she go?' Hannie shrugged. 'She was born there, it was her home, and anyway the stories would have followed her. But it was confused, there was nowhere she belonged even before the stories. You see, her father was Dutch but her mother was Indonesian, and her mother wasn't married to her father. When my father died there was no one to speak for her with the Europeans any more, no one to protect her. And her mother was dead so there was no place for her with the Indonesians either. It was hard.'

Danno was trying to ease out the blackbird's eye with the point of the scissors but it wouldn't come and he had to loosen it from the inside through the beak. When he lifted it out it looked enormous, the black centre surrounded by a firm dark blue rim about three times the area normally visible. He put it in his palm and stretched out his hand to show Hannie.

'You see that lad there,' he said, pointing to a tiny white membrane that ran through the eye. 'That's the optic nerve. Everything the bird sees is carried through that thread.' Hannie looked where he pointed. The sparrow hawk shifted angrily. She didn't like his switch of attention, or perhaps it was the removal of her titbit that upset her. She flew out from the box, trailing her leather jesses, and perched malevolently on top of it, glaring and settling her powerful wings.

'The eye of a bird takes up a third of the head-area.' Danno spoke in the same quiet voice that he used to soothe the hawk. 'More so, if it's a raptor. Is this a secret, Hannie?'

Hannie looked up from the eyeball in surprise. 'No. Why? Who are you thinking of telling?'

'I'm not, but I've read things about Kenya. I just wondered.'

'Oh, Kenya.' She shrugged. 'They could think what they liked, people do anyway, don't they? And it gave them something to talk about. If there'd been nothing they'd have made up worse.'

'And Ned? Does Ned know all this?'

'Of course, why?'

Danno lifted the forefinger of his left hand and pushed his glasses firmly back up on to the bridge of his nose. He swung round and placed the eyeball on the edge of his table where the sparrow hawk could reach it.

'He just went up in my estimation.'

The blackbird lay, an eyeless huddle of feathers and beak on his work table. He'd done enough for now. Feed the dogs, feed the birds, feed himself. He wondered if Hannie talked to Ned about these visits of hers. He knew the way they spoke of him. Peculiar Danno in his peculiar little world.

He hadn't tried to understand Hannie or placate her, he'd just let her come in and talk until it was enough for the time being and she could return to her own life. He'd never meant to like her or talk back to her.

But he was growing more used to her, even the hawk was growing used to her, she flew up on to the top of the box less, sulked less, was generally less of a prima donna. Outclassed in her own act, he thought sourly.

He stopped himself. Thinking badly of Hannie was a habit he'd encouraged himself to get into. It protected his defences and kept her at a distance. He hadn't wanted her to visit, but for a while now he hadn't not wanted her either, he realised. Yesterday he'd even caught himself watching for her to come.

He got up from his chair, went outside and collected the old soup-pan he used for feeding the dogs. It wasn't just Ned who'd gone up in his estimation.

~ *Chapter 25* ~

*I*t was the dogs Danno couldn't forgive, Mrs Coady told her.
Wouldn't forgive – there was no sense nursing grudges when
things were over and done, and Mr Renvyle hadn't acted out
of anger or spite, he'd thought it was the right thing he'd been
doing.

'What dogs, Mrs Coady?' Hannie asked.

'Didn't Danno tell you?' Mrs Coady asked her back.

'No,' she said, 'not a word.'

So Mrs Coady told her about it – about the two black
Labradors that he'd had off Danno when he'd come to live
there, young dogs, but trained up and ready, lovely creatures
and first-rate hunters, his pride and joy as well as Danno's.

He hadn't had them long, five or six months, no more, and
it had been spring, the lambing just starting and the hunting
not long over and he'd been very busy about the place and
inexperienced, and maybe the dogs had got a bit less in the
way of exercise than they'd needed.

Then Micky Cullen over at Maher's Cross had had a lot of
his lambs killed by dogs, and three or four ewes as well. He'd
been out there straight after, standing in the field, slaughtered
beasts all around him, when he'd seen two black Labradors
making off down the hill through the furze ...

He'd had to act fast, they were off down the hill, so he'd
lifted the gun and aimed straight and shot them both dead in
their tracks.

'Did he know they were Ned's dogs?'

'Not at the time,' Mrs Coady answered, 'not at the time,
but that story wouldn't be one to be long staying home, folk

soon started putting two and two together and making four.'

And the way it is in these parts, Mrs Coady told her, there were many would have found themselves two Labradors out of some place a good stretch away, and had them sitting ready in the yard as though they'd known nowhere else. Then when the Guards came looking for someone to pay for Micky Cullen's sheep they'd have pointed at the dogs for answer.

But that wouldn't ever have been Mr Renvyle's way. Mr Renvyle had picked up his chequebook and driven to Cullen's as soon as he'd heard, he'd walked into the yard and said straight out that he was sorry, and Mick Cullen had been right to shoot the dogs, and how much did he owe for the sheep?

So that was that. Mick Cullen had been happy, and everyone bar a few begrudgers thought a lot of Mr Renvyle for the way he'd acted. Mr Renvyle didn't know it, but he was made up after that, people accepted him, he'd never looked back.

Only Danno hadn't been happy. Danno had landed round that night and he'd banged on the door till he had Mr Renvyle up out of his bed. Mick Cullen had shot the wrong dogs, Danno told him, he'd trained those dogs himself, they wouldn't touch sheep, and Mr Renvyle was a fool and worse than a fool not to know it.

Mr Renvyle had given him short shrift, he'd said any dog could turn rogue and there was no point in swearing the moon was blue when a child of two could tell you it was yellow.

But still Danno hadn't been satisfied, he'd said those dogs were clean bar their own wounds, he'd had it off the Cullen boy when he'd been around there asking questions. Mr Renvyle wasn't a fit owner if he didn't know his own dogs and wouldn't stand over them, Mr Renvyle couldn't be trusted with dogs, he was damned if he'd ever have another one he'd bred.

'Was he right?' Hannie asked.

If he was, there was no proving it, but a bare two weeks later there'd been another kill not a mile from Cullens and three other dogs had been shot – knacker's dogs – and after that there'd been no more kills.

Mr Renvyle hadn't held it against Danno, he'd said Danno had trained those dogs, it was understandable that he'd felt the way he had, but it was his heart not his head had been speaking.

And besides, Mr Renvyle had said, what had his dogs been doing loose in Cullen's field in the middle of lambing? At the very least he should have had them properly secured in his yard.

Mr Renvyle had dealt with it like that, then afterwards he'd put it from his mind.

'But Danno hadn't?'

Maybe he had, maybe he hadn't, Mrs Coady told her, but she hadn't seen Danno coming round with another dog when he'd one that was trained up and ready, nor a pup either for that matter. Where had Pip come from, Delaney's, wasn't it? Wherever it was, it wasn't from Danno . . .

'There wouldn't be much love lost between them,' she finished. 'Danno's a proud one and Mr Renvyle would be the same, though I don't think Mr Renvyle knows what Danno thinks of him, I think he hardly remembers what happened, and maybe he's never really acknowledged to himself that he's given offence.'

❧ *Chapter 26* ❧

'*E*llen phoned,' Ned said, coming into the kitchen. 'Aunt Cecily's taken a turn for the worse and she's back in hospital. Making life merry hell for all, Ellen says. Seems she wants to go back to the nursing home. Poor Ellen.'

'They let her do as she liked in the nursing home. The hospital's probably stricter.' Hannie was manoeuvring a rolled neck of lamb out of the oven as she spoke. The kitchen was full of the rich smells of garlic and rosemary and roasting meat. 'Bottles under the blankets, bottles under the sheets, nobody saying a word. She reeked of whiskey. They wouldn't let her do that in hospital.'

'Strictly speaking, she shouldn't be drinking at all.'

'They should put her on a drip. Neat whiskey. Kill her off.' Now she was basting the lamb, spooning hot fat over the skin to crisp it. She might not be very charitable, Ned thought, but she was a first-rate cook. He ate better now than he ever had with Mrs Coady. Paid for it too, the bills were consistently higher.

'Horrible, greedy, old woman.' Hannie returned the meat to the oven and slammed its door. 'More life in the tip of one finger than in both those daughters stuck together.' She lifted a lid, jabbed with a fork, appeared satisfied. 'Kept all the life for herself, I expect, none left over for the girls.' She picked up the pan and drained a stream of orange-coloured water into the sink. 'Stupid, spineless, useless women, I don't blame her.'

'I'm very fond of my cousins, Hannie,' Ned said mildly.

'You're fond of Ellen. She puts her hand on your arm and

looks up at you with her watery eyes and at once you want to protect her.' Hannie lobbed some butter on to the carrots and tipped them into a serving dish. 'You're not fond of Lettie. Lettie is bossy as well as stupid and spineless, no one in their senses could be fond of Lettie.'

'Ellen was very excited. Patrick's come home from Canada.'

'Patrick? The son?' Hannie had a spoon poised at her mouth. She tasted, then put the spoon down. 'I expect he's useless, too. Who wouldn't be with a mother like that? Either useless or selfish or both.' She began stirring flour into the meat-juices for gravy. 'Ran away to Canada, did he?'

'He's an engineer,' Ned said. 'He went to Canada to work. Now he's home for a couple of months to see his family. He's there for the rest of the week, then he's coming to us.'

'Oh? For how long?'

'As long as he likes. Probably until Christmas.'

'There isn't a room ready,' she said flatly.

'He can have Joss's room while you see to one. He isn't fussy.'

'Joss is. He won't like this Patrick using his room.'

'He needn't know.'

She went on stirring at the gravy, her back and her silence so ostentatious that Ned noticed. Irritation rose in him.

'He's my cousin, Hannie,' he said. 'We haven't spent time together for years.'

No response.

'You'll like him, I'm sure you'll like him.'

'I'd have liked to be asked.'

Ned sighed. She expected him to apologise. He was damned if he would, it was his home, his cousin had a right to come to his home, he didn't have to ask permission.

'I didn't think you'd mind,' he said at last, his voice stubbornly reasonable.

Hannie poured the gravy into a jug. She took the plates from the warming drawer.

'Niamh's boyfriend is coming next week,' she said brightly.

'And Joss will be home the week after, we'll be quite a crowd.'

'I didn't know Niamh had a boyfriend.'

'She doesn't, he's a three-night stand, but she wants to turn him into something more so she's invited him.'

'He'll be staying in the cottage?'

'Of course.' Hannie plonked the plates down on the table. 'I expect she would have asked you but she probably didn't think you'd mind.'

Ned did mind. If it hadn't been for the fuss Hannie was making about Patrick he wouldn't have hesitated. He'd have gone straight out, knocked on Niamh's door and told her he had a responsibility to her father and he couldn't allow it. What exactly 'it' was, he didn't get round to formulating.

Now he sat fretting and fuming, his dinner spoiled. The girl was a grown woman, he told himself, she didn't need his protection even though he wanted to protect her, not just for her father's sake, but for her own. She was so lovely and so trusting, it was a much harder world than she knew.

He couldn't say anything now, if he did Hannie would ask him nastily what century he thought he was living in, make him feel small.

But if he was really honest it wasn't just Hannie's fuss about Patrick that kept him quiet. It was those words Hannie'd used – *a three-night stand* – she'd said it like a quotation. Yet he couldn't imagine sweet, grave-faced Niamh saying anything so crude.

He wasn't really a boyfriend yet, Niamh had told Hannie, he wasn't much more than a three-night stand, but she liked him a lot, and she was pretty sure he liked her too.

They'd had a fling in the summer in Dublin, then he'd gone back up to the North without even leaving an address. Her friends said she shouldn't go setting her heart on him.

But she knew she hadn't seen the last of him, she knew he'd be in touch again, and all she had to do was wait.

And he had. And she'd seen him again in Dublin that last time when she'd gone up to buy pastels.

Her friends still warned her, they said he was too good-looking, women went for him all the time, he had it too easy, he couldn't be trusted.

But she couldn't stop thinking about him and she knew it was the same for him.

Hannie had sat listening. She had heard the naked sex in all Niamh said. She'd begun to remember things she had carefully forgotten, emotions and sensations deliberately left behind.

It seemed all women must be fools for men before they got old and grew wise.

But in the drug of the physical there was potent, if temporary, compensation. She'd felt suddenly savage that such compensation should be wasted on Niamh.

Hannie ran the brush carefully along the line of the skirting, making a clean edge of white against the Wedgwood blue of the wall. She was on her knees on spread newspapers, shuffling her way around the edges of the room, turning the big front-bedroom into a suitable retreat for Ned's Canadian cousin. A gas heater bubbled quietly in the middle of the floor.

The cold weather continued. Hannie liked it, she felt more alive, her sluggish blood ran faster. She liked its ancientness, the threat in the air, skies fierce and then soft, mornings smoky and secret with frost. It was quite new to her. Winter's blanket, its thorned weave and rank folds, its clean bitter stars, so unlike the great flowering stars of Africa.

Ned had been tight-lipped over her insistence on the integrity of Joss's room, but her efforts with a paintbrush seemed to be in favour. He was used to the caravanserai, sleeping forms on the floor, a common roof, all thoughts of privacy and ownership redundant. Easy for Ned, who knew who he was, had had this all his life. Not so easy for Joss, moving from school to school, from one of her husband's houses to another.

She picked a brush-hair from the skirting with her forefinger and wiped the sticky gloss down Ned's discarded trousers. She was covered in paint-splatters: mixed blue and white on her clothes and her face, white in her hair from the ceiling. Ned had noticed, he'd touched it approvingly as he got up from the breakfast table that morning, then suggested a visit to the hairdresser when she was finished. She'd got up and started clearing, saying nothing. He'd gone to the study, come back with his wallet, taken out a ten-pound note and laid it on the table.

Later, when he'd come in for coffee, the note was still there, its edge tucked under the milk jug. Didn't she want to get her hair done, he'd asked her, and she'd smiled and shaken her head and said ladies' hairdressers in Ireland must be very cheap. He'd looked surprised, then picked up the ten and put two twenties down instead and asked would that cover it? She had nodded and smiled again and lifted the notes and put them into her pocket.

Now she filled in the last six inches of skirting and got up and stood looking around her. The room looked well with its matt blue walls and white trim, it would look even better when the cleaned carpet was put back and she'd hung the curtains she had washed and pressed and altered. Just the window frame and the door to be done and she'd be through with the painting. She crossed to the window, lit a cigarette and stood smoking and thinking vague thoughts of Joss, of the unknown Patrick, of Niamh's unself-conscious anticipation of sexual pleasure. She could hear Mrs Coady downstairs hoovering the study and Ned in the upper field with the tractor. The house was sombre around her.

Standing there she had one of those sudden reversals of mood that these days often seemed to accompany one of her successful little manipulations or ingratiations. Pleasure in her own cleverness would dissolve into a vague depression. Hard on the depression would come an angry self-disgust.

And she hated it, this enforced awareness. She didn't want

the mirror she kept finding herself looking into and couldn't seem to smash or push away. Suddenly she couldn't stand Ned or this house or herself a moment longer. She was overwhelmed by the need to make some violent, irreparable gesture that would shove things right to the edge and cut at the dragging compromise of daily life.

She put down her paintbrush, turned off the gas and left the room. Then she bathed, changed her clothes, took the money she'd saved for Joss from its place in the back of the wardrobe and put it with Ned's forty pounds. Downstairs, she lifted the car-keys from their hook and crossed the yard. She opened the garage doors and backed out the Volkswagen.

She woke in broad daylight in an upstairs room somewhere in Cork. The man who snored on the bed beside her was half her age and unknown to her. Other bodies, male and female, lay around on the floor, on the other bed, on the sofa. She sat up and someone put a mug of tea into her hand. It was laced with whiskey. She asked for a cigarette.

Some time later, in some pub somewhere in the city, she was searching her pockets for money and her hand met keys and closed tight around them. For half an hour she sat trying to work through the haze of alcohol to reach for a reason for being here. She found none, the last dregs of any purpose had long since fallen away. She stood up, pushed back her chair, picked up her cigarettes and headed for the door. Someone called her name, but she didn't turn round.

Hannie crossed the yard and reached the back door, so hungover and exhausted that she had to drag herself the few remaining steps. She'd lost all track of time, all care for consequences. She felt empty, anaesthetised and ancient.

She paused, her hand on the door, then pushed it open and stood at the entrance looking in. The kitchen was clean and fire-lit, everything glowed and shone, a cave of warm brightness. The puppy lay curled in her basket and the room was fragrant with the rich warm smells of meat juices and potatoes baking. A man was standing over by the fire, a man as tall as Ned with something of his angular, rangy look, despite the extra flesh he carried, the soft bulge over the belt. He cradled a glass of whiskey in his hand. Hannie half turned in an automatic movement of withdrawal. This was a place both domestic and secure. She had no business here. She should go back outside to the darkness, where she belonged.

'Ah, Hannie, there you are.' Ned's voice came to her from across the room. It was quiet and even and matter-of-fact. 'Hannie, this is my cousin Patrick, come to us a few days early. Patrick, my wife Hannie.'

Hannie stood there, her hands shaking, her hair wild, her clothes crumpled and drink-stained and slept-in. She knew what she must look like, what she must smell like. Yet the man who came forward to greet her gave no sign that anything was other than expected.

'My sister Ellen couldn't stop talking about you,' he said easily. 'She is very impressionable and you impressed her very much. She said you were very elegant and wore beautiful clothes and she didn't want to talk about geese at all, but Ned had insisted and anyway she couldn't think of anything else to say. She liked you very much and she hated being so dull for you. She said I was to be sure to tell you and to apologise for boring you so dreadfully.'

~ *Chapter 27* ~

*I*t was late when Ned phoned Mrs Coady, well after eleven, Tom was already in his bed.

'She hasn't come home, Mrs Coady,' he said, 'she went off in the car and she hasn't come home and I wonder if I should be worrying?'

He was calm enough, Mrs Coady thought, no fuss, no dramatics: he might have been asking where she was because he had Ambrose Power standing beside him wanting a decision about paint or tiles or underlay. But she knew what he was thinking and he knew that she knew: he was thinking she'd left him and she wasn't coming back.

It was a lot to take on, Mrs Coady said, a whole new way of life, and it might be that it was all too much suddenly, it might be she'd got into the car for a bit of a drive and gone further than she'd intended . . .

There was a small silence then he said he'd looked upstairs and there was nothing, as far as he could see, that had gone. He paused again then he asked her what it might cost to get your hair done in Dungarvan?

At first she thought she'd heard wrong, but he said it again so she asked was it only a cut she'd be wanting or was it a colour as well?

The next day he phoned again just before ten and said where was she, was she unwell, he'd come and collect her if she didn't have a car?

Mrs Coady said this was Wednesday, it wasn't her day to come, Tuesdays and Fridays were her days – two mornings a week – but she'd come anyway if he wanted her, she'd only bits and pieces of things to finish up here.

When Mrs Coady put down the phone she remembered that Hannie was saving the money she didn't have to pay her anymore now that she was working fewer days. She cursed herself for her mouth and went to get her coat.

Ned had made himself ring round the hospitals, but the exercise only confirmed what he already knew. She wasn't lying injured in a hospital bed, she'd walked out, it didn't matter that her things were upstairs and untouched, packing a suitcase wasn't ever going to be Hannie's way.

His first instinct was to tell no one. He knew what gossip was like here, how each incident was pounced on and shaken to death and the participants held up to delighted ridicule. He would face that when he had to, but he wasn't going to open the door and invite it in.

He was angry with Hannie, he felt that clearly, but what he hadn't expected at all was the feeling of loss. Having Hannie living here as his wife hadn't been as he'd imagined, it had changed his life in ways he didn't always find either positive or comfortable, yet he could find no sense of relief in himself when he thought that she'd gone. Under the anger at what she was doing to him, his strongest emotion was that of wanting her back.

Then she came back. He didn't ask her where she'd been or what she'd been doing. He wouldn't let himself interrogate her, mostly for reasons of honour but also because he was afraid of what he might hear. And Patrick was staying, Patrick was always at his elbow, Ned didn't want to draw any further attention to the difficulties he and Hannie might be having.

Over the next two days Hannie referred once to her absence but her tone was mocking and light and she made no attempt at an explanation. She seemed neither apprehensive at a possible interrogation, nor relieved when none came. He was angry, despite himself, despite his decision to say nothing. It kept coming on to the tip of his tongue, it was harder and harder to push down.

The next afternoon they were coming back from the field above the house where they'd walked with Patrick and old Bess to check on the heifers in calf. It was just after four, dusk thickened, already the trees were lost, dark shapes on the blue of the coming night. Patrick had fallen behind, he was making heavy weather of closing the gate, Ned and Hannie had walked on in silence, then noticed and stopped and stood waiting.

'People can't always be as they intend, Ned. They can't always deliver on what they've said they'll deliver, even when they truly meant to at the time.'

Hannie's words came out of the gloom. Her voice was so low that he almost thought he'd imagined it but he hadn't. Then Patrick was upon them, Bess at his heels, and there wasn't time for more. She touched her hand briefly to his arm and turned from him. Suddenly, he understood why she'd gone missing. He no longer minded that Patrick had seen more than he wanted him to see; he no longer minded her deception over Mrs Coady's hours and money. Mrs Coady was right, it was hard for her, she had lived a different life, a life opposite to the lives that he and his kind lived here: steady and cautious, with every action evolving out of some previous action and tempered by the knowledge of consequences to be lived down the unfolding years.

They tramped home, the dusk loud with the suck of their boots in the mud and the frantic evening chirring of blackbirds in the thorns.

~ *Chapter 28* ~

'*A*nd there she was,' Ned said, 'with her feet in a basin. And when I asked what she was doing she said it was for the chilblains, Mrs Coady said to soak them every day in warm urine.'

Ned swept his eyes round the table. He was enjoying himself, telling his story, making them laugh.

'I got straight into the car, but it was after six when I got there, the chemist was closed, so I banged on the door, made Heffernan come down and attend to me. He didn't like it of course, mumbled about his dinner and emergencies only. "Heffernan," I said, "if it was *your* wife with her feet in the stuff *you'd* be banging on the door."

'"Very good remedy, the urine," says Heffernan, "a lot in these old pishogues. Sure they're drinking the stuff now, these New Agers, or whatever it is they call themselves, you couldn't go far wrong with the odd soak."

'"Like tying rags to a rag tree. We're approaching the end of the twentieth century, Heffernan," I said, "you can surely do better than that."'

Vere was thumping the table, Patrick had his head thrown back, even Joss let out a little yelp that might have been the sound of appreciation.

'Of course Mrs Coady roared laughing when I told her. Said she'd never meant Mrs Renvyle to go trying it, she'd only said it to show her how bad people were with the chilblains in the old days, the things they would do to get rid of them. So I told her not to be telling her such things any more, Mrs Renvyle was the sort that would try anything.' Ned threw

Hannie a look full of pride and affection. Hannie saw it, smiled quietly, looked away.

'Central heating,' Patrick said. 'And proper insulation. Canadian winters are much worse than ours, but they don't just sit back and endure the way people do here, you don't have to have chilblains or rheumatism.'

'Or sit with your feet in warm piss,' Joss interjected.

'Something like that,' Patrick said, grinning at him.

Joss liked him, Hannie thought. Or perhaps he was only getting at Ned. Joss listened when Patrick spoke to him, he even threw the odd remark in his direction, the contrast was hard to miss.

'Don't like central heating myself,' Vere said flatly. 'Awful atmosphere, can't breathe in it, you get sick.'

'No draughts or damp,' Joss said softly. 'Rots the soul, makes you soft, how can the boys grow up to be men?'

Niamh giggled.

'He bought me an electric blanket,' Hannie said loudly, looking at Vere. 'I didn't even know such things existed.'

Ned got up. He crossed to the sideboard and took out a bottle of Drambuie he'd been hoarding. Bloody good dinner, he thought. He'd explained to Hannie about the Beresfords and Patrick, how they'd grown up together, close as first cousins, and she'd understood what he was saying, he hadn't had to ask would she invite them. She'd rung up James and Marjorie as well but they were in Dublin with one of the daughters, so she'd fixed another evening later in the week. Her idea having Niamh, too, company for Joss, stopped him feeling awkward and left out. She'd done them proud all right, not just with the food, but with the way she talked and arranged things and kept it all flowing; the Beresfords were no end impressed.

From another shelf Ned took tiny glasses, sparsely cut, clouded and old. He arranged them on a little polished brass tray that had come from the Yemen. He smiled to himself as he did so, he could nearly see Vere thinking that maybe she wasn't such a total mistake after all. And maybe Vere was right, maybe she wasn't, she could certainly do it when she set her mind to it, that much was clear. She'd had plenty of practice of course, social sort of a life with Andrew, parties and entertaining and the like. Good with people too, easy and natural, sometimes downright charming, the other night at his lecture in Kilkenny she'd really shone. She'd looked terrific, worn her good suit, had her hair done, he'd been proud as punch introducing his attractive new wife. Silly old fool that he was, he thought, smiling happily to himself. At his age. The lecture had gone well too, he hadn't done it for a while, been a bit anxious, surprised himself with his own eloquence in the end. Islam in Sub-Saharan Africa. Surprised Patrick too, he kept saying how good it was, on at him to develop the lecture into another book.

Ned had set one of the tiny glasses in front of each of his guests and was moving around the table filling them. The success of the evening was making him bountiful.

'Ned likes the winter,' Hannie said, pouring coffee into his cup and speaking to the table generally. 'He says he doesn't, but he does.'

'It changes the proportions,' Ned said. 'It's like the desert again, one becomes tiny in an immense landscape.' He looked at Hannie and it was clear that what he was saying was for her. 'There's an excitement, a quickening of the blood. I like that, I like the stars so high and sharp, I even like the darkness, though I wouldn't like it all year round.'

'I had a Swedish friend, once,' Hannie said. 'She said in the north of her country in winter it never got light at all.' She played with an unused fork as she spoke and it shone with the shine of the lights. 'She was like daylight herself, despite all that darkness,' Hannie went on, 'very clear, like fresh water. Her character, I mean, not just her looks. She wasn't dark like the people here, she wasn't secretive.'

'Is that how we seem to you?' Niamh asked suddenly. She had said very little all evening. Now she sat low in her chair, her eyes intent on Hannie, who suddenly saw that she was drunk.

'Poverty, rebellion and endless rain,' Patrick cut in easily. 'Mud floors and history and conspiracy. A race bred to secrecy and darkness.'

He's said these things before, Ned thought. In Canada, over the whiskey, when they ask him about Ireland.

Hannie turned to Patrick. 'Yes, but this darkness is in everyone. In you, and in Ned and in Alison and Vere as well,' she said. 'And you are the outsiders, the rebelled against.'

'Perhaps ruling is the supreme illusion,' Ned said. 'Perhaps the rulers will always take on the characteristics of the ruled.'

'Fiann O'Brian and the molecules,' Joss put in suddenly.

They all stared.

'*The Third Policeman*,' Joss explained. 'It's a book by Fiann O'Brien, about molecules.'

'About a Guard,' Niamh said, trying to help him. 'A country Guard –'

'A Guard who spends his whole life on a bicycle,' Joss said across her. 'Arse rarely absent from the saddle. Time passes and exchange of molecules takes place. The bicycle begins to take on Guard-like characteristics. The Guard in his turn becomes partly bicycle. Literally: he starts standing by the kerb outside his favourite pub propped on one leg.' Joss reached across for the Drambuie bottle and refilled his glass.

'Happens all the time,' he went on. 'See it in Africa. Half-castes. Visible exchange of molecules has taken place.' He gave a little bark of laughter. 'So Niamh is like you, you're like Niamh. You all sit round the dinner table together and everyone's happy. Till you need someone to build roads and die in trenches again. Then there are problems.' Joss flicked his blank blue gaze around the table and settled it on Niamh. 'The bicycle thinks it's the man that rides it.'

Hannie rose, holding the coffee pot. 'More coffee?' she said. 'Perhaps we should have Irish? Patrick has promised to teach me. Joss, fetch the whiskey bottle from the drawing room and bring it to the kitchen. You must learn, too.'

It was gracefully done, Ned thought, hoping she hadn't seen the look Vere'd thrown at Alison but pretty sure that she had. He wondered how much Joss knew about the colour of his great-grandmother's skin.

'He's just weird,' Patrick said, 'don't take any notice of him, Niamh, no one else does.'

'But it's true, what he said. A hundred years ago I couldn't have been in that room except as a servant.' She stood in the yard, her eyes large and thoughtful, clutching an armful of cut logs against her sweater.

'You're being silly, Niamh. Silly and insecure and melo-dramatic.' Patrick was impatient now. '*That room*, as you put it, is only a room in a modern farm, not a turn-of-the-century country house. Besides,' he added more kindly, 'the loss would have been ours, not yours.'

'That's not the point,' Niamh said stubbornly. 'My grand-mother would've been unfit company.'

'Sure. It's the way it was then. It isn't the way it is now. Ned's not patronising you, Niamh, he's not doing you favours. He invited you to dinner because he likes you and he wanted you at his table. Don't be so touchy for God's sake, your father's three times more likely to help Ned out than the other way round. And as for the cottage, you pay your rent, don't you? You're not here on charity.'

Niamh flushed. 'Not much,' she said. 'Not as much as I should.'

'Do you *want* to pay more?'

Niamh looked startled, then she began to laugh.

'Well then,' Patrick said, 'don't suggest it, Ned might just hear you. Anyway, you're talking from gross ignorance, you never knew Ned's mother. If you had you might just think your grandmother a very fortunate woman.'

'Why, what was she like?'

'A true horror.'

'How do you know?' Niamh had cheered up, her eyes shone.

'I remember her. Besides, my mother's her sister, a living reminder, just in case there was any danger of my forgetting.'

Niamh grinned. Her thick blue sweater was matted like an old blanket and she wore mittens in grey and red hand-knitted stripes. Some aunt, over-fond of the knitting needles, Patrick thought. Or perhaps it was the mother. He wondered if she'd wear them when the boyfriend came. Probably, he decided. She had very little artifice. He was glad she was here, he thought of her as a shield or a token, protecting Ned from Hannie and her strange son.

And she was accurate enough, twenty years ago she might have been in the cottage, but she wouldn't have been in the dining room. What no one had said though, was neither would Hannie or Joss. Well, they were Ned's problem. He was naive, Ned, despite all the books and the travelling. Perhaps on account of the books and the travelling: a kind of bubble of unreality he'd deliberately created for himself. Not a bad lecture though, must build him up a bit more, talk him into starting on another book. Something to get immersed in, a sort of inoculation for when everything fell apart.

~ *Chapter 29* ~

'*N*iamh has the polishing cloths,' Mrs Coady told Hannie. 'She was up for them first thing, said she didn't need them for long, just finishing touches.'

'He's hitching down from Dublin, he'll be here late afternoon or evening, depending on how the lifts go. She's told him to start early. *You know what country roads are like,*' Hannie mimicked. '*No cars and no one stops after dark.*'

Mrs Coady laughed. 'She's a bit anxious, all right. She has that place like a palace. *I want everything to be perfect for him, Mrs Coady.* She'll learn.'

'Probably the hard way.' Patrick was standing by the window with a mug of coffee. 'That house looks more like a dowry offering than a setting for an independent woman. I told her she'd defeat herself. "*Do you think so, Patrick?*" she says. "*Oh, but I'm not trying to trap him.*" So I said I didn't mean it, I was teasing.'

'You should've told her to spice things up a bit, ease off on the domestic detail, put in some squalor and sex.' Hannie finished wringing out the floor cloth and fired it neatly into the empty mop bucket. 'I don't know what young people are coming to, nobody thought about soap and water in my day. I hope at least she's had the sense to buy some bottles.'

'The funny thing is that she isn't,' Patrick said. The two women looked at him. 'Trying to trap him, I mean.'

Hannie snorted. Mrs Coady put her hands on her hips, and stared at him in disbelief.

* * *

Hannie slipped the string round the ivy stems and pulled them tight. She wound the cord a couple more times then tied it firmly. She lifted the bundled mass, heaved it on to one shoulder, then bent again for a second bundle, settled it, and began the trudge home.

The sky was racing with cloud but already the light was slipping. The surface of the river shone dully. Two swans drifted past quite silently, their white forms resting on the pewter water, their long wakes catching the shine from the dying sky. On the far bank the darkness was thickening, the land between river and sky was black and lost.

Cold God crouched in the woods and floated on the water. Hannie felt him, his great age, his stubborn indifference. She couldn't remember the sun or its heat. Only the death of the sun, the long shadows cast here at midday in the sunlit fields.

Above her head wave after wave of black birds washed across the sky, great soundings of crows going home to their roosts in the woods across the river. She closed her eyes and stood. The sky reeled with the enormous clamour of their voices. After a time the great traffic of birds ceased, the sky stilled, the darkness came seeping up out of the earth like smoke.

A stick snapped. A blackness broke from the trees and moved out on to the path towards her.

'Oh Hannie, it's you, I didn't know who it was, you were such a strange shape in the dark.' Niamh's white face loomed towards her. Hannie stopped and waited. Niamh turned to the darkness behind her. Another white face moved forwards.

'Hannie, this is Ciaran. Ciaran, this is Mrs Renvyle, otherwise known as Hannie.'

'Hannie as in Hannah?'

'No, not Hannah, Hanneka.'

'Pleased to meet you, Hannie-as-in-Hanneka,' drawled a young man's voice. 'Niamh here was showin' me around, but we couldn't see for the dark.'

The voice was throaty and light and detached. Hannie was suddenly mildly curious to see his face.

'Ciaran's not used to the country,' Niamh said. 'He's not used to the dark.'

'What time do they turn on the streetlights round here? Does everyone go walkabout in the middle of the night?'

'No streetlights, and it's not the middle of the night.'

'Whatever you say, sweetheart.' There it was again, that odd detachment. As though all this was happening to someone else. Someone stupid.

'We were going to Danno's,' Niamh's voice was eager. 'Ciaran wants to see his sparrow hawk.'

'Correction. *You* want to show me his sparrow hawk.'

'I want to show you all his hawks, and you want to see them.'

'That's how it is, is it?'

'That's how it is,' Niamh said, laughing. She was laughing a lot, little laughs of happiness and excitement. Hannie wondered how long it would be before these little laughs of hers began to irritate him.

'What are you carrying, Hannie? Is that ivy?'

'Ned wants holly and ivy, he says it's traditional,' Hannie told her. 'There's plenty of berried holly in the upper field. He'll cut that himself, I've been cutting the ivy, but it took longer than I thought.'

'Tuesday's the shortest day,' Niamh said.

'So everyone keeps telling me.'

'That's a con, so it is, you think you only have to get to it and then the next day everything'll be okay, but it's ages an' ages before it gets any lighter.'

It was odd, standing talking to someone you couldn't see, Hannie thought. He seemed to find it odd too, but Niamh sounded perfectly comfortable. 'Will we skip Danno's?' she asked him. 'Walk back with Hannie?'

They moved off. She had a good fire going, she explained to Hannie, and plenty of booze. They'd be as well going on home and sitting by it, Danno's could wait. Of course if Hannie wanted to join them, she added hastily . . .

Hannie declined.

She dumped the ivy by the step and stood working her wellingtons against the iron scraper, pushing the caked mud out from the insteps. This done, she waggled each foot in turn in the low tub of rain-water beside it. Ned was fussy about cleaned wellingtons. Everywhere Ned, Ned and his systems, everywhere she turned they were in place. He had explained each one carefully to her at the start. When she ignored them he explained them carefully again.

She lifted the bundled ivy and shoved it stem-down into the water-butt, thinking of the young man she'd seen briefly in the spilled light from Niamh's door. Tall with a muscular build, and attractive, just as Niamh had promised. Much good it would do her, except in the short run.

❧ *Chapter 30* ❧

*I*t was all different now: Patrick and Joss in the house, Ciaran with Niamh in the cottage, the house open and warm. Ned liked the generous feeling of the way his life had become, but he missed the silence. Sometimes he had to make himself remember that when he'd had the silence he hadn't always wanted it.

He stayed working outside for as long as weather and daylight allowed. Mostly he toiled alone but sometimes he prised Patrick from the comforts of the hearth and the two men worked together, making their way round Ned's scruffy acres, draining ditches, re-setting hedges, repairing gaps in fences and walls. Ned liked maintenance, the quiet, steady activity of anticipating problems or putting things right where the damage had already been done. It was useful having another pair of hands, though in some ways he'd rather have got Mick up from the village as he'd done in other years. Mick was less chatty than Patrick and cleverer when it came to dry-stone walls, but Patrick was surprisingly competent once he got started and Patrick didn't have to be paid.

Ned suggested to Hannie that he bring Joss out with them, teach him the work. Hannie agreed in theory, it would do the boy good she said, but perhaps he should start in the summer and have these few short weeks just to settle in? She was relieved when Ned dropped the subject, she didn't know herself quite what it was that she feared except that Joss might reveal too much of himself and she needed to keep him concealed from Ned for as long as she could. She was more relaxed when he was at Niamh's playing cards with

Ciaran; he liked that and it kept him happy and away from Ned.

She took basic precautions. It had been easier in Africa.

'Don't let him do that,' she would say to a houseboy without having to explain herself or worry about what they might think.

'Don't leave Pip with Joss,' she told Niamh, and then had to think of a reason. 'He's not reliable with dogs, he'll just take her for a walk and come home without her.' It was a weak excuse even to her own ears, and did nothing to chase the surprise from Niamh's eyes.

Boredom was the danger with Joss. She glanced at the calendar, mentally marshalling her resources. Christmas was almost upon them, Patrick was going back to his mother and sisters in two days' time and Niamh was off home the day after, on Christmas Eve. Ciaran had refused Niamh's familial invitations, he seemed set on going North, but was promising a quick return.

That was something, Hannie thought. Joss was impressed by Ciaran, who treated him with an easy contempt which he seemed to respond to. Christmas itself would be a distraction, and after that there was the New Year. She wondered about a party.

'Where's Niamh?' Ned asked. 'She promised to make us a wreath for the front door, I haven't seen her for days.'

Hannie laughed and said Niamh had other fish to fry just now and he should stop being such an old fogey and try to remember as far back as his youth. She was washing the breakfast dishes, lifting the plates out one by one and setting them in the drainer. She laughed again and turned to him, looking up into his eyes, and he flushed with shy happiness. His hand lifted without him asking it to and he touched her hair, which was silvery-blonde now from the hairdresser she'd gone to on the morning of his lecture. She didn't look away, her eyes held his and there was a humorous gentleness in them. Then

Patrick was at the door with Pippa trotting behind him and for a moment he stopped and then came on and they knew he'd seen them. Ned dropped his hand and made to fill the kettle. He was embarrassed, but somewhere also a little stubbornly proud.

Later that day he knocked on Niamh's door, a big bunch of berried holly dangling by a string from his hand. It was early afternoon, Niamh answered his knock, she was more or less dressed but her feet were bare and her hair was tangled and wild.

'I've been fencing with Patrick,' he said, trying not to look at her, trying not to see her face against the blue-painted door, the puff-lidded eyes that wouldn't look up, the scraped chin, the mouth all gorged and bruised.

'We were just in time,' he heard himself saying stupidly. 'Another day and the birds would have stripped it bare.'

Niamh took the bunch and thanked him quietly.

'The kettle's boiled,' she said, 'I'm making tea . . .'

An invitation was implied but she didn't sound as though she meant it and still she wouldn't raise her eyes. Ned shook his head. He didn't mention wreaths or front doors and he blushed and mumbled as he turned and walked away.

He'd been fencing all right, but she hadn't, she'd been swimming in sex till everything had blurred and merged and lost its edges. He felt irrationally shamed by his age and his innocence and he wished he'd listened to Hannie and had some tact. Then embarrassment overtook him and he began to imagine that they were standing together at the window watching him and he had to make a huge effort not to turn round and look. In his mind he saw the strutting young man he had met but hardly spoken to, and the young man was mocking him, and Niamh wasn't exactly rushing to his defence.

It was different for the young man, Ned realised. He was becoming himself, it was the making of him, at the same time as it was the un-making of her. He even looked different: as though he could see further and run faster. And she was losing herself, that was clear enough, she could hardly even remember who she was.

He thought of Hannie and he wondered if this same losing of herself had happened to her, if sex for women was at the beginning like entering a river where they submerged themselves and became featureless, before finally re-emerging on the further bank.

Abruptly he forgot Niamh. He felt he'd seen a map of a country that he'd glanced at a long time ago and then discarded in favour of other more pressingly interesting maps. He had meant to return to the first map, he knew that now, but he'd forgotten it and left it all too late. Now he wanted to find Hannie, to ask her questions and listen to her answers, to understand through her this country he'd lost sight of years ago and then glimpsed again near to his journey's end.

He looked at his watch. He was anxious to finish the fencing before it got dark, had only come back early with the tractor to fetch more posts. Patrick was working on now, if he went off to find Hannie he'd leave Patrick to run out of posts and they might not finish the job before the light died.

To hell with the posts, he decided abruptly. He picked up the two great bundles of holly they'd cut for the house and made for the back door. He had his hand on the door handle when he stopped himself.

Maybe she'd want to see him as little as Niamh had, he didn't want to feel he was intruding again, he didn't want to be shamed twice in the one hour. He looked down. The holly berries shone against the deep, spiked leaves.

> *The holly bears a berry*
> *as red as any blood.*

The words of the carol sang themselves in his head.

> *The holly bears a bark*
> *as bitter as any gall.*

He slipped the holly string from his hands, laid the bundled holly on the doorstep and went back to find Patrick.

'I must admit I did question the tastefulness of the enterprise at the start,' Patrick said, reaching across and spearing a slice of Niamh's home-made bread on the end of his knife. Patrick and Joss and Ciaran were all sitting in her kitchen, discussing Patrick's mother's parrot, recently deceased. Patrick, in a light mood, had suggested taxidermy on the phone and his sister Lettie had sent the corpse by the next post.

'Then I saw Danno's work and I knew that taste didn't enter into it, I knew the whole scheme was just part of the cosmic fun. Besides, it's What-Mother-Wants, and who am I to deny Mother? This bread's delicious, Niamh, you should go into production, you'd make a fortune.' He helped himself to another slice and smothered it in butter and jam.

'Danno's work?'

'Danno's terrible taxidermy, my dear Niamh, you've surely noticed. A crooked wing on a widgeon, a cancerous bump on the flank of a basking pollock.'

'That's not fair, Danno's quite good,' Niamh said hotly. 'It's not supposed to be exact, more of an approximation.' She stopped. They were looking at her in a way that made her feel about ten years old. 'People come to him from all over,' she finished lamely.

She got up and started to clear the dishes from the rack and put them away. Domesticity – her refuge. More like a permanent state these days. When she wasn't in bed with Ciaran she was standing in the kitchen dishing out food. With a shock she realised she was equating sex with feeding mouths and washing dishes.

She wasn't working, that was the problem, she should just go into the other room and get on with it, then she'd feel better about herself, she always did. But how could she work with her house full, how could she work without quiet? Suddenly she was glad that Ciaran didn't want to come home with her for Christmas: let him go to Belfast, she'd a good mind to tell him not to bother coming back.

And if he didn't?

She found the bottle of aspirin on the dresser and tipped some into her hand. She had a hangover, that was all. She'd feel different when the pills worked.

∽ *Chapter 31* ∽

*H*annie was very busy in the house. They'd had lunches and dinners and drinks, they'd asked friends and relations and acquaintances of Ned's from around the county, all of whom had known Patrick or Patrick's family some time in the course of their lives. These people lived stranded in their big houses, houses crumbling now but still connected up like the knotting in an invisible net, thrown down years ago, then left to tear and rot away.

They knew this, accepted it, but sometimes they spoke as though the country were becoming uninhabited, as though the lands between the dying houses were all empty and laid to waste. It was like Africa, Hannie thought, the white talk of No one-lives-here-anymore, when they meant No Whites. It was like Africa but without the fury, fury that was fear-induced, fear of an overwhelming privilege threatened and soon to be lost. Here there was only resignation and occasional bitterness, the privilege so long lost it was barely even a habit of mind.

Hannie didn't mind this entertaining, especially when she had Patrick for audience and conspirator; she even enjoyed it. She liked showing how well she could do it, liked impressing the Alisons and the Marjories, and she loved the aftermath, the mockery of eccentricity, the ridicule of drunken folly. Patrick colluded with her and encouraged her. Even Ned let himself smile as some of James's wilder expressions crept into his household's daily currency.

Hannie was flirting gently with Patrick. Ned noticed without jealousy; he was glad she was enjoying Patrick, glad that his cousin liked his wife, relieved that her visits to Danno seemed to have fallen away.

Hannie herself felt easier, less trapped and desperate, and with the ease had come a certain caution. Her words to Patrick were light and ambiguous, her husband was always included, she took care to make him feel secure and proud. She wasn't making a play for Patrick – he wasn't husband material, nor was she much attracted to him sexually – but he was pleasant, urbane company, he amused her and he broke the awkward silence around Ned and Joss.

Niamh wasn't careful, except over contraceptives; she was hardly even aware there was anything else to be careful about. She was confused though, she knew that much: confused about Ciaran, confused about her feelings for him, confused about sex and the way it was changing her.

It was as though all of her that she thought of as herself had stopped living tidily some place more or less behind her eyes and had melted like butter left out in the sun. And this warmed butter had run down into her flesh and spread over her whole body, and she was left not knowing anything, not even if she liked what was happening to her until it stopped happening and she ached for it to happen again.

'I'd draw the curtains when I undressed, if I was you,' Ciaran said. 'Yon bucko's not beyond a squint or two.' He hitched his bag over his shoulder and stuck his free hand down the back of her jeans. She felt the shock of its cold intrusion. At the same time her flesh reeled and her body shouted with recognition.

'An' who'd blame him?' Ciaran drawled salaciously. 'Sensible fella I'd say, if you asked me.'

'You'll not be away that long, sure you won't?' She tried to ignore the hand, tried to sound indifferent.

'A few days,' he told her. 'They'll go nuts, so they will, they'll be on at me to stay.'

'But you won't?'

'Couldn't if I wanted to.' He pressed his fingers hard into her buttocks, driving her crotch and pelvis forward to meet his. Her flesh dissolved, she moved forward and pressed into him, he forced his tongue deep into her mouth and worked her till her whole body cried out with need. Then he pulled away from her.

'Have to go,' he said, looking at her and wiping his mouth on the back of his wrist. Then he caught her hand and held it against the bulge in his straining jeans. 'That's just so's you'll remember,' he told her.

'Hm.' Hannie stood in Joss's room, thumbing the shiny paper of the mail-order catalogue. She looked at the young woman in the picture, at her swept-up hair and her downcast eyes and the simper on her glazed lips. '*The Lingerie Collection. The return of the camisole.*' Her voice was casual and dismissive. 'So this is what Niamh's dreams are made of. Get yourself up like a Victorian boudoir and simper about the bedroom: fuck me, oh please fuck me. How very liberated and suburban.' She tossed the catalogue scornfully on to the bed.

Joss leaned by the window, cigarette in hand, watching her. Or at least she supposed he was watching her, his blanked-out, black-swathed eyes were pointed in her direction and the corners of his lips were just twisted up in a smile or a sneer or a snarl, she couldn't tell.

She was coming on too heavy, *freaking out* as he'd put it, and over a few juvenile photos of young women in underwear. She stopped herself. At least he'd been straight about it, had told her where he'd got them as soon as she'd asked.

'Nicked them,' he'd said, blowing smoke at her and looking pleased with himself. 'Off Niamh's dresser where she left them. Silly cow.'

She had no idea what he was thinking now, no idea if her ridicule had sunk in or had slid straight off his trim duck's back.

* * *

'You should get something,' her friend Maeve had said to her in Dublin. 'Anna got the black French knickers, she was showing me, said it was like having a secret weapon on under her jeans, said she fancied everyone she met all day.'

'Anna must be made of money.'

'Twenty quid,' Maeve had said. 'The suspenders are ten. Trust you to worry about the money, Niamh, such a buzz, Anna said, cheap at the price.'

'If I want to feel sexy,' Niamh had said gravely, 'I don't wear any knickers at all.'

Maeve had giggled and rolled her eyes to heaven. 'God Niamh, you're such a puritan, what're we going to do with you at all? Here, take it anyway, have a look at it, something might rub off.'

And she had taken it, though she hadn't really understood why Maeve had called her a puritan. She had looked through it by the fire one night before Ciaran came, had even wondered briefly if black French knickers mightn't increase her chances.

I must have been mad, she thought now. Did I want to spend my whole life on my back?

Niamh stood by the fire after Hannie'd left, the cheap paper catalogue in her hand.

'Joss borrowed it,' Hannie had said. 'You should be careful, Niamh, young boys are suggestible. It's their age, they like erotic stimulation.' She had shrugged. Boys will be boys, the shrug had said.

'Borrowed it,' Niamh muttered indignantly to herself. What was it Mrs Coady had said to her only the other day? *If something goes missing, Niamh, ask yourself if it's something Joss might want?*

Stole it, more like. Then round comes Hannie, behaving as though I've given him pornography to read in bed.

Pornography, indeed. Naïveté. She might be a puritan but even she could see the silly straightforward innocence of the pictures. Fuck Hannie, she thought. And fuck Maeve for forcing it on her when she hadn't wanted it in the first place.

It was unbelievable – like church again – poor decent Adam, befuddled with sex, misled by evil Eve and her womanly wiles. *You should be careful, Niamh, young boys are suggestible.* Well, she would be careful all right. She dumped the catalogue into the fire and felt much better.

Then she stopped feeling better and remembered Ciaran. Draw the curtains, don't tempt the boy. That had been Ciaran's gist as well. The realisation was disquieting.

It never once occurred to her that Hannie might have been trying to warn her.

'The day after Stephen's day,' Niamh said in answer to Patrick's question about Ciaran's return. 'Or the day after that. Depending on how the lifts go. He may not make it down from Belfast in a day.' Niamh broke the thin ice on the puddle carefully with her wellington as she spoke. She liked doing this normally, the creaking sound that it made, the trapped air-bubbles coming free, but somehow today it didn't give her much satisfaction. Patrick was going himself in the morning. She wanted to ask his advice about Joss but she didn't know how.

And even if she'd known, she thought, it mightn't be any good. Patrick might react like Ciaran.

Ciaran was amused by Joss. He was a liar and a cheat, all right, but then who wasn't at Joss's age? Ciaran insisted that Joss was normal, that his behaviour was adolescent only and nothing to get excited about. And he'd gone on insisting, even after Joss had sat one night telling them his hopes and plans for the future. Life here was only a temporary arrangement, it seemed, Hannie was only looking around for something better, Hannie was a mover, she wouldn't stick this dump for long.

'Just wait till she finds something worth getting her claws into. Old Ned won't see her for dust.'

He seemed confident of Hannie's opportunism, proud of

it. He didn't seem to look on her as his mother, more as a partner or a stooge, one who was playing the cards for the moment, but always at his direction. Niamh was horrified but Ciaran had laughed at her, he'd said Joss was only a kid, didn't she know when a kid was boasting to keep himself up?

The truth was Niamh didn't want Joss visiting her any more but she didn't know how to stop him coming to the cottage when she'd been happy enough to have him hang around the last holidays. She had the feeling that calculations were happening in his head and she didn't trust those calculations. She knew now they might be in a language that she barely even knew existed.

'She says I'm not to leave Joss in charge of the puppy,' Niamh said suddenly. Patrick looked startled. 'She says he'll forget, he'll just go off somewhere with Pippa and come back without her.' She felt stupid saying this, it wasn't what she'd meant to say, it just came out in a rush.

'She being Hannie?' Patrick spoke as though she was a child being taught to refer to her nursery-school teacher by name. 'Well, she should know, shouldn't she. I thought Ciaran was going home with you, don't you want to be with him over Christmas?'

Niamh looked up at Patrick, at his bland, amiable, well-fed face, and she knew abruptly that it was no use trying to get through to him, he'd just say something easy to keep her happy, he'd pat her head and soothe her down, lest she disturb his ease.

'Not really,' she said. 'I asked him but I'm sort of glad he didn't want to, it was a terrible idea really.'

She swirled her wellington about with the slices of dirty ice in the muddy puddle. There was no one she could speak to, it was no use telling Ned of her disquiet, he wouldn't even know what she was talking about.

Hannie would though, suddenly she was certain that Hannie would. But somehow she just couldn't say it to Hannie.

❦ *Chapter 32* ❧

'*P*atrick said you fucked up, married the wrong man, you should have married Lannigan.'

'Lannigan?' Hannie nudged the iron into the shoulder of Ned's shirt. 'What are you talking about, Joss? I don't even know anyone called Lannigan.' Her voice was dead-pan, bored, but beneath the feigned indifference she was taut with shock.

'What are you talking about?' she asked him again. 'And who's this Lannigan that I don't even know?'

'The auctioneer. The one in Dungarvan. See – you *do* know him. Patrick said you backed the wrong horse, said you'd have done better marrying Lannigan. More money than old Ned, more future.'

It was Christmas Eve. Ciaran had gone and Patrick had gone, and this morning Niamh's brother Donal had come and taken her home. Hannie hoped these changes accounted for Joss's sudden hysteria. She assumed that it *was* hysteria. Hysteria, and rage at her refusal of his latest project. Joss had come to her that morning with some tale of Ciaran inviting him to Belfast. He wanted money for the trip, he said, he planned to go straight after Christmas.

Hannie set the iron carefully on its end and buttoned the shirt loosely. Then she spread it face down on the board and started to fold in the sides and sleeves. Joss watched her minutely. The only sign was the faintest of tremors in her hands. She was good, his mother, except for the hands you would never have known he'd scored. Serve her right for refusing him, he thought. He felt marginally less savage towards her.

'Joss, stop telling lies,' she said, not looking up from her folding. 'Or, if you *must* tell lies, at least tell lies that are credible. Never attribute a statement that's out of character. Never say someone said something that they wouldn't ever have said.'

'He did say it, he did, he did, he did!' Joss was furious again, his rage the wilder as he heard himself contradicting like a child. She was cheating, diverting, pretending to be instructing him. She just didn't want to face what she'd done: how she'd fucked up, messed up, screwed things up for him and for them both. She wouldn't admit it, wouldn't accept the truth though it stared her in the face. It was all right for her, but he had to take the consequences of her stupid, poxy mistakes.

'You say Patrick told you I should have married Lannigan.' She was speaking now in that calm, even voice, the one she used when she was trying to put him down, to make him feel like a fool.

'Well, Patrick might have thought it,' she said, 'Patrick might even have said it, but Patrick would never, ever have said it to *you*. Therefore Joss, either he didn't say it at all or he said it to someone else and you were just sneaking round, eavesdropping.'

'He told Ciaran, I heard him, the old gas-bag, I heard him tell Ciaran – and I was *not* sneaking around, I was in the room all the time, they knew I was there.' Joss was shaking with fury, oblivious to everything, needing above all else to shatter her calm, destroy her power. Because if he didn't she'd manipulate him, make him do what she wanted, then everyone would turn on him the way they always did and he'd be fucked.

And he could see it and hear it, just as it had happened. Patrick, man of the world, know-all, sitting by Niamh's fire telling Ciaran that Hannie had backed the wrong horse, not caring that he, Joss, was listening, that it was *his* mother he was rubbishing and slagging off.

'It's natural enough,' Patrick had said. 'She threw in her lot with Ned's class because she thought it was the safest, the best bet. But it isn't where the power or the money lies now. She'd have done better with the auctioneer in Dungarvan. Our lot are useless in this new state – useless, sidelined, unable to integrate.'

His favourite theme, the old windbag, he was never done going on about it. Ciaran was into all that too, he'd jaw on with Patrick for hours. Modern Ireland's Brave New World. Nepotism and Corruption and Plenty of Jobs for the Children of the Rich. Meet the New Boss same as the Old Boss. The Provisionals had the measure of them – the only way forward was a clean sweep.

Except he didn't say the last bit to Patrick, he saved it for Niamh and Joss when Patrick had gone.

And Joss had slipped out, unnoticed, sick to the core that his mother was so vulnerable, that she was all he had to depend on.

'Joss,' Hannie said carefully, 'you can't have the money, no matter what you do or say. Do you understand? I haven't got the money, but even if I had, I wouldn't give it to you to go to Belfast. And that wouldn't change, no matter who I was married to. Not Lannigan, not Ned, not Patrick, nor anyone else.'

'So Patrick's on the list, is he?' Joss was on to it like a ferret on a rat. 'Well, well, Mother, not bad. Better than present company, I'll say that.' Joss's pale small face sneered at her through the dusk that was thickening around them. Her heart hurt her with sudden pity for him.

'Canada, eh? Better than this dump, but that wouldn't be hard,' he continued. 'Better make sure Joss keeps quiet, though, Mother. Better pay him to keep the cat in the bag till she's good and ready to let it out, eh? Wouldn't want old Ned getting wind of this change of plan now, would we? Old Ned might just boot her out in the cold before it's properly hatched.'

'You're wrong there, Joss, completely wrong.' The door had swung quietly open; Ned spoke from his stance in its frame. 'Old Ned won't be booting her out, as you put it, whatever she says or does. Old Ned happens to be very glad she fucked up, very glad she married him.' His voice trembled slightly but his face in the half-light was expressionless. 'Very glad indeed.'

Then he turned on his heel and went back down the corridor the way he'd come.

Joss's white face was whiter. He stared at his mother. Hannie crossed to the door and closed it, pressing on the handle till she heard the latch click home. She switched on the light and the dusk at the window thickened abruptly into blackness. She took a pillow slip from the laundry basket and laid it on the ironing board. Then she picked up the iron and moved it backwards, forwards, backwards, forwards, her knuckles showing as white as the linen.

Joss extracted a cigarette from the packet she'd set on the mantelpiece. He lit it with her lighter and crossed to the window. He moved his shoulders once, compulsively, as though to loosen them. Then he picked up his old pose of indifference and swung it around himself like a cloak.

'What will you say?'

'Nothing. He won't ask.'

Joss stared out at the sudden night beyond the panes.

'So, Mother,' he said casually, 'I'm not the only one that goes sneaking around, eavesdropping.'

Hannie's mouth tightened but she didn't speak. The room they were in was at the end of the corridor; if Ned had wanted to find them he must come the way he had come, he had no other choice. But she didn't say it, she couldn't bring herself to defend him, she was far too threatened and angry for that.

How long had Ned been standing there, how much had he heard? That night she lay in the dark going over and over Joss's words, her own words, trying to remember exactly what they'd said. Had he heard the whole lot, or only from where Joss had jumped in with Patrick being 'on her list'? Bad as that was, it wasn't as bad as Joss's account of Patrick's words to Ciaran: his precious cousin not only understanding her motives in marrying him but sitting discussing the whole business quite casually with Niamh's boyfriend.

He couldn't have heard that, she decided. If he had he'd never have said what he'd finally said. She breathed deeply in relief.

But he'd said *fucked up*, he'd quoted Joss quoting Patrick's words. So he must have heard. Suddenly she was coldly certain he'd been standing there listening from the very start.

So why had he spoken out when he needn't have, when he could have just slipped away without ever revealing he'd heard their exchange? Why had he told Joss so firmly he wouldn't be throwing her out?

To subvert Joss's pathetic little blackmail attempt? To bolster her authority with her delinquent son?

She dismissed these thoughts. She wasn't used to magnanimity, she was used to self-interest, had no difficulty in accepting it as she'd accepted Ned's acquisition of her and her own self-interested compliance in the arrangement. Their marriage was a bargain which suited both of them and when it ceased to suit it would be broken or re-negotiated. That Ned should suddenly transcend the bargain was a possibility altogether beyond her experience.

Ned had said what he'd said on account of his own mistake in marrying her, she decided. Once done, he wouldn't disown his action, that would be a worse weakness than the first weakness. He'd done it and he would stand over it, that was Ned. Let Patrick think what he liked.

As for Patrick, she wasn't really surprised. Patrick would be mindful only for himself and his own comforts. That was why he wasn't married now, though he had been once, why he had no real roots or attachments. Too inconvenient, someone else. Patrick was as selfish as she was – one of her kind. No, not entirely one of her kind. She revised her self-judgement fractionally. She wasn't lazy, a love of ease had never marked her out. For a moment she hated Patrick, briefly and completely. Then she dismissed her hatred as she had already dismissed the man.

* * *

Hannie sat forward with her elbows on the pew in front of her and her face in her hands, a sort of leaning crouch that imitated Ned's. Christmas Day. The clergyman droned from the altar regions but she didn't mind him, he was easy to ignore. She didn't mind the crouch either, it was strange but not uncomfortable, and gave at least the illusion of privacy.

Her mind kept returning to Joss's words about Lannigan. She went over and over the conversation, trying to work out its consequences, trying to mediate her fury against Ned.

She couldn't understand herself why she was so angry with him. It wasn't a pretty conversation that he'd overheard, it had put Joss in a bad light and herself in a worse one, but essentially it was information that Ned already knew. Hearing Joss's speculations, having the reality of the way she lived her life spelled out like that might be distasteful, but it didn't actually change anything.

So why did she mind so much, why was she so angry?

It was being known, she realised. Being known and judged and pitied. It was unbearable to her that he should see what her life really consisted of: the narrowness of her options, the sordid smallness of her many shifts and prevarications.

And if it was shameful to her that he should see and know, it was unendurable that she should have to see her life reflected through his eyes, assessed and diminished by his upright unyielding values.

Old Ned happens to be very glad she fucked up. That's what he'd said to Joss. Old Ned was prepared to forgive her whatever she did.

Big deal. She didn't want to be forgiven, she wanted to be young again, young and free and strong. She wanted to live as life took her and to hell with the consequences, to hell with anyone who didn't like it, she wanted to laugh at them as she'd always done, to despise their cowardly, safe self-righteousness, to move on.

There was a peal of organ music from a hidden tape recorder and everyone abandoned their crouches and heaved themselves upright. The recorded carol began. Most people mouthed to it but a few sang defiantly, their voices quavering and rough against the effortless river of joy from the choir on the machine. The congregation was elderly and sparse and well wrapped up, though the church glowed with overhead heaters and was far too warm for these denizens of old and draughty houses. After the initial relief they shuffled uncomfortably and glanced with longing at the chilly mouldering aisles closed off by plate-glass partitions from the sealed box in the nave where they sat.

The church was decked for Christmas. There were great stands of vegetation: chrysanthemums and poinsettias, holly and bay. The brass memorials to dead soldiers on the walls shone with fresh polish, the sills of the narrow lancet windows were snowy with cotton wool, stubby red Christmas candles poked up through clustered holly and trailing green ivy.

Alison has been busy, Hannie thought sourly. It was years and years since she'd been in a church but she recognised an act of solidarity when she saw one: this was a small, carefully tended rock pool on the edge of a great surging sea of threatening otherness. She glanced at Ned's absorbed oblivious face and cursed her own stupidity in making this placatory gesture. It only made her feel more reckless and deepened her alienation from his world. Abruptly she gave up telling herself he'd done nothing wrong and let herself drift on a tide of anger and morose despair.

The rest of the day passed in an agony of slowness. Joss had stayed in bed and she was too relieved to be rid of him to nag about getting up. He came downstairs to eat Christmas dinner and was heading up to his room again directly the food was eaten. Ned called him back.

'Washing-up,' he said. 'I thought we could do it together. To thank your mother for the dinner she's just cooked. Then there's presents.'

Ned gave her two packages. The first held an ebony fan that had belonged to his mother, the second a sea-blue chiffon scarf with a border of pink and orange flowers. She liked the little blue scarf in spite of herself. She shook it out and knotted it round her neck. His mother's fan she would sell later.

Ned gave Joss a book on insects and Joss gave Ned a new clasp knife that she'd bought in a shop in Waterford Ned was always recommending. She gave Ned a pair of extra-thick wellington socks from the same shop. She'd thought badly of them at the time, it hadn't seemed much of a present, just picking out socks and putting them on the account, but what was the point of spending his money on something he mightn't like?

It felt different now. She nearly left them in the drawer and faced him empty-handed, even a pair of socks was more than she wanted to give him. For Joss there was an envelope which he was careful not to open in front of Ned. He needn't have bothered, she thought sourly, there wasn't much in it, Ned wouldn't have disapproved. But that too, was more than she wanted to give.

Ned suggested a walk and Hannie put on her coat and her boots and went through the motions. They tramped through the muddy half-light but she closed herself off and repelled his efforts at conversation. Ned didn't try very hard, he was relieved when he heard himself lapse into silence.

They went by the lower field to check on the sheep. A heron got up from a reedbed and drifted heavily across the fading sky. Bess rounded up wandering ewes and Ned stood counting while Hannie stared at the sheep and they stared back, black-faced, lop-eared their strange diamond-shaped eyes impenetrably blank and alien. The heron went flopping across again, it let out a short sharp shriek of protest at their prolonged intrusion. The rain came seeping out of the dusk.

Hannie thought of all the hot bright riotous Christmases she'd spent with people who longed for Christmases like this and wondered at their nostalgia.

∾ *Chapter 33* ∾

'God, what a disaster.' Niamh closed her eyes at the memory and spoke the words aloud to her empty kitchen. At least she hadn't insisted on taking Ciaran home with her. That was about the only redeeming feature of the last two days. She thought bitterly of her brothers and sisters.

'They just want me to look nice and wear pretty clothes and put everyone else's needs before my own,' she used to complain to Maeve. Well that wasn't true any more. Now they just wanted her to wear odd clothes and to say odd things and to go on being 'peculiar', the baby, their peculiar little Niamh.

So it wasn't even that they were incapable of changing, they were simply incapable of seeing her as she was.

Perhaps it was time for a total reassessment, she thought. Perhaps she should go back to Dublin and eat humble pie. Get hold of Maeve, tell her she'd been right all along, the country was a rotten idea and was there any chance of sharing a studio after all?

But then she'd have nothing to live on. Her father didn't want her in the city. He wouldn't give her even this one year to see what she could do.

Well, so what, she could sign on, couldn't she? She could stop being so bourgeois and spineless? Maeve did, and Ciaran did, and everyone did when they were trying to make it after the end of college and before they'd established themselves as working artists.

It wasn't a big deal or a public shame the way her father made it out to be.

Anyway, it was either that or teaching and once you started the teaching game it was only a matter of time before the work slipped altogether. She'd tried to explain that to her father, but he didn't understand. He asked her couldn't she paint at the weekends?

She'd said it wasn't something you could just turn on and off like a tap, you had to live it and breathe it, or it didn't grow out of you. She had blushed when she'd said this, she didn't know why because she'd meant every word of it, but suddenly she was as embarrassed as if she'd been standing there telling him about her sex life. And then when she looked at him she'd seen that he was embarrassed too. He wasn't looking at her, he was poking with his ash plant at a new rat-hole in among the nettles behind the old harrow. Poking and trying not to hear.

And then she'd felt miserable; miserable, and angry at herself and at her father because she couldn't stop minding what he thought enough to defy him. And after that he had talked to Ned, and he'd come home happy and full of his new arrangement and she'd let herself be manoeuvred.

Ned had continued to pester his friends for commissions. James stubbornly went deaf when he mentioned Jacko, but he'd got money up front from a Mrs Cardew for a view of her cottage garden, and there was a widow who'd sold her dead husband's crumbling birthright and now wanted a picture of it to hang in her bright new draught-free bungalow. Both had supplied photos.

Ned said he understood perfectly that she didn't want to paint people's houses or their pets. Such projects were simply earners, 'potboilers' that paid the bills, let you do what you really wanted to do, that was why you did them.

He had always taken on extra commissions himself, he said. Bits of data-collecting and map-making projects and statistical work. Dull, but necessary, and not a bad discipline. They taught you how to operate on two levels: to work on a potboiler lightly, keeping your passion for the real thing.

Niamh had paid the electricity with Mrs Cardew's advance and then started in on the painting of her garden. She'd blocked it in fairly easily and then put it briefly aside. The aside had been a mistake, she should have just finished it in the one go; in the interval she'd grown self-conscious and then stupidly she'd left it uncovered and Ciaran had seen it. After that it was hopeless, the more she tried the more she hated it. Worse, the hatred seemed to have spilled over into her real work. She'd been doing a painting from a papier-mâché bust she'd made, the head and shoulders of an androgynous figure just looking up as though it had caught some half-heard sound. The bust had been experimental but it had something, a peculiar quick attentiveness, and she'd wanted to see if she could take this further in a painting.

Some hope. She'd been making herself go on trying, but she couldn't get her confidence back, she couldn't put Ciaran's critical appraising glance out of her head. On a good day she dabbed miserably; on a bad day she just stood. She'd stopped believing in herself and it was nearly easier to struggle with flowerbeds and roof angles than to trust to her own fragile vision.

Ned was trying hard to help in his own way, Niamh knew this, but somehow it just made it all worse. Now she had him on her back as well as her father. Ciaran said she was out of her mind to be even thinking of potboilers, or whatever it was Ned called them. You had to do what you wanted to do and not deviate or compromise or you'd end up making crap work and not even knowing it. Niamh, stung, said she hadn't noticed him making any work at all, but he just grinned at her and said no work was better than crap work and the world could wait.

'I hope it's not holding its breath,' she'd said, and flounced off to stare hard at the garden-photos one more time.

Now she wandered into the little studio room and stood trying to look at her canvases with a cool and appraising eye. It was her own fault, she thought, it was no good blaming anyone else, she'd just have to take some decisions and act on them. First, the studio had to be made more habitable. The chimney smoked so badly that she'd long since given up lighting a fire in there. She wore three jumpers and fingerless gloves, and she was still frozen. Jackdaws, likely as not, Ciaran said. A nest in the chimney. She'd asked him to clear it out but he wouldn't.

'Would you wise up, I know sod-all about chimneys. Ask Ned – he's the landlord.'

He was right, but she didn't want to ask Ned, she paid so little rent and she didn't like to bother him. Well, that would have to change, she'd just have to bother him. She'd go straight up to the house now and tell Ned that she wasn't going to do Mrs Cardew's commission or the widow's commission, she wasn't going to do any commissions at all. And even if she wanted to, she couldn't because of the chimney.

'Of course she won't stick at it,' Hannie said, lifting rashers out of the pan and holding them there a moment for the fat to drip. 'All this talk of integrity and jackdaws is just noise. Noise and excuses. Because she is doing no work.' She laid the rashers in the serving dish and put it back into the Aga to keep warm. Joss sat at the kitchen table, waiting. Ned was striding around the room in his stockinged feet, worrying aloud about Niamh. He stopped pacing.

'She will, Hannie, she will,' he said. 'If she gets a bit of support, a bit of encouragement. When she sees money everything will change, when she realises she's making her own way, that she's independent.

'And she's right, she can't work when she's frozen. It'll be different when the chimney's cleaned, I wish she'd mentioned it before, I'll take the brushes down tomorrow, have it clear in a couple of hours.'

Hannie broke eggs into the sizzling fat. 'No,' she said with finality. 'You're wrong, she won't stick at it. She won't stick at it and you can't make her, no matter how hard you want it for her, no matter how many people you persuade into commissioning pictures that she doesn't want to paint.'

'I'm not making her do anything,' Ned protested. 'If she doesn't want commissions she doesn't have to take them. I'm only trying to help her do what she wants to do and become a professional artist. To hear you talk you'd think I was trying to make her do something she *doesn't* want to do.' Ned warmed to his subject, he was glad to see her belligerent, he found it easier than silent antagonism and less confusing. Neither of them had mentioned the overheard conversation, but it was there between them like the smell of decay. Communication, any communication was, to Ned's way of thinking, a definite advance.

'And what makes you so sure she won't stick?' he demanded. 'She got top marks at college. She's got talent, character . . .'

Hannie slid the fried eggs on to the dish and lifted two more from the rack. She cracked them into the pan without turning her head.

'It is not to do with talent,' she said. She flicked hot fat over the bubbling whites. 'Nor character either. It's the way she is bred.'

Ned waited. She didn't seem to be about to add to the statement.

'The way she is bred?'

'Like a Dutch *hausfrau* who knows what the future will hold.' Hannie bent for the dish again. 'Born to a hearth, to shined copper pans and her grandmother's linen. This is what she is, it doesn't matter what she wants to be.' Two more eggs left the pan and the dish was returned to the oven.

'That's nonsense, Hannie, that's got nothing to do with it, plenty of artists come from stable middle-class homes.'

'Male artists . . .'

'Male, female, what does it matter? You underestimate her, Hannie, she's more than that, she wants her life to be more than that.'

'I told you – it's not what she wants or what she thinks she wants, it's what she is, what she can't avoid. She'll marry – it's her nature's imperative – she'll have no choice. Then there'll be children and their care will come first because that's the way she is, and then it will be too late. All this talk of painting is only talk, Ned. I think already she knows this somewhere, and somewhere she accepts it.' She half-turned, saw Ned's face.

'Oh, not Ciaran, she won't marry Ciaran, he's only a passion, he isn't a marriage. And anyway he'll leave her, already he's bored.'

Hannie picked up the dish of bacon and eggs and carried it to the table where Joss waited. 'Perhaps it is *you* who wants her life to be more, Ned,' she said. 'Perhaps you should leave her alone.'

'That's ridiculous.' Ned was stung. 'Why should I care what her life is, so long as she's happy?'

'Oh, because in some way you identify. Your young self with the way she is now. And you don't like her young man, you don't want him to have her affection. But I think it's already too late, much too late –'

Late that night the phone rang and Joss answered it.

'Hey, Joss, how're ye doin', man? Niamh there?' Ciaran's voice was slurred, there were party noises in the background.

'I'll get her.'

'Wise up, would yous? Tell her I got held up, couldn't make it, say to expect me when she sees me, not before. Hell, Joss, say what you like, use your imagination, tell her I'm dyin' for her, tell her I ran out of money and got cut off . . .'

Then he talked for another ten minutes or so. Rabbiting on, this and that. Then he hung up.

Joss passed the message on to Niamh the next morning, putting in some stuff about Ciaran missing her, watching her face light, telling her no, Ciaran hadn't said why he'd got held up, maybe he needed a break?

Watching her face as it made itself go blank.

It was no fun, baiting Niamh. He wished Ciaran would come back. Niamh by herself was poor company.

❧ *Chapter 34* ❧

'– and then she told Ned he was jealous of Ciaran. And he just stood there, the dirty old git, never denied it, never said a word. So it must be true.' Joss was feeding Danno's sparrow hawk with titbits of badger entrail, speaking softly and evenly, not looking at the bird just as Danno had told him, not looking at Danno, either.

'Who'd have thought it, eh Danno? Old Ned fancying Niamh. Young enough to be his granddaughter. And her daddy all gratitude and can't do enough for him on account of his kindness to his little girl. Not half as kind as he'd like to be, eh Danno?' Joss chuckled.

'Ciaran won't be surprised when I tell him,' Joss continued. 'Ciaran was wise to him all along – said the *auld fella* was never done knocking the door mornings, keeping Miss Niamh standing on the step in her nightie, talking away.' Joss was getting into his stride now, relishing the words, mimicking Ciaran's Northern accent. 'And him only just through overhauling her himself, lying out on the bed upstairs too knackered to move, listening to every word the old fool sez to her, laughing away.'

Danno's gaze was fixed on the back of the smooth yellow head, the smooth-packaged self. I'm like a rabbit watching a stoat weave, Danno thought, unable to stop himself. He was mesmerised and immobile, helpless before the undulating death-dance.

'That's something to put in your pipe and smoke, eh Danno? You wouldn't mind being kind to Niamh yourself now, would you, Danno? There's not many would mind, I'd say, and Joss wouldn't be the one to blame them, not a bit, he wouldn't. What's a little kindness between friends, eh Danno? If only Old Ned knew how kind Joss has been. How green he'd be; how – green – he – would – be.'

Joss spoke the last words separately and deliberately, as though he were remembering them to himself. Danno rose abruptly, breaking the spell. The sparrow hawk, startled into rage, scuttled sideways on the perch, jerking furiously at her jesses.

'Joss was here just now,' Danno said.

'I know.' Hannie flicked her cigarette into an empty tea mug. The hot ash fizzled a moment in the cold dregs. 'We are all visiting. Niamh will be the next. She has come rushing back from the bosom of her family, quivering with indignation and new resolutions.' Hannie was wearing an old jersey, full of holes, and a pair of baggy cord trousers stuck into wellingtons. Ned's clothes. Her step was springy, she seemed in good spirits, on the edge of being pleased with herself.

'You should build a barricade, Danno, a high thorn stockade as we do against wild beasts in Africa. But there must be a secret entrance, perhaps an underground tunnel, a souterrain, isn't that what such a passage is called here? Will you dig a souterrain, Danno? A fine one, just for me, so I can visit you while all the rest are held at bay?' She roamed restlessly round the room as she talked. 'Oh, don't look so dismayed, Danno, you can keep a pile of stones handy, lob them at me when you can't stand the thought of me, drive me off. I understand, really I do, there are plenty of times when I can't stand the thought of me myself. Besides, it's only right for people like you to throw stones at women like me, whatever your Jesus once said.' She shot a glance at him, but he was avoiding looking at her.

'You don't speak, Danno? Is it possible you don't believe me? That you don't believe there's ever a time that I can't stand the thought of myself?' She stopped pacing and stood staring at the darkness in the great black window. Half past five going on midnight. She needed something stronger than tea. 'But it's true,' she insisted, 'I assure you it's true.'

'What's the matter with Joss, Hannie?'

'The matter? Why? What's he done?' Her voice had changed, it was casual, non-committal, but underneath it was on guard. She didn't turn round, but he could see the alertness in the back of her shoulders. This was a question she'd been asked before.

'Nothing. He hasn't done anything.' Danno didn't have to look at her to catch her relief. 'But he was here, and he was talking.'

'Human beings do, it's one of the characteristics of the species, some say it's most of the problem –'

'He was talking about sex,' Danno said stubbornly. 'About sex and Niamh.'

'Oh? Was it interesting? What did he say?' She was lighting a cigarette, her back still turned.

'It wasn't so much what he said, more the tone of the saying.' Danno scraped carefully at the inside of the emptied badger's skin. He hoped she wouldn't make him spell it out, that he'd just have to warn her obliquely and she'd do something to keep Joss away from Niamh.

There was a moment's pause. 'What did he say, Danno?' she asked again, her tone quiet and relentless with an edge of contempt in it. She was bullying him, he realised, willing him to let it go. But he wouldn't. Danno braced himself.

'He thinks a lot of Ciaran,' he said, getting the words out quickly. She waited. He opened his mouth to say more but it didn't come.

'And not much of Ned?' she finished for him.

'And not much of Ned.'

'And you think that Ciaran is a bad influence and I shouldn't let Joss spend time with him, is that it?' Again she waited. 'OK, let's try again. You think that Joss is a bad influence on Ciaran and I should protect him from my delinquent son?'

'He – Joss – intimated at a certain ... physical intimacy with Niamh.' Danno got it out in an embarrassed gabble. Hannie was very still for a moment. Then she threw back her head and laughed with relief.

'And you believe *that* – it is *that* that has upset you so? Oh Danno, that's just boasting, wishful thinking, boy's fantasy. You remember boy's fantasies, surely? Masturbation, wet dreams, all that stuff?'

She stopped herself. 'On second thoughts, perhaps you don't. I bet you masturbated with a pin-up of a Labrador and had wet dreams about hawks,' she said nastily. 'What is it with you all? Niamh might as well be a bitch on heat for the effect she's having on you.'

But she'd misjudged him. Danno wasn't to be ridiculed into submission so easily.

'I may be inexperienced, Hannie, but I'm not the sort of prude you seem to think me. This was more than boy's fantasy, there was something twisted about it, something horrible.'

'You're getting this out of proportion, Danno. This is the spoiled priest in you talking.'

'Who told you that?'

'Mrs Coady.'

'Well, you tell Kathleen Coady I'm disappointed in her. Tell her I didn't think she'd be wasting her time on erroneous tittle-tattle, I'd thought more of her.'

'Erroneous?'

'That's what I said. But we're getting off the subject, which is Joss, not me. What's wrong with him, Hannie?'

'Wrong?' She left her stance by the window and coasted around the room again, trying to find the words that would put him off. This was a new side of Danno, she wasn't prepared for his determination.

'Nothing's wrong,' she said coldly. 'He's just not very well-adjusted. A bit odd, if you really want to know. But not schizophrenic or psychotic,' she added bitterly, 'they all seem to agree on that.'

'You've had him tested?'

'Oh, he's been tested,' Hannie said evasively. 'He's had all the tests.'

She got up, strolled over to the window, pausing to look straight into the yellow eyes of the sparrow hawk in a way she knew would anger Danno. Then she stood with her back to him, smoking and staring out at the darkness. Why not tell him about Joss, she thought suddenly, it might be a relief, she'd never just said it out, she was always so locked into trying to prove the opposite. That black was white, that Joss wasn't as she knew he was. And Danno saw no one, it didn't matter what he said or thought, talking to him was scarcely more indiscreet than talking to herself.

'Joss is odd,' she said quietly. 'Not normal. But in a way that doesn't show up on tests.'

'Autistic?'

'No, not autistic.' There was a pause. 'Corrupt.'

'Corrupt?'

'Corrupt,' Hannie agreed. 'That was the word I used, Danno. Sometimes you sound like a bloody parrot.'

Danno laid down the skin he was cleaning. His questions weren't idly curious, he had asked about Joss because he was anxious for Niamh. But he wasn't that anxious, he didn't want to hear what he was learning now, he realised, he didn't want Hannie's confidence, he wanted to tell her the problem and have her take it away.

And she was doing the opposite. He was too private, too unused to human intercourse to accept her secrets lightly. He'd made a mistake in pressing her, had uncovered far more than he wanted to know. So he swivelled on his tatty revolving chair and sat loosely and quietly, his grey eyes averted behind their spectacles and vaguely focused on the floor.

'It's his nature,' Hannie said finally, still not turning. 'That bird there – she's a killer, you can't blame her, it's her nature. Well, Joss is corrupt – you can't blame him, it's his nature.'

There was another silence.

'Hannie, that hawk is a raptor, a bird of prey,' Danno said carefully. 'It's an evolved killer, has spent thousands of years honing itself into what it is. Joss is a human being, not a raptor, it's not his destiny to be corrupt, you can't compare the two.'

'Can't I?' Hannie said, her voice low and stubborn. 'Who says I can't? You, Danno? What do you know? Joss likes corruption. He likes hurting, spoiling, dirtying. Going the crooked way.' She spoke so quietly now that Danno had to strain to catch her words.

'Did something happen?'

No answer from Hannie. She was staring at the great black curtainless window, unredeemed by moonlight or stars. She blew out smoke so it rolled and billowed defiantly across its darkness.

'Was he born like that?'

'Was he born like that, did he get like that? Who knows? What made you the way you are, an old woman fussing away at these horrible birds? Because you were born like that or because they wouldn't have you as a priest?'

Danno gave an almost imperceptible start and straightened very slightly in his chair. 'Is that what Kathleen told you?' he asked quietly.

'She said they wouldn't have you because you're illegitimate. She said that's how things were when you were young.'

'She's got it wrong, I never asked them, I didn't want to go.'

Hannie looked at him, at the stubborn, closed hurt in his face. He'd wanted to all right. It was as Kathleen had said, he just wouldn't give them the satisfaction of turning him down. She crossed to the window seat and picked up her coat.

She stepped out into a darkness that crept and clung at her neck, her face, her hands. The cold had softened a little, cloud hid the stars. She'd left her torch behind at Danno's, could see nothing, her feet found the puddled track and followed it haltingly. She wondered at the black closeness of this darkness that moved and breathed like an intimate against her skin. There was nothing else beside it, nothing in the world but the stones under her feet and the moist black night.

She'd seen his face as she left, the ill-concealed hurt reflecting her over-stepped mark. She'd been almost pleased at the time, she was sick of being patronised, of being the problem, the one always in the wrong. She was a problem and Joss was a problem, but the lives all around her weren't so perfect either, they were just better camouflaged here where they belonged. Sometimes they needed reminding of this. And sometimes it helped your own pain to take a swipe at someone else, even if that someone else came close to being your only friend.

She tramped on. Already the strength she felt from her deliberate little cruelty had all but leached away, leaving nothing but self-disgust in its place. She felt rudderless and directionless, like the dead sheep the November rains had carried down the river. Day after day it had drifted up and down, up and down, moving swiftly away with the pull of the sea's ebbing tide, pushing back again as it rose. Bloated, a perch for the gulls. Till it snagged on some drowned tree and left off its journeying.

❧ *Chapter 35* ❧

*I*t was that dark, dank time that stretched and sagged like a bit of old rope between Christmas and the New Year. It was hard for Hannie to pull herself out of despondency, harder still to stay that way. The tentative easing and harmonising of her relationship with Ned had disintegrated like old silk suddenly restored to light, now parting at the lightest touch. There seemed little to be gained in trying to darn it together again, only to watch it open somewhere else under the strain of the new stitches.

Besides, she had the measure of the life here and of the people who lived it alongside her and she expected little from either. Nothing was going to change, so what was the point of trying? She almost let herself decide against the effort.

Ned's relations came from Galway the next day and saved her. They arrived without writing or phoning, a car drew up and a man got out, walked over the thin gravel, hesitated in front of the heavy iron knocker. Hannie heard and watched discreetly from an upstairs window. When the knocker thumped the first time she made no move to answer it. It pounded again and she went slowly downstairs, leaving whoever it was plenty of time to give up and go back to wherever he'd come from.

He went on knocking. She undid the snib but the heavy door, swollen with winter damp, stuck fast near the top. She heaved and pulled, calling to the man on the other side to put his shoulder to it. The door gave suddenly under their combined efforts, it burst open and he stumbled in after it. He gathered himself. His name was Andrew Clarke, he explained, he was a great-nephew of Ned's by marriage, now come with his wife to visit because they were in the area and didn't want to pass Ned's door.

'It's only a call on the off-chance. I haven't seen Ned since I was a boy, I doubt he'd even remember me.'

Hannie let him run out of words and stand awkwardly. 'Ned's gone to Waterford,' she said, which was true. 'I don't know when he'll be back,' she added, which wasn't. 'You can wait if you want.' Her tone was utterly discouraging.

The man, relieved, started backing out. On the far edge of her vision Hannie glimpsed a movement which she knew was Joss, sidling off behind a door.

'You must come in and wait,' she said, changing her mind abruptly. 'Ned will want to see you – he won't be long now – come in, make yourselves at home, stay for dinner.'

'We wouldn't want to put you to any trouble.' Andrew Clarke looked confused. 'We'll call again some other time.'

'It's no trouble and you can't go now, you've only just come. What will Ned say if he gets back and finds I haven't held on to you?'

Hannie's voice was false and almost arch. Alarm flickered across Andrew's face, he went on trying to refuse but she wouldn't listen. Then he gave in abruptly, looking embarrassed and muttering about having a word with Nora.

Hannie stood and watched him cross the patchy gravel and bend to talk to his wife through the wound-down window of the car. She knew that this great-nephew of Ned's hadn't any idea who she was, nor what was the set-up. He had plainly expected the elderly bachelor Ned, perhaps a housekeeper, certainly not a wife. She knew from the set of his back that the woman in the car didn't want to come in and he was telling her they had to, they couldn't get out of it now. She was arguing, but not very hard, she'd give in soon because he was asking her to.

Hannie didn't care, let them go or stay, it was all one to her. And Ned wouldn't want to see them, she knew that, Ned had had enough of other people's company for the time being. Yet it would be better than nothing, better than sitting silently with Ned by the fire, Joss in Niamh's cottage, she wondering should she go over there or let him alone.

A slim woman, dark-haired and pretty, got slowly out of the car and came with her husband to where Hannie was standing waiting. Hannie put out her hand.

'I'm Ned's wife, Hannie,' she said easily, catching the shock on the man's face. The woman was blank. Either she was better at concealment or simply too preoccupied with her own reluctance.

'Nora,' the woman introduced herself shyly. 'But really we can't put you to this trouble, it was only a whim of Andrew's, we were passing so near to you . . .' She flushed and the words ran out. Hannie took her by the arm and drew her in through the door.

'It's no trouble,' she said again, 'it's a pleasure. You'll stay the night.'

It wasn't a question. Andrew had no choice but to follow.

When Ned came back they were drinking gin by the drawing room fire, Hannie playing the hostess in a dark dress, her hair smoothed and restrained, her manner similar. She said they were staying over and they didn't contradict her. Surprising himself, Ned was pleased.

He hardly knew Andrew, a grandson of one of his dead wife's many brothers, and remembered him only dimly as a lanky youth who had blushed and mumbled when spoken to except when asked about rugby which it seemed he played with flair and talent. He didn't look like an athlete now. Ned saw a big, loose-boned, good-humoured, peace-loving man in his late thirties, the powerful body running a little to fat.

Rugby? Andrew laughed quietly. Those days were long gone, he was his own man now, an auctioneer in a biggish town outside of Galway, his business secure, his peers suggesting to him that he think of standing in the next election.

He hadn't decided yet, he said, he was still turning it over, taking soundings. Of course it was harder for a Protestant to get elected, but Nora was Catholic and her family was long-term Fine Gael; that would help him with the nomination.

He spoke with so natural a modesty, so simple and serious a belief in his life, that Ned could not but listen and warm to him.

He liked Nora too, but he couldn't get her to relax. She was shy and she wanted to stop being shy and open to them, but she wasn't at ease. She was unsure how to behave with her husband's relatives, and over-anxious to deliver whatever it was they expected of her.

Nora was the daughter of a strong farmer on the Offaly-Galway border, one of many children, used to company and noise and laughter, to warmth and work and family. She knew that as a young man Andrew had hero-worshipped his great-uncle and she wanted to do well so he'd be proud of her. But she felt more out of place here than she'd expected to and she wasn't used to such self-consciousness. Everything – her voice, her attitudes, her clothes – seemed suddenly somehow different and open to question.

She had a six-year-old son, she told Hannie, a girl of four and another of eighteen months. A sister of hers was visiting over Christmas and they'd taken this chance to go away together. It was Andrew's idea, for herself she thought Christmas so precious a time that she wanted to be with the children, but still it was only a couple of days, a business visit in Youghal, an overnight in a quiet hotel, a little driving around to show her where his father's family had come from. It was clear that she missed her home and her children and yearned to get back to them.

She was pleased when she discovered Joss. She liked teenage boys, she said, following Hannie out to the kitchen and settling in beside him at the kitchen table, happy to leave the grown-ups to her husband. Hannie fed Joss baked beans and fried eggs while she cooked dinner for the rest of them and Nora did her best at conversation. She made little headway. Joss ate fast, then rose to go.

'I'll be at Niamh's,' he told his mother. He didn't even glance at Nora.

'You feel for them so at this age, don't you?' Nora said, as the back door shut behind him. 'I always remember what it was like – the wanting to join in and not knowing how, it must be harder for an only –' She stopped herself. 'Or maybe it's easier. No competition, no thinking the others are prettier or cleverer or stronger.' She finished with a small, embarrassed laugh. Hannie said nothing. She was thinking that for once Joss had a point.

They had dinner in the dining room. Ned was glad of Joss's absence, he was still recovering from his discovery of the depths of Joss's alienation and the strange complicitous relationship between the boy and his mother. Besides he was tired of making an effort, tired of Joss's odd disruptive presence, tired of his own face reflecting from the mirrors of his stepson's shuttered eyes. He wanted to sit quietly and talk.

Ned saw the ease with which Andrew moved through his life and he guessed that much of this ease must have come through Nora. He plainly liked his relations through marriage, liked the influence of her big noisy family, liked having a foot in both religious camps and feeling neither disloyalty nor any need to convert. For him there was to be no self-imposed silence, no holding a little apart from the daily life of community or state. He and Nora loved and understood each other: life was for rearing your children, making your way, earning the respect of your friends and your community. It was all simple and healthy and straightforward.

Andrew was confused by Ned. He had been in awe of his legend since childhood, and their few meetings had deepened his sense that here was someone different and extraordinary. Now he looked at his great-uncle and wondered what all that adventuring had been about. He saw an old man with an odd wife and a strange stepson, trying to run a bit of a farm and knowing less about it than one of Nora's half-grown brothers. He felt pity for Ned because he hadn't stayed at home and done something with his life, but had frittered it away, travelling with nomadic peoples in forgotten places.

He said all this to Nora in bed that night and she listened and held his hand while he talked. He said he wondered now why he had romanticised Ned, why his life had once seemed so special to him. His own immaturity, perhaps? He saw Ned's travelling now for what it was: a refusal to accept the changing world; ultimately probably an inability to grow up and adapt and take on responsibility.

He didn't know what to make of Hannie, nor why Ned had married her. Could it be that Ned was in love with her?

Nora said she thought Ned had married Hannie because he was lonely. It was a shame he'd had no children of his own, he'd have been a wonderful father, it made sense of life if you had children . . .

The next day they were easier in themselves and not so inclined to be overawed. Ned saw that he had been judged and found wanting, and he saw that Hannie saw it as well. He smiled at her ruefully across the kitchen and she grinned back at him. They were companionable in their outsiderliness.

Ned took Andrew off about the place but Nora stayed with Hannie, insisting that they do the washing up together. Hannie looked at her mutely and handed over the gloves and the mop. Nora could wash up if she wanted, but she could do it alone. She filled a mug with hot water and put a plastic bottle of ear-mite drops into it to warm. Then she knelt on the kitchen floor, clamped the wriggling puppy between her knees, lifted each ear in turn and squeezed in the drops. Joss came downstairs. He ignored Nora and stood watching her.

'Ciaran's come back, Niamh's creaming herself.'

'Niamh that you were round with last night?' Nora asked from the sink.

Hannie released Pippa and got up off her knees. 'Ned's tenant,' she said. 'She's a painter. Ciaran's the boyfriend.'

At once Nora wanted to meet her. It seemed she had a young cousin who might go to art school.

'Joss, take Nora round to Niamh's and introduce her. Tell Niamh to show Nora her paintings.'

'She'll love that.'

Even Nora heard the sarcasm in his voice.

'She doesn't have to if she doesn't want to, it must be so hard to believe in yourself when you're only beginning.'

Joss threw a Who's-This-Moron? look at Hannie. Then he ushered her through the door and followed after her.

Ciaran and Niamh would still be in bed, of course. Hannie hoped Nora would be shocked. Perhaps she'd tell her husband that Ned was allowing all sorts of carryings-on on his property.

Joss seemed to like her, despite the looks he was throwing around; Hannie watched them talking as they walked together across the yard. The damp was on Nora's dark curly hair, there was a glow on her fair skin, she was enjoying herself. Joss looked easy and young and almost animated. Hannie curdled with jealousy.

They were away longer than expected. It seemed Ciaran and Niamh had indeed been in bed and Nora hadn't been shocked at all, she'd lit the fire and put on the kettle and when they'd come down she'd eaten a second breakfast with them.

Ned came back with Andrew and they had lunch. Nora was animated, she tried to draw Hannie into household conversations but Hannie wouldn't have it. She tried again, but Hannie kept on thwarting her so she gave up and talked about her youngest brother who was Joss's age. Hannie caught Ned's eye on her during one of these attempts and she saw to her surprise that he didn't mind that she was stonewalling Nora. Hannie was good at the house, Ned knew that, but there it ended. She wouldn't discuss recipes or getting stains off polished furniture or the perfect kitchen floor.

They ate everything she put on the table and sat over coffee and Nora wanted to help wash up again, but Hannie was firm as a rock. When they finally got into the car to drive away the blue-grey twilight was with them like a witness. Ned and Hannie stood together, hearing the sound of the engine fade off into the distance, feeling the damp silence flow back over them and close them off again in their hidden, frosty world.

Hannie bent to snap a cluster of blackened hips from a long, thorned spike on the Frensham rose. 'Do you think Joss would be more normal if I was?' she asked into the silence.

'You mean if he had Nora for a mother?'

She nodded, her face averted.

'If Nora was his mother he wouldn't be Joss,' Ned said quietly. 'It's a meaningless question.'

She snapped off another cluster of hips. 'Niamh thinks Joss is all my fault,' she said.

'Do you?'

She thought for a minute and then shook her head. 'Not all. Joss is Joss, he was born Joss. But I think I've made him worse.'

She had dropped the shrivelled hips on to the ground and was drawing patterns in the gravel with her shoe. 'Then again, there are times when I think I'm all his fault.' She looked up at Ned, a sad, tired look. 'Nothing is as simple as Niamh believes.'

'When you're young you think that way,' Ned said gently. 'Don't you remember? You think everything could be put right if only people went about things differently. You think there is choice. In twenty years' time she'll be astonished that she thought these things at all.'

'She won't remember,' Hannie said bitterly. 'Niamh will always be sure that she's right.'

Ned smiled and shook his head, but he didn't speak.

That night Ned came to Hannie's bed and tried to please her more than himself. It was a failure. For the first time he knew himself to be hopelessly clumsy and incompetent. He wanted to ask her to help him learn, but he knew he couldn't ever get the words out and if he did it would only make it worse. He saw himself through her eyes and knew himself already far too old and inexperienced. He wished he had known her over years, then at least there would have been the tenderness of friendship to lean on. As it was, she was merely fulfilling the terms of their contract. She would service him efficiently and without resentment, but she expected nothing. He wondered if she thought of old loves, or of nothing at all.

He wanted to stay with her for the rest of the night but he didn't want to impose on her more than he already had. He took himself off to his own room and lay a long time looking into the darkness and thinking about the day. Andrew and Nora's visit had thrown them together, had shown them as misfits, almost outcasts, in this intensely settled and familial society. He wondered if she felt like this all the time, and if it made her lonely. He wondered if it was why she'd taken to Danno.

It was the first time she'd referred, even indirectly, to the scene he'd witnessed on Christmas Eve, the first time she'd spoken of Joss and of his strangeness. He suffered for her now when he saw her trapped or hopeless. He wondered if this suffering was a form of love.

❧ *Chapter 36* ❧

Nora phoned while they were eating. She thanked them for their hospitality and spoke convincingly of how much they'd both enjoyed their visit. She said she'd mislaid a small gold bracelet, she didn't know where. Stupid of her, perhaps they would keep an eye out for it and give her a ring if it turned up? Hannie put the phone down and passed on the message, her voice neutral and indifferent. Later she went through Joss's drawers carefully but the bracelet wasn't there. She searched in the most obvious places but all she found was a woman's high-heeled court shoe under the bed. Probably Nora's, though she hadn't mentioned shoes. No sign of its twin. Perhaps Joss had only wanted the one.

She took it away but said nothing. He'd discover the loss: she wanted him to know she knew.

'Garth Brookes?' Ciaran drawled. 'Bit close to Country-with-its-tongue-*not*-in-its-cheek for my taste. You know the style – sleeve notes all about God and the wife. Songs about men in bars hitting each other . . .'

Joss smirked appreciatively. Niamh, sprawled in the lumpy armchair by the fire, stirred irritably but kept her thoughts to herself. She wished Ciaran would stop showing off for Joss. She'd told him as much only two days ago and he'd said she was jealous.

She'd been dumbstruck. Jealous? The injustice of the word! How did he figure that one?

He'd said it was obvious. They were into stuff she wasn't into, so she felt left out and jealous.

Everything she said about Joss after that came out as though to confirm his verdict, so she avoided saying anything. She'd begun to avoid any subject that might annoy Ciaran, she noticed. She was ashamed of her behaviour, but more ashamed of the besottedness that induced it.

She didn't know how Ciaran felt about her; often she wondered if he even liked her. He wanted her, that was plain enough; he reached for her, unable not to reach, already bored by the imperatives of his body. She was as bad, she knew that, and she wasn't yet remotely bored. More like obsessed. Did she love him? She really had no idea. She'd stopped telling him she did when she noticed that he never said the words himself, only nodded vaguely as if in agreement. She glanced across at him now and decided that he despised her. Well, that was all right, she despised him back.

He seemed always detached and sarcastic with her. With her, but also with the rest of them. Except for Hannie. Hannie took no notice of Ciaran, hardly ever addressed him unless it was a request or an enquiry: he was Niamh's boyfriend, that was all, she was formal with him. With Hannie Ciaran watched, he didn't speak. He spoke disparagingly of her, called her The Hag, but there was a tension in him when she appeared, an alertness.

Ciaran had nicknames for everyone, he called Joss The Spook, he rubbished him, but he didn't seem too unhappy with his company. Unless he wanted to go back to bed with her, but even that wasn't really a problem, Joss seemed to know when they wanted him gone. 'I'll be off then,' he'd say, sliding his blank black gaze across her face, the corners of his mouth turned upwards in a smirk. She thought The Smirk would have been a better name than The Spook, but she kept the thought to herself. Ned was A. R. for Anal Retentive. She'd laughed, despite herself; Ned was so stiff and private.

She sighed now and settled herself deeper in the lumpy armchair and tried to let go of her thoughts and get back into her book. The chair was too small, her long limbs stuck out beyond its confines, but she didn't want to move because the puppy was asleep on her stomach and she liked stroking the soft hairless belly as she read.

'It says here that people with low moral standards have more friends than people with high ones.' She spoke the words aloud before she knew she had intended to; she heard them with a vague surprise.

'Why d'you read that crap?'

''Tisn't crap. She won the Booker Prize.'

'Still crap.' Ciaran extracted a card from his hand and laid it on the table. He threw a quick glance at Joss.

'She says it's because they're easier to be with.'

'Who are?'

'People with low moral standards.'

'Which would be why I'd have a whole lot more friends than you do,' Ciaran said. Joss laid a card on to Ciaran's and took the trick. A little pulse showed for a moment at the corner of Ciaran's mouth.

'More acquaintances,' Niamh said, looking at him, her brown eyes level and steady. 'I have more friends.'

Ciaran shrugged. His lazy voice belied the pulse. 'Have it yer own way,' he said. He was waiting for Joss to lead, watching the back of his cards as though he could read through them. Joss's dark glasses lay on the table beside him. His face looked curiously empty without them, almost bereft, the skin round his eyes very white, the rest of his face still holding the mark of the African sun, his flaxen brows and lashes accentuating both the colour and the absence of it.

'Who is this crappy author that you're reading?' Hannie asked from across the room. She was roaming around with a glass in her hand, picking up objects, putting them down again. She'd come over from the house with a bottle of vodka, ostensibly to return past hospitality, in reality to check on Joss and the chemistry between him and Ciaran. She'd dismissed Danno's words to his face, but nonetheless she was alert to them.

'Anita Brookner,' Niamh addressed Hannie seriously, look-ing up at her from her open book. 'She writes about women by themselves.'

'Spinster moralist,' Ciaran drawled from the table. 'Writes about people too scared to live.'

'How would you know? You've never read her.'

'Have so,' Ciaran said casually. 'Great stylist. Still crap. You should try her, Hannie, put some courage into you. Read two of them books in a row and you'll run out the door and burn the world down just to stop yourself from suffocating in fucking moderation.'

'Hannie doesn't read books.'

'Yes she does.'

'No she doesn't.'

'Yes she does. Tell you what, let's ask her.' He swung fully round in his chair and gave Hannie all his attention. Joss watched from somewhere a long way off. 'D'you read books, Hannie?'

'Not very often,' Hannie said indifferently. She was propped against the dresser, smoking a cigarette.

'D' you think auld Brookner's right?'

'About what?'

'Low moral standards and loads of friends?'

'Of course.' Hannie spoke as though it was too obvious to need stating. She took a drag at her cigarette. She looked thoughtful.

'You think I need courage?' she challenged Ciaran suddenly.

'Courage?' He was puzzled.

'You said it would put courage in me?'

Ciaran hesitated. 'I think maybe you're in the doldrums,' he said slowly. 'Temporary-like. Nothing to write home about.'

A curious atmosphere had sprung up between them, an intimacy that was tangible. Hannie's expression didn't change but she stood waiting, as though she hadn't heard his words. Joss stayed very still, but his right hand came forward as though it was separate and autonomous. It picked up his dark glasses and settled them on to his nose again. Niamh grabbed at the puppy, pulling the little body close and rubbing her cheek against the soft fur. Only Ciaran seemed unaware.

At last Hannie moved. She tossed her cigarette into the fire and looked straight at Ciaran.

'The doldrums,' she said thoughtfully. 'Becalmed, no wind in the sails, nothing to blow you this way or that.' She laughed, a low easy laugh that was utterly surprising. 'Perhaps it's the right place for me,' she said, still speaking to him and to no one else. 'Now that I'm almost an old woman. The doldrums. Respectable. Safe.'

'Would you wise up, Hannie?' Ciaran said. His voice had a harsh authority. 'You're never going to be respectable. And you're never going to be safe, neither. Face facts, stop dreaming dreams. It's not the world that'll stop you – it's yourself.' He stared at her furiously, consumed in the intensity of the drama between them. Then, with a hard effort, he broke her gaze and threw a card down on the table. With a toss of the head he challenged Joss to follow his lead. 'And leave off the fucking glasses, dickhead! You want to play – you play straight. Or as straight as your twisted wee soul can allow for. I want to see your eyes, an' that means no glasses.'

Joss didn't answer. He removed the dark glasses and glanced at his hand. Casually, he laid a low card of a different suit over Ciaran's queen. Ciaran looked at him, wanting to know the catch, then took the trick, sweeping the cards towards him without lifting them off the table so that Joss wouldn't see his hand trembling. Joss saw. He didn't know what had happened but he knew that Ciaran had unnerved himself and he knew his mother was the cause of it.

He'd let Ciaran win the next few tricks, then he'd change the suit with a trump and take the game.

~ *Chapter 37* ~

*H*annie walked back over the yard, the moist black air eddying about her, fine needles of rain showing in the halo around the yardlight. The temperature had changed, it was much milder; she'd rather the frost with its quickness, she felt that the sky had moved down and was pressing in round her. The sky, or was it the sea? She might shipwreck in these waters, she might drown. And she longed for a continent under her feet, for the great empty emanations of a continent, not this small dense island which was like living confined in a single room.

She knew that Ciaran had connected with her and in doing so had shocked himself. A connection of that intensity had always a sexual charge to it, a charge that had passed far beyond flirtation to enter the starker realms of recognition. Sexual recognition, but also psychic recognition. They were two of a kind, she and Ciaran, both physically and psychically, and the strength of this mutual revelation had momentarily bridged the chasm of age.

Hannie hadn't seen it coming: she, too, was caught off-guard, but she knew enough to know what it was when it came. That she'd been unprepared was odd in itself: usually she knew precisely when she had caught a man's attention, knew it long before he did. Then, even to herself, she seemed to forget it. But underneath, she still knew. Her unpreparedness, she decided, was his age. Ciaran was only a boy to her, she had never considered him either sexually or otherwise, unless with a voyeur's detachment, watching Niamh embroiled in her infatuation.

She pushed open the back door and went in. Perhaps she'd

been barking up the wrong tree, she thought, treading off her wellingtons one after the other. She shook the rain from her tangled hair. It was astonishing how wetting was this rain that hardly seemed wet at all. Insidious. Like everything here – nothing clear or straight – everything creeping, wavering, sliding off into something else. Like living inside a house that was underwater but no one knew it. She longed for outdoors and sky, she longed again for Africa, surprising herself, who hadn't thought Africa a place to be longed for.

The wrong tree. The thought brought her suddenly to stillness, the grubby towel limp in her hand, her rubbed hair standing up around her head. Men twenty years younger, not twenty years older, like Ned. For a moment she considered the possibilities of such a reversal, letting herself float on the sweet illusory triumph of having caught, however briefly, the attention of a boy in his twenties.

Only for a moment. She knew too well the reality of the body's inexorable ageing, had no wish to stand at the glass with a young man's reflection floating somewhere in the shadowy room behind her. Rather an old man's, she thought, and she, younger, beside him. That way she kept the upper hand. And she need never learn the science of concealment.

Besides, she had seen him appalled at the connection – attraction – call it what you would. She didn't blame him. It was bizarre, gothic, she didn't want it herself. Had he been older, had she been younger, there would have been no question but of a sexual outcome. As it was, it was simply an unexpected explosion of feeling, grotesque in its inappropriateness, a current far too raw for the delicate social wiring that had failed to contain it. It would fade, she was sure of that; even as soon as the next morning they might look at each other and decide they'd each imagined it. And she wasn't sorry that this should be so. There was no part of her that wanted to be back there garnering what a young man offered. Not the passion, nor the self-absorption, nor the overwhelming drama of the blood.

But how surprising that it should be Ciaran who had seen and understood her. Not surprising: he was, in essence, a worthless young man, worthless and selfish, just as she was herself. Strange, she thought, that Ned should tolerate in her what he couldn't bear in Ciaran.

How wearying to be seeing and judging through Ned's eyes like this. Non-worthless people she had always found close to intolerable, now it seemed worthlessness was become a term of abuse. Perhaps she should seduce him, just the once, before he had time to come to his senses? Perhaps not. She would certainly hate the self-image awaiting her in his eyes. Niamh's shattered complacency might be her only satisfaction.

She had finished with the towel and had thrown it into the empty drum of the washing machine. Now she knelt between the meal sacks and a lean of rakes and hoes and yard-brushes, pulling on her shoe, her thoughts assisted by these small mundane activities. Paulo. His name was in her mind but it hadn't come like a memory, it was more like an involuntary invasion. Abruptly she stopped pulling and just knelt, staring at the wall. The small hatchet hung there and beside it a heavy lump hammer, a tyre-jack, a rusty saw, a length of chain. She didn't see them, she saw nothing of the present. She felt Paulo, his reality almost tangible, like the saturating after-presence of a once-loved figure re-encountered in a dream.

Paulo. Why now? Was it Ciaran, reminding her?

She shook her head, pulled at her shoe again. No, not Ciaran, Ciaran wasn't like Paulo, he was simply unco-operative and a bit rebellious. He would calm down soon, would loiter beside the queue, all the time pretending that he wasn't there and hadn't noticed it. Then when it moved forward, he would move with it. Soon he would be part of it, would speak with its complacency, its convenient, hypocritical morality.

Paulo had been more than that, far more. Paulo was a masterless man, all knowledge in his bleak grey eyes.

Light dawned. It wasn't Ciaran's likeness to Paulo that had brought him so strongly into her mind, it was her own surprise at the connection, her total lack of premonition, her unaware-ness. And Niamh: her thraldom inside her own sexual infatu-ation, so like Hannie's own with Paulo, and yet she hadn't seen the parallel till now.

In her mind she'd left the narrow scullery with its smell of earth and dampness, she'd travelled years and continents to step from the fierce sunlight of a square in a little Moorish town and in through a high narrow doorway, black and deep with shade. There was a narrow, empty room to the left with a heavy, polished counter running the length of it and Salman, the barman, sitting on a wooden chair in the fly-droned quiet, his back against the ochre-coloured wall. She ignored Salman and walked on past the bar (for it was a bar, though there was nothing to show it, no drink of any kind displayed, not even coffee) and on through the empty dining room with its dark polished floorboards that cried out where you trod. She went through the door at the end, stepping from the shadowy room into the sunlit courtyard-garden with its pillars and fountains and dappled light, its tangle of vines and bougainvil-laea, its palm trees slicing up into the dazzling sky. Birds sang, purpled pigeons dipped and drank from stains of water on the tiled floor. To her left, long patterned sofas were arranged in shade against the mosaic'ed wall. Men sat around on them: Arabs, Africans, one or two Europeans. They lounged and talked there, sometimes ate and drank off patterned trays of polished brass.

Who had taken her there, what had she been doing? She couldn't remember. None of it had mattered to her, it was only another episode in a part of her life crowded with places and episodes, with scenes and people, always moving, always changing. There was nothing about it that was different or more important than anywhere else, nothing she had intended to remember. Until Paulo had placed his hand lightly on her shoulder, the touch claiming her.

Even now, over all the years, she had no idea what had happened to her. She'd thought herself indifferent to him, had felt no attraction, no hint of the sexual connection hidden in her flesh. But he'd known, it seemed, he'd been watching her and waiting, knowing the connection to be there, knowing he could have her if he wanted her, when he wanted her.

'Hannie, what are you doing?'

She looked up. Ned was standing in the doorway. She hadn't heard his approach.

'Remembering,' she said, pulling on her other shoe.

'It happens.' He leaned more heavily on the doorknob. 'More and more, these days, but there are warmer places for it. Why don't you come through, do your remembering beside the fire?'

'It's private remembering.'

'That's all right, I won't interrupt you. You'll catch cold here, you're wet through.'

'I thought at first he would be no different from the others. I thought I had the measure of him, that I could amuse myself for a while, then go or stay, as I wished. I didn't realise there would be no choice.'

She sat by the fire, leaning forward in the chair, a glass of whiskey in her hand, her eyes on the flames, the bottle on the hearth beside her. She spoke as though something heavy and dense had laid itself down on her, sopping her up, as a cloth sops a spill.

'It was the measure of myself I didn't have. I drank, I was drunk nearly all the time, early and late, but it didn't help, it didn't dull the way I needed him. And I couldn't endure it, I had to leave him, I knew that, I had to leave him before it was too late and I couldn't.

'He would have destroyed me,' she added, looking at Ned, her eyes very bright. 'I never regret that I left him. But I cannot, altogether, get free of him.' She hesitated, stared back into the fire, began again, her voice quiet and strange. 'Mostly I never think of him, I don't remember him, he isn't in my mind or my imagination, he never comes close. Except in dreams. They come out of nowhere, awful, total, more like visitation than dream. Afterwards I have to fight to be rid of him.

'Sometimes, a long time since a dream, I try to remember his presence and I can't. I can't remember even what he looked like.'

'What was he doing there?' Ned asked from the other side of the hearth. His voice was quiet.

'He had a lot of contacts, his business was his contacts, he was an Italian so the Europeans trusted him and came to him. He's one of us, they thought, he will not cheat us. They thought he'd help them cheat the others who weren't white.'

'And they were wrong?'

'He cheated anyone who'd let him, despised them for letting him. Europeans and Africans were easier than Arabs, he had more respect for Arabs, some of them he couldn't cheat at all. With them he dealt as equals.'

'What exactly was his business?'

'He brokered deals. Deals and double deals – anything illegal or hard to come by, anything for anyone who could pay. You must have come across such men in Africa?'

'Now and then, not ever for very long, I never dealt with them if I could help it. They have no country – great courage, but no country, nothing to hold them back from anything. For them, there is no darkness. They see in the dark, it's their true domain.'

Hannie nodded. He could see her shoulders relaxing, the strangeness going out of her eyes. She seemed easier for talking, less possessed and remote.

'How did you meet him?'

'I sold him my soul.'

Ned stared. She laughed, remembering herself as she'd been then.

'We were sitting one night at a table in the square in a small town,' she said. 'A group of us. We'd no money, we had eaten, but when they came to ask for payment we told them they must wait until tomorrow. No one wanted to go to bed, we wanted to drink and smoke kif, we wanted to lose ourselves, but we were broke. He was sitting at another table, someone knew him, knew he was rich, so I went across and told him what we wanted and asked him if he'd pay the bill.'

A log fell from the fire and on to the hearth, scattering sparks that glimmered and died. Hannie leaned over and lifted it back with the tongs. Ned waited.

'He said he'd pay if I sold him my soul. So I did. He called for paper and a bond was drawn up and I signed. That was the beginning, though I didn't know it at the time. Perhaps he has my soul still, if I ever had one. There are worse things I could have traded for. Money, power, reputation. It seems to me not so bad to have sold it for the satisfaction of the moment.' She glanced up at him and he nodded but said nothing. The fire burned in the silence.

'It was a long time ago,' she said eventually. 'It's odd, the way these things live on in you.' She sat leaning forward, one elbow on her knee, her head resting on her hand, her fingers laced in her hair, her eyes closed. 'You think they've quite gone . . .'

'And then they flare up again. Like malaria. A new bout. Might as well be the first bout.'

She nodded, too absorbed to wonder that he knew.

'I couldn't trust myself when I was with him,' she said slowly. 'It wasn't morality that made me leave him, I didn't care what he did or what he was, but staying with him would have meant giving up myself.' There was another silence.

'You see, Ned, as long as you can act without the time or the need for reflection you can do more or less as you like. It's only when you stop and think about what you are doing, what you have done, that you get caught by morality. Not other people's morality – that doesn't matter – but your own. With reflection comes shame. Not for laws broken, not even for lives broken, but for small meannesses, small acts of cruelty or cowardliness. And when shame comes, it is invariably horrible.

'Paulo never cared about right or wrong, he just acted and moved on. But Paulo was male so he was never slowed down, he never got caught by a child as I did.'

'Perhaps the child was the saving of you, Hannie.'

She looked up, a swift bleak look, but didn't speak.

'What happened to him?'

She shrugged again. 'I never heard directly. But I'm certain that he's dead.'

❧ *Chapter 38* ❧

Joss was kneeling on the floor in his room, stuffing a pair of Niamh's thick black tights with loosely scrumpled newspaper. They looked a bit lumpy and odd but they'd pass; the crude packing had ballooned them into the semblance of lower limbs. He put Nora's shoe on to one of the stuffed feet and it was better – almost realistic – but the newspaper wasn't packed tightly enough and the shoe fell off when he moved the limb. He thought of tying it on, but decided it didn't matter. Once the thing was dumped in the undergrowth, the loose shoe lying about would make it look even better. Thrown off in the struggle. Joss sat back on his heels and rubbed his hands with pleasure.

He put Nora's gold bracelet round the black ankle. Cool, a belly-dancer. Reluctantly he took it off again. It was wasted on the dummy, he'd sell it in the town as soon as he was back at school. He wouldn't get much for it, the second-hand dealers were all rip-off merchants, but something was better than nothing at all.

He took the sanitary towel he'd nicked from Nora's room and daubed it with ketchup from a plastic tomato. The white pad turned dramatically red. Corny, but satisfying, he decided. He put the tomato carefully back into his box of finds. He'd nicked it from a café in Youghal he'd been to with Niamh and Ciaran; heirloom-kitsch, Ciaran had called it, so Joss had taken it with him when they left. Niamh had been uptight when she realised but she hadn't said anything because she knew they'd laugh at her. She wasn't so into standing up for her principles these days, Joss noticed; she was copping on.

He liked taking things, not even bothering to hide them, walking out with them under the noses of the staff who saw but said nothing. It always amazed him how soft people were.

He was pleased with the sanitary towel, it was a real find. Niamh bought those cotton-wool plug-things and stuffed them up herself. He placed the stained towel between the black stuffed legs, and pinned it carefully in place with safety pins. It looked great. Not realistic, but somehow more shocking for that.

He didn't really know why he was doing what he was doing but he knew he liked doing it, and that was enough to be going on with. He sat back on his heels and his eyes closed with pleasure, picturing Niamh and the screech she'd let out when she found it. Then she'd go all white and trembly and he'd laugh himself stupid. He'd say he'd been trying his hand at a bit of soft sculpture, she'd appreciate that. She was always on about soft sculpture, the unexplored potential in the form. The smile on his face widened.

For a moment he wondered what Hannie would say, but he shoved the thought from him and carefully replaced his treasures in his box of finds. It was khaki-coloured and metal, with strong clips that sealed it tight and kept the damp out when he buried it. That was the theory anyway. But he didn't take any chances, he always double-wrapped it in bin-liners to be sure.

He looked at the black legs again. They were good, but they could be better, they needed something more. A top half, or rather a topless half? Perhaps not – it was hard to make naked boobs that were any good. A skirt, ripped up the side? To conceal and not conceal? A red admiral struggled briefly on the blackness of the window pane. It had been there two days now, its wings going tattered and crap, their coloured dust all mussed and messed as it battered itself against the glass. It was weaker all the time, mostly it lay quiet and he thought it was dead, then it would stagger up and have another go.

Joss had an idea.

A double doll. One of those rag-doll things he'd seen somewhere ages ago. He saw one now in his mind in the different light that comes with heat. A double-headed rag-doll, pink-skin, yellow hair, long check skirts. You turned it over and the skirt fell back: a brown doll, big thick lips, black woolly curls . . .

A double-cunt doll. Per-fect. Two sets of legs sewn together, joined up by a skirt that fell back from the waist, revealing all. He'd hang it in a tree where Niamh would find it.

The half-smile on his face widened; his eyes shone.

❧ *Chapter 39* ❧

'*L*etter from Patrick,' Ned said. He sat at the table drinking tea and thumbing through the sparse bundle of post. It came later and later, mid-afternoon was about normal, not that it mattered, it was nearly all bills and Christmas cards that had missed Christmas.

Ned scanned the letter, pushed it back into its envelope, then tossed it on to the table. 'Change of plan, he's not coming back, he'll stay on in Cork for the time he's got left, see a bit more of the girls.'

Hannie was cleaning the dining-room silver at the other end of the table. She didn't speak or make a move to pick up the letter.

Ned was relieved, it was a bread-and-butter letter, but written only to him, a cursory glance would reveal Patrick's quietly ostentatious omission. He hadn't had the grace nor the manners to write her name on the envelope either, but that might pass more easily as forgetfulness.

Ned let his mind go back to Christmas Eve, to Joss's account of Patrick's discussion of Hannie's opportunism. The anger that had flared in him then stiffened now into something more implacable. Patrick had a right to his opinions but there the matter ended. He had no right to such casual speculation on his cousin's marriage, still less to this studied incivility towards a woman who had been a graceful and attentive hostess, however he might judge her to himself.

He glanced across at Hannie. What had she said last night about small meannesses and failures, how they were the deepest shame? Patrick had always been weak and selfish, Ned realised, he had never had much thought for anyone but himself. But he was easy and charming with the manners and assumptions born of privilege, and he was unreflective, it was unlikely that he'd ever spent much time with shame. When the old woman died Patrick would inherit and he'd sell Coolbawn, his sisters' home, without as much as a backward glance, Ned was sure of that now. They might beg and entreat, it would make no difference to Patrick.

Hannie was remote today, Ned thought, but that wasn't unexpected. She had talked last night in spite of herself, had described a past that was painful and private, it was hardly surprising that she should want to re-establish distance now. Yet it was hurtful, however he might rationalise and explain it to himself. Everything was so easy when she spoke openly and truthfully, he felt he could listen for ever, accept anything she told him, his feeling for her only deepening as she revealed herself.

In your dreams, as Joss would say.

He didn't realise yet how passionately she was fighting off self-revelation, that she didn't want to understand herself, still less to articulate that understanding, that the more he knew of her the more she felt herself violated and vulnerable. She was fighting him off and losing ground, after each exposure he was left more tender and accepting while for her it was the opposite: as though his acceptance of her was something malign, something almost akin to rape.

And she felt herself less and less able to resist these exposures. She was alone here, a curiosity, an outsider and a misfit. Andrew and Nora's visit had shifted things, it had revealed them to themselves and to each other. In the end even Danno, the obvious misfit, was further from her life-experience than Ned was. Who could understand her better than Ned if she let him?

Now Hannie went on quietly polishing his grandmother's silver coffee pot in the firelight, her face calm, her hands steady, none of her inner conflict visible. Patrick hadn't put her name on the envelope and she was certain that if she picked up the letter she wouldn't find it written in there either. And only a few years past this same Patrick would have eaten out of the hand she wouldn't have bothered to extend to him. Now his exclusion of her was deliberate and insulting. She was no one, an aberration, an adventuress.

Had she ever pretended otherwise or denied it?

She saw now that he'd despised her from the start but she'd missed his contempt and flirted with him. More fool her. The calm assumption of superiority from this soft, useless man infuriated her but also fortified her resolve and gave her the strength to overcome the aftermath of Paulo's visitation. She placed the coffee pot on a silver salver with a clutter of shining cruets, cutlery and napkin rings, and stood to return the pieces to the dining room where they belonged.

'I think we should have a party,' she said decisively. 'Tomorrow night – for the young people, for the New Year.'

They made a punch. She said it was essential, you mixed up all the alcohol and everyone got roaring drunk before the booze ran out. Ned gave her cooking sherry and supermarket own-brand whiskey.

'No sense wasting decent stuff if you're just going to throw it all in together.'

Hannie added brandy and gin from the sideboard in the dining room. Niamh and Joss were the tasters. Ciaran hadn't appeared.

'He's got a hangover,' Niamh said, 'he'll be over later.'

The punch, they agreed, would blow your head off.

'What about the taste?'

Joss sniggered. Niamh put down her glass.

'What's taste got to do with it?' she asked. 'One swig and no one'll care.'

Hannie was in the kitchen, in the dining room, on the phone inviting people. She organised them all without appearing much interested herself so they found themselves enthused and wanting to join in and help. It was all much more casual than the pre-Christmas entertaining, much more slapdash and fun. Even Ned was enjoying it, though he pretended otherwise.

'Come and eat our food and drink our booze and reduce our house to chaos for weeks to come,' he complained. 'We don't have to do this, we don't owe anyone, we had them all last week or the week before. I can't understand you, Hannie, when other people invite us you say you'd rather talk to the sheep.'

Niamh and Joss were right about the punch. It was a liberator, reducing everyone to the same level of more-or-less-drunkenness after the second glass. People fell on each other's necks, they shouted and roared and guffawed, the noise rose and rose. Hannie fed them with hot food that seemed to Ned to come out of the air, Niamh and Joss were everywhere filling glasses, even Ciaran seemed to get a kick out of playing barman. Later they rolled back the carpet and Ciaran and Joss set up in a corner with Niamh's CD player and did a two-handed DJ act that Ned simply closed his ears to. At midnight everything stopped and they all joined hands and had a go at 'Auld Lang Syne'.

More drink, and the dancing began again. Arms and legs and arses were waggled with grotesque confidence; a historian of country houses fell over someone's shoes and sat happily where he'd fallen talking to no one in particular about nothing remotely comprehensible; a lanky young man in glasses finally persuaded Niamh on to the floor but was sick over her feet a few minutes after they'd started; Marjorie overbalanced doing the twist and fell on her back with her legs in the air until James hauled her upright again, telling her firmly that more drink was what she needed.

Hours later the crowd thinned. Towards morning most people finally wandered off in the general direction of home.

Ned found Niamh curled up on a sofa in his study, passed out or asleep, her dark hair fallen loosely across her face. He fetched a blanket and spread it carefully over her and she moaned and stirred in her sleep but didn't wake. He stood over her and she stirred again and one slim strong wrist poked itself out from under the folds and moved across the blanket as though looking for something. Finding nothing, it left off searching and settled itself, the fingers curling gently in towards the palm. He went out, pulling the door softly to behind him, then moved quietly through the rooms, picking up glasses and paper cups and emptying the overflowing ashtrays. He could hear laughter and voices from the kitchen where Hannie was serving breakfast to the survivors. He felt peaceful and oddly content.

He drew back the curtains. A chill breeze blew through the dropped sashes of the long windows; the air flowed in, so clean and sharp he could almost see it, like coloured ink dropped into clear water. He felt tired and not tired. He had been drunk, but he didn't feel it now, perhaps it had worn off. He wondered about his life, what was happening to it, what he was doing, but somehow he couldn't seem to mind.

He stood at the window, looking out at a darkness he knew would be blue-going-into-grey if he turned off the lights. He turned them off. The darkness paled and shapes and half-tones began floating up towards him like stones emerging from water. Their edges took shape and definition and he saw that it was almost day. As he watched a figure appeared and moved swiftly up the drive, a rucksack looped over one shoulder. Ned stiffened and focused. He thought it was Joss, but it was too tall and the wrong gait. Ciaran. Ciaran was leaving, with Niamh asleep on the sofa in the room beyond. He thought about wakening her, then changed his mind. He'd let things take their course, he decided, she might as well get some sleep while she could.

Instead he went through to the kitchen and took Hannie into the hall to tell her. She stiffened when she heard, her head went up like a deer scenting man on the wind and her eyes scanned the faces in the kitchen through the opened door. Ned's eyes followed hers.

Joss was there, at the far end of the room, sitting sideways on the window seat, his face turned to the thinning darkness. As they watched him he turned his head and looked straight at his mother, his eyes – light and clear and unreadable – meeting hers down the length of the room. Ned realised with a shock that Joss wasn't wearing his dark glasses. With a second shock he realised that Joss knew all about Ciaran, had probably conspired in his departure. He glanced at Hannie and he saw that she was seeing the same.

❧ *Chapter 40* ❧

*J*oss gone, Patrick gone, Ciaran gone. Only the two of them left in the house, and Niamh beyond in the cottage.

Hannie sat at the kitchen table, a glass by her hand, watching a wren working its way along under the overhang of the wall beyond the window. It was like a mouse. Scurry, then stillness. Another quick flick of motion. Stillness. All its movements were neat and brown.

The place was coming down with wrens, even in winter. They lived in the stone walls and the hedges and under the edges of the river banks. They made loops of flight, their small bodies brief against the silver of the river, their small threading movements settling in the corner of the eye.

Joss was right about the brown-ness here. Brown-ness, drabness. All but invisible unless you looked.

Nonsense, Ned said. Ned loved the little mobile tits, the salmon breast-plates of the bullfinches. He thought the goldfinches as exotic as any flame-bright bird of the tropics.

She had begun to learn the names from him. After a while the single stripe of red on the face of a goldfinch jumped out at her, too. She was adjusting. She didn't know if she liked this adjustment, if it boded good or ill for her survival. She didn't want to survive by becoming like them.

Already her life was being sopped up in this place. In the brief daylight hours she sat here watching the wrens, she mooched round the edges of the farm, staring at the black-faced sheep on the rough pasture. Sometimes when she startled them they'd stand and piss. One would piss, then the next and the next, till the whole field was pissing, hard streams of urine drilling into the boggy ground and she, standing watching them. This was her life now. Day followed day. She'd started to drink. Some days she drank all day, some days she didn't touch it. Ned watched but didn't say anything; sometimes she wondered what it would take to make him speak. He withdrew himself, spending the evenings in his study, sorting old yellowing bundles of letters and notes, filing fading photographs. He'd told Mrs Coady not to clean in there, he said he was working on another book, but Hannie never heard his typewriter.

She'd sold the ebony fan in Cork – discreetly, at less than its value, but still not giving it away. A dealer called Slattery. She hadn't used her own name, she didn't have to stipulate no local sales. He looked her in the eye and said the container was full now and would be going straight across the water, the prices were better in the British sales rooms. Then he wished her good day and hoped they would see her again.

Hannie hoped not, but without much confidence. Still, it meant she had money put by against the next emergency, bank notes under the corner of the carpet in her bedroom where she could get at them in a hurry. She had shelved the goose-plan, the rewards were too far away. Would she even be here next Christmas? She didn't know.

Mrs Coady came if Hannie phoned for her, but mostly she didn't. Sometimes Hannie cleaned the house herself, or she just left it, as the mood took her. Sometimes she cooked, sometimes she didn't. Some days she went to Niamh's, talked at her, came back. She hadn't let time swim over her like this since adolescence. Hot nights in Java, her whole being dissolved in an emptiness of waiting. The lizard on the wall, the dredging scent of flowers in the night, the low melodious talk from the servants' quarters. While there were still servants to talk. Her mother had gone this way – floated off down the dark river – alcohol and forgetfulness. There were worse ways, the daughter thought now.

No one had told Hannie that the real winter followed on

behind the solstice, no one had explained the deep dead winter after Christmas, when the light hardly grew and the cold and the long darkness closed like a shroud on the land and only the river shone. She hadn't known the world could be this secret hidden place from out of another age, an older, wilder age, separate from any life or place she knew.

She woke and rose in darkness, began to know the time from its texture and density; if it was night-darkness and she could slip back into sleep, or morning-darkness and she should brace herself, throw back the covers, encounter this freezing parody of day.

All her life she had assumed light, visited by darkness; now she began to see darkness as the reality, the permanent state. She began to understand light as an aberration on the face of the dark, like the slick of shiny light that floated the blackness in the water-butt by the back door. And it made sense to her, it was how life was, it was how she was herself: darkness, visited sometimes by light that lay on its surface but never penetrated to the depths beneath.

Yet the slick was vivid enough when it happened. Sometimes outside, moving stock with Ned on a morning rimed with frost, her spirits would lift and she'd wonder at her own thoughts. Then she could close her eyes and revisit the High-lands of Kenya, the land burning clear of the frost, the plumed breath of the cattle. She would open them and see low mounded mountains, slate-blue, a dusting of snow in the wrinkles and folds of their upper slopes, and fieldfares, like long greenish thrushes, hopping and grubbing for food on the pasture.

But the slick of light never lasted long. A bright morning would give way to endless sodden ones, and even Ned would grow dispirited and downcast. For Hannie this return to the low dark days was like being suddenly re-imprisoned after tasting release. It left her hopeless and without defences, prey to despair and strange imaginings.

Sometimes she saw Joss, a tall wraith by the long windows

watching the light leave, the four o'clock darkness return. Sometimes he would turn to her and she'd see the panic in his uncovered eyes and would better understand her own despair. Joss was gone now, gone even further North to a colder, darker place, hating her because he'd come to her and begged to be let stay and she'd refused him.

'You have to go to school, Joss, you know that. It'll get easier, you'll get used to it, you'll see.'

He'd looked at her, both of them knowing the lie, and then later he'd had his revenge, insisting on the bus, not letting her drive him though she'd had the car serviced in readiness. They had parted painfully in mutual anger.

So it was hard for them all, these slow weeks of January. For Niamh suffering in the cottage; for Hannie, lonely and downhearted and drinking because she could think of no other way through; for Ned, watching the re-appearance of the difficult, resentful woman who was here so frequently now that he often forgot the other had ever been.

~ *Chapter 41* ~

'People make such a fuss about things,' Hannie said. 'And mostly they don't really matter.'

Niamh kept her head down, hoping desperately that Hannie would shut up or go away and not be going over the whole thing yet again. A fuss was exactly what she wasn't making, a huge effort was what she was making and no one, she hoped, would ever know how huge. But she wished she'd had the sense to keep her mouth shut right from the start and her confidences to herself. She should have known better than to talk to Hannie, especially now, when she was drinking all the time.

Hannie, of course, thought it only natural that Ciaran should have been screwing somebody else when he wasn't actually here screwing her. What had Niamh imagined he'd been doing? Hitching all the way to Belfast just to say hello to his parents? Only one thing had surprised her. That Niamh hadn't guessed, that she'd had to discover the truth from Joss after Ciaran had packed his bags and gone.

'It's stupid to trust a man like Ciaran, Niamh, plain stupid. Trust isn't some gift that you give to a man to keep safe in a special place and feel grateful for. It's an indulgence – a self-indulgence – something you may or may not choose to go in for. And if you do, it's your own look-out, there's no point feeling betrayed and humiliated, you've no one to blame but yourself.' Hannie drained off her glass and plonked it down on the table.

Niamh stared at Hannie. She saw a woman in late middle age with dirty clothes and wild hair, drinking a glass of neat whiskey from a bottle she'd set on the table at half past two in the afternoon.

Why did she go on taking this, she asked herself? This woman was standing here lecturing her as though she'd made some sort of success of her life. And she, Niamh, was letting her.

'You're distorting things, Hannie.' Niamh's voice shook with the effort at control she was making. 'It's not about choice or self-indulgence, it's about self-respect. And Aids, a minor fucking detail you seem to have forgotten, probably because it's long since your time . . .'

Hannie's face broke into a grin. 'Go ahead, Niamh, that's the spirit, stand up for yourself, fight your corner.'

Niamh snapped. 'Don't patronise me,' she screamed. 'Don't patronise me, Hannie, and don't ever tell me again that it's all my fault. I've had enough of you, d'you hear? Enough. Take your sour life and your sour views and fuck off out of my house and don't come back.'

Hannie fucked off. Niamh picked up the empty glass and hurled it after her at the closing door. Then she lay across the table in a storm of weeping.

'What did you do to Niamh?' Ned stood in the kitchen door-way, angry and challenging.

'Niamh? Nothing.' Hannie looked up from cleaning sprouts at the sink. 'Why, what did she say I did?'

'She's only a girl, Hannie, she was in love with him, she needs help not bullying and being told she brought it all on herself.'

'Don't be so sentimental.' Hannie went on stripping the damaged leaves. 'If she's not told she'll drown in self-pity. And you're wrong, she wasn't in love with him, only with sex, she knows that herself.'

Ned strode across the kitchen, lifted the uncapped bottle from the draining board and shoved it close to her face.

'You're drunk, Hannie, you've been drinking for days, you

should be ashamed, it's half past four in the afternoon and you're drunk.' He put down the bottle. 'But you're not, are you, you're never ashamed, you're incapable of decency or shame. Not in love with him? Hannie, the poor girl's sitting there all by herself, breaking her heart.'

'So you just said.'

'You should be ashamed, bullying the girl.'

'You said that too. I'm drunk, I'm a bully, I should be ashamed.' Her voice was indifferent. She threw the last of the cleaned sprouts into the saucepan beside her on the drainer. She made a net of her hands in the basin of water, scooped up the discarded leaves and dumped them into the compost bucket. She dried her hands. 'All true, Ned,' she said, 'and just what are you going to do about it?'

He didn't answer. She picked up the bottle and poured until the tumbler beside her was half full. Her hand was completely steady. She lifted it to her mouth.

'You're drinking too much.'

'That's my business.'

'It's my money you're drinking.'

'Ours. Marriage vows, Ned, what's yours is mine, what's mine is yours, remember? Only I haven't got anything, have I? Except Joss. But you don't mind that, do you, you said so – remember?'

Ned looked at her. Rage beat in his white, closed face. He struggled briefly for control then abandoned the effort and brought his face near to hers. 'You're no better than Joss.' He spat out the words and searched around for more hurtful ones. 'And Niamh's right, it's not Joss's fault. With you as a mother, he's never had a chance.'

Hannie's arm jerked back and she threw the contents of her glass at him. Then she set it down on the table and left the room.

Ned stood, pale streams of whiskey running down his face.

* * *

There was nowhere to go to, nothing to do but drink more, so she did. Then she went to see Danno.

Danno almost didn't let her in, he had determined not to, but she stood there on the doorstep asking him to forgive her for the last time. He looked at the ground, stony-faced, not trusting her, and she told him she needed to talk to him, she had no other friend.

He asked her why she didn't talk to Ned.

She shrugged and grinned, the grin half-hearted, failing to conceal her desperation. 'He's my husband. Talking to husbands is a bad idea.'

When she passed out, Danno lifted her carefully on to the cot where he slept and covered her with blankets. Then he sat in a chair for a while, waiting for Ned to come and get her. Then he gave up waiting, put on his coat and walked over to the house.

He didn't knock at the door but went around the outside, careful and quiet, silencing Pip's yelps and old Bess's short burst of barking with a few low words. Ned was in his study, all the lights burning, a rabble of photos spread over the surface of his desk, an old box-file lying open beside them. Danno watched him from the darkness, saw him lift a photo, turn it over and back, stare at it for what seemed a long time and then lay it down. With photo after photo he did this. After a while Danno leaned forward and rapped gently on the glass. Ned started, peered at the black window, left his desk, undid the window latch and hauled up the sash.

'She's over in the house. You'll want to come and get her.'

Ned looked at him, his gaze bleak, but didn't speak. Danno remembered the last time he'd come calling on Ned in the night and he wondered if Ned was remembering too. By the smell of him Hannie wasn't the only one who'd been hitting the bottle. Ned reached up his hands and slowly and deliberately pulled down the sash, shutting Danno out behind the wall of glass. The two men stood for a moment, one on each side, eyes locked together, then Danno turned and disappeared into the night.

In the morning Danno hauled his stiff limbs out of the chair, stretched, shaved and made tea. He went and checked on Hannie, still deep asleep in her huddle of blankets. He stood over her and at once felt so complicated at this undefended insight into her alone-ness that he turned away to give them both some privacy. He wanted to take her tea, even to look after her a little, but he was too uneasy, too unbalanced by the force of his own unexpected emotions. He whistled the dogs to him and went off into the woods with the gun instead.

That's my story, Danno, she'd said last night, *my side of things. What's yours, I wonder? Why do you let me in here, why do you go on putting up with me?*

Because you're lonely?

But you were always lonely.

Because you know now that you're lonely?

Did I tempt you out of your hole, Danno? Did you creep out and sniff at the air and never notice when the door slammed shut behind you?

Once out you can't ever go back, Danno. Never ever ever. Do you know that? Somehow I don't think you do.

He needed to tramp around in the air and settle himself.

Hannie woke, not knowing where she was, and lay in the little room that she'd never seen before, working out how she might have got there. When she had it figured and she thought her head could bear movement, she crawled from her nest of blankets and went in search of last night's bottle. It was empty. She went through the presses looking for drink, but there was none. She struggled with matches and gas and got the kettle on.

She guessed Danno was hiding out in the woods, upset by her presence, unwilling to come back till she'd gone. She nearly opened the cages on all of his hawks just to teach him, but it was too much effort.

Vaguely she wondered what she might have said or done to scare Danno into flight. Perhaps she'd offered to seduce him? Perhaps she *had* seduced him. The thought made her laugh, but the laugh hurt her head so she stopped. She might get drunk again – there was nothing else to do – she might push Ned right to the edge, find out his limit, then push again till he plunged to the rocks below.

She made a face. It seemed she was capable only of melodrama these days. And tormenting Ned. If she was going to be drunk she needed more drink and there was none to be got around here. She abandoned the kettle, washed her face in cold tap water, drank two glasses down, headed back to the house.

~ *Chapter 42* ~

When a knock came to Niamh's door now it was always Ned. Hannie came, but she never knocked, she just opened the door and walked straight in. Niamh accepted her, she didn't refer again to the words they'd had and neither did Hannie. To Hannie, rows were normal, it didn't occur to her that Niamh might be lastingly offended. Besides, she'd been drunk.

Ned hardly ever sat down, he never visited after dark, and he never stayed for long. Mostly he would fix something – the washer on the tap, a stuck window, a loose catch. He seemed only to want to reassure himself, exchange a few words, and be gone.

Sometimes he let her persuade him into a cup of tea. Then he'd stand awkwardly, he'd speak of a heifer in calf, of the prices that day at the mart, of the dealer who'd come to the yard and tried to buy from him for less. He was reading up about lavender, he told her: working out could he make it a selling crop in this climate, did it make economic sense to give it a go? Sometimes he asked her about her work, but she always put him off and after a while he knew to leave her alone. She was fond of him, but there was no ease between them since Ciaran's departure. She learned (though how she didn't know because he never spoke of Hannie) that there were problems above in the house.

One day she went with him into Youghal and he waited with the car while she bought rolls of wall lining-paper, paste, wax crayons, felt-tip pens.

She came home and pinned lining-paper from ceiling to

floor of her little room, sheet butting on to sheet so all the walls were covered. She'd meant to draw but instead she began gluing things on to the paper – leaf skeletons, bits of twig and feather, wings from the dead moths and butterflies she'd collected. Gradually she stopped gluing and began to make marks beside the stuck-on things. Sometimes she wrote random words. She painted around the words and marks – washes in ochres and watery ink-blues and ox-blood reds, the thinness of the washes always contradicting the dense nature of the colours, so it seemed to her that she was always in the process of frustrating them, forbidding their return to what they wanted. She would work in a sort of daze, a waking trance, and then she'd stand for hours and look at what she'd done. Often it looked meaningless and unformed, even to herself.

But sometimes when she came into the room in the mornings she could glimpse, for a moment, what she was making. There was a curious rhythm to these vague islanded shapes, pinned down as they were with lines and words or floating off on pale lakes of colour. She knew this work wasn't an end in itself, but she knew it was leading her somewhere that she ought to go. At such moments her heart would lift into her mouth and the blood would beat in her.

Niamh's brief elation of vision never lasted for long. It faded and she'd work on in weary indifference, knowing only that it was better than just sitting, better than thinking the same thoughts over and over and over. Sometimes her whole effort was only for the vanished Ciaran, to show him what she was, to make him regret his loss. But sometimes she was happy and the work was an end in itself. Whole days passed with the misery of Ciaran numbed. She began to call the little room her studio.

❦ *Chapter 43* ❦

*I*t was Danno who found the stuffed legs, Joss's parting gift to Niamh, as he made his way to a pollarded willow that grew between her cottage and the river. The day was damp with no lift to it, Danno was snuffling and hacking with a feverish cold and for once he'd rather have hugged the fire than gone tramping about in the drizzle. But there was no help for it, he hadn't enough sally rods stored for next year and new ones had to be cut while the sap was still down. At the moment spring might seem like something from another age, another country, but appearance belied reality, and already there were secret quiverings in this dead landscape.

He stopped on the path to wait for a coughing fit to pass over. When he finished coughing he opened his eyes and they fell on what looked like a short black spike in a clump of faded grass. He moved forward and stirred the dark spike with his boot. A woman's high-heeled court shoe was revealed. He picked it up: it was sodden, but hardly worn. Puzzled, he lifted his head and stared about him. A rusty flare of colour showed through the rain-darkened net of the trees. He took off his glasses, wiped them clean of water, put them back on again. An irrational dread in his guts, he followed the rusty flare.

When he saw what the colour was, he stopped dead in his tracks, the blood pounding his head, a mist of cold sweat on his skin. It wasn't that he was fooled by it, it wasn't that he thought it was a real body hanging from its ankles in the birch tree, its scarlet knickers torn, its rust-red skirt fallen back at the waist and trailing nearly to the ground. But he knew with an instinctive certainty that its maker would have liked it to have been a real body, and one that had been treated just like this.

He stood where he was, taking it in, waiting for the shock to pass. The first wave receded. He moved forward, put out his hand and carefully lifted the skirt. He started back for the second time at what he saw.

The basic idea he recognised at once. It was a life-sized parody of a rag-doll – not an ordinary rag-doll but one of those double dolls that his sisters had owned, the like of which he hadn't seen for years. Yet it wasn't quite as their dolls had been, it wasn't two torsos sewn together and joined by a skirt, it was two sets of legs sewn together and joined by a skirt, the one set in pale tights, the other in black. And the pale legs that hung by the ankles wore red knickers, ripped and gaping at the crotch, while the black legs concealed beneath the hanging skirt had a stained and sodden sanitary towel pinned where its genitals would be. The long rust skirt he'd seen light years before on Niamh.

Danno took a knife from his pocket and cut the thing down. He knew it was meant for Niamh and he knew it was Joss who had made it. For a brief moment he'd thought of Ciaran, but he'd put that idea aside. Whatever the drive that had led to the making of this thing, that drive was in Joss not in Ciaran.

He left the legs where they were, a heap in the sodden grass, and began to retrace his steps. A bramble snagged his coat, he bent and freed himself and noticed a blue woollen glove hooked by its thumb to a thorn. Slowly he worked his way back to the path, his eyes on the vegetation. Here a butterfly hair-clip lay in the fork of a birch branch. Further on a string of beads hung from a twig in the stillness.

Danno stood leaning against an ash trunk holding his gathered 'clues' in trembling hands. He was deeply shaken and disturbed. Passionately he wanted to conceal and destroy what he'd found, to tell no one, to remove its complex shamefulness

248

and restore the simplicity of the world. Yet he knew that he mustn't allow himself to do this. It was aimed at Niamh, so Niamh must be protected.

But how to do it? If he told Hannie she'd rush to defend Joss, then belittle the incident and try to bully him into silence as she'd done the last time. And he'd let himself be silenced. Well, he'd been right, all along he'd been right, there was something wrong and horrible brewing in Joss's mind.

Perhaps he had to try to talk to Hannie? If he fought his way through her ridicule, stuck to his guns, he might get her to accept it in the end. If she knew she could at least try and arrest it, whatever it was. If she didn't, she could do nothing.

He could tell Ned, Ned thought the world of Niamh, he wouldn't hesitate if he thought she needed looking after or protecting. Danno saw Ned vividly in his mind's eye, his imperious closed face, his big knotted hands raised to the sash as he'd dragged it down and slammed it against the sill.

No, no point. Ned wouldn't believe him, Ned would think this some sort of obscure revenge.

Not if he saw what Danno had seen.

He had passed Ned checking the heifers in the Chestnut Field behind the house. He could go and find him now, bring him here, he would *have* to believe, *have* to act. And after that it would be up to Ned to tell Hannie: she was Ned's problem, not his, it was time he put his hands in the mud and got them dirty.

Danno shifted himself from the tree and moved off. It didn't once occur to him to go to Niamh and tell her himself directly. If it had, he couldn't have found the words. The ugly intention behind the thing he tried to speak of would have silenced him.

✎ Chapter 44 ✎

She's like a wasp, Mrs Coady thought, you could do nothing right. What was it that was eating her, was it Joss, was it him, was it the Change? Or was she just spoiled – spoiled and bored.

There'd been a time there before Christmas, with the boy home and the cousin staying, when it looked as though things might be working out. She'd done the house, entertained his friends as he wanted her to, made an effort over his lecture, put on a bit of style. She'd worn that beautiful suit she had – the one she said she'd bought to go to Germany with the husband that died – and she'd had her hair cut and coloured a silvery blonde. He was pleased as punch – why wouldn't he be? – at last she seemed to be getting the hang of things and finding her way around.

Then bang, something happened and it changed again. What was it, was it Patrick leaving, was it the boy going back to school, was she just fed up with trying to do things his way instead of hers? Perhaps it was none of these things, perhaps it was January. Whatever it was, they had started to fight. They fought about Niamh, they fought about Joss, they fought about Pip, there wasn't anything they didn't fight about. And then there was something the boy had done that was making everything worse.

He'd gone back into his journeys then: old letters and maps mixed in with the books and articles on lavender-growing he was collecting, old black-and-white photos spread over the study floor. Dark, wild-looking faces looked straight out from them, stared out. Ragged, half-naked men held tight to their spears and guns. Comrades, that's what he called them; warriors and bearers and trackers and guides. Men he took with him, men who'd trusted him with their lives. As he'd trusted them with his, he said, and they never let him down.

I'd believe that, Mrs Coady thought, he's not a man you'd let down lightly. But he always put their trust in him in first.

He's a *mé feiner* – himself alone – it's not that he's selfish exactly, he just doesn't think any further than himself. His life, his needs, his responsibilities. Go along with him, he'll look after you, do right by you, he wouldn't ever allow himself to let you down.

But always on his terms, never on yours, it wouldn't even occur to him that you might have terms of your own, or that they mightn't be the same as his. A decent man, decent through and through, but one who only saw out of his own eyes.

His hip was bothering him, sometimes when he got up too fast you could see the stab it had given him passing across his face. Intimations of mortality, Mrs Coady, he said. So that's what all the photos and the letters were about: he could see through to the end so he wanted to look back on his life, to know what it had been and what he'd done. But it wasn't helping her, him being this way, watching her and saying nothing, retreating more and more into his study, into himself.

Maybe he doesn't want to help her, maybe he's had enough of her already and he's putting in the time till she gives up and goes away. God knows there's many wouldn't blame him, she's not exactly rewarding, not easy, nor good, nor straight, and she isn't what you'd ever expect a wife of his would be. He knows that, he knows that his friends don't like her, whatever they tell him, however they are to her face when they come through the door.

No, there's not many would blame him. And they'll blame him less now she's drinking and letting things go to hell.

'You'll need to stop that,' I said to her, 'to catch yourself on, that's not a road can be walked lightly.'

She looked at me. 'You're right, Mrs Coady,' she said. 'Absolutely right, but somehow I don't give a damn.'

'You've the boy to think of,' I said. She clapped her hands to her ears like a child to keep the words.

Tom was on at me again to give up going there. She won't last, he said, can't you go back when things are as they were? I said nothing. He thought it was on account of the regard I'd have for Mr Renvyle, but it wasn't that.

I'm fond of her. And I don't know why.

❧ *Chapter 45* ❧

*I*t had been hard for Ned, having Danno come to him and insist on his attention. He had listened with scepticism and ill-concealed irritation, but Danno had insisted and gone on insisting, so in the end Ned had followed him to the stand of trees, intending that that would be the end of it. Then he'd looked at the heap of stuffed tights and skirts in the faded grass and he'd forgotten his resentment and his scepticism. He would never have believed that the crudely-made dummy of Danno's description could be so quietly malevolent in its reality.

He had been instantly certain that it was Joss's handiwork, aimed at Niamh, on that he and Danno had been in complete agreement, and even Hannie hadn't argued the point when he'd got rid of Danno and shown her the thing in the kitchen later on that evening. But she'd belittled his shocked concern and she'd poured cold water on his suggestion of a psychiatrist. There was nothing to make such a fuss about, this was just a normal manifestation of an adolescent mind, she'd said. And besides, had he any idea how much such treatment would cost?

Ned had looked at her doubtfully but he hadn't really argued. He'd said Niamh must be told, and she had agreed, she'd said she would do it herself if Ned wanted her to, but he had declined the offer. There was no hurry, Joss was away till half-term, he didn't want her rushing round there when Niamh was still moping after Ciaran, he wanted to tell her gently himself when she was stronger.

Ned said nothing to Niamh straight away, he bided his time

till he judged her recovered enough, then he went to her cottage one afternoon and told her first of the legs and then of his conviction that it was Joss who had made them. He was ashamed of what he was telling her and deeply upset at her anticipated reaction, so it was difficult and embarrassing for them both. Long before he'd finished his story Niamh was trying to fast-forward it, to belittle the legs, and rescue him from his distress.

'It's probably just a phase,' she said calmly. 'Adolescents are obsessed by sex, and adolescent boys are fascinated by menstruation.'

She listened to herself speak and she knew she was being this cool and together because of Ciaran. It was ridiculous, she told herself, he couldn't hear what she was saying, he was miles away with someone else and good riddance. But it made no difference. She would call a spade a spade, she would not make a fuss, no one would ever have the right to laugh at her or to call her naïve again.

'I think maybe I should see it for myself,' she said.

Ned protested, but she was the injured party behaving well so he had to give in and do as she asked. He led the way to one of the sheds and went in ahead of her. She stood in the doorway, smelling its damp earthy smell and letting her eyes adjust while Ned fumbled around in the cluttered darkness. What he pulled out from behind the sacks of stored feed was more like a bundle of old rags than the lurid artefact of his description. The wet newspaper had collapsed into random lumps, the tights were stretched and misshapen, the skirt was sodden and unrecognisable although it had once been hers. The ripped knickers remained but some delicacy in Ned had made him remove the sanitary towel after Danno's departure.

He watched Niamh as she knelt beside it. Now, when he saw what she was seeing, he almost wondered what there was to be so distressed about. She turned the sodden skirt so it fell back, exposing the dark tights, then she turned it again so the pale legs were displayed. She was taking the whole thing very calmly, Ned thought, she was quite matter-of-fact in the way she was looking at it now, and she hadn't seemed so much frightened as embarrassed when he'd told her. Maybe Hannie was right after all, maybe it wasn't so unnatural, maybe women knew something men didn't know, or at least not men like himself and Danno. He was finding it hard not to feel a bit of a fool.

'There'd have been two different fabrics,' Niamh said slowly. 'On the original ones, that is. Two skirts. This one, and then another one backing it, so when you turned it over there were different personalities.' She looked up at him as she spoke. She was so relieved it wasn't worse she'd almost laughed from sheer release of tension.

'The skirt for the black one would've been bright, a loud strong pattern, and rick-rack braid and woolly hair and brass rings in the ears. Black Mama style – not PC – maybe that's why you never see them any more. The white one would've been dressed in a flowery print. And puffed sleeves with lace and yellow hair in bunches. Not children really. Young women with no sexual parts . . .' Her voice trailed away.

And now, sexual parts but no faces, she was thinking. Perhaps she'd go home and make dummies, better dummies than Joss had made, highlighting not racism but misogyny. She got up from the floor and turned to Ned, a distant expression on her face. She seemed almost surprised to see him, as though she'd forgotten what they were doing and needed to be reminded.

~ *Chapter 46* ~

When the rain began Hannie didn't notice, it was only the usual fine damp drizzle, silent and seeping, as though the air wept; there'd been no rains as she knew them, no storms or monsoon downpours. Yet the ditches filled and the streams swelled, the water lay under the fading light in sheets, it gleamed on the roads and moved in dark mass in the great pewter river. She heard it everywhere: the ditch-water sound and the river-water sound and the sound of puddle-water splashing.

Hannie knew about water and the systems for its storage and release; there had always been too much of it or too little in her life, always dams, irrigation ditches, flood drainage systems. Now she picked up a spade and did what she knew how to do without even thinking. She walked around looking for places to drain, she made run-offs and channels, liking the thick mud under her boots, the gurgle of water, the ditches choked with rotting woodbine and the skeletons of umbellifers and old man's beard. She cleared and dug and made new water-courses, found an occupation, forgot about the bottle.

She worked and the water responded, it found her trenches and flowed down her run-offs and gurgled in her channels. But it was hopeless, all she could do was direct it; the ground was like a great sponge, filled and sodden, you stepped on green grass and it pooled under your feet. Water filled every pock and hollow, it lay over the meadows and low-lying fields in smooth thin sheets. Higher up, it ran off the land and into the streams and the streams ran into the river which rushed and swelled, the current swirling and bucking, until it seemed incredible that it could keep its banks.

When the high winds came they brought trees crashing down on to power lines and phone lines, cutting supplies, blocking the small roads, creating chaos. The real rain followed a day later, not drizzle any more but great splashings and sheets, as though the sluices had opened in the sky.

'The rivers are out.' Mrs Coady stood in the kitchen in her waterproofs and dripped. 'Flynn's is flooded and Casey's yard is full of water and the stream behind Costigan's has taken most of the road. Matt Murphy has his stores moved to the back fields and he's feeding them while he has feed left to give them, but if it goes on like this he'll not reach them, hay or no hay.'

Tom had brought her as far as the stream which was over the road, she said, then she'd taken to her feet and paddled through. 'It isn't deep yet, you might make it in a car, and a tractor would get through no bother at all. It's the little small rivers are blocking the roads. They're coming down fast and furious and full up with all kinds of rubbish that's filling the culverts and putting them out from their courses.'

Ned tried to make her take off her wet things but Mrs Coady would have none of it. She'd come to work, she said, not to sit around, and the sooner they had sandbags filled the better, it wasn't unknown for this house to flood. She pulled out letters from an inside pocket and thrust them at Hannie. She'd met the postman, she said, he'd given them to her, she'd nearly forgotten.

Two bills and a white envelope with a Northern postmark, but it wasn't Joss's writing. Hannie turned it over, saw the school crest on the flap. Ned was pouring tea for Mrs Coady from the big brown pot, asking about this one and that one; who had lost stock, who needed help. They were enjoying themselves, the sudden drama, and more being asked of them than was usually required. She recognised it from Africa: a landslide or a flash flood brought the same excitement. She opened the envelope.

'We'll have to sandbag the house and the outbuildings,' Ned was saying, 'keep the drains and culverts cleared, the stock are all right for the time being. It could be a lot worse – who'd be Lambert, with a flooded polytunnel full of Christmas lambs? Thank God we resisted that temptation.'

Hannie read the letter. There'd been a problem with Joss, the headmaster wanted to talk to her, probably he'd need to see them both. He'd tried to ring but seemed to be having difficulty getting through; he asked her to phone him as soon as she could.

She finished reading and stuffed the letter into her pocket. Mrs Coady was listing the neighbours, naming for Ned the houses likely to flood. Hannie picked up the phone. 'Line's dead,' she said, replacing the receiver. 'What about Danno? Is that a house that floods?'

'He's very close to the river but he's high. His feet might get wet, but that's all, it'll take more than this to wash him from his nest.'

She took the waterproof trousers Ned handed her. She'd have to find a phone that worked, find out what Joss had done, she might have to go North. If it wasn't too bad she'd tell Ned, he might just agree to talk to them on the phone. They'd been impressed by Ned, he'd have some clout with them, and clout never went astray when buying time for Joss.

But if it was really bad she'd tell some lie, go by herself, Ned wouldn't stand much more. Either way she'd need more funds. She pushed her feet into her wellingtons and went to fill sandbags.

As she worked she made plans. The first edition Burton on the bookshelf in his study: *First Footsteps in East Africa*. He'd said it was worth a bit now, nearly too much, he'd been told it should be in the bank, but what was the point of a book that was locked away?

He'd notice of course, but not for a while, maybe a couple

of weeks. For a moment she wondered if she should burn her boats like this. Once sold, the book couldn't be retrieved nor its absence concealed, and she mightn't need so much money, it depended what Joss had done, what had to be glossed over, who bought off. She had the money from the fan, but it wasn't much. Just the same, she could take something more discreet, the two sums together might well be enough . . .

She dismissed the idea. She didn't know what else was valuable. And whatever it was, she'd only get part of its worth, they weren't fools, they knew she wouldn't be selling like this unless she had to. And in the end she didn't care if Ned found out, she didn't care what he thought of her, all she cared about was getting Joss out of whatever hole he'd dug for himself and she'd worry about the consequences when they happened.

She carried the filled sacks over to Ned and he laid them carefully to form a wall. He wouldn't trust either her or Mrs Coady to do this, you'd have thought he'd spent his life fighting floods and no one else had ever seen one. Mrs Coady threw her a look which said humour him, let the man be. The two women worked in complicity. It was a long way from Niamh's world view, but then Niamh was stuck in bed with a chest cold and wasn't much use to anyone.

Matt Murphy stopped by with a load of hay for his cattle. He drove the tractor up close and shouted his news without getting down. It was all too local for Hannie to follow, she didn't know the townlands or the back roads, couldn't work out where the culvert was that was blocked or what stream had taken what road. But she understood the last bit.

'They're giving out more storms on the radio,' Matt said. 'If they have it right for once in their lives, then we'll none of us be going anywhere for a while.'

Hannie strained to see through the water that sluiced down over the windscreen. No storms yet, but the rain had thickened and fattened and got much wetter. The wipers threw it off in sheets but it didn't make much difference, there was always more coming. She had got the car through the flooded stream and was heading for Cork now, by whatever road would get her there. She'd stopped further back to phone but the line was dead, the lines might be out for miles for all she knew.

The road ran with shallow run-offs that burst from under the walls and hedges, spreading a litter of gravel and stones as they fanned themselves over the tarmac. Streams filled the old, dry beds as well; they spilled out over the roads, broke up the surfaces, carried them away in lumps.

It all happened fast when the land was as waterlogged as this, Ned said. The ditches were neglected and choked with vegetation, there was nowhere for all that water to go. Ned went on about ditches; how the practice of clearing and digging them out had more or less fallen away. One of his many hobby horses.

At least he'd have the satisfaction of being right, she thought. It might offset the humiliation of being wrong about her.

Standing there in the rain listening to Matt Murphy, she had made her decision in a rush. She'd go to Cork while she still could, phone the school, sell the book, then go North if she had to. What she would say on the phone, she had only the vaguest idea. Find out what she could, she supposed. Play for time. If she couldn't get through she'd put half the money straight in the post with instructions to Joss to try and buy off the complainer. That there would be a complainer she never doubted. There was always a complainer, always someone angry or frightened enough to be prepared to tell.

Maybe she should forget about Cork, she thought, and just fill up the car and head North till it broke down or she got there. She wished she'd had the Land-Rover, but Ned had been shifting feed in it and she'd taken her chance and left while he was offside. She glanced down at herself and wished as well that she'd thought to change her clothes before she left. Schools were pompous institutions, quick to judge, a

260

wild-looking parent arriving unannounced might do more harm than good.

The road ran past a cluster of farm buildings, then veered abruptly round to the right and dipped. She took the bend too fast and felt the wheels slide in the mud. The car skidded half across the road, she righted it and changed down. She gave the road her full attention, felt herself coming alive with the violent veer of the car, the way the wheel bucked and spun with a life of its own. She was happier now, she liked the edge risk gave, the relief from the impotence of anxiety.

She rounded a bend on the crest of a rise. The road dropped and disappeared into a stretch of muddy brown water, then reappeared beyond to run up another rise. She didn't know the road, didn't know if it was merely flood-water or a stream that had overflowed its banks, filling the shallow scoop of the little valley. She peered through the driving rain looking for a clue, for turbulence signalling a current. She couldn't see. Recklessness overcame her.

Halfway across she felt the car slipping, the water tugging at the wheels. She changed down, trying to give the car mass to counter the flow, but the current was too strong. She felt the car rise and lift as it was carried sideways with the current. A stream bed.

She stopped fighting, stopped any attempt at control, let the car drift till it found itself, though it seemed like for ever. She felt the front wheels ground, she pressed the accelerator and for a moment the wheels gripped. Then the engine died. The front wheels stayed where they were but the back wheels went on drifting and the car swung slowly round. Then she felt all four wheels finding ground and the car stopped swinging and stuck fast, two thirds of the way across the brown water, sitting sideways over the road.

Shit shit shit.

~ *Chapter 47* ~

Ned saw the car on the far side of the flooded road, the tractor beside it, the figures peering into the opened bonnet. He set the old Land-Rover at the water and drove slowly and steadily through it. He pulled up beside the tractor and got out.

The tractor-driver was holding the car bonnet open at an angle, trying to shield the engine from the driving rain. Hannie was bent into it, both hands occupied, a bit of old rag clutched between her clenched teeth. The man nodded at Ned.

Hannie finished fiddling. She withdrew from the bonnet, removed the damp rag from between her teeth and rubbed at her wet oily hands.

'Might work,' she said to her companion, ignoring Ned completely. 'Shouldn't think so – plugs' too wet – worth a try.' She ducked into the car and turned the key in the ignition. It fired but didn't catch. She tried twice more. Then she gave up and emerged again from the car, looking through Ned as though he wasn't there. He stared at her. Her clothes were soaked through, her hair hung in rats' tails, her feet squelched when she moved, yet she was utterly defiant.

'Hannie, leave the car, get into the Land-Rover, we have to go to Cork,' Ned said. She didn't move or turn her head, she showed no sign of having heard him.

'We have to collect Joss, Hannie. The bus gets in in half an hour.'

She looked at him.

'The school phoned, they've sent Joss home.' He spoke the words very clearly, as though she was slow or hard of hearing.

She stared. 'The phone was out, they couldn't have phoned, the letter said they wanted to see us . . .' She seemed unable to grasp it.

'Hannie, they phoned, they've sent him home, I keep telling you . . .'

She got it then. She turned and walked over to the Land-Rover, exhausted, all the defiance gone out of her.

He spoke briefly with the tractor-driver, took the plugs out of Hannie's car, wrapped them in his handkerchief. The man took them and put them in his pocket.

Ned reached the Land-Rover just as Hannie scrambled back out of it. She ran through the downpour, ducked into the stranded car and emerged holding a plastic bag with something heavy in it. She stumbled through the rain again and climbed back into the Land-Rover.

'What did he do?' she asked, staring ahead at the rainy glass.

He glanced at her. The bones stood out like knolls on her grey skin and her hand shook as she lifted the cigarette to her mouth. He had the heating turned up full, but the Land-Rover was old, the heater was on its last legs.

'It seems he'd been playing cards in the town and had got into debt,' Ned said. 'He made a list – things his classmates had done that they'd rather nobody knew about. Then he offered to sell them the evidence.'

She said nothing for a while, just dragged on her cigarette and blew out smoke.

'How did they find out?'

'A boy took a lot of pills. Paracetamol. He was all right – just very sick. Afterwards he told his parents all about it.'

'And they told the school,' she finished flatly. 'What had he done? The boy, I mean. What was it he didn't want them to find out? Was it to do with Joss?'

'I don't know,' Ned said slowly. 'I didn't ask.' But Hannie had, she had known straight away that the story might not end with the blackmail. What had Joss done in the past, he thought, to make her think so far and fast?

'So they've expelled him,' she said, as though to herself.

'No, not officially. But they said it looked more serious than they'd thought so they're sending him home while they consider their position.'

She shrugged. 'They will expel him. When they have considered.'

He glanced at her. She had lit another cigarette. She was still staring straight ahead into the darkening afternoon. He switched from sidelights to full beam. The lights deepened the afternoon into dusk and made the rain on the windshield shine. The road was clear of water. They were on the main road now, it was new and properly drained, it would take a lot more rain before it flooded.

'How did you know I'd be on this road?'

'I didn't, Mrs Coady said she thought you'd gone to Dungarvan to stock up, I wasn't looking for you, I was going to get Joss.'

There was a long silence.

'Why?'

'Why what?'

'Why were you going to get Joss?'

'Because he's on the bus. How else was he going to get home?'

For the first time she turned her head and looked at him, a look so bleak and hopeless that it turned him cold.

'I was going to Cork,' she said tonelessly, 'to sell your Arab book.'

'The Richard Burton first edition?' he asked, not seeming surprised. 'Is that what's in the bag?'

She nodded. 'It may have got a bit damp.'

'I expect it did, I shouldn't worry, it'll dry out. How did you think you were going to sell it?'

'A dealer called Slattery.'

'Slattery? Does he really exist? I thought he was just a story people made up to frighten themselves.'

'You know about Slattery?'

'Everyone knows about Slattery. It's just as well I found you. If he's anything like they say he is, he'd have robbed you blind.'

'He's not that bad. And I needed the money. Like Joss.'

'*For* Joss,' he corrected her. 'You should have said, I might have come up with something. I wouldn't have let you sell old Burton, he's your golden egg for when I die.'

She turned her head and stared at him again, but it was almost dark and he couldn't see her face. He could hear her teeth chatter though, she had begun to shiver uncontrollably.

'Ned?' There was a silence, punctuated by tiny clicking sounds. 'Do you think I'll be around that long?'

'Who knows? I hope you will.'

'Do you? You need your head examined. But thank you.'

'What for?'

'Going to get Joss. Not minding about old Burton.'

'Don't mention it.'

❧ *Chapter 48* ❧

What the boy needed was a war; if he found the right niche he would probably do all right in a war. Not as a soldier. Too straightforward and communal. Something underground, undercover. He was brave enough in his own way. And conscienceless and ruthless, he would undoubtedly kill easily and efficiently. Anarchy and excitement – that was what he needed. In the right conditions he might thrive.

And preferably he'd be killed before it ended, Ned added to himself with bitter honesty. *And be buried, heaped with honours.*

Ned sighed. Joss was unfit for civil life, that was the truth of it. The flood had kept him busy while it lasted. But what would they do with him now that the water and the urgency were lessening?

He watched the boy, working the boat in on the current, slipping it into the submerged cut, finding the mooring under the flood-water. The water was dropping fast, the cut was barely covered, you could see its definition clearly beneath the water. Already most of the meadows were clear; in the low-lying fields the drowned tussocks were poking their way up through the last of the flood and everywhere the old order was re-emerging. Soon even the mud and the mess and the work would be forgotten.

Joss leapt from the boat on to the flooded landing-place with barely a splash. He was surprisingly deft and supple. Quick and agile, like a cat.

A cat. That was it. The watching and waiting, the relentless pursuit of its own ends, the cruelty, the indifference to a victim's suffering. No, it wasn't just indifference, it was the same curious atunement that a cat gets when playing its prey. Not exactly enjoyment. More a heightened sense of itself, of its own catness.

Ned had lived large tracts of his life with peoples who were alien to him, he was accustomed to observing and assessing dispassionately, to judging without condemning. He watched Joss now as he would have watched a man who was to accompany him on a dangerous journey, a man whose strengths and weaknesses he must know and then accept. His own emotional reaction to the man he must also know and acknowledge, observing from somewhere slightly beyond this personal response, aware of it and swayed by it, but never overwhelmed by it. It was a discipline that had become a second nature to him and had served him well.

Yet try as he might he couldn't get beyond the personal with Joss. He couldn't get the distance, couldn't not be overwhelmed by his own negative reactions. Joss loved all those things Ned most hated: speed, noise, destruction; the facile heady whizz of the machine age. Only out here by the river could Ned begin to acknowledge that the boy had other qualities as well. Yet still he could not get beyond those that he hated. He stood quietly in the dusk now, tasting his failure.

Joss knew he was being watched but he made no sign. He pulled the boat to him and secured it on the double mooring against the tide's drop, as Ned had taught him to do. He removed the oars and the rowlocks, carried them clear of the water, laid them on the muddy grass. Then he lifted off the outboard, hefting it with both hands, his slight shoulders taut against its weight. Ned moved forward to take up the oars. Neither of them spoke.

The constant rain had stopped but the air was still wet and the wind was patchy and damp. In the near trees the black rooks clustered in the upper branches like high, dark fruits. The woods on the far bank were coloured like smoke, their netted branches rising forlorn into the low white sky, their feet still wading in water.

The river ran swollen and furious, its waters mud-brown, cross-hatched with eddies and currents and pocked with swift-flowing debris. Branches and barrels and drowned beasts jostled together in a wild headlong rush for the sea. For days the light had hardly lifted.

It was dangerous, too dangerous for a fourteen-year-old, though the outboard was powerful and Joss had some experience from his life in Africa. Not enough, though: there was no such thing as enough and even a grown man in full strength would have thought twice before making as free on the river as Joss did. And Ned let him. The neighbours saw and wondered, but they didn't speak of it except amongst themselves.

It had started naturally enough. For centuries the river had been the main highway in the valley, while the little winding roads were only secondary. Then cars had come and the balance had changed, but the lay-out of field and dwelling had gone largely unaltered, and there were still plenty of places more easily reached by water than by road. But as the water rose, these meadows and dwellings were the first to flood.

Ned had a boat hauled up and over-wintering in an out-building, its outboard carefully oiled and stored, the fuel cans filled and ready beside it. He had thought about getting it out but he was too old and stiff, there was too much to be done and Hannie had fallen sick with an infection that had gone deep into her chest.

One morning he'd gone down to the flooded landing-stage and found Joss with three of the local lads and the boat dragged out to the water's edge, the engine beside it, the four of them making it ready. He knew them all, they'd greeted him briefly, not letting themselves be distracted from the urgency of the task ahead.

It seemed Joss had volunteered both the boat and himself. Joss could handle a boat, he wanted to go, so Ned let him.

In the mornings Joss was up without being called and out with the boat before it was fully light. There was plenty to be done. Families and stock were moved, early lambs rescued, feed taken to beasts in pastures flooded or trampled into a waste of mud. Clearly, Joss and the boat were useful.

There were changes in Joss. The dark glasses were gone, his posture had altered, and some of the meanness and slyness of demeanour seemed to have left him. If a week's activity could make a difference like this, Ned thought, then perhaps the boy wasn't altogether lost.

But as the urgency wore off, so did the acceptance. The water dropped and the work of cleaning up and returning began. There was still a need for more hands and another boat and Joss still went out, but more and more he went alone, the young men keeping their distance, the boys of his own age avoiding him. There was no mistaking it, Joss was shunned.

This was the moment, Ned knew, when he should have ordered the boy in.

But he didn't. Partly he was distracted by Hannie's health, partly he was reluctant to take from Joss the one thing in which he excelled here, the one thing that gave him an occupation and a place in this difficult new life that had been thrust upon him. He would have discussed it with Hannie but she was sick and out of commission so he had to take the decision on himself.

Hannie's chest had got worse, she sweated and shivered, her temperature soaring at night. The doctor had come on Ned's insistence and against her wishes, had listened to her chest and said pneumonia. Bed was where she should be – no more of this getting up – bed was where she should stay till she was much better. So Hannie lay in bed and Ned brought her hot drinks and regular antibiotics and when she asked for Joss he told her Joss was fine, he was on the river, he was at Niamh's, he was watching television . . .

People knew that Joss shouldn't be home. There was a gastric problem in the school, Ned told Mrs Coady, a lot of the youngsters had diarrhoea, it might be a bug or it might be something in the water, they'd sent them all home till they got it sorted out. Mrs Coady had looked at him with steady eyes and he knew that she knew what he was saying and she'd pass the story around and stand over it.

But he didn't know what they were going to do with Joss, who was nearly fifteen and in a few months' time could, in theory, finish school. But finish school and do what? They could hardly just leave it at that in this age when qualifications seemed so overwhelmingly important and even good character stood for little. Always supposing that Joss had had that, which he didn't.

So in not ordering Joss in off the river Ned was trying to give him something, some dignity of occupation while they waited for the school's decision.

But also there was another reason, and one that Ned was careful not to investigate very deeply. He wanted to let things find their own level, to give fate a free hand, to see would Joss go quietly under the water and not come back. And he wanted to go and tell Hannie of Joss's death, to watch her overwhelmed and then released, the whole thing like an amputation with no medicines in a stony place, the axe rising and falling, the diseased limb cut away. The agony, then the lost health returning.

Fate would have its chance. But if fate didn't claim the boy, then so be it, he would do his duty and shelter him, he was resolved on that.

~ *Chapter 49* ~

'*F*or God's sake, Ned, stop being so melodramatic, it's not that bad. He's been expelled from school, that's all. Plenty of boys get themselves expelled, go on to lead perfectly normal lives, isn't the first time, won't be the last.' James stared into his whiskey, swished it around the glass, knocked it back.

'All right he's not the way you want him, I can see that. Hard for a chap like you ... But they never are, you know, they never are the way you want 'em, and if you weren't so damned inexperienced you'd know that, you'd make the best of it, stop making your life a misery. What's he done, after all? Gambled a bit, run out of money – blackmail bit isn't so pretty, I admit, but he's young, a new life and all that, adjustment, we all make mistakes, or most of us do.' (A quick glance here at Marjorie.) 'There are other schools, aren't there? Wouldn't have sent him to Northerners, myself – all mad, if you ask me – maybe it's no bad thing they've chucked him out. Cheer up, for God's sake, he hasn't killed anyone.'

James and Marjorie were sitting in the kitchen, drinking whiskey. Old friends, offering themselves for listening and advice. Ned was grateful. The school had written saying the parents of the boys concerned were anxious that the episode be handled with discretion. The school therefore was prepared to overlook Joss's conduct (no charges would be pressed, they implied) but they did not want him back. It was all most unfortunate, they were aware that Ned's connection with the boy was a recent one, they would have liked to have been more accommodating but they couldn't, they were sure that Ned would perfectly understand their position.

The tone of the letter, the way it had insinuated a personal exoneration for him, had so infuriated Ned that he'd almost lost sight of Joss's offence. When he'd calmed down he called Joss in and told him of the school's decision but he might as well have been talking to a breeze block for all the reaction he got. He didn't punish the boy, he thought of reducing his television hours, but he knew Joss would simply spend the time at Niamh's and he didn't want to further encourage that relationship. He cast around for other sanctions but gave up because he didn't think sanctions would make much difference, he just didn't know how to reach him.

So now it was out in the open. Joss wasn't going back.

Ned was relieved to be telling James and Marjorie, he didn't expect a solution but he'd had enough of fretting alone. He knew Hannie wouldn't want him to discuss Joss with them, but he didn't care. They were his friends, he told himself, they would have been Hannie's too if she'd let them, Joss was his stepson, he had every right to discuss him.

As for James and Marjorie, they'd heard Joss was home and Hannie safely indisposed with pneumonia, and they'd come to cheer up Ned. Finding themselves consulted, they responded with a warm attention. It was comforting to find Ned reverted to his old self and their welcome secure.

'Send him to the Quakers,' Marjorie was saying. 'Waterford. Near enough for Hannie to keep an eye. And he can come home the odd weekend if he wants.' She looked at Ned and he was astonished at the sympathy in her bossy grey eyes. 'They did the O'Connor girl, y'know? The bald one – wild as a hawk, thrown out of every school in the country – Shelagh? Siobhan? I forget her name.'

'Sinead,' James said. 'Sinead O'Connor.'

'Singer,' he added, as Ned looked completely blank. 'Batty. Awful-looking creature, boots and stubble, could be a looker, can't think why she does that to herself, voice like an angel.' He had another swig from his glass. 'Not a bad idea, Ned, could be a lot of sense in what Marjorie's saying. If they coped with her, they'll manage Joss all right. Chicken feed to the O'Connor girl, I'd say.'

'If they'll take him,' Ned said, doubtfully.

'Of course they'll take him.' Marjorie was indignant at the idea of a refusal. 'That's what they're there for, isn't it? James is right. Mistake to have sent him North at all. Too rigid, bound to rebel. The Quakers'll sort him out. Enough rope to hang himself. Good at that sort of thing.'

When James and Marjorie had gone, Ned sat on by the fire, thinking it over. They were right, he decided, he was over-reacting. As usual, where Joss was concerned; he was getting het up when nobody else did. Look at the Legs, how disturbed he had been, and the girl hadn't minded, seemed to think it was more or less normal. He'd felt a fool, all the fuss he had made.

Perhaps he was wrong about Joss, too. Not wrong altogether, but perhaps the boy wasn't bad through and through as he thought he was. He'd been wrong about Niamh, had thought her more fragile than she was. And a lot more innocent.

And he *was* inexperienced, James was certainly right there, but he wasn't too old to learn. He would do as they suggested, go and see that school, fix it all so Hannie needn't worry. He got out of his chair, banked the fire, switched off the lights, picked up the pup and went and stood in the yard as he liked to do last thing if the night was fine. The light was still on at Niamh's so he tipped the pup into her run and left the door unlocked for Joss, and for once this small concession didn't anger him.

Upstairs, he went in to say goodnight to Hannie, but she was asleep, her hair straggled over the pillow, the violet shadows strong beneath her eyes. Sometimes she stirred and coughed. He had never known a woman in this way: unpresented, unadorned, mortal and sick and in his care. He could not get over the everydayness of her, of her life lived so close to his. Very quietly, he turned the lamp off, backed out and closed the door.

But he woke in the night and remembered the dread in Hannie's eyes when she'd asked him in the Land-Rover what Joss had done. He lay a long time staring into the darkness and knowing his friends for false comforters.

Ned was carefully and thoroughly interviewed by the headmaster and his deputy. He didn't lie to them or try to conceal anything, he told them what had happened to cause Joss's expulsion and he told them he thought there'd been problems in the past. He didn't know the details he said, the boy's mother had pneumonia, he didn't want to bother her while she was still so ill.

They said they'd talk to Hannie later when she'd recovered. In the meantime they would ask the boy. Ned stared, but the two men seemed perfectly confident in what they were doing. They sent him off to the bursar's office to discuss the financial side of things. They wanted to talk to Joss alone.

In the end they said they'd take Joss, but suggested that he drop back a year, starting after Easter. That way he'd have a term just to settle in and then he'd move into the new school year with surroundings and classmates already familiar to him. He'd also have a couple of months at home to get used to a new country and a new way of life.

Ned felt his bones sag with surprise and relief but at the same time he couldn't help feeling that somehow he was cheating these people, that he'd deceived them into accepting Joss when he should have been warning them against him.

Ned's relief was short-lived. The flood dropped and Joss lost all interest in the river. He abandoned the boat like a child leaving down a toy he has tired of, it rocked on its moorings, dirty and forlorn. Ned told him to get it cleaned up and out of the water and Joss obeyed him with sullen ill-will. Ned watched his resentment. He had always worked alone or with people who wanted to be on his payroll. If a guide or a bearer had had Joss's attitude he would simply have let him go.

But he couldn't let Joss go. For the first time it occurred to him that Joss might refuse an order. He wondered how he'd deal with straight defiance from his stepson.

It was all very well, this talk of Joss settling in at home, but the truth was, Ned didn't know what to do with the boy. There was plenty of routine farm maintenance and clearing up in the flood's aftermath to be done, but Joss wasn't interested in such work and Ned was not prepared to take on the duty of motivating Joss, or of bullying him into accomplishing the tasks he set him.

Nor was he prepared to give up his solitude and work with Joss. Solitude was precious to him – solitude, aloneness and separateness. He had always refused to travel with fellow Europeans whose language he understood. He wasn't a natural linguist: with native peoples he had been protected and separated by his inability to understand the daily chatter. Solitude was now far more than a drug to him: in it he found rest and refreshment and no task was dull.

So Ned tried, but only half-heartedly. He required Joss to be up in the morning, he directed him at a task, explained it, and left the lad alone. If it was done, it was badly done. More often it was left half done or hardly started. Ned quickly grew angry. Joss was never going to be any good on the land because he didn't want to be; he could do it if he wanted to, he had shown that with the boat. Ned could not bring himself to use himself up on Joss when he knew the boy was trying to wear him down. Sometimes he couldn't bear the sight of Joss, his blankness and resistance. He was afraid of his own rage.

The doctor dropped by and was astonished that Hannie was still in bed and so ill.

'Why didn't you call me?' he asked Ned. 'I thought she'd be up and around ages ago, I'd no idea she wasn't responding to treatment.'

Ned muttered about pneumonia. The doctor, involved with his prescription pad, growled dismissively. 'That's the dark ages. Pneumonia's not what it was, she just needs a different antibiotic. Here.' He tore out the prescription and handed it to Ned. 'We'll try her on that. I'll leave you a few to start her off. You should see a big change in a day or two – three at the most. But for God's sake call me if it's not working. I want her out of bed and hopping around the place in a week.'

When the doctor had left Ned carried Hannie's supper tray down and put it on the table. It was hardly touched, the soup cold and congealed, the bread uneaten. He felt downcast and sorry for himself and generally angry. The doctor clearly considered him hopelessly behind the times. He might not be able to give Hannie what she wanted when she was well, but he'd thought that at least he was looking after her now she was sick. He was doing his best, and he just got accused of making things worse.

Niamh was mooching about the kitchen, picking things up, putting them down again.

'Two to be taken three times a day.' She had Hannie's pills in her hand. 'Stronger and stronger antibiotics, that's all doctors can think of, no mention of nursing or rest. This one doesn't work fast enough – change to another one. And all those illnesses they thought they'd got rid of – all back, stronger, more resistant. She shouldn't be taking these things, she should be getting over it herself, in a natural way, using her own resources.'

'She *was* using her own resources,' Ned said tiredly. 'And she wasn't getting over it. I've just had a bellyful from Malone and now you start in from the opposite direction.'

Niamh looked at him, her dark eyes stubborn and determined. 'They'll weaken her in the long run.'

Ned sat down and opened the paper. He wanted to eat his supper, read the newspaper, take himself off to an early bed. He had never lost his temper with Niamh, had never even imagined that the situation might arise.

'Is your work going well, Niamh?' he asked her without looking up. 'I hope you haven't forgotten Mrs Cardew's painting, I know you've decided you don't want to bother with commissions but you did say you'd finish it, since you've already been paid for it. And it might be civil of you to let her know your intentions.'

'Ned?' said a woman's voice on the phone. 'Ned, this is Nora.'

Ned didn't know any Noras. He waited blankly.

'Andrew's wife,' said the voice. 'Nora – Nora Clarke.' She finished a bit desperately, as though she was asking him to confirm her name.

Ned got it. Nora, the dark girl with the pretty ways, Andrew's wife, they'd been to stay at Christmas. He made himself put warmth and recognition into his voice.

'Hello, Nora. How are you, what can I do for you?'

'Grand, thanks,' she said, ignoring the second part of the question. 'But we heard that Joss is home and Hannie isn't so good. We wondered if there was anything we could do?'

'How on earth did you hear that?' His tone was sharper than he'd intended. There was a slight, anxious pause at the other end.

'Oh, you know,' Nora said brightly. 'This is Ireland – everyone hears everything.' A nervous little laugh.

'Anyway,' she went on in a rush, 'we wondered if you'd like to send us Joss for a week or two – I've a nephew staying, it'd be company for him – give you a break till Hannie gets back on her feet?'

'That's very kind of you, Nora,' Ned said. 'Very kind indeed. But it would be a lot of trouble for you.' (And would Hannie want it? She hadn't said anything against his school arrangements, but she hadn't been as relieved as he had expected.)

'Oh no, no trouble at all,' Nora was saying into his ear. 'I like having young ones around, and it'd be great for Conn. That's the nephew – my sister's son, fifteen. Just the right age for Joss.'

She wouldn't take no for an answer. She had it all thought

out, her plans for Joss's transportation were swift and practical, she seemed completely au fait with bus routes and timetables, naming the towns and the changes with practised ease. Joss would leave the next day and return in a couple of weeks. It was all fixed before Ned had time to think.

To Ned's surprise, Joss wanted to go. He stood in the kitchen, taking in the details, his face blank. Then he pulled at each of his fingers in turn till they cracked in their sockets. Ned told himself to be patient. Joss turned to leave the room.

'Where are you going?' Ned asked him.

Joss looked surprised. 'To pack.'

Ned had a moment of contrition. 'You don't have to go if you really don't want to, Joss, I don't want to force you – it's just that with your mother being sick like this and school not starting for you till Easter . . .'

'It's cool,' Joss said. 'I want to go. I like Nora.'

'You do?' Ned couldn't keep the surprise out of his voice.

'Sure. She's cool. And she lives in a town. She told me.'

'Would you rather we lived in a town?'

'Sure. It's boring here. No one to talk to but Niamh.'

'But you get on with Niamh?'

Joss sighed. 'Niamh's all right,' he said. 'But she's boring. It was better when Ciaran was here.'

Ned didn't say anything.

Joss stood. After a moment or two Ned realised he was waiting to be dismissed.

'All right, Joss,' he said. 'You can go and pack now.'

Joss turned to go. At the door he turned back. 'Does *she* know?' he asked.

Ned looked blank.

'Hannie,' Joss said. 'Have you told her?'

Ned almost lied.

'No,' he said reluctantly.

'Best not,' Joss said. 'Not till after I've gone.'

'You think she might not approve of the arrangement?'

Joss grinned suddenly. 'She'll go nuts,' he said. 'But she'll calm down when she gets used to the idea.' He disappeared through the door.

☙ *Chapter 50* ☙

*T*he next day Hannie's fever was down and she slept through for twenty four hours without waking. When she did she sat up in bed and announced that she wanted a bath and something to eat. She had both, then Ned told her that Joss was in Galway with Nora.

It wasn't quite as Joss had predicted. She did go nuts, but showed no sign of calming down or getting used to the idea. Instead she got up, got dressed and went down to the kitchen. He was doing farm accounts at the table but she didn't seem to see him. She sat by the phone, leafed through the address book, then dialled the Clarkes' number. When Nora answered Hannie told her that the school in Waterford needed Joss for tests because they wanted to assess his progress-to-date in all his subjects. He'd be ahead in some areas, she explained, but would probably need some extra help in others. Unfortunately it meant that Joss's stay in Galway must be cut short.

She listened while Nora replied.

She said she was glad Joss was enjoying himself, and yes, he did need to be brought out of his shell, but she still felt his education must come first. No, the school wasn't being arbitrary, this had always been the arrangement, it was simply that Ned hadn't realised they would need Joss so soon.

Her tone was straightforward and matter-of-fact but she was very firm. She wanted Joss put on a bus the next morning. She got Joss on the line and told him the same thing.

She put down the phone and went and inspected the fridge. She removed all the pre-cooked portions that Mrs Coady had prepared. She bagged them and labelled them and despatched them to the freezer. Then she cleaned the fridge, cleaned the sink, cooked a fresh, hot meal, set out the food and sat down and ate in complete silence.

Ned was at once relieved, apprehensive and angry. She had undone his arrangement seamlessly, concealing nothing from him, not blaming him to Nora or making him look a fool. Nonetheless she had reversed his decision as though he'd had no business making it in the first place.

This annoyed him. Joss was his stepson, in his charge, he had a right to his say in things, whatever she might think. But he should have withdrawn from the arrangement as soon as Joss had told him she wouldn't like it, he should have asserted Hannie's authority and taken no part in conniving with the boy – of this he was well aware. And he had a guilty conscience because she didn't know Joss had said what he'd said, and he certainly wasn't about to tell her.

'Hannie, you're being unreasonable,' he accused into her silence. 'When he wanted to go to Omagh you were all for it, you said there was no one for him to talk to here, no one his own age.'

She reached for the salt without even looking up.

'Well he's happy in Galway, he's got Nora's nephew to talk to, I don't know why you're making such a fuss.'

No response.

'You were sick in bed, Hannie, you weren't around. And I don't think it's a good idea, him being too much at Niamh's.'

Silence again. He tried another tack.

'Hannie, I'm sorry if it wasn't what you wanted, but I can't understand why you don't want him to be at Nora's, at least we know he's in good hands.'

She got up, lifted her plate and crossed to the sink.

'It's because of the shoe,' she said quietly, running water into the bowl, not turning round.

'The shoe?' He didn't understand.

'The black high-heeled shoe Danno found by the legs that Joss made. It was Nora's shoe.'

She turned and looked at him then, a steady, wordless look, her face quite grey with fatigue.

Joss came home. He no longer got up in the mornings or reported to Ned for tasks. Ned said nothing, he used the break from their barely established routine to let things drift. It was easier so, they were both relieved, and the school had phoned (Hannie's lie proved no more than the truth); they wanted Joss for tests in a couple of weeks. Hannie's infection had passed, but she'd got up too quickly, she found herself drained and exhausted after only a few hours out of bed. She, too, was ready to leave Joss alone and let things be till school kicked in and kept him at least occupied.

The doctor came again. Ned walked him to his car when he'd finished with Hannie. They talked briefly of the livestock and the latest political scandal and the weather. Then Ned asked about Hannie.

The doctor thought for a moment before replying. 'Basically she's a strong, healthy woman,' he said slowly. 'She's responding to treatment, the infection's receding, yet somehow she's not picking up in the way she should . . .' He paused and looked at Ned. Ned said nothing. 'She seems a bit low, not much interested in life,' he went on cautiously. 'I wonder – perhaps she's found the transition a bit difficult? She's used to the sun, they tell me?' He paused again and looked amiably into the distance. Still nothing. Oh well, might as well be hung for a sheep as a lamb. 'Would you think maybe of taking her for a bit of a holiday?' he asked. 'Somewhere warm, a package maybe. A bit of a break for you both?'

He felt Ned stiffen beside him, but he didn't look round. Ned mumbled vaguely about not being able to leave the farm and her boy. The doctor let that pass. Ned said money didn't grow on trees.

'It doesn't have to be the Caribbean, you know,' the doctor said gently. 'There's grand holidays these days without going all that way. Turkey, perhaps. North Africa. They tell me

Tunisia isn't dear. And the great thing is you can go direct from Dublin. No trailing off to London, waiting around for hours for a connection. Not too hot when you get there, either. Not stripping-off-and-lying-by-the-pool weather, but pleasant, strolling-in-the-sun sort of heat.'

He shook hands with Ned and got into the car and rolled down the window. 'Might be worth your while having a look in at Shea's the next time you're over in that direction. Think about it, anyway . . . And let me know if there's any change for the worse.'

He drove off down the bumpy drive, avoiding the potholes. These Anglo-Irish types were the divil. Inbred and touchy and close as a well-planed door. And you never knew what they had or didn't have, outside of a horse and a picture or two. Poor woman. Stuck down there with no company and a husband twenty years older. Still, Ned Renvyle was a decent man and probably a kind one, it could work out well enough when it settled down. And he just might bite on a holiday – a holiday might do the trick. Wouldn't like spending the money, though. Well, if he wouldn't, he wouldn't, you couldn't force people. He'd give her a month, maybe try her on anti-depressants if she wasn't picking up . . .

Ned dismissed the doctor's suggestion at once, but it itched at him like flea-bites for the rest of the day. Malone meant well enough, but he was interfering with his talk of holidays and sunshine. Hannie would do very well once she was properly over the infection, she was an active woman by nature, she *would* be low after so long in bed. And there simply wasn't the money for holidays, it was tight enough to begin with, and Joss's schooling was an enormous extra drain.

Maybe he should think about involving her more with the farm, he thought, get her roped in on his lavender plans, encourage her to go ahead with the geese. The farm machine show was coming up in Dublin, they could go there together, there'd be ideas for farm development, information on geese, maybe something on lavender as well. And after that there were race meetings they could go to, she liked race meetings, there was a good winter calendar, much of it within fairly easy reach. Ideas leapt into his head.

Thus Ned talked to himself, proving easily that if there was money to be spent it would be better spent so; more outings and expeditions, a gradual steady change. He'd show Malone he could do better than a week in Turkey or Tunisia.

He was infinitely relieved by his conclusions. In the end it wasn't even the money, it was the thought of some high-rise hotel in some tourist resort and other people at breakfast, and traipsing around on bus tours looking at curios and belly-dancers and souvenirs. He hated tourism, its superficiality and inanity, he hated what it did to countries and peoples and their immemorial ways of life. He'd felt violated by Malone's well-intentioned suggestion.

Later, in the house, he waited for Hannie to go up to an early bed then picked up the phone and dialled Vere and Alison.

Vere answered. Ned asked him to recommend a modest hotel in Dublin.

'Hang on a minute.' Vere went off to find Alison. Alison came on the line and she gave him the name and number of a hotel and told him the price, which seemed to Ned exorbitant, but he wasn't going to let that put him off. Alison asked when he was thinking of going and he explained about the doctor and the need for a weekend away, and Alison listened to it all and then asked gently if he thought Hannie liked farm machinery shows?

Ned stopped in his tracks. With anyone else he'd have clammed up but because it was Alison he hesitated and then he said he hadn't actually asked her, but he'd thought about involving her more in the farm and the show might be a good way to begin.

'It was going to be a surprise,' he finished lamely. 'D'you think it's a bad idea?'

'Not necessarily, not if she likes shows.' There was a small

284

pause. 'But it might be quite strenuous and noisy, walking round all those stands, perhaps she'd like music or the theatre better? And maybe some shops in the day?'

'The theatre's noisy too.'

'True, but at least she'd be sitting down.'

'She won't want to go to the shops, she doesn't like shops, shops are hell.'

'I couldn't agree more,' Alison said, 'but she might like to buy some new clothes? That's always good for you when you've been ill, it gives you a boost.'

Ned thanked her and put down the phone. Hannie had clothes, it hadn't occurred to him that she might want new ones, any more than it had occurred to him that she mightn't like a farm machinery show. Suddenly it all seemed hopeless, he didn't have the faintest idea about her or any woman and if it hadn't been after seven he'd have lifted the phone to Shea's then and there and booked them on to some God-awful package to some God-awful place, as Malone had suggested.

❦ *Chapter 51* ❦

*I*t was suddenly milder. The sky had cleared to a soft, light blue, higher and airier than it had been for weeks. There were dribbles of birdsong, stripes of pale light on the straggly grass, blackbirds poking and scuffling about in the hedges. Under the apple trees the snowdrops had pushed through.

Hannie walked about in the garden, little clouds of floppy grey gnats swimming towards her through the warmer air. The garden looked like a field, the grass tussocky and rank, the flowerbeds frost-blackened and clogged with rotting leaves. But everything smelled different. Bands of rooks flew over, their wings swishing the quiet air.

So, she thought, that was the winter.

When she came in Alison was standing in the kitchen with a biro in her hand, a cardboard box and a brown envelope on the table beside her.

'Oh Hannie, how are you? Much better, I can see that, I'm so glad. I was just writing you a note. I've brought Ned's Burton from the National Library –' she patted the box – 'it's all right, no serious damage, but they said to tell him not to go leaving it around beside open windows, he mightn't get off as lightly the next time.'

Hannie put on the kettle and took Ned's teapot down from the shelf. So he'd sent off Burton to be checked, had he? How like him. And all the time protesting that it didn't matter. Still, she shouldn't complain, what was it he had called the book? *Your golden egg for when I die.*

'It's so difficult, isn't it?' Alison said. 'Awful to lock things away just because they're valuable, but they were really quite disapproving when I said Ned thought books were there to be read. They got very stuffy and looked at me as though I wasn't entirely a fit person and muttered about reading the Penguin Classic and keeping the real thing. I almost thought they were going to say I couldn't take it away, but Ned had written them a letter so they couldn't *not* let me have it, even though they clearly wanted to . . .'

Hannie set a tray with a milk jug and biscuits and bone-china cups, and ushered her guest into the cold dampness of the drawing room. Alison protested all this formality but Hannie wouldn't listen. She put a match to the laid fire and drew the curtains against the twilight. She poured the tea and handed Alison a cup.

'You've been in Dublin?'

Alison sipped and nodded. 'Yes. Vere's ancient aunt, she's getting quite meandery, poor old thing. Everyone keeps wanting to put her into a home, tidy her away, but she won't hear of it and I can't say I blame her.'

Alison sat back in her chair. 'And then we looked in on the farm machinery show. Vere wanted to look at balers, he's had an idea for an improvement and he wanted to check that no one else had got there before him.'

'And had they?'

'No, but they might as well have. It's all so hi-tech now and Vere's idea was just a simple modification of the old ones, he really got quite depressed. I've got some information on geese for you, but nothing on lavender, we couldn't find anything at all I'm afraid. Vere thinks daffodils would be a better plan, but Ned's not interested in daffodils, is he, he wants to grow lavender?'

'I've really no idea,' Hannie said coolly, 'I didn't know he'd asked you to get information on geese, much less lavender.'

Alison flushed. 'I expect he forgot to tell you. It's my fault, he wanted to take you himself, but I thought you might not be well enough, I'm afraid I was rather discouraging.'

'Wanted to take me where?'

'To the farm machinery show.'

Hannie stared at her for a moment, then threw back her head and laughed. Alison looked startled, then she laughed too. The two women laughed like giddy girls, Hannie clutching her stomach and Alison holding a cushion to her mouth, her eyes dancing above it. Every time they looked at one another they started each other off again.

'I've never even heard of the farm machinery show,' Hannie said when she could speak. That started them again and they couldn't stop. A door opened in the hall. Abruptly Alison stopped laughing and sat with one hand raised in warning. Footsteps and a door closing, then silence.

'It's all right,' Hannie said, not laughing any more, picking up the pot and refilling the cups. 'This is what he wants of me – afternoon tea, in a drawing room, with someone like you. He'll be pleased to hear us laugh, it'll never cross his mind we might be laughing at him.'

'It must be very hard for you,' Alison said slowly. 'Not belonging . . .'

'Hard for me? No, it isn't hard for me. I have never wanted to belong anywhere or with anyone. The opposite.'

'You must have a great many friends.' Alison said this thoughtfully and it wasn't a question.

'Why do you say that?'

'So you don't have a need to belong.' Alison leaned forward. 'I'm sorry, I don't really understand, I've always lived in one place, it's hard for me to imagine another kind of life.'

'We are very different people,' Hannie said coolly. There was a moment's lull in the conversation, then she picked it up again. 'No,' she said, 'I don't have *a great many friends* and I wouldn't want them, I like to be free and alone. I only ever had one real friend and she's dead now. That's all right, it means I rely on myself.'

'Not on your husband?'

'No,' Hannie said gravely. 'Not on my husband. I have never had a husband that I trusted. Have you?'

'I have only ever had one husband. But yes, I do trust him. I trust that he will always do his best for me.'

'But not that he will always do what you need of him?'

'No. But I don't think you can expect that of anyone.'

'You can expect it of yourself.'

'Yes. But what if it's too much for you and you need to be helped?'

'You withdraw from the situation.'

'Sometimes you can't.'

'There is always that danger . . .'

There was silence again. The two women looked at each other as though baffled. Alison sensed that Hannie wanted to talk to her, but she didn't know what it was that she was trying to say and she was afraid of missing it.

'But one can never be quite self-reliant, can one?' she said at last. 'Not once one has a child? A child is an extension of oneself, the boundaries are breached for ever, even when they are grown up and gone away.'

'I don't know.'

'But Joss – ?'

'Joss is not my son.'

Alison opened her mouth to speak, then realised what had been said to her. There was dead silence in the room.

'Whose son is he?' she asked at last.

'The son of the dead friend that I just spoke of. Joss is Ilse's son, not mine.' Hannie got up and went over to the long window. She pulled the curtain back and stood staring out into the darkness. There was a peculiar atmosphere in the room.

'Who was Ilse?'

Hannie answered without turning.

'Ilse was Swedish. Very young. She married my husband.'

Alison struggled with Hannie's words but she couldn't make sense of them. 'I'm sorry,' she said gently. 'I don't understand what you're telling me.'

'Joss is Ilse's son,' Hannie explained from the window, 'by a man who was my husband when she met him.'

'Ilse took your husband from you?'

'That's one way of looking at it. My husband then was a man named Rolf. Ilse was a young au pair from Sweden, very naïve and beautiful. Later, when she was dying, she asked me to take Joss for her.'

'Why did she do that?'

'She didn't want Rolf to have him. And there was no one else, her family were estranged.'

'But why did you agree?'

'Because she was my friend.'

'But she took your husband?'

'Yes, but it didn't matter, things change, people move on. And anyway I wasn't in love with Rolf, it was just a convenient arrangement.' She stopped and looked at Alison's bewildered face and tried again.

'I used her, she was useful to me, I exploited her naïvety, her guilt. Then, years later she helped me for no reason and looked after me when I was sick. So when she was dying she asked me to take her son Joss.'

'But why didn't she want her husband to keep his own son?'

Hannie shrugged. 'Joss is a strange boy and Rolf was a hard man and a heavy drinker, he was bad for him. Bad for Ilse too, I shouldn't have let her marry him, I should have stopped it at the start.'

'But if he left you for her,' Alison said, bewilderment in her voice – 'if he left you, how could you have stopped it?'

'There are ways. One can often stop things, if one really wants to. But I didn't know her then, I didn't care about her, so I didn't bother. Her family tried but she wouldn't listen to them and in the end they never spoke to her again.'

'But if Joss isn't your son, why do you say that he is?'

'When you marry a man, he must take your child. If it's not your child, then things are not so clear.'

'And Joss is . . . not an easy child.'

'Exactly. Joss is not an easy child.'

Alison sat back in her chair, taking in this flood of strange new information. For a moment she was certain that the woman standing at the window was deliberately misleading her. Then Hannie half-turned her head and Alison saw her face against the light-coloured curtain and she wasn't quite so sure.

'But Hannie,' she began very cautiously, 'since Joss is not easy, and since he is ... not your son, why do you go on doing this?'

Hannie stared at her. 'I just told you,' she said, surprise in her voice. 'Because Ilse asked me to.'

There was another silence. Hannie left her position by the window and sat in the chair she had left.

'Why are you telling me all this?' Alison asked.

'Because I think perhaps someone somewhere should know but I'm not sure why. Maybe it's because I have been ill again and when you recover from illness it changes everything around you for a little while.'

Alison stirred uneasily. 'Why don't you tell Ned?' she asked, her voice worried. 'Ned is a good man and he's your husband and he cares for you. Don't you think he deserves to be told the truth?'

Hannie shook her head impatiently. 'Joss is a lot to ask of anyone. It's easier for Ned to accept him if he thinks he's my son.'

'What if I were to tell Ned?'

Hannie sat back. 'I think you won't do that,' she said quietly. 'I think you wouldn't allow that of yourself. Or not till it became necessary.'

Alison thought for a moment and then nodded.

Driving home through the darkness, Alison turned Hannie's words and gestures over and over in her mind.

Was it true, what she'd said about Joss not being her son? And if it was, why didn't she give up on Joss, leave him behind somewhere? No one would blame her.

Could it be as she'd said, some sort of loyalty, some sort of debt of honour? Was it possible? Was this woman whom she'd thought more or less without morality motivated by gratitude to a dead friend?

Alison shivered; it had turned cold again, she regretted believing the afternoon's warmth and leaving off one of her sweaters. She banged the heater hard with her left hand but it only gulped and settled back into a low-grade luke-warm hum, refusing to crank itself up even half a notch.

She thought about telling Ned, but she knew that Hannie was right and she wouldn't. Why not? she wondered. Was Hannie also right in saying it was easier for Ned if he didn't know? She thought about telling Vere and she knew she wouldn't do that either. She could hear Vere's voice in her mind.

'So you're planning to swallow all that are you, Ali? Come off it, old thing, it's lies, just a tissue of lies, she knows you're a soft touch, she's buying sympathy, simple as that. How do I know? Well, she's not telling Ned, is she? And why not? Because the little monster would be out on his ear in the morning, that's why not. You think I'm being hard? Well then, answer me this – if he's not her son, why on earth is she doing it?'

'Honour,' she would say to him. 'Because her dead friend asked it of her.'

'Balls. She's just shifting the focus, making herself out to be a martyr. Ali, the woman's a walking crisis, she can't function without chaos, Joss is the same, he guarantees chaos wherever he goes.'

Alison sighed. The weather forecast was giving out change. A cold front moving rapidly in from the north. Heavy frost. On high ground, sleet and snow. She gave the heater another half-hearted thump.

Chaos. Was Vere right? A nursery jingle sounded inanely in her mind: *rings on her fingers, bells on her toes, she shall have chaos wherever she goes.*

~ *Chapter 52* ~

*I*t was much colder again, the weather forecast stopped limiting the snow to high ground and gave it out as general and widespread. Yesterday's floppy gnats must have frozen to death in the night, Hannie thought. It was amazing how fast it all changed, the brief warmth seemed like a dream-memory, the rain and the flooding were distant and unreal as a folk-tale.

She was finishing up in the kitchen, sweeping and washing the floor when some change in the light made her glance out. The sky was blank and heavy and loose grey blobs were coming flying out of it, vanishing instantly into the waiting mud. This must be snow, she thought, astonished by its greyness, by the bleak wet dreariness of it. The sky grew denser in its discoloured whiteness, the blobs grew larger and faster, they thickened and whitened and clung to the shed-roofs and the twisted branches of the apple trees. She strained her eyes through the soured light. Beyond the roofs, the thorn hedges showed black against the whitening fields.

When the light changed in the room she knew without looking out that the snow had stopped. She fetched the lead, called the puppy and walked her up the road towards Danno's. At first Pippa romped and bit at the snow, then she settled down and sniffed her way quietly through this strange, changed world. At the corner where Lambert's field ran off from the road, she stopped in her tracks and stood there sniffing and watching.

Lambert had early lambs out. They looked cold and unhappy in the snowy wastes of the meadow; they bleated and fretted and picked their way on impossibly long legs. The ewes stood stolidly, very yellow and dirty-looking against the blue-white of the snow, like large fat maggots on the pale skin of a corpse. Hannie let Pippa watch, she was only a pup but the ewes panicked when they saw her, they called their lambs to them and lumbered heavily away. Pippa didn't move, only the muscles at her neck quivered. Her fluffy fur stood out.

A belt of heavy grey cloud lay stretched out on the rim of the field. Above the cloud was the empty sky – very cold – a clear, far blue. The ewes were all moving off, lambs at their flanks, bleating and fussing like over-anxious mothers. She heard a sound behind her and turned her head. A man was standing there watching her as she was watching the ewes. She turned away. He didn't look local and yet she was sure that she knew him. She looked again. Ah yes, she remembered, she had him now. The man in the bar-tent at the races. The man who thought he was Lord Tung.

It was already beginning to thaw when he drove her back to the house. He'd suggested leaving her off where he'd found her, but she'd vetoed his suggestion.

'D'you want the whole world putting two and two together and making four?' she'd asked. 'They will if we sneak around the place being guilty.'

He hadn't liked that. He was a lot less confident after the event than before, she noticed. In fact he had looked not Lord Tung-ish at all, but rather as though he wished her at the bottom of a well. She shrugged to herself, she didn't care, he was vain and arrogant and self-centred, she wasn't about to lose sleep over him. Still, it was nice to be corrupted so pleasantly, to slip under his guard without even trying. Granted, he was at a loose end, the lovely twenty-eight-year-old had dumped him and gone off in search of livelier pastures. But he'd had to humble himself and ask, it was a good warm revenge for his previous disdain. And they were both aware of what they wanted, both skilful and practised enough to ensure a satisfactory coupling.

Ned had been in the yard at the back when she got home, he'd made a fuss of the pup but he hadn't mentioned the strange car, nor asked her where she'd been. He didn't ask, so she didn't volunteer an explanation.

Instead she took the colander from the hook in the kitchen and went down to the vegetable patch to pick spinach beet. They ate little else these days, the sprouts were over but the leeks and cabbages she'd planted in the autumn were still a long way off. She bent to the frosted beet. The bird-net had stretched with the snow, which clung in its sagging hollows, weighting and dragging them down. Gobs of cold slush from the net dripped on to her back and her head and her hands. Her toes, still swollen with chilblains despite the electric blanket, pressed painfully against the hard rubber of her wellingtons. The darkness was coming, cobalt blue against the whiteness of the thawing snow.

~ *Chapter 53* ~

*T*hings were easier. Even with Joss, it was less ominous. Hannie was taking the boy into Waterford for school assessments, dropping him off and picking him up again later. He seemed less odd and more open. There were even times when Ned wondered if James mightn't be right after all and Joss's behaviour wasn't rather the norm than the exception. What did he know about teenagers? Nothing. Nor, he had to admit to himself, did he much want to.

Hannie, too, was easier, her health and vitality restored. Things were different between them, less charged and more matter of fact. Ned was relieved but under the relief he felt as though he had somehow lost something of her. It wasn't that he wanted her to be sick, or unhappy, or desperate over Joss, but he wanted her to need his help. He had always wanted the essence of things (why else had he made those extraordinary journeys?) and now he felt her eluding him. He couldn't quite pin down the change in her. She was relaxed, almost warm, but he felt that her gaze had minutely shifted. When she looked at him now she saw slightly past him to somewhere else.

Oddly, this change made her more accessible. They talked more, spent more time in each other's company, and she was freer with him than she'd been since they were married. He was too old to be journeying, yet with her he still journeyed. New landscapes opened before him, sometimes familiar, sometimes dangerous, sometimes merely surprising. He liked the way she looked at things, said what she really thought, didn't feel the need to be consistent. Without realising it, he was getting over his initial disappointment. He was adjusting to her presence and he was less lonely.

He was right about Hannie, something had changed in her, a part of her that had been asleep had woken again, a sexual part. But she wasn't in love so it didn't overwhelm her, it just diverted her attention, cheered her up, and made things easier with Ned. She knew it was risky, these things were never a secret for long no matter how you tried to conceal them. So she was as careful as she could be, especially with Joss. She didn't want to unsettle him and she didn't want him getting ideas about another change.

She liked going to Waterford and having time that she didn't have to account for. She liked parking by the quays, walking about, watching the cattle boats and container ships and the bright, dissolute trawlers berthed in crowds by the bridge. She went into pubs, read the paper, had her hair done, bought a sweater. Sometimes she went to the accountants or the solicitors on farm business for Ned. She liked all this, liked the bars and the shops and the offices, the feeling of life going on, of people who had never seen her before and didn't care if they never saw her again, indifferent as the herring gulls watching from the railings, their eyes yellow and cold. The world was still there, she hadn't dreamed it or made it up.

She didn't get much out of Joss on their drives back and forth. He was opaque to her, silent and watchful, never letting his guard slip. The more she tried to talk to him the more he baffled and refused her. The casual intimacy of his childhood seemed lost for ever, puberty had barred all access to him, all she could do was watch and wait.

Sometimes she didn't go to Waterford at all, instead she put Joss on to the bus in Dungarvan saying she had chores to do and went to Thornton's place instead. Sometimes she met him in Waterford and he bought her lunch or a drink or took her to a hotel he had an arrangement with for such occasions.

Ned didn't know what Hannie did while she waited in Waterford for Joss and he didn't ask. If she was back in the afternoon now she came and worked alongside him and he liked this so well he forgot his preference for solitude. She worked hard and efficiently. Sometimes she talked as she worked but she never just downed tools and chattered.

Ned knew Thornton slightly himself and had no interest in him. He'd seen her getting out of Thornton's car on the day of the snow and he'd waited for her to mention it, but she hadn't and then he'd remembered seeing them talking together in the bar-tent at the races. Thornton had bought the old Cantalon place and was doing it up; Ned supposed that he'd asked Hannie over to look at it, perhaps to give him advice. He felt he should be glad that Thornton was interested in her opinion, but he wasn't, he didn't like her going there, he was afraid she might fall in love with the man.

It didn't cross his mind that Hannie might simply go to bed with Thornton, he didn't conceive of sex as something she might do for its own sake, without passion or affection or even the contract of marriage; the truth of the situation didn't once occur to him. But because he was jealous of Thornton's possible place in Hannie's affections, Ned remembered the doctor's words and he cast around in his mind for ways to make her life more outward-looking and varied.

'Mrs Cardew was on the phone. She wants to know when she's getting her picture.' Hannie tossed the words over her shoulder.

The weather was wild and cold again and she was bundled up in layers of his old jackets and coats, a motley of brown corduroys and greyish wools and tweeds. They were clearing out one of the sheds together, the lambing was still a week or so off, but there were more ewes this year and Ned liked to feel fully prepared and in control.

'I can't understand Niamh,' Ned said tetchily. 'Mrs Cardew's paid in advance. Sylvia Roche didn't pay, Niamh can do what she wants about her picture, but Mrs Cardew's paid.'

Hannie didn't say anything. Ned went on lugging fertiliser sacks.

'You have to deliver what you've undertaken to deliver, surely Niamh understands that? It isn't always plain sailing, quite often commissions turn out to be more trouble than they're worth, but you don't just dump them because they're inconvenient, you still have to stand by your word. I'm surprised at Niamh. Disappointed . . .'

'Niamh doesn't live in the real world,' Hannie said. 'Which is just as well, she'd last about five minutes. Anyway, she's busy, she's making papier-mâché legs for an exhibition.'

'Papier-mâché what?'

'Legs. Like the legs Joss made. Only better, more life-like, more shocking.'

Ned stopped spreading hay with his fork and straightened up and stared at Hannie. Hannie didn't stop work to stare back.

'Several of them. Different models. One of them has chained-together ankles and a padlock on the chain. A reference to chastity belts, she says. Chastity belts and possession. Another one has scarlet slashes painted across its cunt. She's going to hang them by their ankles in some gallery, just as Joss did.'

'Has Joss seen them?'

'Joss is helping her. She wants him to, that's why he's there so much.' Hannie straightened as well and looked at Ned. 'I told Joss he shouldn't go round there all the time and he said she'd asked him to give her a hand. When I checked with her she said it was true.'

'But what's she doing it for? Why's she making these things?' Ned sounded almost more bewildered than shocked.

Hannie shrugged her shoulders. 'I told you, for some exhibition. She says that they're a metaphor for misogyny in marriage, hence the chained ankles and the mutilated genitals. Nothing subtle – she says that's important: "I want it to look as though its cunt has been slashed."' Hannie turned back to her work as though tired of the subject.

'What about Joss?'

'What about him? Perhaps it'll do him good, you never know with Joss. Occupational therapy. Like Danno making baskets ... Maybe she'll rope Danno in as well, get him to teach her some basketry, make woven legs out of willows. I wouldn't put it past her. She's always on about old skills, adapting them, using them in new ways.' Hannie pulled out a nest of blackened sacks from a corner and heaved them on to the growing pile of rubbish. 'On second thoughts, perhaps not. Danno would have a fit and anyway she's such a puritan.'

She pulled again and a tangle of rotting ropes followed the sacks. A rat ran across her foot and made for the open door.

'Young women, what chaos they do cause; I never noticed it when I was young myself. But maybe she's right about old skills, Ned. Danno's selling baskets faster than he can make them. Maybe you should give up this lavender plan and try your hand at growing willow. At least you wouldn't have to fight this bloody climate quite so hard.'

'I won't be here tomorrow,' Joss said from the top of the ladder. 'He's taking her to some pile of old stones. She says I have to go with them.'

'Couldn't you get out of it? I need to hang the frame for the next one and I need someone to hold it while I get it right.' Niamh stood back and half closed her eyes. 'A bit higher. That's enough. Now lower again – not much – an inch or two should do it.'

Joss pulled on the rope and the papier-mâché legs rose. He gave it some slack and the legs dropped slightly. Niamh walked all round them, looking at them critically, but with mounting excitement. The wire frame she'd built the model on had been suspended from the start, but this was the first time she'd seen the work with the proper elevation. It looked good, well-made and powerful and shocking. It had a potency and presence beyond what she'd expected. She was glad she'd abandoned the print dresses. The white tulle of this skirt was perfect and the white satin overskirt, now reversed and become an underskirt, was quietly redolent of weddings.

'Okay, that's fine, that's exactly the height I want. I didn't know Hannie was into ruins?'

'She isn't.' Joss wound the rope round a bracket he'd fixed to the ceiling and secured it with a couple of hitches. 'Not remotely, but he wants to take her and she says she's not about to leave me to my own devices.' He came down from the ladder, hammer in hand, and Niamh tossed him a cigarette. They both lit up. Niamh had gone back on the fags after Ciaran had left. Might as well kill herself with her own smoke, she'd decided, there was always someone else's around to breathe.

'Where's this heap of stones you're off to visit?'

'Don't know. Clon-something. Some monastery he rates, up on the Shannon –'

'Clonmacnoise?'

'That's it. Used to be where it was at about a thousand years ago. He's creaming himself. Bore the pants off anyone else.'

'It's famous,' Niamh said, 'it's supposed to be really interesting. Everyone had a go at it – Vikings, Irish, Brits. You should go, you might just learn something.'

Joss made a face. 'Lay off, will you? I'm going, I'm not being given the choice. Want to come with us?'

'Flattened,' Niamh said, 'twenty-six times in twelve years. Can you believe it?' She turned from the scattered grey monastery ruins to Joss. 'Wake up, strap on the old sword, jump into the boat and we're off. Now, where'll we go today? I know – Clonmacnoise.'

'Nah,' Joss said. 'Boring. Did that last year.'

'So?' She rounded on him. 'It's a really good raid, they have great altar treasures, churches to burn, monks just waiting to be disembowelled. You don't even have to walk far, you can get really close in the boat.'

'I told you, we did that last year. You're such a nerd, Niamh, we can't just do the same things over and over, we'll lose respect.'

'Okay, wise-guy, you think of somewhere better.'

Joss pantomimed thought, his forehead on his fist. Then he looked up brightly, as though a light had just gone on inside his head.

'I know, let's do Clonmacnoise. It's a really great raid – altar treasures, nuns to rape, monks to skewer, plus we haven't done it for at least six months.'

'You're on,' Niamh said. Together they took off down the boggy slope, arms and legs flying, Pippa plunging and bouncing behind them. A great cloud of lapwings got up from the rushes and took to the air, turning and weaving, loose wings dark against white bellies; the racing grey sky was filled with the wheeling birds. They broke and scattered and the sky scattered with them, they dropped and rose again and the sky rose too. Niamh and Joss stopped their wild flight. They pointed up at the birds, waved their arms about, ran on. Pippa plunged through the bog, sleek as a seal with dark mud, desperate to keep up. The Shannon gleamed and wound through its sombre flood-plain.

No one had much liked Clonmacnoise, its neat, sealed ruins and lawns and concrete paths, but they all liked the river, the empty jetty, the wide flood-meadows, the rainy wind. Pippa, used to the steep banks and inaccessible flow of the Black-water, splashed cautiously about in the shallow fringes of the Shannon. Joss found a stick and dropped it almost in front of her nose. She stood in the water, quivering, then stretched her neck, seized the stick and carried it carefully in. Joss dropped the stick further out, tempting the puppy into deeper water. Again, she brought it back.

Then the stick was too far out and she baulked and wouldn't risk it. Joss waded out up to his knees in the icy water. He stood patiently by the stick, encouraging Pippa to come for it. Pippa plunged, sank, swam a few frantic strokes, grabbed the stick and made it back to the shore. They all cheered. She laid the stick at Hannie's feet. Joss waded back again, water pouring from his jeans and mud-soaked trainers.

The wind strengthened, it was getting colder, the sombre light had deepened, they turned and faced back up the rise. Niamh plodded ahead, Hannie followed with her arm linked into Ned's, Joss and Pippa came behind, the puppy staggering with exhaustion. Joss reached down, caught her by the loose skin of her neck and heaved her on to his shoulder. She rode there, shivering and content, licking at his ear.

A few days later Hannie skipped a Waterford liaison with Thornton. She hadn't intended to, but she saw a ship leave its moorings on the quay and suddenly nothing would do but she had to smell salt water. She turned the car round and drove out to the coast and walked in the cold rainy air by the grey heave of the sea. Then she went to get Joss.

It was the effort he made to impress her that was getting to be too much. The house, the grounds, his things, his plans, his past, his future: everything endlessly displayed for her admiration. And she'd never cared for things or success, neither his possessions nor his attainments remotely impressed her. Sometimes she'd catch him looking at her and really seeing her (her un-twenty-eightness), and she'd see him wondering to himself why he was trying so hard to gain her admiration. Yet he couldn't seem to stop. Which made her still a challenge, despite her willingness to be bedded. He'd move on when something better presented itself, they both knew that, but in the meantime she had his attention. And she didn't give a toss about him, she hardly even cared about the sex.

She found that she liked going home to Ned, who was quiet and modest about the place, though he was no use in bed.

❧ *Chapter 54* ❧

*H*annie was settled deep in the big mangy armchair, legs stretched in front of her, feet propped on a torn leather pouf. They had got through dinner and had moved to Vere's study to drink whisky in front of a modest fire.

The study was narrow and high-ceilinged; there were sagging shelves heaped with jumbled volumes and piles of National Geographics and Sotheby's catalogues. The walls were smoky and studded with fox heads and photos of hounds and horses. A poster showing breeds of sheep was pinned up over the desk beside a portrait-study of a lovely young woman with fine skin and dreamy eyes that might once have been Alison. There were dogs everywhere, mostly old.

At least it's half warm in here, Hannie thought, most likely the only warm room in the house. A large part of Alison's energies seemed to be absorbed into making ends meet: recycling was second nature, economies were complex, far-reaching, and always uppermost in her mind. Alison would be ruthless where her own welfare was concerned, Hannie speculated, but would preserve a few creature-comforts for the beloved Vere. Suddenly Hannie was relieved that Ned hadn't landed her with a House: his friends and relations were quite enough without a mouldering pile as well.

She shifted herself further down in the chair and looked owlishly over her glass in parody of James. After the trials of dinner it was good to be completely comfortable. And the whisky helped one forget the food. 'One'. Any minute now and she'd be talking like Marjorie. Her mind wandered. Perhaps she'd end up looking like Marjorie too? No Lord Tung then. At this moment that seemed like a definite loss. Ah well, perhaps she'd be past it by then anyway. It was even possible, if she hung on that long, that she might have *got her bearings*, *settled down*, *learned to belong*, or some other such euphemism for giving up and giving in.

'Wrong climate,' Vere was saying to Ned, 'better off with daffodils, northern sort of flower, temperate, doesn't mind rain, easier all round than lavender.'

'Likes a bit of decent soil just the same,' James put in. 'And what about marketing, what good's a field full of flowers? He has to get them cut and bunched and sent off to where someone's going to buy them.'

'Could be done. Not impossible, take a bit of organisation . . .'

'Cost a bloody fortune. He'd never get his money back.'

'He'd have to do his sums,' Vere argued stubbornly. 'Identify his market, cost his labour, that sort of thing.'

James snorted.

'Change of plan,' Ned said before Vere could get in a reply. 'Change of plan, Hannie had a better idea, I've given up lavender, we're going into willow.'

'Willow?' The brothers looked at him in disbelief. 'You mean sallies?'

'Exactly,' Ned said. 'Sally wands for basket-makers.'

'You're out of your mind, Ned,' Marjorie announced firmly. 'The country's coming down with sallies, if you want to make a basket you can cut what you want when you want, no one in their senses is going to part with hard-earned cash for them.'

'They do already,' Ned said confidently. 'A skilled man – or woman for that matter – a skilled man wants to spend his time making, not cutting and drying and sizing and storing, he's buying in willow that's ready-to-use and he's buying it in from England. There's a demand, I tell you, I've done the sums, collected up some information, basket-making's on the up and up.'

'Hmm. Haven't noticed Danno going in for conspicuous consumption recently. Haven't noticed him driving a new car around the place or putting a decent engine on that boat of his.'

'Not Danno, Danno cuts his own sallies, he makes a few creels and log-baskets when the fancy takes him, bottom end of the market, that's as far as he goes. It's not Danno I'm talking about, it's people who do it seriously, the ones who fill the orders in the smart craft shops, foreigners mostly, people who've come here to live an alternative lifestyle and found that basket-making's an economic way of doing it.'

Half an hour later the argument was finally losing steam and Alison was filling up the glasses. Hannie had taken no part in it, she'd sat deep in her chair, half-listening to Ned and the stream of information he'd acquired from somewhere, half lost in her own wandering thoughts.

'Did you see that Dimbleby programme?' Vere was addressing her.

'Not Dimbleby, Vere, Attenborough. He means that Attenborough man,' Marjorie announced.

'Do I? So I do. Fascinating. Speeded-up film. Plants and seeds and the right places.'

They all looked blank.

'How plants try to ensure their seeds have the best possible habitat,' Alison said quietly.

'That's what I said – the lengths they go to. Always thought it was up to the birds and the wind. Not a bit of it – all organised – nothing left to chance. Showed you a plant on a wall – nothing foreign or exotic – just a little toadflax you'd see any day on any wall. Then they showed you what it does –' Vere paused dramatically and looked at their waiting faces.

'Speeded-up film,' he announced. 'Fascinating. It feels around on its wall, earmarks a crack or a crumbly bit, then reaches up where it wants its seeds to go and puts them there itself. Amazing. You could actually see the thing performing . . .'

'Not so different, after all,' James leered. Vere looked at him blankly. 'Puts in the seed where it wants it,' James crowed.

'Oh. Oh, yes, exactly so,' Vere said. 'It was incredible. And all sorts of examples . . .'

'What's a toadflax?' Hannie asked lazily.

'That little mauve pea-flower with the roundy leaves,' Alison replied. 'A yellow stain on its lip. Common – likes old walls.' She smiled quietly at Hannie. 'Vere likes these natural history programmes,' she explained. 'He'd never watch the television to begin with. We got it for the children, Vere never wanted it, he only agreed because of the Olympics.'

'Sport and wildlife,' Vere said at Hannie. 'I like the wildlife programmes and the natural history.'

'I like a decent documentary myself,' James said. 'Hate chat shows. Can't stand that Gay Byrne fellow. Pat Kenny makes me puke.'

'You always watch Pat Kenny,' Marjorie said indignantly.

'Still makes me puke.'

'I watched the other night,' Ned said. 'Annaghmore was on. Or that's what they told me in the post office. But it wasn't on at all, it was only an interview with Thornton about the record business. Waste of time, really, Hannie had more sense – went to bed – but I wanted to see what he'd made of the place.'

There was a small queer pause in the room which Ned didn't appear to notice. Hannie did, though she didn't stir or try to move it on. At least now she knew how the land lay.

'We watched it too,' Marjorie said. 'To see the house.' She swung round suddenly and addressed Hannie. 'Weren't you curious?' she asked, something close to belligerence in her voice.

Hannie seemed to have slithered deeper into the chair; she had long since discarded her shoes, she wriggled her stockinged toes on the pouf.

'Curious?' she said to Marjorie. 'No – why should I be? I have seen it, he has shown me all over, for me it is just a big house, the inside very clean and expensive and new. Really, it is wasted on me . I didn't know it before when the Cantelons had it, as all of you did, so the changes meant nothing to me. You should go and see it if you want to, he will show anyone, he is very proud of it, but you must be very interested and have lots of time. Really, it is rather boring.'

There was gaiety in Hannie's face, and amusement. The slight foreignness of her voice and diction was accented. She looked up candidly at Marjorie. James snorted and Alison looked at the floor, but no one spoke. They were careful not to let their eyes stray to Ned, who had brought into their lives this woman who was making a fool of him and didn't know how to behave.

'Oh, come on, Niamh,' Joss said, 'don't be such a scaredy. Take it, it's a gas, you'll have a great time.'

Niamh looked at the little pill lying in the palm of her hand. She took a big swig from her glass. The vodka tasted clean and cool.

'Where did you get it?' she asked him.

'Off Nora's nephew. Con, his name is. Good name, eh? Con by name and conning by nature, that's what I told him. He liked that. He's cool, she never knew a thing, the stupid cow. Thinks he's innocent and pure. She said we were a good influence on each other. Far out, eh? A good influence!'

Joss spoke fast, his voice was light and excited, he was pacing restlessly round the room as he talked. Niamh wondered what he'd already taken. Aside from the vodka he'd drunk with her, that was. She thought of telling him he'd had enough, but she knew that'd be red-rag-to-the-bull.

'She was right there, wasn't she, Niamh? Joss is always a good influence. Stupid fucking cow. She said I was good with the kids as well. And so I was, with my lovely bedtime stories out of this big old book that had been in Andrew's house when he was a kid. Ghosty poems, scary stories, Edgar Allan Poe, stuff like that. There was a great one about an earwig

308

crawling into this man's ear, laying its eggs and the eggs hatching and maggots eating his brains out. All that stuff.

'Alana – that was the girl – she was younger but she was wised-up – if she didn't like something she just stuffed her fingers into her ears and watched my mouth till she saw I'd stopped reading. But the boy couldn't get enough and he had nightmares, wet his bed. Andrew went on at him, made him tell what scared him.

'Andrew was mad with me at the start, he was a whole load more copped-on than she was most of the time but he was silly about her, he let himself be talked round. Plus he was in a difficult position, he'd told her he'd read the book himself when he was a kid, but he couldn't have – obviously – he wouldn't have forgotten stuff like that. Anyway, Andrew says he doesn't like what I'm reading to them, says it's too frightening – which it definitely is.

'So I stop and the little kid goes off his food, he wets his bed worse, he's afraid to go to sleep cos he knows about the earwig that's eating out his brain on account of him telling his daddy. And you know what she does? You'll love this, Niamh, you really will. She decides it must be school, she rings the other mothers and it's the same story, half their kids have got the jitters as well, cos he's been telling them about the earwigs in their brains. Then she goes to the teacher and she wants to know why the kids are scared, what's going on, is that new priest that's coming in for religion *really* all right?' Joss sniggered delightedly.

'Too much, isn't it, Niamh? And she says to me, it's okay to read to them again, but maybe something a bit younger? *She* knows it's all right, of course she does, Alana's fine, but Andrew was an only child, he doesn't understand that children love being scared. And then she starts on about being little and her big sister telling them scary stories and them all sitting there, goggle-eyed and loving it, the fear and all that – and she gives me the Flopsy Bunnies to read to them, but by then it's way too late, I can read about lettuces and baby rabbits till the cows come home but every time Mr McGregor comes on the scene I just whisper earwigs and hey presto – who needs Edgar Allan Poe?'

Joss stopped pacing abruptly and dumped himself sideways in the armchair with his legs over one arm. He lit a cigarette. Niamh watched him, despising him. She hated Joss like this: how degenerate and wicked he was, how clever and cool and immoral. She knew he was lying to build himself up because he was lonely and insecure, she knew she should ignore him and never ever act shocked or even surprised, but sometimes she wanted to tell him what she thought of what he was saying so badly she had to bite her lip to keep the words in.

It was like that now. She sat there, sipping at her vodka, saying nothing. She didn't dislike him as a human being, she told herself, she just wished he'd take his fuck-ups and his hang-ups somewhere else.

'It's amazing, it really is,' Joss was saying. 'If you showed a video of the stuff that's in that book, they'd lynch you, but it's a book and it's got a leather binding, so it must be okay. I mean, have you ever *read* Poe, Niamh? Bizarre. What a mind! He must have been on everything. They were, you know, those Victorians, it was the way they liked things. Quiet and neat on the surface and *wild* underneath, just wild. I mean, Elizabeth Fry was a laudanum-head, did you know that, Niamh? This famous Quaker – in there, reforming the prisons, giving everyone a piece of her mind – and she was a laudanum-head! I said that to one of those Quaker teachers at that poxy school and he just looked at me. "It's very possible," he said, "yes, very possible, we are all human." Joss sniggered quietly to himself. 'We are all human – I mean to *say* . . .'

Abruptly he stopped sniggering, threw his cigarette-end into the fire, swung his feet off the chair, and was up and pacing again.

'What are you hanging about for, Niamh, haven't you dropped that thing yet? You won't be scared, I promise, you won't have a bad time or anything, you'll have little bubbles in your blood and one huge big smile wrapped round your face and new red dancing shoes on your feet . . .'

'I know what E is, Joss.'

'Then what're you hanging about for? Come on, Niamh, throw it into yourself, I've got her car-keys, we'll go into town, find ourselves a club, they won't be back for hours.'

'I haven't got a licence.'

'So? You can drive, I can drive, who needs a licence? What's the problem?'

'The problem is, Joss,' she said, wishing she didn't feel so drunk, 'the problem is, what if it's cut?'

'Cut? Would Joss give you stuff that's cut? What are you talking about, man? I've had this stuff, it's A-one, Niamh, believe me, it's A-one cool.'

'It all looks the same, Joss,' she said carefully, aware that her words were coming out a bit slurred, 'but it isn't the same any more. You have to be dead careful now, some of it's cut with a whole lot of shit. Dangerous shit. And a little bit of smack in it to make you think it's what it says it is and like it used to be.' She finished in a rush and had another swallow from her glass. Joss was watching her very intently, a funny expression on his small white face. He pulled a chair out from the table, spun it round and sat down on it, his legs astride it and his arms folded across its back. He rested his chin on them and went on staring at her.

'You know something, Niamh,' he said very quietly and gently, 'I bet you were always careful. I bet you were so careful, you never took it even when it was *all* good stuff. In fact, Niamh, I bet you've never taken anything at all. Oh, I know – speed, acid, coke – you've tried them all, I heard you telling Ciaran. But I've just sussed you, Niamh, you're one of those Talk-ones, you're one of those ones that stashed the stuff and watched the others. Cos you want to be in there but you're much too careful to do it yourself, much too scared of losing control.

'I might have known what you'd be like.' There was no missing the hard sneer in his voice now. 'You're all pretend, Niamh. You're a fake, a rotten fake. If I hadn't heard you with my own ears moaning your head off under Ciaran I'd say you'd lied about that as well. And to think I was planning to give you some later on, just to make your night. To think I was going to dirty my beautiful cock on you.'

For a moment Niamh thought she hadn't heard him right. She went white, then red. She sat numb. Then she pushed the pill across the table towards him. Her hand shook but she kept her hold on herself.

'And to think I thought you might be all right if someone gave you a chance,' she said. 'To think I thought you might be growing up. You're just a little boy, Joss, a smutty little wanker in the literal sense of the word. All boast and shit. And I knew that. I said it to Ciaran right at the start. And then, between the two of you, I forgot. For a while there – I have to admit it – I just forgot. So thank you for reminding me, Joss, thank you very much. It's one mistake I'll not be making again.'

❧ *Chapter 55* ❧

Vere and Alison came out with them to see them off. It was two in the morning, cold and still. No moon, but the sky clear and mazy with stars. 'Like the tropics,' James said.

Not like the tropics, Hannie thought. These stars were glittering and sharp, not soft and large, like blossoms or moths. She moved away and stood waiting for Ned. Ned, knowing both worlds, Ned who could have bridged them for her if she'd let him.

She didn't want a bridge, that was the truth of it. She didn't want this new world, didn't want to think and adapt and review her life, just wanted to go on living it, such as it was, without the pain of reflection.

But deeper down she yearned for something beyond even that, she yearned for her first life, a world lived milky and close to the ground, the lost voices in the darkness like small birds talking.

And she could never have that back. Never, never, never, no matter how she longed, or what she did, or how she tried.

Behind her Vere had started to sing and the others joined in.

> Oh little town of Bethlehem,
> how still we see thee lie
> above thy deep and dreamless sleep
> the silent stars go by . . .

They went on singing, carol after carol, everyone knowing most of the words, someone always knowing the bit where the others forgot and the voices thinned. They'd waver, wait for a familiar phrase, resume; a sort of gladness in them when they had the words again, a peace and contentment in their faces and their voices that was so tangible that Hannie had to look away.

Peace and contentment. Like a built wall, Ned thought, and his wife there, standing alone on the other side of it. And how could it be otherwise? She was of another race, another world; she didn't know even the simple sweetness of these carols that they'd sung together in this valley since their earliest childhood. He should cross the wall to be with her, he knew that, but he didn't want to leave off singing, he didn't want to leave belonging with his comrades now he stood beside them after years away.

It was late, Niamh had polished off most of the remaining vodka. But she wasn't shaken any more, she had got over Joss and his little outburst, had retreated into her adult self and put his juvenilia into perspective.

And there was a certain steadying satisfaction in having been, at last, proved right. It wasn't just her imagination. Joss *did* fancy her. He *did* fantasise about her, she was right to be wary of him.

She remembered Ciaran's ridicule when she'd suggested it. Joss was just a kid, he'd said, lonely, trying to find his bearings after Africa. Sure, he would fantasise in a general sort of way – it was a sexual age – but not Niamh, Niamh at twenty-one would seem about of an age with his grandmother. Always supposing Joss had anything as normal as a grand-mother.

She should relax, Ciaran had said, stop being sexually para-noid. Less paranoia, more sex.

Niamh remembered the look she had given him. Then she remembered the next bit. She *had* relaxed, but she'd made him climb the stairs for it. In case Ned called, or Hannie called, or Joss called. He'd said she was ridiculous, but worth it.

She'd forgotten everything for a while, but afterwards the uneasiness was still there with her.

And then she'd forgotten the uneasiness as well. She'd disregarded her own warnings, let Joss confide in her, opened herself to his influence, let his thoughts slide into her mind.

Like the shadow of a hawk, she thought, sliding over the yellow grass.

Yellow grass. Now where did that come from? The grass here wasn't yellow, it was green. And yet she could see it, the dark shadow slipping sideways and very fast. Yellow grass: African grass. But she'd never been to Africa . . .

She'd go to bed now, she decided, she wouldn't drink any more or think any more, she'd just go to bed, sleep off the booze and get it all straight in the morning.

Now, where was the top of the bottle? She fumbled around on the table, picking things up and putting them down again. There it was, where she'd already looked, there beside her gloves and Hannie's car-keys. Funny how much easier it was to think than do when you'd had a few drinks. She screwed the top down on the dregs of the vodka. Nothing like locking the stable door when the horse has mostly gone.

'Now Niamh,' she said aloud to herself, 'fire, lights, doors. Then you can fill your hot-water bottle and crawl into bed and sleep.'

She banked the fire, positioned the guard and put the kettle on to boil. She was standing beside it, hot-water bottle at the ready, when she heard the cough outside the window. She was startled, but no more, there was always some animal or other with a cough, it sounded more like a heifer than a sheep but Ned didn't have any cattle in the near field.

The coughing noise came again, but this time it was much louder and there was the sound of a bin lid falling. Perhaps it was a cat, perhaps it was Joss, drunk and stoned, bumbling around bumping into things.

She hated Joss, his crawly voice and his ugly words and his small white face, but it didn't occur to her to be afraid of him.

315

It never had, that's what Ciaran hadn't understood, he was just ridiculous and nasty and she was a fool to have tried to help him, to have let him hang around. She took the torch down from its hook and pulled open the door –

She was scared when she saw it, who wouldn't have been? The blazing cross with the great bird on it, its wings stretched, writhing and twisting, black against the leaping flames.

For a moment she almost panicked, then something strong and detached and self-observing came up inside her. She was scared all right, but not as scared as she might have been, not terrified, it was too kitsch, too Klu Klux Clan, and besides she'd been thinking Joss when she saw it, and she knew Joss, knew the gothic coils of his imagination. She made a huge effort, made herself look at it for what it was: a silly farce, no more, a cheap stunt like the legs, just bits of tarred wood, just a crucified bird – not a bird at all – just one of Danno's mangy old stuffed pheasants.

These thoughts flashed through her, then the detachment was gone and rage came in its place to save her.

She clutched tight to the torch and stormed out, shouting as she ran – 'Shite, pig, bollix, dirty-minded-little-shyster' – she didn't know what she was saying, she didn't care, but she wouldn't let him put this on her, the fucker, she wouldn't let him beat her.

She ran right up to the stupid hackneyed blazing thing, she flew at it, kicked at it, her boot hit the rotten timber, the arm of the cross fell slantwise, burning feathers flew up into the night, the bird writhed as though it was alive or newly dead, one claw lifted horribly through the licking flames –

She was still attacking it, kicking and swearing, the tears running down her face and her breath coming in sobs when she saw the other thing, the long slim form hanging from the branches of the apple tree, dark ropes looping from it, turning slowly in the fiery light –

She stopped kicking and moved closer. And all at once, without even looking again though she did look again, she knew it was Pip, hanged Pip, her soft little belly slashed, her guts spilling out in thin black ropes.

Joss.

She turned and ran hard for the light and the open door, plunged through it, slammed it shut behind her, turned the key, plunged on through the house to the other door, her shaking hand already on the key to lock it fast against him.

Then she heard his laugh, low and soft and coming from the room behind her.

Her hand flew to the knob, she yanked open the door, fell into the night, terror at her back, terror driving her forward, feet slipping and sliding on the muddy path, running and running, heart pounding, breath coming ragged and wild, his feet coming closer and closer behind her . . .

Hannie was sitting hunched into herself in the car, staring sightlessly out of the side window. It was her usual don't-speak-to-me-posture, so Ned didn't. He was tired anyway and fed up with the effort of it all, with feeling angry with her, with feeling bad about her, with feeling a failure.

There was something going on about Thornton, he didn't know what, but the others knew, he'd felt it in the room when he brought up that programme he'd watched that hadn't been about Annaghmore after all, but about the record business. Something – he didn't know what – but whatever it was, it wasn't good.

Ned knew now that this marriage had been a mistake. He was too old for her, their backgrounds were too different, he couldn't make her happy no matter how he tried, he couldn't give her enough to make her life here meaningful. And he'd no one to blame but himself, he'd married her because he wanted her here, simple as that, he should never have let himself persuade her to it.

He'd got nothing for himself either; she had turned his life upside down, filled his waking hours with an unbearable, unfulfillable yearning for what she couldn't give him, destroyed his peace of mind. Even Joss had done badly, had gained little beyond a certain material security; it might even be that this marriage had brought his demons closer in on him.

Suddenly he didn't like anyone – neither himself, nor his friends, nor her, either. He wished profoundly that he'd stayed at home and never found her, that he had accepted his lot and gone quiet and lonely into old age and death.

The lights were still on in the cottage when they turned into the drive, the yellow squares of its windows shining through a net of branches. Joss would still be at Niamh's, Hannie thought, she'd better go and winkle him out, though Ned hadn't nagged about Niamh's so much since the trip to Clonmacnoise. She sighed and fished around down the side of the Land-Rover seat for her other glove. Scarves, hats, gloves, coats, boots – she couldn't get used to the clutter of things you needed here every time you opened an outside door.

'Where's the Volkswagen?'

Hannie was bent sideways trying to retrieve the errant glove. She could feel it, could get a hold with the tips of two of her fingers, but when she pulled her hand came away and the glove stayed where it was.

'Bloody thing must be caught.'

'Hannie, the Volkswagen, surely you put the Volkswagen away before we left?'

Hannie hauled herself upright. 'What? Of course I did, what's wrong with you, you must be going bli—' She stared at the shadowy space between the Land-Rover and the tractor. 'Oh shit, shit, shit, shit, shit.' She had the door open and was out of the Land-Rover in one movement. 'Joss!' she yelled into the darkness beyond the shed door. 'Joss, where are you, you bloody fucking little nuisance! Where's the car, where's the keys, and where the hell are you?'

No answer. She set off furiously for the cottage. Ned saw its outside light go on, heard a door open and close, a pause, and then all the lights went off at once and a few minutes later Hannie reappeared.

'There's no one there now, but they've been there, they must have gone off in the car, I must have left my keys out.' She stared at Ned. 'I didn't know Niamh could drive?'

'Neither did I, but she's farm-reared, she'll drive a bit though she probably hasn't a licence. Can Joss?'

'Same. He can drive a bit but not very well, and no licence. Plus they're drunk, there's an empty bottle of vodka on the table.'

'Where could they have gone?'

'Sin city – Dungarvan. Joss is always pestering me about some club there, I don't know what it's called but it shouldn't be hard to find, I can't imagine there'll be more than one.' She had her hand on the Land-Rover door as she spoke. Ned put his hand on her arm.

'If that's where they've gone then you might as well leave them to it. It's nearly three, they can't be much longer, at this hour in the morning Dungarvan's like a grave.'

'They might go back to someone's house.'

'Then you won't be able to find them anyway.'

She turned and faced him. 'Something's wrong, Ned, I'm sure something's wrong, I want to try –'

Ned shook his head. 'Go to bed, Hannie, they'll be home soon, and if they're not then driving around looking for them isn't going to help. Besides, the Land-Rover's tank's nearly empty and the spare can's in the Volkswagen.'

'I might find them.'

He shook his head again. 'There's three different roads they could take, you'll just go round in circles till you run out of petrol.'

She stared at him. 'Shit, shit and shit again. I hope to God Niamh's driving.'

❧ *Chapter 56* ❧

*H*annie lay awake. Sometimes a floorboard creaked, a door eased shut, a window rattled unaccountably in its frame. Each time a sound came she tensed and lay in the cold dark straining for more sounds, for steps on the stairs, water moving in the pipes, a too-carefully closed door. Some time after five she knew it was hopeless, he hadn't come in, she wasn't going to sleep, she might as well get up and go and check at Niamh's . . .

She woke with a start; a noise had disturbed her, steps on the landing, a bright narrow light-stripe was shining under the door. She sat up. There was something she had to remember. She stared into the thinning darkness, at the shapes that were forming themselves in the room.

Joss.

The steps had stopped but the landing light was still on. She listened again, then threw off the blankets and reached for a sweater. She pulled trousers over her nightdress, bundling its thick folds up around her waist.

There was no light on in Joss's room, no clothes were tossed around, the bed was empty and unslept in, the room icy and uninhabited.

But the footsteps she'd heard?

Ned, going out to the loo, making his way back again to bed.

Hannie laid breakfast but she didn't eat, nor had she meant to, she just wanted to give him a few more minutes in which to have got back; to delay a fraction longer before opening Niamh's door and finding him really there. Then she put on her boots, took a coat from the hook and went out into the yard. It had rained heavily in the night and the dank air clung to her face, the thin daylight creeping and licking like a cat, insinuating for a place in this interlude between dark and dark.

She went into the long stone shed where the cars were kept. A smell of mould, a scuffle of rats in the corner. No Volkswagen.

'They're not back, Hannie.' Ned was standing behind her. 'No one in the cottage, no sign of the car. I think it's time we thought about the Guards.'

'Not yet.' The words came out too quick and hard; she made an effort, dropped a key, she wanted her argument to sound like reasoned thinking. 'It's early yet, they might have stayed over with someone, they both had a skinful, they're probably still sleeping it off.' She glanced at Ned. She was getting through. 'I don't think we should go panicking,' she went on. 'We should give them an hour or two, let them wake up and get to a phone, after that we can think about calling the Guards.'

'Something might have happened.'

'But it might not. And they've neither of them got a licence and they must both have been well over the limit. Why don't you go and have some breakfast, then phone the hospitals in case and check admissions? I'll take the Land-Rover, have a scout around, I can get petrol at Delaney's on the way.'

'I can't find Pip, either –'

'Don't worry about Pip, she'll turn up, and so will they.'

When Hannie got back two hours later the local Garda car was in the drive and a muddy blue Cortina was parked in front of the house. She swore to herself, bit her lip, took a deep breath and prepared, once more, to perform.

There were four of them in the kitchen when she walked in: Ned and John Comerford were sitting at the table, Garda Mahon was talking quietly into the phone and a tall rangy brother of Niamh's called Niall was standing at the window drinking a mug of tea. Ned got up and came towards her. None of the others moved.

'Hannie –' he started and stopped.

Hannie looked at him. Her hands wanted to fly to her mouth but she held them rigidly by her side. She could see anger in Ned's face, anger and shame, and behind this darkness she could see compassion and she knew it was for her. She stood very still. 'Something's happened,' she said, and it was a statement not a question.

❧ *Chapter 57* ❧

*T*he facts seemed to tell their own story: a chase in the dark, the path to the river trampled and beaten down, skid-marks on the bank where someone might have lost their footing and gone in. Plus the missing car, the cross, the hanged and gutted dog.

Frogmen came, and Garda specialists. For five days they dragged the river and searched through the woods and the bogs and the fields. They found nothing, neither a drowned body nor a live one nor any sign of the Volkswagen. At the end of the time they packed up their gear and left. The radio said that the search had been abandoned, it was possible that a body or bodies had been washed out to sea.

The radio had given out a description of both the missing young people. There were also reports of a hanged dog, a Ku Klux cross and some unusual sculptures that the Guards had found in the cottage where the young woman lived. There were no reports of foul play, or of either of the young people being wanted for any reason other than to ascertain their whereabouts, but there was speculation in the newspapers and locally everyone was way ahead of what was written down.

– *It's murder, so it is, let no one tell you different, he's after raping her and then pushing her into the river . . .*

– *There's no body, no proof that she's dead even . . .*

– *They'll find her, she's drowned sure enough . . .*

– *If she slipped, it isn't murder, it's an accident, even he frightened her into it . . .*

– *Accident? I suppose you'll be telling me next she was traipsing about in the dark for her health . . .*

– *Maybe it was the other way round. Maybe it's the boy went into the river . . .*

– *It was the girl all right, they know from the footprints . . .*

– *Maybe she crawled out and legged it, maybe he helped her? Maybe the two of them's driving around the place right now, listening to the radio and laughing?*

– *You've been at the videos. They say she was a quiet sort of a girl, not one of your Bonnie-and-Clydes . . .*

– *Then what about them things the Guards found in her house? Sculptures, isn't that what they called them in the paper? Naked legs, hung from the ceiling. Maybe that's what gave the boy ideas . . .*

– *There was more to it than just ideas. There was another fella living there with her, wasn't there, a fella that cut out and left her? Well? If she'd do it with one, sure why not with another . . .*

It was eight days now, eight days since he'd found Pip's hanging body and phoned Niamh's parents' home to ask was she there. No, she wasn't there, John Comerford had said. Nor had he been prepared to wait while Hannie went looking. When he'd finished speaking to Ned he had phoned the Guards.'

Ned couldn't think that Niamh lived, he believed her drowned, her body trapped in long streamers of weed or caught in a tangle of mud and sunken branches. The search might be off but he still spent hours walking the banks and staring at the brown flow of the river. Sometimes in his mind he saw the drift of her hair in the silted, underwater light.

At these times he felt he could bear anything if only they could find her body and bury it. He dreaded the thought of a funeral, but he wanted her laid to rest.

Laid to rest. The euphemism that had once angered him in its blandness now seemed like literal truth. He wanted to see her lowered into the sanctuary of the earth, private and quiet and safe from any further violation. *Here lies all that was mortal of Niamh Comerford.* It would be settled then, her mortal death could begin to take its due proportion.

But part of Ned wouldn't believe what was happening to him. He felt that it couldn't be true, she couldn't be dead, she'd come back from wherever she was and explain where she'd been these last days and all that had happened. And if she didn't come back, if the nightmare was true, then it was really nothing to do with him, it was some hideous and unjust visitation. He'd been given no warning, had done nothing to earn this disaster, was entirely innocent and unprepared.

Then sometimes it seemed the opposite. He remembered John Comerford's face when he'd looked at the sculptures his daughter had made, how he'd turned and asked Ned if he'd known of them and what they meant. If only he'd had more foresight, Ned thought, if only he hadn't allowed himself to hope for the best over Joss, if only he'd acted on his own forebodings when he saw the legs . . .

Sometimes he thought none of these things, he was just lost in the squalor and uncertainty of it all.

He tried not to think of the puppy, her belly slit open, swinging from the apple tree.

He tried not to think of Hannie, except as his wife who was innocent and in great need.

And he tried not to hear the voices that said there was no innocence, the boy wouldn't be as he was without the mother.

Hannie was taut as a spring; she had smoked and drunk coffee and answered the Guards' questions with a strange, robotic concentration. Ned was amazed at her self-discipline, the weight was falling off her and the circles under her eyes were black and deep, but she spoke always carefully and evenly, as though her patience could have no end. He watched as the Guards began to assemble the facts and arrive at conclusions. He heard the tone of their questioning change from sympathy, to suspicion, to a hostility that was barely veiled. He tried to speak of this shift to her, he thought he should help her to talk, but she only glanced at him and reached for another cigarette.

'They've made up their minds,' she said, lighting it carefully, blowing out the match.

He looked away then; the Guards weren't the only ones who'd made up their minds, he didn't know what she thought or believed or hoped and he didn't want to ask, he didn't want to hear her try to make a case for Joss, he didn't want to have to go along with what she said.

When she wasn't answering questions she worked. She started on the scullery then she did the other rooms downstairs, mindless keep-yourself-occupied activity, everything pulled out and scrubbed and scoured and put away. Then she began on the fabric of the rooms: walls were washed, skirtings and window-frames filled, broken tiling scraped and cleansed and re-cemented into place.

When the divers and searchers packed up she stopped pulling the house apart and putting it back again, she seemed less taut, she even seemed to be making an effort to eat. Ned was relieved; he thought it was release from the constant pressure of their presence. It was only later that he realised that that must have been about the time she heard from Joss.

Vere and Alison came, and James and Marjorie. Ned took them into the drawing room and poured them whiskey. Hannie hadn't said anything when she saw the cars, but she'd cleared off.

It was awkward. Ned wasn't, at that moment, glad to see them, but he was glad that they'd come, he understood the extent of the gesture.

James had plainly been briefed to keep his mouth shut, so they talked about anything except what was on all their minds. At the very end Vere said stiffly that they were all very sorry about 'this awful business'. They were old friends, he continued, Ned could, of course, count on their support at any time and in any way . . .

Everyone had stared hard at their glass or some picture on the wall. Even James refused a refill when it was offered and it was with relief that Ned ushered them out into the chilly March darkness that smelled at once so empty and so fresh.

Alison hung back. She caught his arm urgently and lifted her face up to look directly into his eyes.

'So hard for you,' she said. 'For both of you. If Hannie wants to talk . . . ?' Ned tried to say something polite and reassuring but nothing came out.

'I know she doesn't now,' Alison said, 'but I'd like her to know that she can. It must be a very lonely business.'

Ned nodded and watched her walk across the thin gravel and get into the car. When he turned round to go back into the house he felt like weeping he was so sorry for himself and for them all.

Hannie was in the hall. She was leaning against the opened door in the shadows, her arms folded, watching.

'Poor Ned,' she said into the darkness, her voice bitter and light and mocking. 'Poor Ned, what a mess, what a stupid mistake you have made, consorting with a woman like me.'

He couldn't see her but there was something in her voice and he knew that she was close to breaking. 'No, Hannie,' he answered her quietly, 'you are wrong, a mess it may be, but I've made no mistake.'

And he meant it, but he didn't know why, because it was hard to bear what his life had become.

Chapter 58

When Joss rang the Guards had just left, Ned was out in the fields, it was Hannie who picked up the phone.

He was in Galway, he'd dumped the car and hitched, he said, he was staying with people he knew, people he'd met through Nora's nephew Con. He was all right, they were cool, everything was cool, but he needed money. He wouldn't tell her any more than that, wouldn't answer questions or give her an address, he said he was just letting her know the gist so she could work on the cash situation.

He sounded high as a kite and jittery with nerves. She asked him where Niamh was and he said he didn't know and he didn't care. Then he told her to get off his back and he put down the phone.

She waited. A day passed, two days passed, the Guards rang to say they hadn't found the car or Joss. Another day passed.

The phone rang when they were both in the kitchen. Ned answered it, listened to the silence and put it down. 'Must be a wrong number.'

She nodded and said nothing, her face blank. People locally were garrulous, they never just listened then hung up, if they got a wrong number they wanted to know why you weren't who they thought you should be.

She was ready for Joss, she had the money from the ebony fan still, and a bit more that she'd siphoned off from times when Ned had forgotten himself and given her cash. It wouldn't do Joss for long, nothing would ever keep Joss going long, there would always be another phone call, he would always always need more money than he had.

She was trying to keep the affair with Thornton going, making her absences a little obvious so Ned would smell a rat and draw the wrong conclusions when Joss rang. She did her best but it was hard work, she was sick and tired of him and he was growing leery of her now he'd caught the sort of talk that was going around.

Joss phoned again. This time he caught her by herself and he had an address for her to send money to. He wasn't living there, he said, he was moving around, but he'd tell them to expect a letter and they'd get it to him.

She drove to Youghal and posted the money in cash. Afterwards she went to visit Thornton. She wanted to be seen doing something she shouldn't be doing so people would remember that and forget whatever else they might have noticed.

The lambing started, the inexorable spring cycle, a busy, urgent relief from the tense hours of watching and waiting. Ned needed help; Mick came every year, but suddenly he was promised to a cousin near Clonmel.

Ned showed Hannie the basics and that was enough; she picked up the rest, she had the knack, which he didn't have, despite his experience. She liked the whole process, but especially the difficult births, liked plunging her soapy hand into the hot depths of the ewe, feeling around for the lambs' tangled legs, aligning them for easy passage. To her surprise she found she liked the ewes as well. They were different in the shed, not just stupid and infuriating, but female creatures, patient and suffering and courageous. She enjoyed being with them and helping them; it was practical, immediate and satisfying.

At night they worked in shifts, each one calling on the other if there was a run of lambs, the births bunching together, the ewes needing more help. They kept erratic hours, left out food for each other, fell in and out of their unmade beds, lived frantic, unreal lives and were grateful for the urgent occupation. Anything, so as not to have to wait for news and think.

Ned tried not to watch Hannie, he tried not to wonder who might be putting down the phone when he answered it, nor to register when she came back in the car and didn't say where she'd been. Once he stepped out of the lambing shed and saw her through an upstairs window, standing dressed against the light when he'd thought her dead asleep in her bed. Instinctively, he took a step back into the shadows, stood a moment, then made himself re-enter the shed. If Joss was in the area and she was going to him, then so be it, he would not spy. But neither could he play blind and deaf much longer. He knew he must make himself talk to her soon, but he desperately didn't want to.

Ned was on his way out through the scullery when the next call came. He kept going, pretending he hadn't heard, though she knew that he had. She let it ring a dozen times while she watched Ned disappear round the corner of the shed, then she lifted it and said her name quietly into the mouthpiece.

Something had gone wrong, he'd trusted someone who'd let him down, the scumbag, he'd had to move on –

He didn't know these new people, but they were cool, they were into things in a big way. It was all working out, he'd be laughing in a couple of weeks, but he had to show cred, to buy into the deal, he had to have more money and he had to have it now –

'How much?' Hannie asked. Joss named a sum.

She laughed out loud, a bitter, disbelieving laugh, though she didn't know why she was surprised, she'd always known Joss would get more expensive as each year passed.

'How much d'you have left?'

'Nothing, not a bean – that scumbag Doran ripped me off. I trusted him, just wait till I see Con, I'll tell him all about his so-called friends . . .'

Hannie interrupted. She had no more money, there was no chance of a sum like that and there never would be; he'd better wake up, stop day-dreaming, and put it out of his head for good and all . . .

He laughed, the laugh high and wild.

'Come on, Mother, I've told them all about you, what an ace mover you are, how you can get anything together, no problem at all, Mother, *pas de problème* . . .'

Mother. That word. He only ever called her that when his back was to the wall, when he was trying to make her do what he knew she would not or could not do, when he was at his wits' end.

So she told him there were no more moves, this was it, the end of the line, she had nothing left to sell; she would try to borrow something but it wouldn't be much and he'd have to make it last.

And if and when she could get some more he would have to make that last too, and it would be like that always, there would be no deals, no windfalls, not now, not ever, so he'd better take a long hard look at just what lay ahead.

He had a choice. He could come home and face what had happened and she'd fight for him and support him and it would be hard – she wasn't pretending otherwise – but it mightn't be as hard as he thought. Or he could stay away, change his name, find some work. She'd send him what she could when she could, but that was the future.

'Home,' he said, his voice incredulous. 'When have I ever had a home? When have I ever had anything except trailing along behind you, Mother? What have I ever had but what you've got left over when you've finished shagging some man, or doing whatever it was you had it in mind to do?

'Face things? You mean tell them my side of the story, Mother? Tell them the truth, tell them their precious Niamh was drunk and out of her head, tell them Virgin-Mary-Niamh was trying to make it with me, that all that Klu Klux Clan stuff was her idea, that she was so bombed nothing would do her but to go swim in the river, nothing would stop her, and if I hadn't held back I'd be as drowned as she is . . .'

Hannie went cold and still. She held the receiver tight, with part of her mind she watched the knuckles stand in bluish knolls on her hand.

'Tell them all that, Mother?' Joss was saying. 'Hold out my hands for them to lock the cuffs on, Mother, for them to send me down and throw away the key?'

He was crying now, she could hear his sobs in the silence. She steeled herself. Her voice seemed to come from a dingy room a long way off. 'What about Pippa, Joss?'

'Pippa? What about her? I told her and told her, she kept following me, wagging her tail and yapping, wanting to be picked up, getting on my nerves. I tried to shut her in the kitchen but she got out, the stupid little cunt, she was stupider than Niamh, she wouldn't leave me alone, I couldn't help it...'

His voice was high and hysterical and he started to beg. He begged her not to abandon him, to find some money, any money, even if it wasn't enough to cut him in on this deal, to stand by him, not to tell, to save him. He couldn't come back, she knew that, she knew what would happen if he came back, how everyone always took one look at him and hated him, how they wouldn't believe Niamh had slipped, how they wouldn't stop till they'd fucked him and destroyed him; and she was all he had, he'd do anything except come home, anything, anything she wanted, he'd promise anything...

Hannie stood clinging on to the phone, letting the silence run on. Then she took hold of herself. She told him she loved him and would never abandon him. She said he should come back – no one knew what had happened – no one thought he'd pushed Niamh – if he came now, of his own accord, it would go better for him. But if he couldn't, it was all right, she'd leave Ned, find work, they would manage somehow.

But he didn't want that. He didn't want her around, interfering, messing things up, he just wanted the money. If he had money he could do it by himself, that's what he was saying, didn't she understand English?

He'd do fine by himself, much better than when he was with her, but he needed a start, he had to have money.

He was away then, high as a kite, he said he knew she loved him really, but he couldn't have her around just then – maybe later – or she could stay with old Ned, he didn't mind, he'd come and see her, take her out, give her a spin in some decent wheels . . .

But he wouldn't give her his address in case she went all motherly on him and had to come and see him. He'd ring again, he said, he was counting on her, he knew she could get it together, she always did, she was the best he knew, he'd be in touch to tell her where to send it.

Hannie put down the phone and sat on the chair beside it. She knew then that Joss was doomed whether he came back or stayed away. He would never find work, he would go on the game or deal or steal or all three, and even in that world he wouldn't make it, he was too wild, too unbalanced, it would destroy him or he would destroy himself.

She knew she couldn't help him or change him and this knowledge made no difference, she still had to go on trying, she still had to act, to act against judgement, to act without hope.

And she knew she couldn't bear it but she'd have to bear it, and she could tell no one, and no one could help her. Then she thought of Niamh, drowned in the river, and for the first time since it happened Hannie wept; she wept for herself and she wept for lost, crazy Joss and she wept for Niamh, whose life had been swept away in this sad, ugly game they must go on playing to the end.

'Was that Joss on the phone?'

Hannie didn't turn round. She went on washing the dishes, lifting them out of the water, placing them on the rack. She mightn't have heard him.

'He's been ringing you, hasn't he?' Ned asked her back. 'The Guards think you're sending him money, they think you

333

know where he is. Is it true, Hannie? Have you sent him money? Do you know where he is?'

'No,' she said, still with her back turned. 'I don't know where he is. I did, but I don't any more. I did send some money. Then he moved on. Any more questions?' She hauled a big saucepan out of the suds and dumped it down on the drainer. Ned didn't answer her challenge.

'He phoned once, but we had a row, he wouldn't leave an address. He hasn't phoned since – that was someone else – it was a bad row we had, he won't ring again, the Guards can follow me, open my letters, tap the phone, it won't do them any good.'

'Don't be so melodramatic, Hannie.'

'I'm not being melodramatic. And stop hiding behind the Guards – *you* think he's phoning, *you* think I'm sending him money . . .'

'Well you are, you just said so.'

She ignored him. She swished the cloth around in the water, wrung it out, wiped down the draining board with sure strong hands.

Ned stood watching her. He wanted to believe her but he didn't.

'Where did you send the money?' he asked, aware that he wasn't asking her where she'd got it.

'Belfast.'

'Belfast?'

'He went to Belfast. Someone he knew through Ciaran.' She started on the table where they had just eaten.

'And where did the last phone call come from?'

'England. He took the boat.'

'That was convenient.'

She went on wiping. There was a silence.

'Sit down, Hannie. I want to talk to you.'

She looked at him then.

'And what if I don't want to sit down? What if I don't want to talk?'

Ned sighed. He took off his reading glasses, pinched the bridge of his nose as though to ease something.

'Hannie, you're not helping him, you're not doing him any favours. You think you are, I can see that, you think you're fighting for him, but you're not, you're only fighting off the consequences of the things he's done.' Ned spoke slowly and carefully, his eyes shut, his fingers still pinching his nose. 'You can't put the clock back, Hannie, you can't change things for him or make them all right, all you can do is help him to face what he's done.'

Hannie tossed her head back. It was a small, impatient movement of scorn. 'How would you know what he's done?' she asked bitterly. 'How would anyone? No one was there, no one saw anything, but you've all made up your minds.'

Ned stared at her blank, hostile face, its cornered exhaustion, and his heart went out to her. He forgot Niamh, forgot her family, his duty, the talk about Richard Thornton that was reaching him now round every corner, all he thought about was helping her through this despair.

He said she was making things harder for Joss, that the longer he stayed away the worse it looked.

He spoke gently, not hectoring her as he might have done.

He said he knew she loved Joss, but sometimes love wasn't about shielding, it was about letting the person you loved move forward to meet their fate. It was about helping them to do it.

Hannie stared at him with contempt in her eyes.

'Who'll believe Joss?' she asked. 'Who'll believe him or help him or take his side? The Guards? Niamh's family? You?

'Spare me, Ned. There isn't even a body, but Joss has been found guilty. It's all his fault, he did it all, and Niamh is white and Joss is black and there's no colour called grey.

'And afterwards? After he's come home and faced this impartial reception committee? You know how he is with authority, you know how he puts people's backs up, you know what would happen to Joss if he went to prison. And yet you can preach to me? You can say I should help him meet this fate of his? This is your best advice?'

She stood there, challenging him, all anger and defiance and despair.

He was suddenly sick of her. He was sick of it all – his life, this mess, the raw wound inside him that was Niamh. He wanted no more to do with her. He hit down on the table hard with his opened hand, then slammed out through the door.

He'd only really let himself think about Hannie, he hadn't allowed himself to think about Niamh, except to go on looking for her body. Partly because things were as they were, and there might yet be some miracle. Partly because of his own loss. He couldn't walk past her cottage, couldn't bear to think he'd never talk to her or hear her laugh or meet her steady, serious gaze again. Butterflies and moths he found unendurable.

Hannie was right, he had made up his mind, Joss's restless brittle delinquency had destroyed her.

He stood now in the darkness, his back against one of the cherry trees, pressing into it, seeking the comfort of its old hardness. He heard a dog in the distance, then another, the bleat of lambs, the small hard scream of a rabbit taken by a stoat. He smelled the wet grass, the river meadows, heard the sough of the wind rustling the ivy massed in the hearts of the unleafed trees. The darkness was soft, clouded, complete. Without moon or stars.

He thought of Niamh, how she'd come into his life like a trust, how he'd been excited by her, had thought the world of her and tried to help her. He'd identified – Hannie was right there too – he'd thought she was as he'd been himself when starting out. Then slowly he'd come to see that she was different.

And he'd minded that. He'd been disappointed in her and had stopped thinking the world of her. And then, when he was used to his disappointment, he found he'd grown deeply attached to her.

He thought of Hannie. How he hadn't loved her when he'd married her, had simply wanted to have her in his life.

How he loved her now, but at a price that was too high.

How he set this love of his on the scales against everything else in the world that he lived by and valued, and it did not weigh heavy enough.

He felt like a man who wanted to leave something down and walk away from it, something precious that he'd wanted very hard for a long time. Then, when he could nearly have it, the effort of it had proved too great, all the good had been driven from it, and all that he wanted was not to want it any more. He felt there would be a flat calm peace in such a withdrawing, an end to hoping and wanting, an end to uncertainty and pain.

But he could not make this withdrawal. In spite of himself, he could neither erode nor negate his feelings.

And he could not leave her so undefended, even though he longed to.

He left the sanctuary of the cherry tree. He got out the Land-Rover and drove away from the shadowy house in its nest of trees. He didn't want to talk to anyone or be with anyone, he was too low and ashamed to want anything but the night.

He headed south, drove the dark empty roads, turned on to winding, unmarked byways, kept on till he smelled the salt in the air and felt the road run out and the wheels muffle on sandy grass. He left the Land-Rover and found a hollow under the lip of a field where it fell away into the sand of a long white beach he had known since his childhood. He sat there, hearing the roar and slap of the sea, its rising and falling, the low notes of the roosting waders talking in their sleep.

Funny thing, loyalty, he thought. You never knew what would call it up or where you would place it till it was placed and your choice made. Not your choice at all, but your heart's choice, and there was little you could do to help yourself, even when most of you wanted no part in your heart's decision. He had thought it was about ethics and codes, what was right, what was wrong, but he was discovering a deeper, stronger way of being that could not be gainsaid.

He had gone to the Comerfords' farm when the search was called off, but Niall had come out to intercept him even before he reached the door.

Had he news? Niall had asked, and Ned had shaken his head and said he'd only come to say again that he was sorry. Niall had said his father wouldn't see him. Ned had nodded and turned away.

Then he'd turned back. 'Tell your father she's my wife, the boy's her son.'

There it was. Hardly a wife at all except in the eyes of the law. A companion of seven months. And he was poised to stand against his own morality, against his society, against his tribe. Because of her, because of her loyalty to her deranged son. And he felt that nothing in his life had prepared him for this moment, nothing had prepared him for the exposure and ignominy that had come to him here, in his own place, among his own people.

And yet everything had prepared him, everything he had learned from remote peoples in far-off places who lived within the laws of tribe and family and answered to these codes in every detail of their lives.

Sometimes the demands of the heart ran contrary to the demands of the tribe, sometimes a choice was forced. He had seen men discover their own loyalties, where they ran deepest, he had watched the struggle, the decision, the outcome. Submission, and the tribe closing around; defiance, and the outlaw's life.

But always he'd been an observer and a recorder, that was his temperament and his training, he hadn't ever thought to be participant himself.

He felt that all his life was for nothing now, that all his

precious achievements were meaningless and stupid, like a child's treasured toys when childhood has fallen away.

Then he stopped thinking, he listened to the waves and to the waders; if he thought at all he thought of the comrades of his journeys, all dead or scattered now, their lost worlds changed past recognition. He sat with his ghosts, feeling the comfort of them, feeling the old comfort of empty, roofless places. After a long time, very cold and wet and tired, he got back into the Land-Rover and slept for an hour. Then he drove home and was washed and out round the farm before Hannie was out of the lambing shed.

❧ *Chapter 59* ❧

*R*ichard Thornton wouldn't lend her any money. She asked him as she was getting dressed, her arms in the air, her sweater around her neck. He said no, he didn't think so, in a casual voice, his back to her as he buckled his belt, behind him a great fall of clear, underwater spring light in the tall Georgian windows of his immaculately refurbished home. She nodded, accepting his decision, finished getting dressed and walked from the room as though to fetch something she'd left next door. She went down the stairs, crossed the hall, opened the front door and descended the steps.

She felt empty and neutral as she walked down his well-kept avenue, a small figure on the gravelled drive, the big grey house behind her and the chestnut trees to either side. She stared at the fat swooping chestnut buds, how they swung around in the windy white light and the cold wind blowing. Bright fields bordered the drive, a cruel acid new-grass brightness, like drought-fields in Africa after rain.

She wouldn't have asked if she could have taken, but everything was wired to alarms, the pictures were bolted to the walls, silver and china stared from locked glass cases. His refusal had changed nothing, it was only the punctuation mark at the end of a completed sentence, he meant less than nothing to her and she had no appetite left to satisfy.

Gangs of fat Christmas lambs ran about on Thornton's smooth green pasture, noisy and lusty and innocent, different altogether from the little leggy new-borns picking their way round Ned's straggly fields.

Ned's fields. She knew their bounds now, had even learned

how to look at a field, but that was it, the full extent of her involvement. Alison spoke of *our* fields, saying the words with tenderness and protective pride, as though of a delicate child she had reared against all the odds. And such fields as Alison wrung her pride from – stony and boggy – all the good land long since sold to pay for a stretch of roof, a rotted floor, a failed venture. No wonder they spoke of Richard Thornton's house and fields with that soft confused longing in their eyes.

Some of the ewes were beginning to shed their wool, they looked like skinny middle-aged women shrugging out of their fur coats. That was her, she thought, only she'd no fur coat to shrug out of and small chance of one around a man like Ned. Nor was she completely skinny yet, despite Joss's best efforts. She wondered about this new mood she'd drifted into; distant and unreal, so she no longer felt the weight of Joss like a sharp stone lodged in her belly.

She had almost no more cards left to play, she thought, as she turned out of Thornton's drive and walked up the road; there was only Ned she could ask and all she'd get there was a lecture. She stopped and stood with her hands in her pockets, staring about her. The land was laid out in stretches and plains, pale green and blue, soft and misted like water-colours put down on a wet ground. The air was different. It was somehow thicker and whiter and there were pools and streamers of scent that you hit, like swimming into warm pockets in the sea. The trees still looked lifeless, except for the chestnuts, their fat phallic buds, straining up into the cold sky.

'You should see it in spring,' Alison had said. 'Like paradise.'

Could she ever feel as Alison felt? No, she didn't think so, this spring of theirs could never negate the winter, Ned's fields would never be *our* fields, no matter how long she lived here, nor how she worked and tramped about in them. Yet her ties with Africa were looser, she no longer dreamed its landscape at night, nor woke in the mornings flooded with longing for its smells and sounds. She was losing her connections with the past, but still she had almost no ties to the present. She was as a blown leaf now, belonging nowhere.

She didn't hear the car till it pulled up beside her. Then Mrs Coady was leaning across the seat, pushing the passenger door open. Hannie got in.

'Smelling the air?' Mrs Coady's face was neutral, the irony only just there in her voice. Hannie shook her head.

'I was at Thornton's,' she said, lighting a cigarette. On an impulse she offered one to Mrs Coady. Mrs Coady took it. Hannie raised her eyebrows, lit it for her, said nothing.

'I like a cigarette, once in a while,' Mrs Coady said. 'I don't buy them. Tom was a smoker once, he can't stand them about the place, the temptation would be strong still.' Hannie nodded. The two women drove on in silence, the car hazing with smoke. The road narrowed and Mrs Coady slowed and swung out to pass a thick-set old man in a jacket and sweater, walking towards them. His hand lifted at sight of the familiar car and then dropped abruptly when he saw who was in the passenger seat.

'The old fella from Cummin's Cross, out walking on doctor's orders,' Mrs Coady said in a neutral voice. 'It'll take more than walking to cure that heart.'

'He saw me in the car,' Hannie said.

'I wouldn't be much liked around here, anyway,' Mrs Coady said as though she hadn't heard. 'People think me stand-offish, they say I keep myself to myself.' She wound down the window and fired the butt out of it. 'They can think what they like.'

'I asked him to lend me some money, but he wouldn't,' Hannie said out of nowhere, staring at the road as it unwound in front of her. It was Mrs Coady's turn to nod. She rounded the next bend and then pulled the car in suddenly by the field-gate just before Ned's drive. She turned off the ignition and pulled on the handbrake.

'I'll see you all right for money, you needn't be asking Thornton,' she said. 'How much do you want?'

Hannie stared at her. She named a quarter of the sum Joss had asked for. Mrs Coady nodded, reached down and fished around at her feet for her handbag. She hauled it up and opened it and began counting twenties off a roll she took out of its zipped inner pocket.

'You may not get it back,' Hannie said stiffly.

Mrs Coady laughed. 'Sure I know that,' she said easily, not looking up from her counting, 'that's always a risk, but I think maybe I will ... And if I don't, what harm? I suppose I can bear the loss.'

'It's for Joss,' Hannie said, even more stiffly.

'Sure I know that too,' Mrs Coady said. 'When did I ever see you wanting money for yourself?'

'What if Niamh's drowned?'

'She's drowned all right. She's not the kind of young one would be staying away and worrying people if she'd the choice.' Mrs Coady handed Hannie the money. 'I'm not condoning what's after happening and I'm not saying I don't think Joss had a hand in it. But it's happened now, I can't change that or bring her back.'

Hannie couldn't look at Mrs Coady, she felt as awkward and grateful as a gauche girl, and suddenly she needed to play straight, she needed to give her the chance to change her mind.

'Aren't you going to say I should make him come home and account for himself?' Her voice was small, her eyes on the money in her hand.

Mrs Coady didn't answer the question. Instead she waited for Hannie to look at her, then she met her eyes, her gaze grave. 'What else can you do?' she asked quietly. 'Who else has he, only yourself?'

Hannie walked up the drive with Mrs Coady's folded notes in her pocket and heard the phone start to ring before she reached the door. She wanted to run but she dug her nails into her palms and made herself walk. She got the door open. It was still ringing.

She called Ned's name into the silence but there was no answer. She lifted the phone in the hall. His breathing came ragged and excited.

'Joss?'

'Mother? Have you got it, Mother?'

'Some – not much – you'll have to make it last.'

'I can't talk now, I'll phone again, here's the address.'

She wrote the words down on the pad beside the table, then tore off the sheet and put it into her pocket. Joss was in Limerick.

∾ *Chapter 60* ∾

*H*annie stood at the front door watching the magpies in the trees. All winter she'd stood like this and watched them, their flaunting black-and-whiteness, their dip-tailed snaking undulations out along the branches. Today they were different, they were silhouettes in the wild cherries, moving shapes on the luminous air.

She closed her eyes. The forms of the cherries were printed onto her mind, the three grey trees stepping out like dancers, their long arms held gracefully above their heads. She opened her eyes, breathed deeply and her shoulders eased a little from a weight lifted. She stared around her. She had been careful, had told Ned she was going to Dungarvan, but had headed north instead to Mitchelstown where they never went and nobody knew them. She'd done her errands like any normal shopper, then dropped the letter casually into the box at the main post office, safe from the sharp eyes of the postmistress in Cappoquin. She hadn't sent all the money, she'd kept back half for the next time.

Nothing had changed or improved, she told herself, her action had solved nothing, she must try to will herself back into a numbed indifference.

But somehow she couldn't. Hope had crept in.

Hope of what?

Danno found Niamh's body. He saw a bit of old cloth in the slob a long way downriver and pulled his boat over to take a closer look.

When he saw what it was he wanted to mark the place, to

go and find the Guards and leave the pulling out to someone else. But the tide was on the turn, in half an hour the slob would be covered and she might not be there when it dropped again. He knew he had to try to get her into the boat.

So he did, but she'd been in the water a long time, it wasn't a pleasant experience. He put her in face-down, then took off his coat and covered as much as he could, started the engine and made for the nearest quay.

The Guards came again, the questioning started again, there were descriptions of Joss broadcast on the television and the radio. The broadcasts said only that the Guards wanted to speak to him, but the tabloids speculated openly about the missing boy in connection with Niamh's drowning. The word Satanism cropped up. It was widely known that a dog had been mutilated and hanged.

People talked, they said Joss had crossed from Cork and vanished into France, they said he'd gone to the North, they said he was living wild in the woods somewhere beyond Lismore.

They said Danno was taking it hard, he had shut himself up and was drinking, the Guards had come but he'd roared at them to go away. He was breaking his heart, they said, she came to him in his sleep, he'd been in love with her and was drinking now to forget.

'Isn't it wonderful what people know?' Mrs Coady said. 'Know for a fact, and will swear to.'

Mrs Coady was staunch, she shopped for them and spoke for them and generally kept them informed. People tried to get news out of her but she'd gone blind and deaf.

And most of what was being said, she didn't tell them. It would have been too painful.

When the urgency of the lambing eased Hannie started to dig. The light had stretched, the darkness was folding itself back like the tall wooden shutters in Alison's house, she wanted to be outside in the air and she wanted to be active because it helped her bear the weight. The vegetable garden, the flower beds, the potato patch, they were all receiving their neglected autumn dig.

Early one evening Ned went out into the garden to find her.

'Hannie, come for a walk,' he said and she thrust the fork into the ground and stepped out from the tangle of blackened perennials. He took her hand and led her like a child across the field to the river.

But as they walked he began to doubt himself. The spring was late, what was so much to his eyes might be nothing at all to hers. And truly, there was little enough to see: a softening everywhere, silver shoots on the long whippy stems of the young willows, buds like tiny seed-pearls on the whitethorn, the docks thrusting up their red-veined leaves. It was all caught in a silvery caul of almost-birth; a net of light was round the unbroken buds like flame.

She would walk that walk every evening in the days to come. Sometimes he went with her, sometimes he walked down and found her there, sometimes he left her alone. There was a truce between them. He had emerged from the despair of the night by the sea, but only just, and he knew it was close beside him and might claim him again at any time. He felt an intense tenderness towards her, but beneath it there was also horror and distaste.

Once, beside the river, he asked about Richard Thornton. Were they true, he asked – the rumours he'd heard?

'Probably,' she said. 'It depends which you heard.'

'Aren't I worth lying to, Hannie?' he asked.

She walked on slowly, not looking at him. 'It *is* true,' she said. 'Or rather it *was* true. And it doesn't matter at all, it never did.'

'Isn't that for me to decide?'

She didn't answer. A heron flopped slowly past in the cold white air. A flight of duck got up from the fringes of the shiny water. Sometimes Ned hated the river now. Niamh's was the fate he had had in mind for Joss.

Sometimes he'd go looking for her and he'd find her standing watching a single tree, its bark swelling with buds, or a hazel hanging with catkins like yellow rain.

'Why don't you leave me alone, Ned,' she asked him at last in exasperation. 'I can't abandon him, I can't just throw him to the wolves. I'm not taking anything away from you that's yours and giving it to him, why don't you let me be?'

After that he didn't question her any more. He knew she wasn't talking about possessions.

She seemed aware of him, but separate, distant and impenetrable. His words and actions seemed to have little effect on her. If he spoke or kept silent, he felt it all the one to her.

She ate little and she wandered about in the night. Sometimes he woke and heard the floorboards creak, saw the glow of light around his closed door. He would get up then and go looking for her and often as not he found her at the table in the kitchen drinking hot milk heavily laced with whiskey. He would sit with her, but she never seemed to want to talk, so he'd talk instead, sometimes of his journeys and the peoples he'd lived with, sometimes of his childhood in the valley. She didn't say much but his ramblings seemed to soothe her and then he'd go back upstairs with her and sit propped up with pillows in the big double bed, a glass in his hand, talking of things long gone till she fell asleep beside him. Sometimes he couldn't sleep himself after one of these sessions so he'd stare into the darkness at his vivid life passing before his eyes. Often when he woke in the morning she'd be already up and gone.

The cause of death was drowning, the state pathologist told the inquest. She had also suffered lacerations, bruising, and a fracture of the left leg but these injuries had almost certainly occurred after death. The coroner adjourned the matter till

May twenty-seventh as a Garda investigation was still underway.

At once the rumours spread. Everyone agreed on one thing: whatever about the violence, there'd been sexual intercourse before death, the state pathologist had found evidence but the coroner was keeping it under wraps, hushing it up, like suicide a few years back.

– *It was rape, they were hushing things up, saving the family's feelings. Wasn't it bad enough without making it all worse?*

– *Sure it didn't have to be rape, it might have been voluntary.*

– *Hardly voluntary. The boy was too young for her. It was rape sure enough, they just couldn't prove it, they were saving no one's feelings . . .*

– *She'd taken drink, the autopsy found she'd taken drink, they were saving the family . . .*

– *Or saving the boy. Renvyle was an old name, he had connections still, a word in the right place . . .*

– *It wasn't Renvyle's son. It was that woman he'd brought in. Mad about her, for all he'd never see seventy again. And her going straight from his bed and into the bed of that Thornton man, the one had Annaghmore now. She was no chicken either. No wonder the boy was like he was . . .*

Ned heard the speculation and his shock was very great. At first he dismissed the talk – it was idle, credulous gossip – but as the rumours solidified the strain, the isolation of his position began to erode his certainty. The more he thought about it the more he had to admit that it was possible. Then he had to go further: if intercourse *had* happened, it had to be rape. That Niamh could voluntarily have had intercourse with Joss, was altogether beyond credibility.

For two days he turned it over and over, like a dog turning a bone as it tries to get at the marrow in its core. Only it wasn't marrow he was trying to suck, it was poison. He was sure enough in his mind that Hannie knew where Joss was, despite her protestations. Hitherto he had believed Joss responsible for Niamh's death, but he'd tried to stop short of interpreting the boy's actions as culpably deliberate until they'd heard his side of the story. Despite Pip's fate – the deliberateness of which there was no avoiding – he still believed that Joss had not intended Niamh's death and that the full extent of the disaster was unintentional.

Now he began to revise his position. Drunkenness and mindless cruelty were one thing, rape was another altogether. If it was rape and Hannie knew where Joss was, then he must confront her and persuade her to give him up.

But was it really rape, or was it simply gossip wanting it so? He decided that he couldn't act on rumour. He would go to Dungarvan, speak to the man in charge of the case and when he knew the facts he would see more clearly just what must be done.

He reached this decision while he was blocking gaps in the long acre against the lambs breaking out. He was pleased with the plan, it would be a relief to hear straight facts, he should have acted days ago. He picked up the wire and the cutters and left the thorn branches lying.

He was edging the Land-Rover carefully up the drive, climbing the verges to avoid the potholes, when he saw the squad car nosing towards him. He stopped, and Garda Mahon stopped, then both men got out and shook hands.

'How are you, Mr Renvyle? It's a beautiful morning, though 'twould be a rash man would put money on a clear run through.'

The Guard was a well-liked man, a bit overweight, shyer than he seemed, shrewder than he seemed, a countryman by birth from west of the Shannon. When they'd passed through the formalities, Ned volunteered that he was on his way to the superintendent in Dungarvan.

Mahon looked down at a clump of celandines by his left boot, then said slowly that he'd be glad to save Mr Renvyle a journey if he could. On the other hand, if his business was with the superintendent, he wouldn't want to be keeping him standing here talking.

Ned hesitated. His instinct was to go to the top, but if he did that he would automatically alert their attention. This way the thing could be done in privacy and without commitment. And he knew Mahon, he knew him to be decent, reliable and discreet. Mahon went on gazing steadily down at the celandine while Ned made up his mind.

'There's a report going around,' Ned said quietly, 'a report about the way Miss Comerford died.'

Mahon waited, saying nothing.

'About what happened before she died,' Ned went on. 'I wanted to know if it was true or if – if it was – all just talk,' he finished lamely.

'And what would that report be, Mr Renvyle?'

'The report was . . .' Ned cleared his throat and began again. 'The *rumour* was – is – that certain information was withheld by the coroner due to lack of the necessary confirmation. Information about sexual intercourse. Would that be true, could you tell me, or would it be just – speculation?'

'Speculation,' Garda Mahon said firmly. 'Officially, it would be pure speculation.'

'And the injuries?'

'It's a big strong river, she was gone a long time, she could have been caught on a drowned tree or trapped on a bit of an old fish weir and battered around for weeks. No, the injuries aren't a problem, she was drowned before the injuries, it's what put her into the river that's the problem.'

'And the thinking on that?'

'Unofficially, and between the two of us, I'd say we don't know but it's very disturbing. And disturbing's no good, you can't go putting things about without proper evidence, much less charging people.'

He folded his arms round his big body and stared hard at the springing grass. 'Let's just say we don't think the young woman was pushed, but she didn't go jumping into the river for fun. Something frightened her, frightened her badly enough to make her keep running even when she wasn't pursued.'

'She wasn't pursued?'

'Only part of the way. The path was churned up to about halfway along but only her prints went as far as the river.'

Ned was aware of a flooding relief, but Mahon hadn't finished. 'She kept going, she just kept going, she didn't care what was in front of her, only what was behind.'

Ned's relief evaporated. He looked at the smooth round stem of an ash sapling on the ditch. There was a long pause.

'Perhaps it's more than the dead we should be thinking of,' Mahon continued thoughtfully.

Ned didn't say anything. Mahon shifted his feet and looked steadily at Ned. 'I've two little daughters at home, Mr Renvyle. I don't know what happened, but I can't sleep at night if I think of it happening again . . .'

Ned didn't go to Dungarvan. Instead he went back to the field and finished his task. They'd get through somewhere else, they always did, but at least there'd be one less place.

All Ned's instincts were clear: Mahon had been emotional, he'd said himself there was no evidence for what he was suggesting, therefore his suggestion had to be discounted.

Nonetheless, he made himself look at it from Mahon's point of view. It *could* have happened as he seemed to imagine it had happened. And if rape had either occurred or been threatened, then it was fair to suggest that it might occur again. But Joss was innocent until proven guilty and there was no proof that there'd been the crime of rape, much less that Joss had committed it. The only crime Joss had unquestionably committed was the slaughter of Pippa. Yet Niamh was dead and Mahon was right, she hadn't jumped into the river for fun.

This field bordered the road, he was afraid for the lambs but more afraid for the accidents they might cause. He cut more thorns and blocked two other places. He checked the ewes while he was there, then went back to the house. Hannie wasn't around.

The phone rang as he was washing his hands in the scullery. A few rings only – it stopped just as he got to it. He stood beside it waiting for the ringing to start again. The clear light fell slanting on to the table, and Ned could see the imprint of an address Hannie must have scribbled down on the pad before she tore off the page. The phone sat there, malignant yet quiet, it didn't seem to be about to ring again. He picked up the pad and fished in his pocket for his reading glasses. The address was clear enough. There was no way of knowing how long it had been there.

ᔆ *Chapter 61* ᔆ

*D*anno made her tea and she sat on the window seat, sipping quietly at the hot liquid, not smoking or roaming around, just staring out at the river.

He had been varnishing his ash plants when she came, letting the glaze slide over the carved and painted handles, the long clean lengths of the sticks. He liked this task, it was the last stage of a long process and it brought its own peace.

He had opened the door to her without wanting to see her, he would have put the ash plants away, but he was already deep in the job and there were tacky half-dried sticks propped all around the room. He would concentrate, he decided, sink into what he was doing, then he wouldn't be disturbed by what she said.

Only she didn't say anything much, she just sat there sipping her tea in the silence and the room was filled with unsaid words and loud with unasked questions about Joss and Niamh. He needed her to speak or to go away, but she did neither.

'You want to know about Niamh?' he asked at last, surprising himself.

'Not much,' she said. 'Do you want to tell me?'

'Not much.' He took the next unglazed ash plant from the stand, turned it this way and that to check its preparedness. 'Why did you come?'

She roused herself. 'For a drink,' she said. 'You're supposed to be poleaxed with drink, I thought I'd get something stronger than tea.'

He looked at her; it was a horrible misplaced effort at gaiety, he could think of nothing to say.

'I came to see how you were,' she went on, 'to check you weren't secretly in love with Niamh the way they're saying you were – to assure myself you're not drinking your way into an early grave.' She paused. 'And I came to ask you a favour.'

'What else do they say?' he asked, ignoring her last statement.

'That she's broken your heart, that she comes to you in the night.'

He made himself look at her. She was sitting sideways at the window, her head resting against the wall behind her. Her hair looked longish and unwashed, strands of it stood around her face, her skin was papery and thin but still held the hint of a tan. Not a tan, he realised, a brown pigment, the only visible legacy of the racial mix that was somehow common knowledge now. He felt the fury rising in him and he bowed his head so that she wouldn't see.

'What's the favour?'

She stared at the river. 'Something has changed, Danno,' she said, her voice low. 'Something has changed, it's to do with Joss, I felt it last night, but I don't know what it is.'

He waited, his eyes still fixed on the stick in his hand.

'I came to ask you to look out for signs of Joss when you're in the woods. I want you to come and tell me if you find them.'

Danno raised his head now and stared at her, but she was still looking away.

'What makes you think you can ask this of me?'

Her head turned and she stared, a startled confused expression on her face he'd never seen there before. Tears sprang into her eyes.

'We were friends once,' she said slowly. 'Remember?'

'That was before all this. That was a long time ago –'

'A few brief weeks –

'– and on the strength of it you're asking me to help you help Joss get away.'

'They're all talking about rape, and I don't know why, where did rape come from, why does everyone suddenly think she was raped? He didn't rape her and he didn't kill her.'

'I suppose he didn't hang the puppy either.'

She stopped. For a moment his hostility seemed to penetrate through to her. She sat back suddenly, her eyes went dead, her body sagged, her shoulders slumped like a sawdust doll. For the first time she seemed to lose Joss, to get a sense of Danno and how *he* felt. She seemed to realise what she'd asked of him.

'I understand that you feel like this, Danno,' she said quietly. 'You found her, that's very strong, very emotional, it is looking the reality of her drowning straight in the face. But remember one thing. We know she died, but we don't know what passed between them. And remember too that Niamh, as well as Joss, was drunk, and young ones don't handle drink so well, they get a little wild and excited, they get frightened when there's no real cause.' The words came out fast, she was pleading now, she held up her hand as though to ward off his snort of derision.

'I'm not making excuses for him and I'm not trying to pretend he didn't do wrong. The puppy, that stupid burning cross, those things were deranged and bad. But I think it has wrecked his life already, I know he'll never ever forget those hours, he will carry Niamh's death till he dies. And he isn't guilty of rape or murder, Danno, whatever you feel about Niamh, however much you want someone called to account for what you found. He didn't push her, even the Guards say that. He is guilty only of wild and excessive behaviour.'

'Wild and excessive behaviour caused her death.'

'I think if Niamh had been sober she wouldn't now be dead . . .'

'Is it a crime to be drunk? Punishable by death?'

'No, it's not. But if you're going to be drunk you must look out for the consequences . . .'

Danno studied her in silence and she seemed to hear what she'd just said.

'Have you finished, Hannie?' he asked.

She nodded miserably.

'Then listen to me for a change. You're right when you say we don't know what really happened, perfectly right, and I don't suppose Joss is going to tell us so we'll probably never find out. But there's one thing we *do* know. Someone scared the living daylights out of her and no one else was there, so that someone must be Joss.' He paused and looked straight at her, challenging her with his eyes and his voice and his words. 'You say he didn't kill her, but who did, answer me that? No one?' He took off his glasses, sighed, put them on again, looked down at the stick in his hands. 'If I found him Hannie,' he said quietly, 'if I found any smallest sign or trace of him, I'd have no hesitation, I'd go straight and tell the Guards.'

In a quick, desperate movement she clapped her hands to her ears.

'Oh, Danno, stop, stop, please stop! You don't know what'll happen to him if they catch him, you don't know. It may seem nothing to you – a short time in a borstal or a prison – it may seem only justice, but it isn't justice, if it happens he'll never recover, I'll never ever be able to get him back, no matter what I do, or how I try, he will be lost for ever . . .'

'He's lost already.'

'No, Danno, it isn't like that, it isn't set in stone like that. Once I said it was his nature – like a hawk's – that a hawk killed things, that Joss spoiled things – and you criticised me, you said I was wrong . . .'

'You were right, I was wrong. Joss has done what he's done, he must pay the price.'

She didn't move or flinch, though he might as well have struck her. He glanced up, met her eyes, looked down again. She went on staring at him.

'Something has changed you, Danno,' she said softly. 'You weren't like this the last time I was here and everything then was the same as it is now. What was it, Danno, was it finding Niamh?'

'Yes,' he said, 'it was finding Niamh. And I'll tell you something else, Hannie. They're right when they say that she comes to me in the night.'

ᴀ *Chapter 62* ᴀ

*T*he Guards phoned for Ned just after Hannie had gone to visit Danno. They said the Limerick Guards had raided the Limerick address the previous night but had failed to apprehend Joss.

Ned asked what that meant and was told that they'd missed him by chance. It seemed Joss had been at the shop round the corner and when he came back he'd seen the squad car and scarpered. Did Ned have any idea where he might have gone?

Ned put down the phone and went and stood in the doorway. Before his eyes the whitethorn was coming into leaf and the blackthorn's frail stars of blossom were dying. He felt how small their lives were, how soiled and helpless and unheroic. A snail was making its slow way up the door frame. It had paused at about his head-height and was looking around, its slim grey horns feeling tentatively into the warmer air. He put out his hand and lifted it off, then walked down the steps and placed it in the damp earth under the wall. He bent and watched it making its careful way till it reached the sanctuary of stone.

He looked up. Alison was standing by the steps, her grey eyes with the red veining at the inside corners looking steadily at him, her soft lined face full of pity and defeat. How old they were all getting, he thought, how old and irrelevant, living their small lives in this small lost backwater of this suddenly thriving little country that once their families had ruled like petty kings.

He rose to greet her. Alison put out her hand and touched

his left forearm and he covered her hand with his own. They stood like that, both looking at their hands, one on the other, not saying anything. He was surprised and touched and embarrassed and then he found himself wondering how they were going to stop doing this and he thought of that childhood game of piled hands, how when your hand was on the bottom you slipped it out and put it on the top, hand on hand, faster and faster till the game ended in a wild jumble of slapping hands. And as he thought this, Alison slipped out her hand and his own dropped.

'I came to see Hannie, it must be quite dreadful for her,' Alison said, settling her mac around her shoulders. 'I know she doesn't want to see me, but she ought, you know, whether she wants to or not . . .

'She has you, of course, but she ought to talk to someone else, someone detached and her own sex. It's really too much for anyone, this sort of thing, and she has the boy to think of. She must keep herself up to the mark.' She put up her hand and tucked a lock of her faded hair back under her headscarf as she spoke. 'Perhaps you'll tell her that I'd very much like to see her when she has time?'

She touched his arm briefly once more and turned, but suddenly Ned's relief at seeing her prepare to go changed and he wanted her to sit in his drawing room drinking gin and talking to him in that steady, responsible way that was so unlike Hannie, so like his mother and his dead aunts and all the admirable women in whose drawing rooms he'd sat long years ago.

He asked her to stay and talk to him. He sat her down and gave her a drink and unburdened his troubled conscience a little. Then she asked him what he knew of a woman called Ilse who had once been Hannie's friend.

Alison unlocked the back door with the big iron key that was always left in the keyhole. That was the system, had been the system since Vere's childhood. You went out, you locked the door, you left the key in the keyhole. There was no logic to it, but didn't matter. No self-respecting burglar would bother with their possessions, Vere said, there was nothing in the house that wouldn't have been marked down in a junk yard.

He was sitting at the kitchen table with James and the account books and a bottle of cheap whiskey. They pretended they'd been talking shop, but she knew they were waiting for her. Vere got up and rinsed a cloudy tumbler vaguely under the tap. He poured her a drink.

'All sorted, then?'

She sat at the table, sipping at the grubby glass, shaking her head sadly up at him. 'Not that simple.'

'No, I suppose it isn't. Pity. A great pity.'

'No fool like an old fool,' James said brusquely. 'Throw her out, only thing to be done. Throw the boy out too, the minute he shows up. Whole thing a mistake, mistake from start to finish . . .'

'Oh, I don't think it's a mistake,' Alison said quietly. 'I think the boy's in very serious trouble . . .'

James snorted. 'Course he is, so he should be. It's marrying *her* I'm talking about.' He glared at Alison. 'Well, so be it, we all make 'em and what's done is done. But he should put it behind him now, wash his hands of the whole sorry business.'

'I expect he wants to,' Vere said. 'But he can't, can he? Not his style.'

'Can't? Not his style? Don't talk crap, Vere, course he can. What's this about style? Honourable chap, old Ned – is that it? Stands by his wife and her mad son, won't let her down no matter what? Blah. He's in love with her, that's what's wrong with him, that's what's stopping him doing what he should do, throwing her out, setting an example. He's besotted, nothing to do with honour. Showing us all up. And at his age!'

* * *

Vere found her later, standing quietly on the landing in the darkness, staring through the great window at the garden beyond. He placed himself beside her.

It looked quite decent in the moonlight. Roses in the border all pruned and neat, the beds half-way weeded, the old fountain showing white in the silvery light.

You couldn't see the moss and scutchgrass in the lawn, the rain-filled potholes in the drive, the ground-elder clogging the fountain.

He didn't mind all that, he even liked it, though he'd never say that to Ali, she worked so hard.

'D'you think James is right?' she asked him.

'That he should throw her out?'

'That he loves her.'

'I suppose he could be...'

❦ *Chapter 63* ❧

'*H*annie,' he said gently, 'whose son is Joss?'

There was a fraction of a pause.

'Rolf's,' she said, without looking up from the book she was staring at, not reading or even turning the pages.

'I don't mean who is his father. I mean who is his mother?'

She closed the book and placed it beside her on the sofa. She looked at him. 'Alison's been here, you've been talking to Alison.'

At once he felt as though he had betrayed her. He struggled against guilt, told himself they had to have the truth out.

'Yes,' he said.

'What did she tell you?'

'Just what you told her.'

'And what was that?'

'That Joss is Ilse's son, not yours.'

'Ah yes.'

'Are you angry that she told me?'

'No, that's why I told her. I wanted to tell someone in case something happened.' She sat quietly, her hands placed one on the other on her lap, her eyes downcast. He couldn't read her. He got up and went over to the sideboard and poured himself another drink, though he'd already had the two that were his normal limit. He refilled her glass without asking her. 'What do you mean, in case something happened?'

'In case I died or went away.' She looked up, met his eyes, didn't look down. 'I thought you'd be kinder to him if you thought he wasn't mine. If you thought he was a victim, like you.'

He ignored this last remark. 'Are you planning to go away?'

'No, not now. But I thought of it.'

'And you'd have left Joss?'

'Joss needs a home.' Her voice was matter-of-fact. 'That's why I came here in the first place. He couldn't go on moving from one place to another, from one stepfather to another, it was getting harder and harder for him. But I thought I couldn't stand it here and I knew you'd look after him. At least until I came for him.'

'Even when you left me?'

'Even when I left you.'

Ned threw back the contents of his glass. 'Why are you telling me all this?'

'Why not? It's all passed now, everything's changed.'

He stood planted, his feet apart, a sort of inertia upon him. He seemed baffled, unable to advance in the conversation. He made a pincer of his thumb and forefinger, closed his eyes, held the bridge of his nose, made a great effort.

'Look Hannie, I can't get this straight. Who is Joss, what are you saying? You told Alison he wasn't your son but that you always said he was so there'd be a place for him in your marriages. But now you seem to be saying that everything you told her was just a carefully planted lie. So that I'd be better disposed towards Joss if you left.'

He kept pinching at his forehead, speaking with his eyes shut, getting it straight in his mind.

'But at the same time you said to Alison that *someone ought to know*. She told me you said it very urgently – as though it was the clue, the core of what you were saying.' He straightened up, dropped his hand and looked at her directly. 'Know what, Hannie? Whose son is Joss anyway? Yours? Ilse's? Whose?' His voice rang. He was staring at her, challenging her.

Her eyes rose to meet his, then they dropped again. 'What does it matter?' she asked wearily. 'He's mine – my responsibility – the rest is irrelevant.'

'My responsibility too, or that's what you seem to have intended from the start. I have a right to know. And to know about Ilse. Oh, I know, I know, you've told me, she was Swedish, she was your ex-husband's second wife . . .'

'Third wife. I was the second.'

'*Third* wife. But who was she, Hannie? What was this hold she had on you?'

There was a silence. She stared at him for a long time, saying nothing. Then she shrugged, lit a cigarette and drew the smoke in deeply. Ned took his glass from the mantelpiece and sat down across from her. When he was settled he looked at her and she met his eyes.

'All right, Ned, I'll tell you, since you so badly want to know. But there's no point, it will change nothing, nothing at all.

I had a husband and his name was Rolf. He was wealthy. He came from a Czech family – very well-bred – who lost their lands but got their money out before the war. We were good together, there was no deep feeling between us but it was fine, we both liked life and money and the way we lived. It worked very well – for a year, two years, three years – and then Ilse came.

'Ilse was Swedish, the daughter of a bank manager from a not-large town beside the sea. A happy family, bourgeois, innocent, church-going, with this sweet, pretty daughter; it would be nice for her to learn good English, to travel a little, and then to come home and marry. The father had a client who had friends in Africa and so it was arranged. She came to be an au-pair to their children.

'Well you see, Ned, she was so young and shy and so very blonde – that white Scandinavian blondeness – her hair a dusty oat-colour, but fine, like ivory silk. She had perfect skin and a perfect mouth and a perfect figure, slender but full, and when she was with the children she was always smiling and laughing.'

Hannie stopped and stared into space for a moment. Then she reached for another cigarette and lit it.

364

'I am telling you all this stuff about how she looked because it is the reason for what happened to her. If she'd been plain, she'd have been left alone. But she wasn't plain. She would have stood out anywhere, but in that society – with its alcohol and easy sex, its darker colouring, its ageing beauties – she shone. And it wasn't just how she looked, it was because she didn't know her currency. She didn't sway or pose, her clothes weren't new or good, she didn't like drink or parties, she liked to be with the children. You see? She was so natural she was a beacon.

'Rolf had to have her from the start. I saw this, but I thought he'd just have her and tire of her, I thought all that artless simplicity would soon be too much. He pursued her. At first she disliked him and feared him, but she couldn't resist him, he was so relentless when he wanted something. I waited for him to discard her, but he didn't, she was an obsession with him and the obsession didn't grow less.

'I was young still, I was barely thirty, men came to me easily. Rolf didn't mind that – some men find it erotic – and I was easy with him, I accepted what he did, I even advised him. This time I gave him good advice, I told him not to marry her, that if he married her she'd be like a poison in his life because she was too far from him and could never under-stand him or accept him. I told him he should use her till the way he felt had run its course. Or give her up. But he couldn't do that either.

'It wasn't altruism on my part, you understand. I liked the life I had with Rolf, I could handle him, I didn't have to worry about surviving, yet it wasn't dull. But he couldn't listen to me and I grew tired of the situation. I thought, I'll let him go ... And then I thought, why should I? She's so pure and good and yet she's sleeping with my husband, she's no different from the rest of us. So I went there to the house of her employers who were our friends. It was quite early and the servant let me in and went to call her, only I followed after him and I stood on the verandah outside her room

365

waiting for her to come out. And when she did she was wearing a long nightgown and she was carrying the teething baby and she smelled so sweetly of sleep that I wanted to be sick.

'She was bewildered when she saw me, but not defensive. She thought that for a man to be unfaithful to his wife the relationship between them must already be over. That's how naïve she was.

'Of course I knew then there was no point trying to hold on to Rolf. And I knew that Rolf would destroy her and I didn't care. I think I began to hate her then, though I hadn't bothered before. I went on hating her for a long time before I started to love her.'

Hannie stopped suddenly, as though she was afraid of what she'd just said. She got up, went over to the sideboard and poured herself another drink. Then she offered the bottle vaguely in Ned's direction, but he shook his head. She sat down again.

'You know, Ned,' she said thoughtfully, 'when I saw her there on the verandah, it was the first time I realised I was decadent. Before that I thought the way I was was normal and that people like Ilse – little, ordinary people – were afraid to live. I had never lived inside affection and I never wanted to, I had never seen a family that didn't make me want to scream with claustrophobia, I'd never seen a contented couple but I had to make him want me in front of her, just to show them how things really were.

'I couldn't see their bonds, these small, dull people, I thought what held them together was simply self-interest and fear.

'But when I saw Ilse so tender with that teething baby that wasn't hers but had kept her up half the night I knew she was different from the people I knew. And I knew she knew something that I didn't know, and didn't want to know and never would.

'Anyway, I told Rolf I would divorce him and not long

after they were married. Ilse's family wouldn't come, they'd made enquiries about Rolf and they tried to threaten her out of it, they tried to save her though she didn't want to be saved. She loved Rolf, you see, it was all she could think of, though it was a big thing for her, losing her family, her parents, her younger brothers and sisters. But her parents were bourgeois and hardworking, their relationship was very happy and she thought hers would be too.

'Poor Ilse. She should have lived and died a Swedish wife.

'She made sure of Rolf's behaviour to me after the divorce. I thought she must feel very guilty, it never crossed my mind that she did it because she felt it was right. He was useful to me through her, gave me money and help when I asked for it, though at that time I didn't need much of either, there were plenty of other men around. But I asked for money anyway – why not?

'I didn't know she had to fight him for me, I thought he was still besotted with her and he'd give her anything, she had only to ask. She never hated me, no matter what I did or said to her. She would look up at me with her soft eyes and I would grow more vicious to her. I despised her.

'Then I went away. When I came back some years had passed. I was sick, I had a fever that seemed to go and then came back, each time worse, so I would be half delirious for days and weeks. I could not get well. I had a little boy – Paulo's child, Paulo that I told you of – I had gone back to Paulo then I had left him again, he never knew I was pregnant. I was thirty-seven when Joss was born, not so young any more, it was hard, and the child wasn't strong, he had had malaria and he needed good food and care and I had no money.

'So everything was different. I had a room in the city, a horrible room and more than I could afford, but it was all I could get because of Joss. I was behind with the rent, and the landlady threatened me.

'I went to Ilse in their place in the hills and I told her my situation. She had two children, a girl, and a younger boy, almost the same age as Joss. It was all so green and orderly and well-tended, money and servants, but no Rolf.

She said she would pay off what I owed and she'd help me to get on my feet again, but she had to wait for Rolf to come home because she'd no money of her own. She told me to come back in a week and she gave me some cash to keep the landlady quiet, but of course I didn't use it for that, and I got sicker again and I was very weak and I knew the woman would put us out if I left the room, so I didn't go back there as we'd arranged.

'She came to my room. I don't know how she got the address, I didn't give it to her, she must have made enquiries. But there she was and I had a fever and I thought she was a dream, and other things that were dreams I thought were real. I don't know what happened or what was said. The next thing I remember I was in their place in the hills and she was tending me. That was Ilse's way, she had plenty of servants, but no, it wasn't some servant who nursed me to her orders, it was Ilse herself.

'Anyway, I slowly grew less sick. The house was large and low and rambling, with many bedrooms, and my room was in one wing and it gave on to gardens and trees. In the early mornings I lay and I watched the monkeys in the leaves against the sun, just as I'd done in my childhood so far from there. Joss thrived, he was fatter and healthier, he sat on my bed and told me of the other children and the games they played and Ilse came and sat with me every day.

'Then Joss said the children's daddy was home and the servants told me there was a big house party as well. I didn't want to see Rolf, so I stayed where I was and I kept Joss with me. I heard the comings and goings, the voices and cars and music at night, but I was sick still, I was glad to stay where I was and I didn't see Ilse either, she didn't come to my room.

'Then the parties stopped, it grew quiet again, and I knew that Rolf wasn't there any more. I began to be strong enough to be out of bed and I spent my time with Ilse and the children. I learned the story of the marriage.

It was as I'd predicted. Rolf had turned against her a long time ago and the more she tried, the darker he became and the more violent. There were women too, and friends that she hated, and he didn't bother to conceal any of it from her, it was as though he was trying to goad her and goad her until she finally gave up her stubborn love and agreed to hate him, but she never did. It was very hard for her. He couldn't stand the way she was bringing up the children, he hated to see them tender towards things and full of pity, the same as she was. He ridiculed her in front of the children and he ridiculed the children when they showed her values. He taught them how cruelty worked and he taught them about fear. Especially the boy, he wanted the boy for himself. The girl was safer from him – she was older and very strong for her mother – but he claimed the boy against these two soft women, the mother and the sister.

'I didn't see all this to begin with, but I noticed how the boy was different after Rolf had been there and I saw how patient she was with him, how she tried to rebuild the bond, always through gentleness. And he was confused, he couldn't understand which world he should live in. Perhaps she should have left him in his father's, but she couldn't. It wasn't in her.

'And you mustn't think that Rolf wanted this either, he didn't want to live in the dark place he lived in, but he couldn't live in her light place, he wasn't like that. They should have parted but they couldn't. She couldn't leave him because she couldn't take back her love and he . . . Well, sometimes I think he was afraid of her. Afraid to stay with her, afraid to leave her. She was too much for him.

'She trusted me, I don't know why. Perhaps it was the same flaw of judgement that made her love Rolf. At first I tried to stop her, I tried to make her understand that I was untrustworthy and would let her down, I didn't want her trust or her love, they were too burdensome, I only wanted her help.

When I had what I needed I wanted to go away and forget her.

'But she was too much for me, too; in the end she got what she wanted from me. Or perhaps it is wrong to say she got what she wanted, because I don't think she wanted anything, she tended me as naturally as she tended the wounded things the children brought her, fixing a splint, removing a thorn. She seemed to have no fear – only tenderness and pity. Sometimes I was angry with her because I wanted more than this mindless pity. I began to understand Rolf.

'And I did become trustworthy, I even came to love her, though I never showed it. It was strange, the effect she had on me. She used to sew at night, the lamp beside her, the soft moths batting out of the shadows. I would stand outside on the verandah, smoking, watching the night, knowing she was there behind me in the lamplight. I loved that, I felt so lonely and complete. I never wanted to be like Ilse, mostly I didn't even want to be with her, but I wanted to know that she was there. I knew then that I was an outsider, would always be an outsider, would perish if I tried to be anything but what I was.

'I began to talk about moving on. She accepted that, though I think now she wanted me to stay. I suppose she was lonely, there on that land-bound ridge on that great continent that was as endless as the sea. Ilse was always, always homesick, she never got used to Africa or the heat. She used to talk of those northern harbours of hers – sunlight on cold blue water, white dresses, hems fluttering, everything sparkling and flashing – I see them now quite clearly, though I've never seen them.

'She knew I was getting restless, that I wanted to be gone. Whatever she wanted for herself, she put from herself, that was her way. But she wanted to find a place for me, to make it safe for me, she didn't want me just to go off as I'd always done, seeing what might turn up. She said I had a child now, I was responsible, I couldn't just trust to luck or fate. So she found a job for me in Nairobi – in charge of a place for white people who'd grown old and lost their luck. I don't know how she did it, I had no qualifications or experience, but she told them I was entirely capable.

'It wasn't stupid, this plan of hers. I could take the boy and yet there wasn't much work to be done, it already ran smoothly with native staff, I would only be a figurehead, a *white* figurehead.' Hannie stopped abruptly and laughed slightly wildly. Ned regarded her steadily. She put down her empty glass.

'It would be very suitable for a while, Ilse said. Of course, she meant till I was married again. She knew men liked me. She would write letters, arrange that I be suitably invited, I would be settled before very long and there would be a home for Joss. She meant well.'

'Like Alison . . .'

Hannie stared at him as though she hardly knew who he was. Then she laughed mirthlessly. 'Poor Ilse,' she said, 'I've wronged her badly, I have made her sound like Alison. And she wasn't, you know, she had no security, no family to fall back on, no social position, no caste to belong to. All her life she was just a girl, a naïve girl who never grew up or learned life. She knew nothing, anyone could do anything to her, she just let them.'

'I know the feeling.' Ned heard the anger and self-pity in his voice too late. She looked at him, a blank exhaustion in her face.

'No you don't,' she said wearily. 'You don't do what you don't want to do, or what your conscience won't let you do, you are stubborn and strong and selfish and you have no idea what it was like for Ilse, no idea what it was like to be helpless and soft and alone in a strange country with no one to help you and your husband a drinker and a shit.'

'And you do?' Ned said bitterly. He was ashamed of his tone, but he couldn't stop himself.

'A little, but only a little.' Her voice was quiet, almost

thoughtful. 'I was alone, yes, but I wasn't soft, it makes a difference. And I wasn't beautiful as she was, I didn't have that thing that made men fight to own her. And when I was helpless she looked after me. That is the hold she had on me, Ned, the bond you find so sinister.'

She got up, went over to the window, pulled back the curtain, looked into the night.

'We both had sons,' she said, without turning. 'Sons only a little different in age. Sometimes I see the pictures in my mind and the memories are all mixed up. What is true, what isn't true? I had a son called Joss, but I never had a son by Rolf. Sometimes I feel I can't sort it out, can't ever know for sure . . .'

It was too much for Ned. He felt too bruised and confused and exhausted to stand this change. He could handle the truth when she told it, how could he do otherwise when she set it before him as she did? Like a woman bringing her worldly goods to morning market, placing her bundle on the earth, unfolding the cloth, revealing its sparse contents (for are not all our bundles mostly empty or filled with junk?) in the bright, clear, pitiless light.

But he couldn't go from that to this.

'Come on, Hannie,' he said savagely, 'don't give me that half-baked twaddle. As though you don't know, as though you're only half there. If you're not going to tell me, then don't tell me, but do it straight.'

She swung furiously round to face him. 'What do you know, Ned?' she came back at him. 'What do you know – you with your home and your family name and your moral standards and your self-respect? What do you know about living? Nothing. Why? Because you never do it, you just watch other people. Detached, objective, safe.

'You're afraid to live, Ned. You're a coward, posing as a hero . . .'

'In all my life, Hannie, no one has ever called me a coward.'

'Well, *I* am calling you a coward, *I* am saying that your courage is not true courage, that bravery coming from strength is easy. What do you know about courage? You've never been soft or helpless or tricky or shamed or wrong. You've never been humiliated or disgraced or hated . . .'

'What about now?'

She stared at him. 'What about now?' she said furiously. 'They hate Joss, they hate me, but no one hates you. And if you think what you're feeling now is hatred you should see what it looks like from our end . . .' She whirled from the room, slamming the door as she went.

He thought about going after her but it was hopeless, he'd lost her and he wouldn't get her back now. She'd told him more of herself than she'd ever done, but something was missing still, nothing was finally explained. He needed a lens that would shift it all into focus and he wasn't going to get it. He cursed himself for not keeping a tighter control on himself. Rage was the other side of the tenderness that he felt for her, a molten rage that lived in him like lava, erupting at the slightest pressure. It shook him, he didn't recognise himself like this, he didn't like himself.

❧ *Chapter 64* ❧

*I*n the morning Ned decided that his life had been on hold
for too long and enough was enough. He wasn't going to
skulk at home avoiding people any more, he was going to go
about his normal business modestly and respectfully and in a
way that he hoped would give offence to no one. If he met
any of the Comerfords, then so be it, he would have to face
them and they him, but he hoped he wouldn't and he hoped
his action now would make it easier for them in the long run.
People would see him about and report back to them and
they'd get used to the idea of a meeting. Then, when the
inevitable finally happened, they'd be less unprepared. He told
himself it wasn't a matter of pushing things, but of facing
them.

He took himself to Waterford and began with a long over-
due meeting with his accountants. After that he went to the
car insurance people, talked to them about the still-missing
Volkswagen, then called in at one or two garages and priced
what they had in the second-hand line. He had some lunch,
read the paper, folded it into his pocket and prepared himself
to go and do what he'd been dreading most.

He drove through the school gates, parked the car and got
out. The old stone building was sombre and quiet in the chill
sunlight, the grounds were studded with great trees, their
branches netted with veils of bright leaves. He could hear
shouts and yelps and laughter from the playing fields and
snatches of something choral and familiar from what must be
a music room. A little flock of starlings wheeled and dropped
and rose again and pigeons sounded softly from the roof. 1798

– the founding date of the school was carved up there in the dark stone under the eaves. The place had been established by the Quakers in the aftermath of the '98 Rebellion the bursar had told him, an attempt to build on ruin and devastation, to create a future out of chaos and terror and bloody suppression.

Suddenly Ned knew he couldn't walk in as he'd planned and ask them to spare him a few minutes, couldn't stand there saying his piece about bringing them up to date, couldn't even cross the threshold or find the office or meet anyone's eyes. Nothing would happen to him, he told himself, nothing had happened all morning beyond a slight distance, an unwillingness to let the conversation drift beyond the immediate business, a certain fumbling of hands and shifting of eyes. But it didn't matter what he told himself, he couldn't do it, and that was something that he'd never experienced before.

He went the long way home for no other reason than that he didn't want to arrive; he drove back with the thoughts so loud in his head that he didn't see road or cars, or fields and trees. He had a new respect for Hannie, for her courage and single-mindedness and endurance, but much stronger than the respect was a fury at what she was and what she'd got him into.

He wanted a stiff drink, but more than a drink he wanted a cigarette, he hadn't smoked for years but he wanted a cigarette. Hannie smoked like a chimney, the kitchen was always full of smoke, she didn't care about her own lungs or anyone else's, she didn't care about anything but getting her own way, all the rest could go hang. She didn't care what she said either, had no thought for consequences, all the subtleties, the allusions, the necessary ways of sidling up to things were swept away leaving nothing but pain and chaos in their wake.

If this was what she meant by living, he thought, she could keep it. And she was right when she said he didn't do it for himself. He didn't, and he didn't want to either, no one in their senses would.

Why should he try any more? What did he care who Joss

was, or what cul-de-sac in Hannie's sordid past had produced him? Why should he go on picking up the pieces when she wouldn't listen or co-operate and showed nothing but contempt for other human beings and their feelings?

He would cut his losses and ask her to leave, he decided; it would cost money, but it would be worth it. He'd have peace again, a quiet way of living, the respect of his friends and neighbours. He gripped the steering wheel and his hands hurt from the arthritis that was starting in them.

He pulled in at the next town to buy cigarettes. He didn't know how much they cost now, and after he'd paid he held out his hand with the change spread on it, convinced that he was being cheated. When it was explained to him, he didn't apologise, he just walked back across the street towards the car, his rage deeper because he knew now how much money she was wasting every day. He had forgotten Niamh, forgotten grief, he no longer felt pity for Niamh's family or for Hannie or for Joss or for anyone but himself. He felt soiled, humiliated, shamed.

A dog ran out under his feet. He stumbled and a woman caught at his arm to steady him.

'Watch yerself, now,' she cautioned him tetchily. 'We're none of us gettin' any younger.'

A young lad leapt after the straying dog, grabbed at his collar, and ran with him. His friend appeared alongside him, grinned complicitously up at Ned, and made vivid ribald faces at the cross woman's back. They sped off down the pavement, the dog loping between them.

Ned stood where he was, looking after them. A red-haired girl was standing waiting by the Allied Irish Bank, her hair a dark flame against the cut stone, and beside her leaned an elderly man in a rusty black suit. Ned watched them, the clear rainy light showed their clothes and faces in calm detail, their quiet waiting, their patient incarnation, their acceptance of it.

Inside Ned everything suddenly smoothed out and went simple. Youth, age, it was all the one, you lived and life passed, nothing mattered but this quiet, attentive acceptance. He stood there, empty and still, with the life of the street flowing round him. He didn't think about what he was thinking, nor wonder where the thoughts came from. And after a short time it was enough.

He walked back to the car, got in and started the engine. He saw everything now, the clean lines of the houses, the sudden pink flare of an almond in blossom, the filling station on the road out. He saw where the edge of the town changed to countryside, the tall chestnuts lining the road, their spires of unopened blossom, the green towers of their leaves.

And he saw that he'd been someone in his life, that he'd got used to being someone, that now he was old and was becoming no one, and this being old and becoming no one was his next great task.

He knew he wouldn't write the book he was planning, that his dream of writing one last book was just a way of trying to hold on to importance, of trying to put off for a little longer this becoming what he really was.

And this was his business, this was his task, whatever Hannie did or did not do, whatever happened around him, whoever else lived or died.

All the way home he went on seeing everything, the fields and the trees, the hedges standing in the greenish, underwater light, the whitethorns breaking where the pale sun reached. The fields were full of lambs and young cattle, the rowans carried big bosses of creamy blossom, the mountains were soft and blue and close with the coming rain.

When he pulled up in front of the house it was grey and still. Rooks beat and clamoured in the empty ash trees and the first swallows flicked through the chilly air. He saw Hannie through the boughs of the young fruit trees, moving about in the garden. He was no longer angry. He felt neither hope nor despair.

∽ *Chapter 65* ∽

*H*e saw her cross the yard and for what seemed a long time he stood watching and waiting for her return. There was a big moon up there but the clouds came fast and the shadows blew over the uneven ground. He had to stay alert. When she did come, she was so quick and so quiet that he would have missed her if she hadn't made straight for the door where he stood.

She didn't see him till he moved. She started and gave a little sharp cry which she cut off even as it came out. Then she saw that it was him and she tried to push past. He grabbed her by the shoulders and held on to her though she pulled away. He yanked her round to face him and she went limp in his hands and he spoke low and fast and shook her to be sure she understood.

'You can't do this, Hannie, you have to stop helping him, you have to let him face it . . .'

He stopped, he'd seen a movement over her shoulder. Only a small movement and only for a moment, but enough. He froze and she did too. They waited. He saw a shadow move across the gap between the sheds. Then stillness again. He pulled her inside and shut the door, stopping it at the last moment so that it closed softly to.

She understood at once. Even in the unlit darkness of the scullery he could see her eyes widen, he felt her body taut beside him. He went to the square of window and stood quietly watching. She was there with him.

'Where?' she asked, very softly.

'Over there – by the shed door.' He only breathed the words.

The moon had gone in. They both peered into the darkness. The cloud passed and they saw the shed door and the shed's thrown shadow, its outline sharp and blank. Nothing. They waited for a long time. Nothing moved, even the cloud-shadows were absent, the moon sailed round and clean through the high sky.

At last Hannie left the window and moved to the door. Her hand was on it. He was beside her.

'Where are you going?'

'He's trying to reach me . . .'

'Hannie, I don't think that's Joss out there . . .' They were whispering still.

'Not Joss?'

He shook his head. 'Wrong shape. Didn't move like Joss . . .'

'Are you sure?'

'Pretty sure. It was only a glimpse –'

And Joss would have to have travelled pretty fast, he thought, he'd only skipped the Limerick house three nights ago. He wondered if Joss had phoned again – she seemed so sure that he was heading home.

'The Guards?'

'I don't think it's the Guards, I think they think he's long gone. Nora phoned, they've been questioning Con.'

'If it's not the Guards, then who is it?'

He hesitated. 'Someone local,' he said quietly.

She turned to him there in the darkness by the door. 'What shall I do, Ned?' she asked simply. 'I can't just wait here, I can't, I can't . . .' Her voice cracked.

'Did he phone?'

She shook her head. 'No. Not for more than a week. I just feel him coming near, I just *know* . . .'

He believed her. 'It could be someone who thinks he's around here and you know where he is. Someone waiting to follow you when you go to him . . .'

'Moonlight plays tricks, you could be mistaken, it could be him . . .'

'No. You were out there, whoever else was out there must have seen you. If it was Joss he'd have shown himself. It isn't Joss . . .'

'One of Niamh's brothers?' she said slowly, shame in her voice.

'Possibly. Feelings run high, it could be anyone. I think you should go back to bed.'

'No,' she said urgently, shaking her head. 'I'm going to sit at the window with the light on so he'll see me when he comes.'

'But if whoever's out there is still out there . . .'

'Then Joss will run straight into him . . .'

'I'm going to put the kettle on.'

He moved the kettle on to the hob and busied himself with mugs and sugar and milk, his back carefully turned from her because he was afraid too much was written in his face. The kettle boiled and he wet the tea and put the cosy on to the pot and went to fetch the whiskey from the drawing room.

When he came back she was standing by the door with her back to him, smoking. He asked her if she wanted her whiskey straight or in her tea but she didn't turn or answer. Some instinct made him cross to her. He put his hands on her shoulders and swung her round to face him. Her body shook with sobs and her face was wet, though he hadn't known she was crying. Her eyes were shut tight against him, the only privacy she had left. He was shocked by the exhaustion and despair he felt in her.

He held on, gripping her hard by the shoulders, trying to penetrate through to her.

'Hannie,' he said, 'Hannie, listen to me, you can't go on like this, it's tearing you to bits. You can't do it all alone – you against all the world – you must trust a little, you must let yourself think about giving him up, he may be safer with the Guards.'

She shuddered and sobbed. 'I know, I know, but I can't

bear it,' she said, her eyes still shut tight. 'And I can't bear not knowing where he is and not being able to do anything, and everyone against him and hating him – I can't bear to think of him alone at night . . .'

'You have to, Hannie,' he said. 'You have to bear it, there isn't any other way.'

She drew in her breath in a long shuddering intake. She let it out and then breathed in again. She stood, her arms wrapped round herself, her eyes closed tight, drawing breath in, letting it out. He still held her shoulders, he wished she'd lean into him and let him comfort her, but she wouldn't. When her body no longer shook, he let his hands drop from her shoulders. He moved away from her and carried the tea to the table and after a moment or two she picked up her cigarettes from the dresser and came and sat down.

She looked awful, her face at once gaunt and swollen, her hair wild, her eyes almost closed. She moved the mugs around as she always did, then she lifted the pot and poured the tea. He opened the bottle and laced each mug with whiskey.

'I'll tell you the rest, now, Ned,' she said. 'Everything this time. It will change nothing, but I want to tell you . . .'

So she began, at first hesitantly, the words stumbled and halting, then more and more easily. She seemed to forget Joss, to forget the darkness and the figure waiting in the darkness, she re-entered the past and lived again in the far bright world she had known before ever she thought of Ned or this hidden place or what it might hold for her.

'I told you about the job in Nairobi that Ilse had found for me, but I didn't tell you that I never meant to take it. I didn't want her letters or her introductions, I didn't want her job or her concern or the sort of men she'd know. But I didn't tell her this, I let her plan. And while she was planning, Rolf came back. It was as before, there was drinking and music and revelry, the bedrooms were much in use. I was well now, I found I no longer wanted to avoid life, to live like Ilse, like a ghost who flits around the place and is at once ignored and avoided. I knew some of Rolf's friends from way back before I'd gone off, before the second time with Paulo. I was forty, I wanted to live again, to laugh with this bright fast crowd, to forget Paulo and sickness and even my little son. To enjoy myself once more before age closed down the party.

'There was an expedition that started off when everyone was drunk. One of the guests, a man called Abercorn, had bought a horse off an Arab on a trip up north. He couldn't stop talking about it, boasting about it, bets were laid. In the end nothing would do Rolf but we all had to get in the cars and go to Abercorn's house and see this horse.

'The house was five or six hours' drive away, we set off and drove through the night and when we got there it was dawn. The horse did its stuff, it was better even than Abercorn had boasted, he picked up his IOUs, we drank more and ate more and slept a bit and got more drunk again. By the time we were ready to leave another night and a day had passed.

'Everyone was drunk, drivers and passengers, everyone. And there was plenty more in the crates we carried for anyone who got sober. The journey back didn't seem long.

'On the way up the hill to the house the Land-Rover that Rolf was driving turned a sharp bend and hit a car head-on. In the car were Ilse and the three children and one of the servants. The little girl had been bitten by a snake, a kutzu snake, which is venomous but not usually deadly. Ilse had administered the antidote and dressed the wound but she was taking her to the doctor to be sure. The child had been frightened so Ilse had made it into an adventure and the two little boys had insisted on coming too.

'The little girl was killed in the crash and also one of the boys. Rolf's passenger, a woman named Eva, had a broken shoulder. Ilse and Rolf were both very badly injured and the servant who'd travelled with Ilse and the children had concussion and a fractured hip.

'Ilse died three days later, while Rolf was still in a coma. Before she died, I promised her that if Rolf regained consciousness I'd tell him he'd killed both his son and his daughter, which wasn't true. Rolf's daughter was dead, but it was my son who was killed, my little son Joss. Their son had been scraped and concussed, but he was all right. I also promised her that I'd take her boy and bring him up as my own, that I'd call him Joss and Rolf would never know the boy was alive. If he did, she said, Rolf would get him back, he wouldn't rest till he had him. Rolf must believe his son was dead.

'I went to Nairobi, to the job I'd never intended taking up, and I took the child with me. Rolf's spine was damaged, it took him a long time to get back on his feet and they said he would always have pain. He went on drinking.

'I never thought about what I was doing. When Ilse and Joss were killed, a kind of despair came into me, sometimes I think it has never entirely gone. It was a hard time for me, very hard, so it was easy to make the boy the reason for going on. I called him Joss, I spoke of him as my son, just as she'd wanted, and very soon that was the way it was. Then I met Stan and he had a farm and after a while I married him and Joss came with me. Then there was Andrew. I was his mistress at first and later his wife and Joss came there, too. Why wouldn't he? Wasn't he my son?'

It was getting light in the kitchen, Hannie sighed and sat heavily back, throwing her arms over the hard ridge of the chair-back, letting them fall loosely down behind her. She tipped her head up towards the ceiling and spoke with her eyes closed.

'Rolf never knew the child was alive, I made sure of that.'

'No one told him?'

'No one told him. The servants knew things were as Ilse wanted, they were her household, not his, they wouldn't betray us to Rolf. There would have been talk, of course, some of it might have reached him, but he sold the house without ever going back there.'

'And his guests?'

'They weren't interested in children, most of them couldn't

have told them apart in the daylight, much less in the dark. They went away as soon as they could – all that blood, every-one screaming – there was no one to turn round and say, *I was there, this child lived, this one died.*'

'What was this Joss called before?'

She stared at him. She brought her arms forward and joined them in her lap. 'James,' she said after a long pause. 'His name was James. Why? Do you think it matters? He was so young, only four years old –'

'And you've never told him?'

'No. At first I was trying to help him forget. Because of the accident, because of Rolf. Later, when he thought I was his mother, it seemed simpler to let him go on believing. He was so insecure always and moving around has made it worse, I thought if he knew about Ilse and Rolf it would be even harder. He would have no solid ground at all.'

'Does he remember?'

'Yes and no. He remembers Rolf and I've told him he was my husband before Stan and Andrew. I've also told him Rolf was his father, which is true. He used to ask where Rolf was and sometimes he dreamed of him and woke afraid. A few years ago, when he asked again, I told him Rolf was a drunkard and was probably dead by now, which is also true. He hasn't asked since. He remembers Ilse but he thinks she was his nanny. I told him she was killed in an accident years ago.' She had her elbow on the table now and was leaning her head on it. She sounded infinitely weary. 'He doesn't remember his sister or the accident . . .

'In school – in his first boarding school in Africa – there was a boy who took Joss's place on a football team, a place he wanted very badly. This boy wasn't better at football, he got the place by telling on Joss – something he'd said or done, I don't remember. Joss caught a scorpion and kept it in a box. One night he put the scorpion into the boy's bed but another boy saw and told the matron. They sent for me. They said they'd keep Joss if he told the boy he was sorry, but he wouldn't, he absolutely refused, I had to take him away.

'Afterwards he told me his daddy said you must always strike at your enemies. Forgiveness was soft and for girls. He said his daddy would be very proud of him when he knew. Yet he never asked to see his daddy. Not once.'

Ned didn't speak. She got up and crossed to the window and scanned the yard. She came back and sat down and rested her face on her hand again. It was very white and intent.

'Joss caused Niamh's death,' she said. 'I'm not disputing that. But I'm certain that it wasn't deliberate like the scorpion, I'm certain he didn't see it as a striking-at-his enemies or anything like that. He caused her death but he didn't mean to, it was just one of his *things* that started for kicks and got completely out of hand. He thinks of it as bad luck, an accident, he told me that on the phone. Even the thing with Pip he thinks of as bad luck. She annoyed him, he said, she was so stupid, he wanted to stop her following him around, to hurt her a bit because she was so trusting. He says he didn't mean to do what he did, but he was drunk, it just came over him, he couldn't help it. And I believe he couldn't help it. I believe that Joss is bad, has bad instincts, and can't help himself against them and I don't know what to do to help him, I've never known what to do . . .'

They sat in silence.

'Do you think he raped her?'

Hannie laughed, an ugly sound. She lifted her head off her hand and sat up. She placed her two fists in front of her on the table. 'He didn't rape her,' she said harshly. 'You don't understand Joss, it's not his style, I don't think he's even capable.'

'What d'you mean?'

'He's odd.' She shrugged hopelessly. Ned waited and she tried again. 'He's passive sexually. He watches, he is done to. But he doesn't do himself, he never does –' She broke off and sat silently. Still Ned waited.

'You remember, before we were married,' she said, 'that I

told you things had gone very wrong between Andrew and Joss? That it was because of Joss that I left Andrew, that Andrew didn't want him around any more?'

He nodded.

'Joss was offering himself to Andrew's friends for money.'

'He's homosexual?' Ned almost sounded relieved.

'No, not entirely – he is and he isn't.' She stopped, then went on. 'He likes to watch others. Both sexes, he doesn't seem to mind. And to have things done to him. But he doesn't seem to want to *do* anything himself.' She stopped again. 'It wasn't only the thing with his friends that angered Andrew so much. Andrew had two children from his previous marriage, a boy and a girl, just into puberty. They lived with us when they weren't away at school, they were very close, it was the age when children like to experiment. Joss paid them to do things together in front of him and Andrew found out.' For the third time, Hannie stopped. 'So you see,' she went on desperately, 'he'd never have raped Niamh. He might have threatened her, but he would never ever have raped her because he couldn't.'

There was a dead silence.

'You are disgusted,' she said flatly. She got up slowly, pushing back the chair so it scraped across the floor. She crossed the room and switched off the light.

'It is not his fault, Ned. If he was born this way, or if he was made this way by all that's happened to him, it's what he is like now. Whether he wants to be or not, and I don't think he wants to be. He can't help it, Ned, he can't help the way he is or what it makes him do . . .'

Ned sat looking down at his hands which were spread on the table. 'It's not that,' he said at last. 'I just have to get used to it, Hannie.' He looked at her. 'I will,' he said, 'but it'll take a little time.'

❧ *Chapter 66* ❧

*I*t was dead easy, getting out of Limerick, he was standing in this Texaco shop scooping sweets and stuff into his pocket with one hand while he waved a Crunchie bar round in the air like he urgently wanted to pay. She was down the other end but she came after him as he was leaving. He was jumpy, he thought she'd seen him nicking, but she hadn't, she only wanted to ask him where he was heading.

'Timbuktu,' he said. It was a nothing answer, mouldy as old cheese, but she giggled and squirmed and batted her eyes as though it was a sparkler.

She'd seen him thumbing back down the road, she said, and she'd wondered if he mightn't be going in her direction? She'd missed her bus and there wasn't another, she wanted to hitch but she knew she shouldn't try it on her own. Would he mind if she hitched with him? She felt stupid asking, it was only because it was safer.

Depends where she was going to, he'd said. Clonmel, she'd said. That was okay by him, he'd said, he would put Timbuktu on hold.

So he did and they got a straight lift all the way through and he'd sat in the back and let her do the talking. He'd heard the man who was driving refer to him as her boyfriend and she'd smiled, not contradicting him. She'd wanted the man to think that, it made her feel safer.

He'd had to leg it most of the way after that though. He'd got a short lift from a farmer crawling home from the pub; he'd driven very slowly, his two front wheels straddling the white line. 'So's to keep meself straight,' he'd said.

He'd taken a chance on that one, but it wasn't really a chance, the guy was too blocked to see where he was going much less remember he'd given anyone a lift. Anyway, he was frozen and knackered, he needed a lift, he needed to sit in a comfy seat with a heater blasting away at his wet boots and his wet socks and his soaking wet jeans. His top half wasn't as bad; wet, but only up to the elbows where the rain had seeped in. Further inside he was almost dry.

The worst bit had been coming over the mountains. The road was completely exposed, every time he'd heard an engine he'd had to hop off and hunker down behind some rock or flatten into the heather. And no sleep for two days, just a bit of a kip in a place like a wet rabbit burrow half-under the side of a boulder. He'd kept waking. Every two minutes he'd woken, imagining he was hearing some noise, someone coming. Even when he'd been asleep he'd been dreaming he was waking up, so sleeping hadn't helped because it hadn't felt like sleep. He'd fought up out of a dream, tight as a spring and ready to run, then he'd opened his eyes on nothing but dark, and wet rock and the wind blowing over the mountain. He'd whimpered a bit then, whimpered and curled up tighter. He'd imagined he was wrapped around Pippa and she was snuggling and wriggling against him, keeping him warm. Then he'd gone back to sleep for a bit and it wasn't so bad once it got light.

He had some pills, he'd been taking them to keep going, he would take an upper so's to give himself a bit of a blast, then he'd drop something else to smooth himself out and take off the jittery edge. He'd lost track of what he'd taken and what he hadn't taken; anyway it was hard to work out what was doing what to him, or what he needed next. Everything was confused on account of him being so cold and tired and hungry. In the end he'd decided he couldn't do anything about the cold – pills couldn't stop you being cold – but he'd drop-ped something whenever he felt hungry so at least that was one less problem. He felt very spaced though and it wasn't all that pleasant. Things were definitely getting weirder all the time.

He needed some food inside him now, he knew that, just because he wasn't hungry didn't mean he didn't need food. He'd had water but nothing to eat since he'd got to this barn, all the bars and the stuff he'd nicked had gone in the time on the mountains.

He should have gone home with that girl in Clonmel, she'd wanted to take him to her mother for a feed, but he wouldn't, he'd been fretting to get back on the road. The Limerick house hadn't exactly been into cooking either, he couldn't remember when he'd last had a decent meal.

He had to get to Hannie, she'd get him some food, if he couldn't get to her himself, he had to get word to her. She was mad with him over Niamh, he knew that, but she'd help him just the same, he was her little boy, she wouldn't let him down.

It was nearly dark again now and the rain was getting heavier, he would try again to reach her later, at least all this cloud and rain would shut out that pissing moon. He'd been close last night, close enough to see her, she'd been standing at a lighted window and he'd known why she was there. He'd watched her leave the window and he'd waited for her to come downstairs and outside and place herself where he could find her.

And she'd done exactly what he'd wanted, she'd come out of the yard and stood herself in the dark by the shed and then, just when he'd decided this was the moment, the pissing moon had come sailing out from a cloud and he'd seen a movement off to his left where she wasn't looking.

He'd frozen again. He'd been lying flat in the trampled bit under the little thorn tree where the cattle went for shelter, and he'd stayed lying there, and whoever was off to the left had stayed where he was too. Then after a long time she'd given up and gone inside and over to his left this patch of darkness had stirred and moved off quietly behind her.

So he'd given up too and come back to this barn; he was

tired anyway, and cold, so bloody cold, and he knew the daylight wasn't far off and he had to hole up and hold on till the next time it got dark.

It wasn't really a barn, it had been a house once, a long time ago, but the lower windows had been blocked up and the ceiling had fallen in and it looked like someone had been using it for cattle, though they weren't using it now. Part of the roof had fallen in – the bit in the middle where the chimney must have been, you could see this old blackened hearth mostly lost in a heap of beams and roof-tiles and stones. It wasn't too bad, there was light from the roof-hole and from the empty doorway and from these little window-openings high up in the gable-ends. Rain blew through the hole so it wasn't really dry, but it was a lot dryer than anywhere outside.

He'd made a place for himself behind the rubble of the roof-fall, a kind of nest-place in among the earth and tiles and stones. He couldn't be seen from the doorway, he'd stuck a stick into the ground – a longish stick – and he'd gone and stood by the door to check and it was fine. He was hidden but he could still move around a bit, he just had to remember not to stand up to his full height. He could see out, too, there was one of those blocked up windows right beside him, he'd pulled out some of the stones and made a viewing hole.

It wasn't much of a hole; he'd had to be careful, the stones had shifted a bit as he worked a few of the lower ones out, and he knew if he took the wrong one the rest would come down in a crash. He couldn't see much out of the hole, just a bit of earth and some wet grass and some long whippy briar stems with thorns on them and small new leaves. Not much, but better than nothing, he could watch things, there were birds around, they'd hop across his patch, then they'd hop away. And there were spiders in the grass, he'd watch them scuttling about, he'd watched one making a web all afternoon.

There was a robin too, a little small robin that had found a big worm, double its length, and so fat you knew the robin would never get its beak open wide enough to get it down.

It was like Pippa that time Ned gave her the fishskin without cutting it up first; she'd kept biting at it but it wouldn't sever, then she'd tried taking a chew and a gulp and had to gag it all out again.

The robin was the same, it couldn't work out how to eat this worm it had, which wouldn't stop wriggling and was too big to peck into bits or to swallow all in one go. The robin tried all ways, then it jumped on the worm and threw it around and banged its head so hard that it finally quietened down. Then it got hold of the end of the worm and started to swallow and soon it couldn't stop, there was too much of the worm already inside to start sicking it out again. So it swallowed and swallowed and swallowed and in the end all of the worm was inside and none of it was outside. Then the robin stopped swallowing and just stood there looking stunned. Joss laughed at the robin, he laughed and laughed, he was sorry when it hopped off beyond the viewing hole to do some private digesting.

It was very dark now, he must have been asleep, though he didn't feel like he had, he didn't feel refreshed or anything, his bones ached and his muscles ached and he felt like he wanted to die. At least he was warm – hot, not warm – at least he was too pilled-out to be hungry or bored. He was thirsty though, he could drink a lake dry; he reached across for the plastic bottle but it was almost empty. He drank the half-inch that was left and lay back. He'd go out soon, fill it from the spring well in the field, he was sweating and hot to the touch.

No water, no cigarettes, he might die. Perhaps he was sick – he'd take another pill – he reached in his pocket and pulled out a wrapping of foil. He opened the wrapping to see what he had left, chose a pill, worked his tongue back and forth in his mouth till he had enough saliva made to swallow it.

Not late enough to go and find her yet, might as well lie back, might as well make it easier for himself, though he wasn't really worried. He'd get to her this time, he knew he would, he'd get to her and she'd give him stuff to drink and put him to bed and when he woke up she'd have it all sorted out. He lay back and fantasised iced fizzy drinks with cold sweat-beads on the bottles and bubbles pinging up through the sweetness.

He heard a noise.

At first he took no notice, he was too busy with the 7-ups and Fantas and Cokes, lined up now and open, ready to drink. He heard it again. It wasn't a big noise, it was just like someone outside had stepped on a stone that had rolled over under his foot. A sort of clanky rattle as it turned over and rolled against another stone. Then he heard nothing for a bit, and then another of these small rattling noises, but outside still and down the other end of the barn. It had stopped raining, he realised. And someone was walking around outside. He sat up slowly and turned himself quietly over on to all fours.

Then the noises stopped and a pencil of light walked over the wall, flicked up to the roof, flicked down again to the floor. Someone was standing in the doorway. He stayed very still, he wasn't frightened; he knew Hannie was waiting for him and he'd be quite safe if he stayed exactly where he was. A few minutes passed. The light-pencil seemed to have gone away and he couldn't hear any more movements. After a bit he looked cautiously out over the wall of his nest. Darkness and silence. He crawled out and kept crawling till he got to the doorway. He looked out past the dark shapes of bramble and thorn, he looked over the wide sea of darkness he knew was the field with the well. Nothing. Then he saw the light flick on somewhere on the far side of the meadow. It moved further away, then suddenly died.

He needed some height, he wanted to see what had happened to the light and where it had gone. He pulled himself up the vertical barn-wall, his fingers finding holds in the rough stonework, his feet placing themselves in cracks and on jutting-out stones. He was nearly there, he liked climbing, it felt good to be moving and stretching, he was a spider shifting up the wall.

He stopped and listened again. Nothing. He had his hands on the sill of the gable-window, he hauled and one foot found a gap where a ceiling beam had been. He got the other foot into a hole, swung one leg over the sill and he was sitting astride in the window.

He looked out. Oh-oh. The light was much nearer, it had turned around, it was circling back and was heading for the barn. The cloud shifted, a chink of bright moon looked out from behind its mass. The light-carrier halted and switched off the torch. Whoever it was had stopped and was standing still, his head moving slowly from side to side as though he was scanning the ground. A bit more moon emerged. The head moved again, something shone on the face, the light-carrier was wearing glasses. There was something familiar, something about his gait and his shape. In a flash Joss knew. It was Danno.

Joss nearly laughed out loud, he nearly yelled out Danno's name and came scrambling down from the window to give him a message for Hannie. Nearly, but not quite. He was catching himself on about trusting, he'd trusted too much in the last few days and look what it had brought him. A cop-car outside the house in Limerick, and another one waiting round the corner. Magic. The Guards had sat in their cop-shop and looked into a crystal ball. Like hell they had, no magic about it, someone had picked up a phone and talked.

He leaned slightly back from the window and into the shadow, though he knew he needn't bother, everything was fine now, his luck was running, he knew he was completely invisible until the moment came when he chose to show himself. Danno was scanning the building, probing with those flickery eyes of his behind the glasses. Yes, it was definitely Danno.

Danno had switched on the torch again, he was running it over the ground, wasting the batteries, wasting his time. No prints there, the rain had turned the trampled earth at the entrance into a sludge of mud. The torch flicked off again.

Danno turned and began to trudge slowly back across the long black field. Joss watched him for as long as he could see him. The moon kept coming and going, Joss kept losing the little figure and then finding it, smaller and smaller, further and further away.

The moon went. Joss stretched and smiled, he felt good now, it was time he came down from his perch and went and found Hannie. He didn't think he was into all that spider stuff this time, he thought he might just play birds and jump from the sill. He swung his leg back inside, pushed forward and jumped loosely down through the dark to the floor below. It was further than he'd thought, a lot further. When he landed he twisted his foot and fell sprawling, his hand hit a slate which split with a crack, his head thudded on a lump of stone. There was a moment's complete silence, then a little rumbling noise, then a dull roar as a section of the roof fell slowly in.

Joss's hand, sticking out from the pile of rubble, opened and closed once, then lay still.

∼ *Chapter 67* ∼

*T*he formalities had been blessedly quick, the funeral swift and quiet. Joss was buried in the little local church; people muttered a bit but it was done before they could gather themselves and Ned had a family plot so they didn't have to go looking for vestry permission.

James turned up with Alison. He looked flustered and angry and muttered about Marjorie and prior commitments. Alison didn't mention Vere or offer any excuses but she brought a great sheaf of fresh garden flowers that must have taken her hours to pick and assemble.

Mrs Coady came with her husband Tom. Her arms went round Hannie as soon as she saw her. To Ned's astonishment Ambrose Power the builder arrived, a wreath in his hands and his workmate Liam at his elbow. After the burial they went over to where Hannie stood by the grave and shook her hand and spoke the traditional words of comfort. Ned saw her eyes fill and suddenly Ambrose's handshake had become a strong embrace.

It was the same with James. He made a dive for Hannie, grabbed her in his arms, squeezed hard, then let go and turned away, his face wet.

Danno came. He stood at the back of the church in a jacket and tie but left without words as soon as the service was over.

There was no one else.

Niamh's body was finally released and she was buried two days later. A massive funeral; everyone went.

Ned didn't go, he decided it would be kinder if he stayed

away. But he wanted to pay his private respects so he went to the church the night before. At the last minute Hannie said she'd go with him.

It was late, they parked the car, pushed open the heavy door and walked slowly up the aisle to where the coffin stood before the altar. The church was empty, the lights were dimmed, the service of removal was long over. Hannie went and sat on a seat in the shadows. Ned stood by the coffin, his head bowed, he stroked the pale wood with his hand and tried to realise that it held Niamh.

Not Niamh, he told himself. All that was mortal of Niamh.

There was the sound of the church door opening and shutting. Heavy footsteps, burdened and slow, but Ned didn't move or look up. When he did John Comerford was beside him. There was a moment of utter stillness, then both men moved at once and stood held in each other's arms.

Hannie watched from her seat in the shadows. As simple as that in the end, she thought: arms reaching and folding and holding. As James had held her. She didn't begrudge Ned his grief, nor this reconciliation. She might have grieved for Niamh herself had she been less lost in the sorrow of Joss.

As simple and as difficult. People could only do what they could do. She knew that when it came to her, John Comerford would be able neither to forgive nor to forget.

Nor would he want to.

~ *Chapter 68* ~

'*I* had earrings like two little lanterns. Inside each one was a tiny plastic candle painted with luminous paint so it shone in the dark. I would put them on for him at night before he went to sleep and I'd turn out the lights and he'd laugh with happiness.'

Ned was standing on the ditch cutting thorn branches and throwing them down. Hannie was hauling them off and blocking the near holes in the hedge as she talked. Everywhere there were new holes, butted open by the lambs that grew daily stronger and more independent.

Hannie worked vigorously, pushing the spiked branches firmly into place, ignoring the inevitable cuts and scratches. She was happier when she was active, he noticed. She came with him all the time now, these days they were rarely apart.

'He was very attached to me when he was little. There was a lot that wanted to be soft in Joss but he couldn't allow it, he was too insecure. When he wasn't being – as he was – when he trusted, which wasn't often – then he was gentle and affectionate. Perhaps he thought it wasn't safe to trust.'

She had hardly talked about Joss to begin with. People said grief needed an outlet so Ned had asked her questions, offered kindness, said words that were meant to show he cared. There'd been no response. She was silent and stunned and closed.

After a while he'd fallen silent himself. It was too difficult, too complex, she knew his feelings were ambiguous. She shook him off and he didn't blame her; she pushed his platitudes away.

When he stopped trying she started to talk of her own accord. Slowly at first and then with a growing momentum. He left off trying to prompt her and he left off telling her it wasn't her fault and she'd done her best. She didn't want that or need it, she wanted him to listen, so he did.

'I think it must have been hard for him when I married. I thought it would give us both a home, but it didn't. He gained a place, but he lost his home, which was me. And I wasn't entirely honest. I said I was doing it for him, but I was doing it for myself as well. Particularly this last time. Perhaps I was getting old and tired, perhaps he was my excuse.

'And then when I'd done it, and I was unhappy, I told myself it was only for Joss –'

'You don't have to explain yourself to me, Hannie.'

'I'm not, I'm trying to understand what happened. To all three of us – to him and to me and to you.'

It was strange for Ned to hear himself included like this. He still thought of Hannie-with-Joss as something that was separate and independent from Hannie-as-she-was-with-Ned.

'Do you remember I told you how I would stand on the verandah at night, with Ilse inside, sewing? How I knew then there was somewhere in the world that was completely safe and still? Even if I didn't want it – which I didn't?

'Well it must have been like that for him, too, only he needed it, he needed it very badly. And he lost it when she died. I think his father's influence was very strong, very confusing. And I didn't see it and I didn't give him anything instead of that lost safety. How could I, when it isn't in me?'

The ewes were standing off, watching the hole-blocking activity, the lambs were bunched together, the dog, Bess, was sitting apart in the grass. Rain came on the wind. It blew across, fine and grey, smearing the edges of things, dampening the soft, damp colours.

She was looking at the past as though it was a bolt of cloth, he thought. She'd laid it out, unrolled it; she was checking the weave for flaws and for places where the pattern had smudged and changed.

'He was not so cold-seeming when he was younger,' she said, reaching for another branch. 'And then when this coldness started I thought it was his age, I thought he needed privacy, so I left him alone. But it was the wrong response.

'I have made so many mistakes, it was always so much easier to focus on the things about Joss that were peculiar and a bit horrible, the things that made people give up on him and decide he was just bad. I think I often forgot the little lovable things because they were so small and ordinary and hardly seemed worth remembering.

'Sometimes I hear myself and it's always the bad things I say – said – I always blamed him when maybe it wasn't his fault.'

'It wasn't your fault either, Hannie. *He* wasn't your fault.'

'I wasn't a good mother, he was at least partly my fault. Partly, not all. Joss was Joss, just as I am me. I'm not only the sum of my mother's genes and my father's genes, I'm not only the sum of what has happened to me either. I am me as well. It was the same for Joss. He was what I did to him and what was done to him – but he was also himself.'

The more she talked the more she found she could talk. Talking brought her comfort and she needed a little comfort. Ned was steady and calm and unsurprised, whatever she said.

Sometimes she looked at him and she was amazed that he could accept her so totally when what she was and the life she had led contradicted everything he'd so sternly required of himself. She felt his tenderness for her and she did not feel inclined to reject or ridicule it. He was closer to her than he'd ever been, than she'd ever allowed him, close in the way that a loved dog is close when it wants to sit so its body touches yours. She was comforted by this desire of his to be with her, it relieved and warmed her, for the first time in her life she felt cherished. And feeling like this was painful because she saw more clearly what had been lacking for Joss.

A heron got up from the reedbed in the next field. It crossed slowly over the meadow, its long stiff legs trailing, its big loose wings flopping at the unresisting air. It voyaged above them letting out short, hoarse shrieks of protest, as distinctive and ungainly as its carriage. Hannie stood and watched.

'It's like you, Ned. Solitary, distinguished, bad-tempered, stiff in the knees.'

'I didn't even know I had a temper till I met you, Hannie.'

She smiled an almost-smile. She'd begun to believe that there might, after all, be a future. Sometimes things seemed nearly possible out here in the fields in the daylight.

Ned was strangely content. Everything was in ruins about him but the end-result was an almost-happiness that was true for them both. She was very grey and strained still, but she was slowly becoming less desperate and less taut.

She drank heavily in the evenings, but in a distracted way, like someone drinking too much coffee out of habit. She never seemed to get drunk. Once he caught her eye as she refilled her glass and she looked at it in a surprised way as though she'd only just noticed what she was doing.

'Does it help?' he asked as gently as he could. She didn't answer at first and he didn't know how to tell her he wasn't judging. Then she started to shake her head but stopped herself, mid-gesture. She grimaced at the glass.

'It numbs things.'

She was talking to him directly now, not trying to hide or evade, and he understood what she was saying. He felt he could face anything – Niamh's death, Joss's death, even Niamh's family and the loss of his own good name. Life wasn't easy, he reasoned, tragedies happened, they wouldn't be tragedies if they didn't carry pain.

He had all but forgotten his epiphany on the road home from Waterford. When he remembered, he remembered it only as a moment of softness and defeat. He thought they were rational – his deeds, his thoughts – he didn't realise she

400

could say anything, do anything – he didn't care as long as she went on living with him.

Part of him knew the depths of his dishonesty but the rest of him pushed this knowledge aside. There was a sort of euphoria of relief in him because he knew her at last. He let himself believe that she would stay.

Hannie saw his belief and she didn't challenge it even to herself. She was at once too numb and in too much pain to know clearly what she felt for him, but she knew that she trusted, even liked him, and his cherishing of her sustained her.

❧ *Chapter 69* ❧

*T*he wind was up. It lashed at the long green limbs of the whitethorn, it blew the swallows about the sky and shunted the magpies into purposeful earth-bound flights. It tossed the creamy elder flowers and streamed their silver-bellied leaves and tore the green fans from the chestnut trees.

The mountains were grey-white wraiths, haunting the near-distance. The rain came.

Ned sat a little back from the window in the sitting room, holding the paper but not reading it, watching for Hannie coming up the drive. It was Sunday, the first Sunday in May, a month since Joss's death. The rain blew against the window, the panes rattled.

He must have dozed because he didn't see her return. He knew she was back when he heard the scrape of the heavy door.

She came in; she'd left her coat in the hall but her hair was wet and plastered back off her face. She stood at the window and stared at the rain running down the glass. He folded the newspaper carefully and put it on to the low table beside him. He sat watching where she watched.

'How was Danno?'

'He said to tell you he shot a dog-fox behind the earth-slide below the long acre.'

'When was this?'

'Last night. He said you asked him to keep an eye out. He thinks there might be a vixen around but he hasn't seen any cubs.'

'He's all right then? What about this talk of him hitting the bottle?'

'He's not hitting the bottle, he doesn't need drink, he doesn't need anything, he was very specific. He doesn't much like human beings, he said, he doesn't like the rooms people live in behind their eyes, he'd rather be outside under the sky.'

Ned winced.

'He asked me why I'd come. I said I wasn't sure, I thought perhaps I wanted to hear him say he was sorry about Joss. He said he wasn't sorry about Joss, Joss was like a homicidal goshawk he once had, one minute she'd be normal, the next she'd be off her head. You never saw it coming. In the end he wrung her neck.

'He said death was a sanctuary – the last inviolable sanctuary. He said it was better that Joss was killed like that than killed by somebody else. He seemed to think it had to be one of the two. Then he said the Guards raided the house Joss was hiding out in and that was why he came back here. He said the house was in Limerick, which is true. He said someone phoned the Guards and gave them the address.'

There was a dead still silence. Ned stared at the window. He watched how the drops of rain built on the inside of a pane where the grouting needed to be replaced. He felt that he stood on an endless flat plain and a great tower was falling on him, falling and falling. He could do nothing, not even run, all he could do was stay in the dread of this great falling weight that he couldn't escape or avoid. It was like one of those endless black dreams of nightmare, only worse because he was awake and it was real. He knew he was losing everything, finally and forever, just when he had won it.

She turned to face him.

'Tell me it isn't true, Ned, tell me, and I'll believe you, even though I know it is . . .'

Her voice was quiet and very tired and he knew she couldn't bear much more. He wanted to say it was just a malicious lie but he couldn't.

'How did Danno know?'

'He had it off his cousin. She's married to a Guard in Lismore.'

Ned almost smiled. Whatever had made him think he'd get away with it?

'You'd written down Joss's address on the telephone pad in the hall,' Alison said carefully. 'You pressed hard and the paper's soft, Ned saw what you wrote. He wished you hadn't, he wished he hadn't seen. But once he had, he felt there was no alternative. He had spoken to Mahon you see, and Mahon had implied that the rumours were right and Niamh had either been raped or was running to escape it.'

Alison sighed deeply and put down her cup. She folded her hands in her lap, and continued.

'The next day the Guards phoned to say that they'd raided the house and Joss had gone. I'd come to see you but you'd gone to Danno's, so I sat and talked to Ned and he told me what had happened. Don't hold it against him that he told me, Hannie – he had to tell someone, he was terribly worried about the consequences of what he'd done.'

She looked at Hannie but Hannie sat motionless, her body a rag-doll's with no bones in it. Alison looked at her folded hands and made herself go on.

'Ned knows what rumour is like here, he knew his action was emotional, but at the same time he still thought it was right. And Joss was a minor, he'd have been dealt with very lightly, Ned could have no idea that things would end the way they did . . .'

Alison stopped. She thought she was probably making things worse but she had to keep trying for Ned's sake. Hannie raised her eyes and looked at her. Alison would have preferred the averted gaze to this bleak one.

'He concealed what he'd done,' Hannie said. 'He wanted to get away with it, he didn't want me to find out, he pretended he was supporting me and was on my side.'

Alison moved her hands up in a gesture of protest, but Hannie took no notice.

'He didn't tell me when they rang to say that Joss had gone. He knew I knew something had changed, he knew I was half out of my mind with worry, but still he didn't tell me.'

'He should have told you,' Alison said. 'He should have told you, but he thought you wouldn't forgive him and he wanted you to stay with him. He loves you.'

'If he'd loved me, Alison, he would have put this love of his above his integrity. If he'd loved me, he would have made a different choice.' She stopped, looked away, looked back again at Alison. 'I thought he was different from me,' she said quietly. 'I thought he had a right to things I didn't have a right to – to truth, and honesty and integrity – because that's how he was himself, above all the lying and expediency that I live by.

'But he isn't, he's no better than I am. He only seems better because he stays out of it all.'

'He did what he did because he believed it was right when he did it,' Alison said stubbornly.

Hannie stared at her.

'Fine, that's his choice. Let him have his public integrity.'

'Can't you just forgive him, Hannie?' Alison pleaded. 'It's done now, it can't be undone, can't you forgive him?'

'If he loves her, then why did he do it? And why didn't he tell her Joss had skipped? That's how she sees it and nothing will shift her.'

The kitchen was full of greenish light from a great over-branching chestnut they could not bring themselves to fell. Alison always associated this light with early May, with the bright intense greenness of the young leaves in the translucent evenings of late spring.

Soon it would change. As the leaves thickened and darkened the kitchen became merely gloomy. She put up with the gloom for the sake of this time. And for the thinning gold leaves of the autumn, the soft September light sifting through. Her life was full of such small and numinous gratifications, awaited and hoarded in the intensity of her innermost nature.

'Well she's right, isn't she?' Vere said. 'Ned wanted it both ways. His conscience clear and her hanging around his neck being grateful ... Much as I hate to admit that she's right about anything.'

'Yes, she's right, or at least she's right by her own ethics. It's what she did for Ilse. She took the boy because that was what Ilse wanted, whatever about the rightness of the action, whatever about the consequences.'

'Tosh, Ali, romantic tosh. She took the child because it suited her. That's the way she is, she wouldn't lift her little finger if it didn't suit her.'

'Perhaps, but I don't think so. I think her action was beyond herself – beyond her own nature.'

'It's no good, Ali, you can say what you like, I dislike the woman too much to want to see any good in her. Those lettuce seedlings you planted out aren't taking. Too cold still, got ahead of yourself ... Don't take on so about Ned, Ali. She'll bugger off now, he'll mope a bit, then he'll settle. Do him good in the long run, bring him down to earth.'

⊸ *Chapter 70* ⊸

'*T*hey say you're thinking of leaving,' Kathleen Coady said. 'So I came to find out if they're right for once, and if they are, to persuade you out of it. And to ask if you need any money.'

'I don't need money. Richard Thornton came and he brought his wallet,' Hannie said. 'He asked me to accept his help.'

'And did you?'

'Does the leopard change its spots? He gave me a lot of money, more than I need, enough to pay you back for the last time. He was relieved when I took it. Now he can relax, he's tidied me away.' She lifted the pot and poured the tea. 'Ned wants to give me his money as well. Cash and no pre-conditions. He says I'm his wife and he should support me whatever I decide to do. Funny, isn't it?' she continued bitterly. 'You ask from your heart and they give you nothing. Then suddenly everything's changed and they insist. So thank you, Kathleen, but no, I don't need your help this time. Not financially, anyway.'

'Is your mind made up, are you set on leaving?' Kathleen Coady took the cigarette Hannie offered.

'I can't stay here. There's nowhere I want to go to, nowhere I want to be, but I can't stay here.'

'Why not?' She leaned in, accepting the light. 'You're too old to be traipsing around the world without a home. You're used to this now. And we're used to you.'

Hannie smiled. Her face was like a skull with the smile stretched over it. 'You're used to me, Kathleen, no one else is. They point me out in the shops in Dungarvan.'

'You're a scandal, that's all, they'll get over it. It doesn't mean you have to leave.'

Hannie shook her head. 'I can't stay, Kathleen.'

'Because of him?'

Hannie nodded.

Kathleen Coady smoked for a few minutes in silence, drinking her tea. Then she put down her cup and looked thoughtfully into Hannie's face. 'You have to forgive him, Hannie, there's no way round it,' she said quietly. 'If you won't forgive him, he'll never forgive himself.'

Hannie looked steadily back at her. She said nothing.

'He's an old man,' Kathleen said, 'he'll die with it on his conscience.'

'Let him. He can think about Joss.'

Kathleen's mouth hardened. 'Then you'll have it on yours,' she said.

'One more thing won't make much difference.'

'Dying isn't so easy, you should know that by now.' Her voice was sharp.

Hannie looked away, then down. She stared at her hands, which had turned into fists on her lap. 'I'm not pretending that I think things would have worked out for Joss,' she said. 'But I'd rather he hadn't died the way he did . . .'

'We can't choose,' Kathleen said, her voice gentler.

'I know.' There was a long pause. 'It's for myself as well. I feel betrayed.'

Kathleen Coady flicked the ash off her cigarette and took a drag. She blew smoke out through her nostrils.

'Why must he be better than you, Hannie?' she asked, her face softening slightly to match her voice. 'Aren't we all made from the same clay?'

Hannie stared. 'He's better than me without even trying,' she said bitterly. 'He'll *always* be better than me, so what he does is worse.'

'If it's as you say, then he needs forgiveness the more.'

Hannie looked away. 'Do you ever get used to it, Kathleen?' she asked, pain in her voice. 'Does it ever get less?'

'It never gets less,' Kathleen said flatly. 'Never. But in the end it changes. Then it's clear and cold inside you. A spring well on a hot day. Clear and cold, so you see to the smallest stone on the bottom.'

'The last time – the first time – with my little Joss, I had this Joss to take his place . . .'

'Well, you haven't that now. You haven't anything to keep you going now but hating Ned. You can hold hard to that if you want . . .'

Hannie looked up. 'That's what I intend.' There was a flat finality in her face and voice.

'Then good luck to you. You're a stubborn woman and a strong one. Enjoy your hate and guard it well, for it's all you'll have.' Kathleen put down her cup, got up off her chair and reached for her coat.

'Where are you going?'

'Home. I'm getting too old to be rubbing shoulders with hate. It upsets me.' She put her arms into the sleeves and shrugged it on. Hannie made no move to rise or to stop her.

Kathleen turned at the door. 'I ran into James Beresford on my way here. He said I was to tell you you're to stop this bloody stupid carry-on. "Tell her she lives here now," he said. "Tell her she might-as-bloody-well start getting used to it."'

It was evening. The river ran dark and greenish-brown, dimples and whirligigs raced along its surface. The swifts shrieked in the cold white air, the swallows dipped and swooped above the shiny water. Cattle moved about in the blue rushes of the flood-meadows, cow parsley floated its pale lace on the banks, the willows flared grey-green over the water, the oak and beech were new-leafed and built in their beauty.

'What do you want to do, Hannie?' he asked.

'I don't know.' She spoke without looking at him, the words

coming out slowly, the sentences broken with pauses. 'I thought I might go to Sweden. Try and find Ilse's relations, tell them how it ended. It's all I can think of to do for them both. But I don't know if I can – I think my courage is quite used up.

'After that, I don't know. There isn't anywhere I want to be, but I don't want to be here. Not because I don't care for you. I just can't bear to be near you.'

Ned had been trying to register her words but not feel what she was saying, but she'd never used such words before so they got through to him despite himself. He was suddenly involved with the zip on his waxproof. After a while he spoke.

'Do you want a divorce, Hannie?'

'I hadn't thought of it.'

'I'm not trying to stop you, Hannie. You can't go on like this, I can see that. You don't eat, you don't sleep . . .'

'Kathleen says I have to forgive you. She says there isn't any way around it. She may be right but I don't know how.'

Ned looked at the river. 'I'll need some help with the lambing if Mick won't come back. I'll need help with the willow as well.'

'You forgive me, I just take it for granted . . .'

'Less to forgive. Anyway, easier for me, always was, always will be. Different nature.'

'I couldn't bear to stay because I was too tired to go. I couldn't bear the thought of living like that.'

'You have to go, I know that, you have to find the courage and do it. Go and do whatever you need to do. But when it's done, think about coming back . . .'

She looked at him, then she looked away. She put her hand on his arm.

'Let's just walk, Ned. Let's not talk any more . . .'

What Shape is a Snowflake?

What Shape is a
Snowflake?